THE
Girl
from
CHARNELLE

ALSO BY K. L. COOK

Last Call: *Stories*

THE
Girl
from
CHARNELLE

K. L. COOK

WILLIAM MORROW
An Imprint of HarperCollins*Publishers*

FIRST EDITION

Designed by Sarah Maya Gubkin

Printed on acid-free paper

Library of Congress Cataloging-in-Publication Data

Cook, K. L.
    The girl from Charnelle : a novel / K. L. Cook.— 1st ed.
    p.   cm.
    ISBN-13: 978-0-06-082965-0 (acid-free paper)
    ISBN-10: 0-06-082965-6
    1. Working-class families—Fiction.   2. Teenage girls—Fiction.   3. Texas,
West—Fiction.   I. Title.

    PS3603.O572G57 2006
    813'.6—dc22   2005050234

---

06 07 08 09 10 WBC/RRD 10 9 8 7 6 5 4 3 2 1

For Anita and Brandy
&
for Charissa

No one will retrieve my lost heart
from all those roots, from the fresh-bitter glare
of the sun multiplied on the water.
That's where it lives, the shadow that does not follow me.

——PABLO NERUDA,
"Sonnet XXX"

And through some strange, perhaps accidental, combination of
circumstances, everything that was of interest and importance to him,
everything that was essential to him, everything about which he felt
sincerely and did not deceive himself, everything that constituted the
core of his life, was going on concealed from others.

——ANTON CHEKHOV,
"The Lady with the Pet Dog"

CONTENTS

PART ONE

A New World

May 1958

✦

Gone

*L*aura watched the thunderstorm from the living room window. The clouds bloated and darkened, common in the Panhandle during late afternoons, and then it poured—a gusty, whipsaw wind driving the rain sideways against the house. The rain hardened into thick white hail, which soon sheeted the yard. Her younger brothers, Gene and Rich, joined her at the window, and their mother stopped cooking in the kitchen and stood behind them, drying her hands on a dish towel.

The boys soon tired of the show, but Laura and her mother continued to stare at the white pellets pouring down—dumped, it seemed, from a huge bucket in the clouds. Lightning crinkled the gray sky, and to gauge the distance, Laura counted slowly until she heard the thunder. One, two, three, four, BOOM! The time between the light and the sound shortened, and then in an instant the hail stopped, the sky opened up, and a bright beam of sunshine shone on the street. They squinted.

A moment later, simultaneous thunder and a flash of silver heat cracked in *their yard. The house shook as if bulldozed. Rich screamed. Laura was blinded for a few seconds. Her body vibrated, jangled, and her teeth kept clicking, as if she were sending a signal in code.*

Her mother stood in front of the window, frozen, her face cut by the sudden shadows after the light. Gene led Laura to the couch.

"Are you okay?" he asked.

"The . . . the tree," Laura stuttered, "the tree."

Her mother opened the door and went outside. The old oak was split in half, a bright black burn down the center, the heavy-leaved top branches strewn across the white-pelleted lawn and porch. The ends touched the door.

"My God," Mrs. Tate said, shuffling through the melting hail. She placed her hands on the dark center of the trunk. "It's hot," she said. "It's still hot."

Laura moved to the door, the muscles in her thighs and calves quivering, the joints of her knees still vibrating. Her teeth wouldn't stop clicking. Small lines of blinking silver crosshatched her vision. The sky darkened again. She and her brothers stood on the porch, afraid to move into the yard.

Their mother touched the trunk, the branches, the leaves, as if searching for a heartbeat. "So hot," she muttered, "so hot."

The next morning, the destroyed oak lay about the yard like a huge, stricken animal. Mr. Tate and Laura's older brother, Manny, had cleared away some of the debris that night, but the large job of cutting the heavy branches and uprooting the burned base of the trunk would take longer and would require special equipment. Leaving for school, they had to maneuver carefully around the fallen branches and the blackened husk of the split trunk. It was a mess.

Coming home on her bicycle later, Laura rounded the curve, saw the tree, and felt again the lightning in her body. Faint silver lines again blurred her vision. Her teeth involuntarily clicked. All this triggered, miraculously, by the presence of the tree.

She got off her bike in the front yard and wheeled it around to the side of the house. The front door was slightly ajar, and she pushed it open.

"I'm home." No one answered. "Momma? Rich?"

Still no answer, which made her nervous. She went through the kitchen and opened the kitchen door, expecting them to be in the backyard. But all she saw was Fay, scratching around the fences.

"Where's everybody?" she called.

Fay trotted over. Laura patted the old dog's coat and head, careful around the wounds that their younger dog, Greta, had gouged in her face. Fay licked Laura's wrists and cheek with her bad breath. Inside, on the kitchen table, Laura found the note, quickly scrawled, in her mother's crooked handwriting: "Rich is at Mrs. Ambling's."

"*Where did my mother go?" Laura asked old Mrs. Ambling.*

"*I was wondering the same thing. She just asked me if I would watch Rich until all of you kids got home. She seemed in a hurry. She headed down the road with a suitcase."*

"*A suitcase?"*

"*Yes, a brown one. Not that big."*

Laura inhaled sharply. She knew the suitcase, could picture it clearly in the back of her mother's closet, rarely used. It had a hole in the bottom, patched with duct tape, and one of the grips was frayed and threatening to come loose. Laura thanked Mrs. Ambling and grabbed Rich's hand.

"*Ouch!" he whined as they walked across the yard to their house. "You're squeezing too hard."*

"*Sorry."*

She went into her parents' room, not something she usually did without invitation, and opened her mother's dresser drawers, found them half empty. From the closet, six of her mother's ten dresses were gone, the brown suitcase gone, the wedding picture on the end table (the only picture in their house) gone, the postcard of a cathedral in Rome that her older sister, Gloria, had sent just last month, gone. Maybe something's happened to Aunt Velma, *Laura* thought. Maybe she went to Amarillo. *She sat on her parents' bed and closed her eyes for a few moments. She could smell her mother's presence in the room—a faint whiff of sweat and talcum powder.*

The front door opened. It was Manny. He came to the bedroom, an apple from Mrs. Ambling's front yard in hand, a greased black curl falling over his forehead.

"*You ain't supposed to be in here." He smirked, leaning against the doorjamb.*

He doesn't know either, *she thought.*

"*Where's Momma?" he said, chomping the apple.*

"*I don't know."*

Rich appeared beside Manny's legs, watched his brother's mouth working slowly over the fruit. "I'm hungry," he said.

"Where's your mother?" Mr. Tate asked when he and Gene got home.

"We thought you were going to tell us," Manny said.

"Huh?"

"She left Rich with Mrs. Ambling and told her we would pick him up when we got home. Laura found the note. Give it to him, Laura."

"Where did she go?" Mr. Tate asked, glancing at the paper, turning it over as if there had to be more to it.

"We don't know," Manny said.

"She took a suitcase," Laura offered. She hesitated before adding nervously, "The brown one."

"A suitcase? She walked to town with the brown suitcase?" he asked.

"That's what Mrs. Ambling said."

Mr. Tate went into his room, searched her dresser and nightstand. He opened the closet and grabbed the empty hangers and dropped them to the floor. The hangers bounced. He pulled the covers from the bed, looked under the pillows, threw them on the floor. The kids watched him warily from the doorway. His lips twitched. His forehead broke into a wrinkled frown. He eyed them as if he were going to say something but then didn't. Suddenly he slammed his hand down on the top of the dresser, and they all jumped. Rich grabbed Laura's leg. Her father whipped the drawers out of the dresser, overturned the contents onto the bed and floor. Laura and her brothers continued to stare from the hallway, not crossing the threshold.

"Damn it!" their father shouted, and then struck the lamp by his bed. It crashed against the headboard.

He looked at them as if they were to blame. Then he shook his head, sighed heavily, and brushed past them into the living room. "Stay here!" he ordered, then opened the front door and slammed it behind him. They ran to the window and watched him walk to Mrs. Ambling's house, kicking aside the dead branches from the oak. They did not follow him.

Mrs. Ambling answered her door. With his arms folded across his chest and his forehead still furrowed, he asked her questions they couldn't hear. Mrs. Ambling did not open the screen door, though Laura could see her frail and weathered face and white hair through the screen. Laura couldn't blame her for *wanting to keep a barrier between herself and his anger. Mrs. Ambling nodded and shook her head. After a few moments, Mr. Tate looked up and saw Laura and her brothers at the window. Laura felt suddenly embarrassed for him, but also for herself and her brothers shamelessly watching him. Mrs. Ambling turned to them, too, and then she opened the screen door, and he went inside her house, his arms still crossed.*

"What did she say?" Manny asked when their father returned.

Mr. Tate didn't answer, just hurriedly grabbed his keys. "I'll be back later."

"Where are you going?"

"To look for your mother."

"Where is she?"

"That's what I aim to find out."

They ran to the porch as he started the truck and backed out, shooting gravel. They all jumped down and skirted the tree and stood at the edge of the road as he drove away, tires squealing. The truck shimmied down the road and turned the corner, but they remained there, looking at the tree and the darkening sky.

"Can we eat?" Gene asked nervously, unsure if hunger was appropriate.

"Yeah," Laura said, putting her hand on the back of his thin neck. "I'll make some peanut butter and jelly sandwiches."

By midnight he hadn't returned. Laura made Rich go to bed. The child was cranky, unsettled, and had been crying off and on in jags, "Where's Momma? Where did Momma go?"

Laura said, "She'll be back soon. Don't worry." She helped him into his pajamas. He needed a bath. His thick blond hair was dirty and his neck ringed with dust. She lay down with him on her bed and rubbed his back and sang songs quietly until he nodded off, and then she went into the living room.

"Gene, you should go to bed, too," she said. Skinny Gene, the most frail of them all, just stood at the window, looking out. "We have school tomorrow."

"No," he said.

"It's after midnight. You'll be exhausted."

"I'm not going to school tomorrow."

"Yes, you are."

Manny said, *"Give it a break, Laura. None of us are going to school to-morrow."*

"We don't have a choice."

"We goddamn sure do!"

"Momma won't stand for it," she protested.

"She's not here, you idiot! And she ain't coming back either. Just like Gloria. Can't you see that?"

Gloria had eloped to Mexico with an air force pilot less than a year ago, and according to the last postcard, she would be in Europe indefinitely.

"Dad's going to find her."

"Fat chance! Are you blind? She's gone. Long gone."

"You're wrong," Laura said.

Gene sat down on their father's chair, covered his ears, and began to cry.

"Quit yelling," she said to Manny. *"See what you've done?"* She bent to comfort Gene.

"Who gives a shit?" Manny shouted.

"Shh. You'll wake Rich."

"He might as well be up," Manny said.

"It's okay, Gene," Laura said, stroking his head.

"No, it's not!" Manny shouted again. *"It's not okay."*

"Will you just shut up?" she said.

"You fucking shut up!" Manny lurched toward her, his face red and knotted. She put her arm up as if to ward off his blow, but he stopped himself. Still, he hovered over the chair.

Gene yelled, through his tears, *"Stop it, stop it, stop it!"* The intensity of his voice startled both of them.

Rich screamed shrilly, an animal cry, then called, *"Momma!"*

Laura shook her head and grimaced at Manny. *"What is the matter with you? It's not our fault."*

"Laura!" Rich called again.

"Rich, I'm right here," she said. She went into the bedroom and made him lie back down. *"I'll check on you in a minute."*

"Don't leave!" he cried.

"I'm just in the living room."

"Stay with me," he whimpered.

She lay down on the bed next to him and rubbed his back again. She thought he was asleep several times, but whenever she moved, he woke, clutching her.

"I'm right here," she said.

She remained as still as possible and closed her eyes and tried not to think. Gene and Manny spoke in hushed whispers in the living room, and then they opened the front door and went outside. Their father wasn't home, though. She hadn't heard his truck. She relaxed for a second, nodded off, and then woke, startled, afraid that she'd slept too long. She looked at the clock. Only twenty minutes had passed, but she felt groggy, disoriented. Rich was deeply asleep now.

She grabbed her sweater and slipped on her shoes and went outside, where Gene and Manny sat on the ground in the debris of the halved oak. She turned on the porch light, left the front door open in case Rich woke again, and then sat down with them.

"I'm sorry," Manny said.

"It's okay. Let's go on to bed. He'll be back soon, and we'll wake up then."

"You two go on," Manny stated. "I'll wait here."

"I'll wait, too," Gene said.

"No, you come on to bed with me," Laura said softly, taking his hand. "We'll get up when he comes home."

"Go on, Gene," Manny said, nodding. "She's right."

"I don't want—"

"I don't care what you want," Manny said. She could hear their mother's voice in him—a hard, flat finality. "Go on with Laura."

Gene and Laura went into the house and then on to bed, without changing into pajamas. Gene slept fitfully. Laura heard him tossing throughout the night. She wanted to do something for him, rub his back or temples as their mother used to do to soothe each of them to sleep, as Laura had done earlier for Rich, but Gene didn't always appreciate her efforts to protect and comfort him, though she often felt the impulse to do so. Rich wouldn't stay on one side of the bed, but he kept waking when she moved him. Finally she sat in the chair by the window and watched Manny, standing now in the split of the tree, his fingers laced behind his head, staring down the dark street. Waiting.

Mr. Tate still hadn't shown up by the next morning, and so they did not go to school. Laura tried to busy herself and Gene and Rich with chores—making breakfast and lunch, washing some laundry and hanging it on the line, pulling weeds from the garden. She offered food to Fay, who had lost her appetite and moped about, as if she also knew what was happening. Then they watched television, but nothing good was on—no baseball game, just a silly soap opera. So they played Crazy Eights, but Gene started crying in the middle of the game, and that set off Rich, and then soon she was crying as well.

Manny left on his bike right after lunch, said he couldn't wait around anymore. He was going to try to find their father and maybe figure out what in the hell had happened. A little past three in the afternoon, he rode wearily back down their street. Sweat stains darkened his shirt, and his face was flushed. She figured he'd ridden all over Charnelle. Of course, that wasn't all that difficult. The town was only three miles by two miles, not counting the little farms and ranches that peppered the outskirts. But he was clearly worn out from his effort—or from the news he'd received.

"Did you find him?" Laura asked tentatively.

"No. The man at the bus station said he came by last night, asking questions."

"Did the man know anything about Momma?"

"He said she caught the bus yesterday."

"Where?"

"He couldn't remember. Maybe Amarillo, maybe Denver."

Denver? What was in Denver? Nothing Laura knew of. She felt suddenly like she might faint, so she sat on the porch steps. "Where is Dad?" she asked.

"Still looking for her, I guess." After a few moments of silence, he added, more quietly, "She left us." He stared down the road, his eyes glassy, his face puffy with shock, as if he'd just been punched.

"Why would she do that?" Laura asked.

"How the hell do I know?" he said, not angrily this time, just confused. "She hates us, I guess."

"It's my fault," Gene said, startling Laura. He stood behind her in the doorway, his head down.

"No, it's not," she said.

"Yeah, it is. On Sunday I stole a dollar from her dresser, and she caught me and whipped me."

"It's not your fault," she said again, and reached out her hand, encouraged *him to sit beside her. She put her arm around his shoulder and said, too gaily,* "*Besides, Dad will find her.*"

Manny was conspicuously silent.

Mr. Tate didn't come back home until three days later, close to dawn. His truck rolled into the driveway, and they all jumped from their beds. He'd not called. Laura had started to wonder if neither of her parents was coming back. She ran to the window.

He was alone. She felt her stomach drop. She and her brothers all stood at the window now, staring at him. He had turned the ignition off, but he didn't get out. He put his head on the steering wheel. She wondered if he had not slept the entire time he'd been gone, and now, exhausted, home, he didn't have the energy or will to even get out of the truck. He was there for five, then ten, then fifteen minutes.

"*I'm gonna get him,*" *Manny finally said, his anger rising again.*

"*Maybe you should just let him stay there a little longer,*" *she suggested.*

He ignored her and opened the door. She, Gene, and Rich stood on the porch as Manny walked cautiously to the truck.

"*Dad,*" *he said, but their father didn't stir. Manny placed his hand on his shoulder, shook him.* "*Dad!*"

He lifted his head slowly. Black stubble grizzled his sagging face.

"*It's almost six,*" *Manny said.* "*You fell asleep.*"

Mr. Tate opened the truck door and eased out. He didn't speak. He started for the porch but stopped by the debris of the oak.

"*What happened?*" *Manny asked him.*

He didn't respond. It was as if their father didn't even register their presence. He moved among the branches of the tree. He crouched down at the base and put his hand on the charred wood.

"*Dad,*" *Manny said, more insistently, which frightened Laura.* Let him be, *she thought.* Give him some room. "*Tell us what happened,*" *Manny said.*

Their father rubbed both hands over the dead wood and then smelled the burn on his fingers. He put his face down to the tree. When he lifted his head up, his cheeks and nose were black. Manny's body stiffened, and then he inhaled deeply and waded quickly through the branches and closed in on their father. Gene, Rich, and Laura moved instinctively down a step toward the yard.

"Damn *it!*" *Manny demanded. "What in the hell* happened?"

He grabbed his father's arm.

Mr. Tate whirled and, quick and vicious as lightning, struck Manny across the face. Manny fell among the branches. He did not rise. Black finger marks were streaked across his cheek. He lay there in the branches and started to cry. Even though he was fifteen, only a year older than Laura, he seemed like a small boy crumpled there. Mr. Tate looked down at him for a few seconds, and then he crouched and placed his hand on Manny's head. He began to cry, too. Laura had never seen her father cry before, not even when Gloria eloped.

The other boys sat down on the porch, and first Gene and then Rich began to weep. Laura breathed deeply and looked up at the sky. It was cloudy and pink. The light spilled over their house, but the sun was blocked from view. Their street, out on the eastern edge of the town with only half a dozen houses, all still sleeping, seemed far too empty. She stood on the lawn—her two younger brothers on the porch, crying; her father and Manny, huddled by the tree, crying. She stared at the western horizon. It seemed right there, but so far. She could picture that bus, disappearing over the edge, rolling away from them, her mother not looking back.

1

✴

New Year's Eve, 1959

$\mathcal{S}$he'd only tasted beer before, never champagne. It was sweet and sharp and stung high in her head, and it gave her a tingling jolt, akin to her father's black coffee. The more she sipped, the better it tasted. Soon she was finished with the whole cup. She stood by the punch bowl. The dance floor was swollen with people. The Pick Wickers, a six-piece band from Lubbock, plucked out a country waltz. The Pick Wickers had become minor Panhandle celebrities, had even opened for Marty Robbins in Lubbock, Amarillo, Fort Worth, Austin, and Houston. They had played the Charnelle New Year's Eve celebrations twice before, in '56 and '58, and were regulars at the Armory dances. Laura had seen them only once and was glad that they were playing tonight. Though billed as a country act, they played a little bit of everything (rock and roll, the blues, swing, bluegrass, gospel) and would, rumor had it, get wilder as the night wore on and they drank more beer. The lead singer was a pudgy, gray-haired man with a string tie who sang like Fats Domino and sometimes played a screechy fiddle, and most of the other members of the band were in their thirties, except for the guy on the stand-up bass, a tall, thin boy with Cherokee cheekbones and a suit that looked too big for him. He would close his eyes during the songs and sway back and forth on the balls of his feet. Earlier in the evening, he popped his eyes open in the middle of "Blue Moon of Kentucky" and caught Laura staring at him. He winked at her, smiled, then closed his eyes again and continued plucking his bass as if that wink were a dream and the real world was in the rhythm of his fingers.

A little after eleven now. The decade almost gone, Laura thought. Another coming. Though her mother had left them a year and a half ago, it seemed at times like it had happened just yesterday and at other times like her mother had never existed. Time slipped or seemed stuck, but never the same. She didn't know how to judge it, and it no longer mattered, or at least it didn't matter in the same chronically aching way.

And on nights like this, it certainly didn't matter. Her first New Year's Eve party. Except for Rich, who was staying with Mrs. Ambling, her family was all here. Manny with his girlfriend, Joannie. Her father at the bar. Gene with his friends. They'd arrived late, almost eight-thirty, and the whole time she'd been dancing—the twist with Gene, a polka with her father, and other dances with boys she went to school with. Though chilly outside with the threat of snow, the inside of the Armory felt warm. On the deck were three barbecue grills with chicken and ribs and brisket. Inside were chips and a thousand variations on potato salad, bean salad, and fruit cocktail. Mounds of cookies and cakes and brownies. And a table full of champagne bottles, a few opened each hour, plastic cups filled. Her father had said she should try some, see if it tickled her fancy.

When she finished her champagne, John Letig suddenly stood by her side with a bottle in his hand, smiling, twirling around in goose-step foolishness.

"Let me top her off there, Miss Tate."

She liked Mr. Letig. No one called him John, except his wife. Everyone else referred to him simply as Letig. He worked with her father at Charnelle Steel & Construction, and though he was younger—early thirties, she guessed—he played poker and went hunting and fishing with a group of older men, including her father. She sometimes baby-sat Mr. and Mrs. Letig's two boys. One was almost five, Rich's age, the other only three.

Laura held out her cup, and he poured too quickly. The foam bubbled over the rim and splatted on the floor between them. She jumped back but could feel the wetness on her legs and the laced hem of her dress. She wanted to protect the dress, a green-and-white-striped one with small white satin bows on the sleeves and waist—a dress she'd had her eye on for more than a year and a half and had only recently saved enough money to buy, even though her father thought it frivolous to spend seven dollars on a dress she'd probably outgrow in a year or two.

"Whoops!" Mr. Letig chirped. He set the bottle on the table, gathered up a wad of napkins, and blotted the dance floor. "Here, let me get that," he said and wiped at her shoes and leg.

He was handsome, she'd noticed before. A big man with a thick chest, but also delicate features, a long face, his eyelashes thick and practically white, his nose angular, Scandinavian. His lips always very red, like a lipsticked girl's, and white teeth only slightly crooked. His fingers were long and slender, and he moved with the grace of a large cat.

"No, that's okay. I'm fine." She stepped away quickly and spilled more champagne.

"I'm not gonna bite you," he drawled, looking up at her, smiling. His cheeks were flushed. His blond mustache wriggled comically. "Unless you want me to."

She laughed nervously. He grabbed her foot. He pulled his handkerchief from his back pocket and snapped it open. "Never let it be said that John Letig besmirched a lady's shoes."

He enunciated slowly, carefully, and she couldn't tell if it was because he was drunk or because he was trying to be funny. She figured a combination. And it *was* funny and sweet in its way, and rather than call any more attention to herself—already people standing around the punch bowl were looking over—she let him finish polishing. He stood up, neatly folded the handkerchief, put it back in his pocket, and reached for the bottle of champagne.

"Thank you," she said.

He winked at her. "My pleasure. Do you know what time it is?" he asked.

She could see now that his eyes were bloodshot and slightly glazed, but it didn't scare her. He wasn't a mean drunk, she could tell, not like a couple of Manny's friends, who she knew got drunk as a precursor to fighting. He was having fun, and the alcohol brought out a comic foolishness that she found disarming.

She looked at the big Armory clock behind his head. "Eleven-fifteen," she said.

"Right. And at midnight you're gonna owe me something." He smiled and tapped the bottle against her cup. "Cheers!"

"Cheers," she said.

"Don't worry. I'll find you." He walked away, his shirttail dangling over the back of his pants. He walked straight, though, and she wondered—had she noticed this before?—if he used to be an athlete. He had an athlete's natural agility, even for a big man, a lithe fluidity that suggested he was at home inside his body.

And what was that thing about finding her? Just him drunk, she guessed. She knew that at midnight there would be toasts, everybody kissing. She knew it was a custom. In the past, their family had always stayed home, sometimes listening to the New York City special on the radio but often not even making it to midnight. She took a long swallow of champagne, and it felt like all the bubbles popped in her head at once. She laughed, and an old couple turned to her from a table by the dance floor.

"Are you okay?" the woman asked.

"Yes, ma'am."

Dean Compson, whom she'd known forever, swept by and grabbed her hand and said, "Come on," pulling her to the dance floor.

"Wait!" she called. "Let me put this down." She raced to the corner and set her cup on a chair, ran back and slid across the floor into Dean's arms. The Pick Wickers had begun a fast-flying version of "The Rock Island Line." Dean spun her so wildly that she almost fell, then pulled her close. They fumbled with a two-step, tripping clumsily over each other's feet before parting. A couple danced by quickly. The man bumped Laura's shoulder, hard, and knocked her off balance. She fell to the floor, landing flatly on her bottom, her dress flying above her knees. She felt stupid. Dancing couples gawked.

Dean and the man who'd bumped her crouched on the floor, hands extended toward her. "Are you all right, Laura?" asked the man. It was another one of her father's coworkers at Charnelle Steel, an older welder who looked perpetually sunburned from the torches. She'd met him before, a dim memory from a picnic several summers ago.

"Yes." She laughed nervously. "I'm fine."

She took both his and Dean's hands, and they lifted her up. She brushed off the back of her dress. The dancers on the floor formed concentric rings of activity around her. In the far circles, the couples spun on, yellow and red skirts whirling, felt and straw cowboy hats spinning around and around like tops. The closest rings looked to make sure she was all right. "I'm fine," she said again louder, assuring them, not wanting the attention, and the couples reclasped their hands and were absorbed into the beat. She felt embarrassed and silly. She shook her head slightly to dispel the fog.

Dean asked, "You had enough?"

"No," she said and moved close, placed her left hand on his shoulder. He slid his palm to the small of her back, and they danced more slowly, an off-kilter two-step that seemed out of sync with the music. The Pick Wickers didn't pause. The last note of "The Rock Island Line" led into a wordless rockabilly number. At the end of that piece, the lead singer announced that they were going to take a short break. The musicians put down their instruments and began moving from the stage to the bar. Laura wiped the sweat from the corners of her forehead, picked up her drink, and watched the bass player onstage drinking from a beer bottle, his eyes still closed, body still swaying.

"I'm hot," she said to Dean. "Let's go outside."

Behind the Armory, they found a cluster of teenagers gathered around a small fire. Manny was among them, with Joannie by his side. They and the others—four boys and a girl named Claudette—were all older than Laura. Seventeen or eighteen. Juniors, seniors. The boys smoked cigarettes, as did Claudette, and one of the boys was telling a joke—something about a camel and a wetback—and suddenly the joke was over, and the boys erupted into laughter. The two girls smiled weakly.

"That's fucking hilarious," said one of the boys, and then he belched.

Laura didn't get it. She stared at the parking lot, full of cars and trucks, the road empty, a thin spit of snow caught in the halo of the streetlight. She held her palm up but didn't feel anything. The band began playing again. Two boys took final drags from their cigarettes, tossed them into the fire, and headed back inside. Manny and Laura exchanged glances, Manny smiling widely. He was drunk. She knew that look, that serene blank stare. He nodded as if to ask her whether she was having fun, and she smiled back. She sipped her champagne, but it had warmed and tasted sickly sweet.

A boy poked his head out the door. "It's almost twelve! Everybody inside!"

She didn't want to be standing near Dean when the kissing began. They were friends, and he was fun to dance with, but he had a zitty face and thin lips. She'd rather be inside in the comforting circle of girls, or maybe close to Gene or her father.

"Bye," she said and strode quickly to the door.

Inside, the Armory was hot and smelled of pine, sweat, sweet champagne, and barbecue sauce. The band played Patsy Cline's "Ain't No Wheels on This Ship," though it didn't sound right with a man singing it. She found the punch bowl and ladled a cup of red juice, frothy with ginger ale and melting raspberry sherbet, into her cup. She drank it quickly and refilled it and then surveyed the Armory. Gene was with a group of other kids at a table playing cards. Her father was on the other side of the dance floor, leaning against the bar with a beer in his hand, talking to Jimmy Cransburgh, who was nodding and eating peanuts from a bowl. She studied her father for a moment.

Did he look like a man whose wife had abandoned him with four kids still at home?

The question surprised her. She used to think about it often, but it had not occurred to her in a long time. He was still a good-looking man, she guessed, though he'd aged in the past couple of years. His hair had grayed at the temples, and when he forgot to shave for a couple of days, his beard came in more white than black. His cheeks had thinned. She wondered if he sometimes forgot to eat, especially when he worked too much; he had a lean, hungry look.

A bosomy, dark-haired woman in a purple dress sauntered to the bar and clinked bottles with him and Jimmy. Laura's father smiled politely. The woman wedged herself between them, and Laura could see her father's discomfort. Since the night, over a year ago, when he'd brought a woman back to the house after going dancing, he'd never once been out on a date. One day Laura had asked him if he ever thought he'd get married again. He looked at her harshly and said, "I *am* married," then walked outside and began pounding with a hammer on the toolshed. She didn't pursue it. In fact, she was relieved in a way. It meant that her mother was still part of the family, connected to her father, legally if not literally. Even if her mother was dead, which might be the case for all they knew. Her mother's death was something Laura had definitely thought about, though it frightened her.

This woman at the bar boozily swayed side to side. Jimmy Cransburgh threw his head back and laughed, then leaned in to hear what the woman said. Her father also laughed but not in a Jimmy Cransburgh bust-a-gut way. The woman must have said something to her father because Jimmy looked at him, and her father looked down at his feet, shyly. He seemed boyish, even, and Laura felt a pang of protectiveness come over her, a desire to help him, as she often felt with Gene and little Rich.

She sipped more punch. A group of girls on the other side of the room fluttered nervously, all of them looking out to the dance floor. Laura recognized three of the girls—Jeanette Winters, Marlene Shopper, and Debbie Carlson. She thought to join them when suddenly the music ceased and big Bob Cransburgh, Jimmy's older brother, hopped onstage and whispered in the lead singer's ear. Bob Cransburgh smiled and tapped the microphone a couple of times so that it thudded loudly in the hall.

"Give us a break, Bob!" his brother shouted.

Mr. Cransburgh said, in a low voice, over the microphone, "Aw, shut up, Jimmy."

Everybody turned toward the bar and laughed at Jimmy, who picked up a handful of peanuts and hurled them toward the stage. The peanuts flew like buckshot.

"What an embarrassment," Mr. Cransburgh said, shaking his head, and everybody laughed again. "Keep him upright, will ya, Zeke?"

Laura's father stuck out his right arm as if to prop Jimmy up. More laughter, and Laura felt a surge of pride.

"Okay, now that we've taken care of that little problem," Mr. Cransburgh said, "I want to thank you all for coming tonight."

The crowd cheered, whooped, whistled.

"And I'd like to especially thank the Pick Wickers for keeping us on our feet. Let's give them a big hand now, folks."

Everybody clapped louder and whistled while the band took their bows. Then someone from the audience shouted, "One minute, Bob!"

Mr. Cransburgh turned back to the band, and they nodded and picked up their instruments. "Okay, everybody. Have your drinks in hand. Make sure you boys are standing next to somebody pretty. Get ready to kiss the fifties good-bye."

At thirty seconds, everybody started counting backward, loud rhythmic shouts. Someone handed a bottle of unopened champagne to Bob
Cransburgh. The crowd chanted five, four, three, two, one . . . and a beat
afterward, the cork popped near the microphone—a high-pitched, whistling
thwat—and shot toward the ceiling. Four boys on both sides of the stage
threw multicolored crepe paper streamers across the dance floor. Confetti
glittered in the light. Bottles and champagne glasses clinked. The band
began to play "Auld Lang Syne." The crowd clapped again and then quieted,
and a surprisingly harmonious chorus of voices sang along. When the song
ended, there was another eruption of joyous whistles.

Mr. Cransburgh poked his head back in front of the microphone and
said, "By God, let's see some kissing!"

And suddenly men and women, husbands and wives, boys and girls,
were lip to lip. In the corner, teenagers made out modestly or in clutching
gropes. Old couples closed their eyes and leaned into each other for gentle
pecks. An old man who worked in the hardware store, Mr. Dale, danced by
and kissed Laura on the mouth. "Happy New Year," he said, and grinned.
Two women, old friends of her mother's, kissed her on the cheek. Gene ran
over, grabbed her, and swung her around quickly, then ran off, chased by
two younger, pigtailed girls.

And then Dean was by her side. "There you are," he said. "I thought
you'd disappeared." She felt a strange fluttering in her chest at the mention of
that word, "disappeared," which she associated with her mother. He bent over
and quickly kissed her on the lips, a thankfully dry kiss, not bad, but she could
smell cigarette smoke and lasagna on his breath. Barbecue sauce, too.

"Happy New Year!" he shouted and leaned in to kiss her again, but she
was already gone, calling over her shoulder in a singsong voice, "Happy
New Year." She started across the Armory, but the band began "Rock
Around the Clock," only the fourth rock and roll song of the night, and the
dance floor immediately swelled with jitterbuggers. She had to sidestep
several couples to get to the bar. Her father saw her coming and nodded as
he raised his beer bottle. At that moment, the dark-haired woman in the
purple dress grabbed his neck and pulled his face to hers and kissed him
passionately. Laura felt embarrassed.

She turned toward her friends clustered in the corner. Another boy she
went to school with, Mike Hargrave, grabbed her, kissed her sloppily, and
said, "Come on." He pulled her to the dance floor and flung her around like

they did on *American Bandstand*. After five minutes, she was hot and sweaty and laughing. The band plunged into another hard-driving blues song, and they danced again, this time better and faster, with whirls and ropy arm loops and lots of swinging.

She was out of breath afterward and really hot. She licked her lips and brushed away the sweat from her hairline. "Thanks," she said, and when the band began yet another fast song, she begged off. "I gotta get something to drink."

"Yeah, okay," he said, turning away to find another girl. Laura felt strangely shunned. She walked to the punch bowl and ladled a cup, drank it quickly. The dance floor seemed to groan and give from the weight of the dancers. She saw Dean and decided to go outside before he tried to kiss her again.

Snow fell now, a layer of fluff on the cars, trucks, windowsills, street, and sidewalks. A green radio light glowed inside a truck across the parking lot, two heads locked together, the windows foggy. She seemed to be the only one outside. The snow and cold felt good. She walked across the lot and watched the thin, translucent lines coming down. They reminded her of Christmas tinsel. She closed her eyes, felt larger flakes splash against her cheeks, the heat from her body melting them. She thought about Gloria, who now lived in West Germany. They received letters and postcards from her every once in a while. Laura wondered if the sky looked the same there, could imagine her sister outside with her young daughter, Julie, another child on the way, staring up at the sky where her husband, the pilot, might be flying past.

Laura rubbed the back of her hand against her face, then straightened her bra, an old one that chafed under her arm and beneath her breasts. Behind the Armory, she heard a commotion and turned around. Two kids raced off, leaving behind a tipped trash can spilling cups and bottles and plates. She righted the can and, with a napkin, picked up the trash that had spilled and replaced the lid. She cupped a handful of snow, ran it over her fingers to clean them, and shook her hands until they were only damp. The snow came down in much fatter flakes now, softer, like small leaves, and she watched the swirl of white in the air. It still felt miraculously warm, though her breath misted in front of her. She listened to the thumping of the drum and the muffled lyrics from inside the hall. The whole building vibrated and buzzed with voices and stomping and laughter and music.

The screen door slapped open, and boots clomped on the wooden stairs. A tall man emerged from around the corner of the building. Mr. Letig. She stepped back into the shadow of the building and spied on him as he walked, a slight dancing stagger, to the edge of the parking lot. He put his hands down, wriggled his torso, and she could hear, after a few moments, the splash of urine on the gravel. She turned her eyes away at the sound, moved farther back into the shadows of the building, and leaned against the brick wall in the corner. The sound seemed to go on for a long time. His boots crunched over the crushed, snow-covered gravel. He crossed back to the Armory, walking slowly, moving right toward her, humming to himself. She was just going to let him pass, but without really thinking she said, "Hi, Mr. Letig."

He spun around toward her voice but couldn't locate her in the darkness. "Hello," he said, still searching. "Who's that?"

"Me," she said.

He bobbed his head until he found her. "Me who?"

"Laura."

He took a couple of steps toward her. "Laura Tate?"

"Yes, sir."

He laughed. "You don't need to 'Yes, sir' me. I'm not your father."

"Yes, sir," she said, out of habit, and they both chuckled. She stepped hesitantly from the shadow.

"You're a proper one, aren't you?"

She didn't know how to answer that. She shrugged.

He laughed again. "Happy New Year," he said and leaned in suddenly and kissed her on the mouth. The light stubble on his chin scratched her cheek. His mustache surprised her, tickled.

"Happy New Year," she said quietly, looking down, embarrassed.

"You're quite the dancer," he said.

"Not really."

"I've been watching you. You like it, I can tell."

"Yeah," she said. "It's fun, I guess."

Inside, the band began "The Cotton-Eyed Joe." The crowd chanted, clapping in rhythm and stomping their feet. The building shook. Shouts of "Bullshit!" were followed by shouts of laughter. Mr. Letig glanced toward the building. His face caught the light spilling out of the kitchen. His eyes and blond mustache seemed to glitter. Her stomach fluttered.

"I better be getting back in there," she said.

He turned to her, his face now in the dark. She lost his eyes. "I told you I'd be looking for you. I wanted to ask you something," he whispered.

Everything slowed down. She felt paralyzed. She caught a quick, bright vision of his face passing through a shaft of light that separated them. His mustache brushed her cheek. His breath was sweet, and she expected him to move away after a moment, but he didn't. His lips were against hers, and then she felt the shadow of his entire body against her own. His big hands were suddenly on either side of her face. She smelled his flannel shirt and a combination of beer, smoke, champagne, and peppermint. He felt warm. His tongue darted against her lips. She pulled away, surprised, but he eased her face back to his, and she opened her own mouth slightly and felt his tongue lightly tapping against her teeth and then touching her own tongue. This was the same as kissing boys, which she did and often liked, but it was also different, heavier, more deliberate and relaxed. She felt strangely disconnected. It seemed as if she were watching what was happening in a movie. She knew that she should stop right now, push him away, run inside. A voice whispered, *Wrong*. But the voice sounded weak, muffled, and mocking, like it didn't really mean it. Her body was somebody else's body, and she watched from above, curious and calm. He kissed her lips again and then her cheek, and then his breath on her neck was hot and oddly soothing.

He pulled her forward gently as he kissed her neck. And then his fingers swept up the curve of her hips, across her ribs, and brushed lightly over her breasts. She'd thought about this sort of thing before, sometimes late at night, or when she had kissed this boy or that, or after seeing a movie, and it had always made her feel both excited and frightened, but what she felt now was only this fluttering inside her chest and now in her head, like that first sip of champagne. She could hear breathing. Her own breathing. He was kissing the top of her chest, just above the collar of her new dress. His fingers swept across her neck and through the back of her hair, and then he kissed her again more forcefully on the mouth, his tongue entangled with her own. He pulled her close and breathed harder now, too.

The rear door suddenly slammed. Letig pulled away sharply, swiped at his mouth. Laura shook in a spasm of fright. Bob Cransburgh peered into the shadows.

"What's going on here?"

There was a slight, incriminating pause. Then Mr. Letig said very calmly, "Hello, Bob."

"Letig? Is that you?"

"Yep."

"What are you doing out here?"

"Just cooling off."

"Who's that with you?"

"Laura Tate."

"Well, what's she doing out here?" he asked, moving from the steps closer to the corner where she and Mr. Letig stood. "With you," he added.

"You're not on duty now, Bob." They both laughed. "I'm just trying to talk Laura into watching the boys for me next weekend, so Anne and I can go skiing in Colorado."

Laura didn't want to say a word, was afraid of what might spill out if she did. But she was impressed with how he sounded so calm, so convincing. Like he'd had practice.

"Where you going?" Mr. Cransburgh's voice seemed to shift noticeably, as if he'd suddenly rounded a corner and decided everything was all right.

"Outside Aspen. If we can."

"I should go in," Laura said, not looking at either of the men.

"Well, think about it," Mr. Letig said to her. He touched her shoulder lightly. "And let me know if you can do it."

She didn't speak for a second, unsure exactly what he was referring to. "Huh?"

"About next weekend."

"Oh. Yes, sir," she said. She glanced quickly at him, saw him smile. A blister of heat spread across her face. She looked down so they wouldn't see the blush and darted into the lit din of the Armory.

The band now played a mellow waltz. The floor was only half full, mainly married couples, young and old, cheek to cheek, smiling. Despite having been in the snow outside, she felt hot again. It was suffocating in here. She walked quickly to the bathroom. Two middle-aged ladies were applying lipstick. An older woman fussed with her hair. Laura darted into a stall, adjusted her dress, and wrapped tissue around her fingers and wiped her face. She waited until she heard the other women leave, then came out and leaned into the mirror. Her face was flushed, her lips swollen. Anyone would know what she'd been doing. But hadn't everybody been kissing? Her dress collar was up in back, her blond hair tangled on one side. She patted it down, then sniffed her fingers. They smelled faintly of the trash she'd picked up earlier, so she washed them quickly. She splashed water on her face and neck, too, pulled on the towel roller, and dried herself. She looked again in the mirror, and her reflection startled her, made her think of both Gloria and her mother, as if they had suddenly inhabited the features of her face. She closed her eyes and could hear herself still breathing hard, her heart thumping fast. *What have I done? Nothing, nothing.* The door opened. Laura stepped back into a stall, shut the door, and put her head against the wall. She closed her eyes. Her legs were rubbery and weak, and her head swam as it had before with the champagne. *Get a hold of yourself.* She breathed deeply several times until she felt calmer. She waited until the woman who came in washed and left. Then, finally, she opened the door and reentered the Armory.

She spotted her father by the bar at the other end of the room. He stood talking to Manny, who nodded. Gene gathered his coat and gloves and the new deck of trick cards he'd received from Aunt Velma for Christmas. Laura joined them.

"Where you been?" her father asked.

"Outside. Cooling off."

She wiped her forehead, as if wiping away sweat, then faced the dance floor. She was afraid if she looked at her father, she might say something she would regret.

"You ready to go?" he asked. "Or do you want to come home with Manny?"

The dance floor had thinned out. But moving in a slow two-step were John and Anne Letig. Mrs. Letig had her head on his shoulder, and she was smiling. She was nice-looking, with dark red hair, almost auburn, plump across the middle and in the hips. Laura liked her face—a warm, generous smile. Mrs. Letig and her mother had been friends. Not close—it seemed no one was ever very close to her mother—but they had spent some time together and liked each other's company. Laura watched Mr. and Mrs. Letig turn slowly. Although she'd baby-sat for the Letigs, she'd never thought about them as a couple. She rarely thought about her parents' married friends that way. But she wondered now. What was it like for them? She felt like she knew things now about Mrs. Letig that she shouldn't know, as if her husband had whispered secrets about her behind her back, an intimate knowledge that made Laura's stomach knot. At that moment, Mrs. Letig caught Laura's eyes. The whole night, she realized, she had felt off balance, knocked over, suddenly caught—the boy on the bass, Dean, John Letig, Bob Cransburgh, and now Mrs. Letig. She didn't know what to make of it.

She nodded at Mrs. Letig, as if they had been in conversation, but the woman only smiled and turned away.

"Laura," her father said again.

"Yes, sir?"

"Do you want to come with me or with Manny?"

"I'm ready to go," she said.

"Well, we better get a move on. I told Mrs. Ambling we'd pick up Rich by one."

She grabbed her coat, and they walked toward the door, people calling good-byes to them. She told herself not to look at the dance floor, whatever she did. She wasn't going to look. But at the front door, her father and Gene already outside, she turned back for a split second, and there was John Letig, standing at the edge. His wife was leaning over a table, talking to another couple. He stared right at Laura, as if he'd been waiting for her to turn around. Or willing it. She didn't know. She didn't wait. She lunged out the door, jumped from the deck toward her father and brother.

The snow was coming down hard and fast now, big flakes eddying in a white confusion. It felt cold through her shoes, and the draft whipped around her legs. She trotted to the truck before turning back to the Armory. The snow swirled around it like a cloud, the flakes silver and glistening in the light. She watched the Armory door, people starting to mill in and out, a few men smoking cigarettes on the deck.

Her father honked the horn, and she jumped. She opened the truck door, hopped in.

"Do you want to stay?"

"No, I'm ready."

He started the engine and turned the wipers on to slash away the powdery snow. He backed up, and they slowly eased from the parking lot, following the tracks left by the early departers. She looked over her shoulder and saw Mr. Letig standing on the deck, under the awning, the snow seeming to circle him. He raised his beer, as if toasting her.

Her father turned onto the snow-covered road, and the Armory disappeared through the trees. Within seconds Gene was asleep, his head bobbing on his chest. It began snowing harder as they drove along the old highway back toward town. The snow blew harmlessly in front of them. The slow rocking of the truck and the falling snow began to calm her. That fluttering feeling was fading now. Within a few minutes, she felt surprisingly as if all that had happened tonight, even in the last hour, had happened long ago and to someone else, someone in a book or movie. It felt exaggerated, silly. A white blanket covered the trees and fields and roads, except for the tire marks ahead of them. Charnelle lay hidden beneath, she thought. Laid to rest. The fifties gone from them now. The only time she really remembered. An amazing thought.

"It's gone," she said.

Smoke slipped from her father's lips and nostrils. "What's gone, honey?"

"The fifties," she said.

He nodded, sighed. His mouth curled around the cigarette, and he inhaled deeply, the end brightening in the cab. "Good," he said. "I'm ready for a new world."

That was an odd thing to say: "a new world." She supposed he meant a new year. A new decade. Or a new era. That's what the newspapers and radio stations called it. Maybe he'd had a few too many beers. But she liked "a new world" better. It was somehow appropriate. And slightly exotic. The last few years had been difficult for him, no doubt. For them all. Maybe they all were ready for a new world.

She closed her eyes and, leaning her head back, listened quietly to her own breathing and the hum of the truck engine. She thought she would always remember this night. What did it mean? She didn't know. What had happened had happened. And yes, she'd liked it. Some part of her had wanted it to happen. Was that possible? She breathed heavily. *Foolish*. She watched too many movies, read too many novels. She could picture Mr. Letig—Letig? John?—standing there on the deck, his beer bottle raised to her, the snow coiling around him like her father's cigarette smoke in the cab.

"Did you have a good time?" her father asked.

She opened her eyes. "Yes, sir."

He nodded. "I'm glad."

2

Foolish Things

*I*t snowed a foot in Charnelle on New Year's Day, 1960, and then the temperature dropped into the teens, so the snow didn't melt and the roads were slick with black ice. School was canceled the following Monday, which elicited a hurrah from the four Tate kids, even Rich, who didn't go to school yet but was excited by the enthusiasm of his siblings. As usual, Mr. Tate left early for work that day but was home by lunch, because the power lines were down at Charnelle Steel & Construction. The generator wouldn't be up and running until the next day, and with the acetylene torches not working, there wasn't enough light or heat to do anything except get in the way of those trying to fix the problems. He was happy to have another day off, especially at the company's expense, though it wasn't clear yet if this would be counted against his vacation days. Charnelle Steel wasn't unionized. "So you never know," he said, and went to take a nap.

Manny had trudged through the snow to Joannie's house. Gene and Rich wanted to build snowmen, so Laura helped bundle everybody up, and they went outside. Soon they had constructed a big three-tiered figure in the front yard, and without their talking about it, the snowman became a snow*woman*, sticks outlining an apron, dead branches the hair, black pecans and rocks the eyes, mouth, nose—definitely a woman. They just kept building and adding, and then they all stood back, sweaty now around their cap lines, their coats and gloves and scarves drenched from the snow. They stared at it for several minutes, and then Gene took the broom out of the hand of the snowwoman and whacked the center ball. Twigs cracked and fell. The wooden apron dropped to the ground. Laura and Rich opened their mouths in astonishment. Gene swung at the head, and it flew off.

"Hey!" Laura shouted.

But Gene struck again, and Rich ran and jumped at the two remaining balls, and the whole thing toppled over, with Rich buried face-deep in the mounds, his short arms wrapped in a wrestling hug around what was left of the body. Gene and Laura guffawed and then pulled him out of the snow and brushed him off, and as soon as they did, he dove back into the squashed remains of the woman. Gene jumped on top of Rich and shoved snow in his face, and then they turned on Laura, pelting her.

"Okay, you've had it now!" she shouted. And by the end, they were all soaked and lying in the snowy yard amid the ruins, giggling.

Her father opened the door. He wore his blue long underwear and his "home" overalls. "What happened to your snowman?" They looked at one another guiltily, then broke into laughter. "What's so funny?" he asked.

Gene and Rich couldn't stop laughing. Mr. Tate shook his head, smiling. He was glad to see them laughing. "Laura," he said. "Telephone call."

"Who is it?"

"Anne Letig."

She stopped laughing. *Had he told her? Would she know without him telling her? Did Bob Cransburgh say something?*

"What does she want?" she asked, as offhand as she could manage.

"Beats me. Said she needed to talk to you."

"Hello," Laura said tentatively.

"Hey, honey. John said he asked you to watch the boys this weekend."

"Yes, ma'am." *Was that all he said?*

"Well, change of plans. We're not going skiing, which I'm thoroughly disappointed about, but we're hoping to get out to eat and play some pinochle with the Brewers if you can come for a few hours on Saturday."

"I'll need to talk to my father about it," she said, relieved.

"Okay, you get back to me. You can bring Gene and Rich if you need to, or I can drop the boys by your house instead."

"I'll check."

Maybe it would be best if she dropped her boys off here, Laura thought, but something in her rebelled against that idea. And she didn't want Gene and Rich over there either. She wanted to be in their house by herself.

By Saturday evening, the snow was mostly cleared. Walter Clemons, the Charnelle deputy mayor, ran his plow all week. Laura thought the walk would be more treacherous and take her longer, but she made it, without slipping much, the mile to the Letig house, which was closer to the heart of the town and on a nicer street with bigger, more carefully groomed homes. She was nearly forty-five minutes early, so rather than knock on their door, she walked one more block to the downtown square.

The red granite courthouse still sported Christmas lights and large foam candy canes and wreaths, though these looked ragged and droopy from the bad weather, and Laura figured everybody had been so busy with the ice and snow that they hadn't had time to take down the decorations. Spenser's General Store and Thomason's (both owned by Glenn Thomason and connected by a brass-lined revolving door in the wall) were open until seven on Saturdays. Laura ate a couple of caramels and sucked on a sourball as she strolled through Spenser's. At Thomason's she tried on a pair of shiny black high-heeled shoes and a trim green wool collarless dress; the front of the dress fell just below the knees, and it came with a wide silver-buckled black belt. She'd seen a woman at the dance wearing one just like it, and she now felt that her own dress, with its stripes and satin bows and lacy hem, was old-fashioned, too girlish. This dress cost twenty-two dollars and the shoes another eight, which was way out of her league, but it was fun to try them on just the same. Cathy White, who worked at the store but also substitute-taught art classes at the high school, said that the dress made Laura look much older. "Twenty at least."

Cathy shook her head admiringly and whistled, saying, "You'd have to be careful walking down the streets in that, darling," which made Laura wish she had the thirty bucks for such luxuries.

She stopped in at the Ding Dong Daddy Diner, spun around on the bright red counter stool, and got a free cherry soda from Dean Compson. Under the bright lights of the diner, his faced seemed more ravaged with pimples than usual, as if he'd suffered a recent eruption, and he scuttled about sweatily busing tables and refilling hot teas, hot chocolates, and coffee mugs. He wanted to know if she would come back later, near closing. He'd be happy to drive her home.

"Can't," she said, slurping her straw noisily.

When she arrived at the Letigs' house, on time, she was disappointed to find Mr. Letig gone. He had run some errands and was going to swing back by and pick up Mrs. Letig. Laura wondered if it was an excuse, if he just didn't want to see her. Maybe he was embarrassed or ashamed of what had happened on New Year's.

Mrs. Letig looked spiffy in a nice paisley dress, which fit her loosely enough so as not to make her hips or stomach appear too thick; in that dress, Mrs. Letig looked a little like Laura's mother, though younger, prettier, even if a little heavier. Her dark red hair was pinned up in back, however, which made her face seem severe. But when she smiled, it was the same smile, generous and friendly. Laura had worried all day that maybe Mr. Letig had broken down and told his wife what he'd done. When he wasn't at the house, fear suddenly pierced Laura. She thought that maybe Mrs. Letig had kicked him out of the house, and Laura, too, would be in for a harsh scolding, or that something more terrible might happen. Just last Thursday she read that in Amarillo a woman had found her husband with another woman and shot him in the stomach, though he didn't die. But Laura's worries were not grounded, and she felt both relief and an odd disappointment. It had meant nothing, it seemed. And hadn't she spent just a little extra time in the bathroom, brushing her hair? And why had she worn her nice dress? her father wanted to know. "It's freezing outside," he'd said. "What's wrong with your overalls?"

When she arrived, Mrs. Letig said, "Now don't you look pretty." Laura blushed.

Mrs. Letig gave her the usual instructions—no dessert, easy on the liquids close to bedtime, under the covers by eight—and said they'd be back by ten or eleven. Then Mr. Letig was in the driveway honking, and Mrs.

Letig was out the door, the boys at the big window waving good-bye, Laura behind them, waving, too, smiling, feeling slightly foolish with Mrs. Letig holding her palm up, wiggling her fingers, and Mr. Letig looking behind him as he backed out. She kept waiting for him to turn around and see her. But he didn't.

John Jr. went by Jack, and the younger boy's name was William, but they called him Willie. They were good boys, not as wild as her brothers, very polite. Which must come from having Mrs. Letig for a mother—or just having a mother around, period. They played Go Fish, and the boys wrestled, and then they watched a quiz show on the Letigs' new television set. The Letigs' house was nicer than her own, newer, and it seemed bigger, though maybe it was because there were fewer people living here. Laura's father had told her that Mrs. Letig "came from money," and so while Letig didn't make a hell of a lot of money at Charnelle Steel, Anne Letig provided "the frills"—the decorations and furniture, the ski trips. "A mixed blessing," her father called it. And Manny said he wasn't sure he'd want to marry a woman who had more money than he had: "You'd be pussy-whipped for sure." Manny talked like that more and more around the house. Her father didn't seem to mind. Manny'd never say that if their mother were still at home.

By eight-thirty, the boys were asleep. Laura turned the television back on, but she wasn't really interested. She wanted to look around, didn't she? She'd been thinking about it all week, the thoughts hiding slyly at the corners of her mind. She'd been planning it. She was sneaky. She didn't want to take anything, nothing devious or mean. Just curious, curious about . . . well, just curious. It's why she didn't want Gene or Rich to come with her, wasn't it? Why she'd said no when they asked. "You can't come," she'd told them, though Mrs. Letig had said just the opposite.

She checked on the boys again, shut their door tight so she'd hear if it opened. She just wanted to take a peek. The bedroom wasn't forbidden. The door was open. No one had said, "Don't go in there." And what was there to see? She flipped on the light. Two dresses laid out on the bed, a blue cotton one and an olive green linen. Discards. She touched them, the fabric soft in her fingers, much nicer than her own dresses.

Mrs. Letig's vanity table: lipstick, rouge, an orderly array of makeup, hair spray, a red velvet jewelry box. One of her drawers was half open. Laura could see a white girdle, the big cottony bras like her mother left behind, and something red and shiny underneath, something black too. Frilly. Is this what her father meant by "frills"? She thought of the woman he'd brought home that one time. But never again. A kind of frill he didn't allow himself anymore, it seemed.

And his dresser. Nothing much there. In fact, not much different than her father's. A work watch, the face scratched. Some scattered pieces of folded paper. A pack of Wrigley's gum. A white handkerchief. What was she hoping to find? The top drawer was ajar. She could see inside: T-shirts, socks. She felt funny, her heart racing. Okay, she'd open it just a bit. She put her hand on the drawer, eased it slowly out. The wood scraped. She held her breath, then peeked in. Behind the shirts were a couple of pairs of boxer shorts. One white, the other with little red diamonds, like on a deck of cards.

She heard something. She froze for a second, terrified, then shut the drawer quickly, skipped out of the room, flipping the light. The boys' door was still closed. She raced to the living room, jumped into the chair. Her heart thundered in her chest, in her neck. She could feel heat spreading over her face. She pretended to watch the television, Nat King Cole crooning on some variety show. But no, it wasn't them. No car. She listened again. Just a branch blowing against a window shutter. She took a deep breath, let it out slowly. She got up and looked out the window, then went back in the bedroom and made sure the drawer was closed except for the small opening, everything left in exactly the same place it had been. The dresses exactly as before. Nothing disturbed. Nothing out of the ordinary. Then she returned to the kitchen, washed the dishes left in the sink, picked up the toys. The sort of thing that might earn you a little extra, if you were lucky.

Mrs. Letig took a dollar from her purse and handed it to Laura, light electricity passing between them when their fingers touched. "Thank you," Laura said, putting on her jacket and starting for the door.

"Oh, honey, you can't walk in this cold. John'll take you." She called toward the bedroom, "John, are you ready to run Laura home?"

There was no answer.

"Really, it's not so bad. I don't mind walking at all."

"Nonsense. Your father would have my hide if you caught cold. It won't be a second." She walked back to the bedroom. Laura could hear her muffled high voice. "Sweetie, Laura needs you to run her home."

Laura wished Mrs. Letig hadn't said it that way. It made it seem like Laura's idea. She heard the low register of his voice but couldn't make out the words.

"Stop that," Mrs. Letig whispered. "Now put your shoes back on."

A minute later they both emerged from the bedroom. Mrs. Letig had pulled out the pins, and her hair fell over her shoulders in soft ringlets. It was prettier that way, beautiful even, which surprised Laura.

"Ready?" Mr. Letig asked without looking her in the eye. His hair seemed unusually blond in the light, his mustache a sandy brown. Those red lips. But he was avoiding her, she could tell.

"Yes, sir," she said deliberately. But he didn't acknowledge the joke.

"Go hop in the car. It should still be warm inside. I'll be right there."

"Thank you again, honey," Mrs. Letig said.

"You're welcome."

From the car she saw him kiss his wife good-bye. It was a long kiss, and he did something else with his hand that Laura didn't quite see, but Mrs. Letig pushed him away playfully, smiling, her head tilted. The front door opened and out he came; Laura looked through the side window, agitated. She had the strange feeling that he had been carrying on for her benefit.

"Oh, it's colder than I thought," he said inside the car. "Let me warm her up." He flipped on the heater. "Were the boys good for you?"

"Yes, sir." He smiled nervously, and she could tell he got the joke this time.

"Good," he said.

"Did you have fun tonight?" she asked.

"Yes. Thanks for coming."

"You're welcome."

They drove for a minute in silence.

"Did you have fun at the New Year's Eve party?" she asked. She said it fast and tried to make it sound casual, but her heart started beating quickly in the quiet after she spoke. She was suddenly aware of her breath misting lightly in front of her.

He glanced sideways at her, pursed his lips, and nodded his head slowly. "Yes, ma'am," he drawled, smiling, and there was a joke in that. "Yes, I did. Probably too much fun."

"You drank a bunch, huh?" She laughed.

"Yeah, I guess I did. I felt it the next morning, too."

She looked at his mustache. She remembered the way it had felt against her cheek, above her lips when he kissed her, like the bristles of a toothbrush. "So did Manny," she said. "He was so sick he didn't even want to watch the Cotton Bowl on New Year's."

There was an awkward lull. She held her hands in her lap and stared out the window.

"Did *you* have a good time?" he asked.

She nodded, then realized he couldn't see her. "Yes."

"You sure do like to dance," he said, and she remembered he'd said the same thing that night. "You're good at it, too."

"I don't know," she said dismissively. "It's fun."

After a minute of silence, he said, "Listen, Laura, I sometimes do foolish things when I get a little drunk. Sometimes I remember them, sometimes I don't. Well, I vaguely remember doing something a little foolish that night. And . . . well . . . I'm sorry about that."

So that was it. He didn't even remember. Or not all of it. Or maybe he was just sorry. She realized that she'd rather he didn't remember than be sorry.

"Don't worry about it," she said.

He turned down her street and pulled into her driveway. The lights were on in the living room and at Mrs. Ambling's house next door. He shifted the car into park.

"Thanks again," he said. "For baby-sitting, I mean." He smiled, and at that moment she felt a bold thrill run through her. She nodded and started to open the door, then turned and leaned across the bench seat and kissed him on the cheek. His face was clean-shaven, smooth. Then she kissed his mouth. She pulled back and looked up at him in the dark, smiling. His thick, nearly white eyelashes seemed to shimmer. She liked that expression on his face—slack-jawed, stunned, astonished really, his eyes wide open.

"You're welcome," she said and scooted over and out the door. She ran to the house, her arms swinging freely, and hopped up the cement porch stairs, still rimmed in snow. She looked back at his car but could only see the two white globes of the headlights. She could not see inside but could imagine him peering out, fixing her on the porch. It was risky, she knew. Her father, her brothers, Mrs. Ambling—anybody could have been looking out—but she didn't care. She liked the recklessness of it. He'd done it to her. *Turnabout was fair play*. Isn't that what Manny always said, needling her? She smiled and waved and then was inside, where Gene stared up at her from the floor where he was working on a model airplane. Manny just barely acknowledged her with a nod, his ear next to his transistor radio. Her father walked into the living room, wearing a yellow apron of her mother's, a gray dish towel in his hand.

"How'd it go?" he asked.

"Good," she chirped and pulled the dollar from her coat pocket, waving it so they all could see.

3

✳

Don't Tamper with It

*I*n school the next week her English teacher, Mrs. McFarland, told them—quoting some German writer, Laura couldn't remember who—that "boldness has genius, power, and magic in it." And that struck Laura as perfectly right. Anytime she'd done something that scared her, just plunged in—dancing wildly, walking on the edge of Palo Duro Canyon, swimming across Lake Meredith with Manny and Gloria one summer, running outside in her underwear in the snow on a dare at a slumber party, and now kissing Mr. Letig in his car—she always felt wonderful afterward, triumphant and graceful. And yes, like there was some touch of genius in the act itself. She'd have to remember that. Yes, she would.

The following Wednesday Mrs. Letig called and asked if Laura could watch the boys that weekend. "Sure thing," she said, this time without consulting her father.

———————

The next Saturday night she dressed nicely, but not too nice, not like before. She had washed her hair and braided it, and when she undid it, her hair was wavy. She had been thinking about him, and she looked forward to seeing him. She planned to gauge from his eyes how he felt about her kissing him in the car. But there would be no secret trips into the bedroom this time. None of that foolishness. That was crazy.

She couldn't figure out what to call him. Not so much in public—in anybody else's company, she would always refer to him as Mr. Letig, and she doubted there'd be another "incident," as she now thought about it. But for herself, she wanted a private name. "Mr. Letig" seemed too formal, and "Letig" too much a man's way of talking to another man. It made her think of locker rooms and Manny's sweaty gym clothes. "John" was what Mrs. Letig called him, but still she liked that name best of all. It was simple, familiar, intimate, and when she thought of him as John, she could see the boy in him. It must be odd to have many names, she thought. She could see herself only as Laura. She'd never had a nickname. Her father called her sister Morning Glory. When her brothers were little, they'd sometimes called her Laalee, but it was something they grew out of soon enough. Miss Tate. She could imagine that, though it seemed proper, too proper, what some of her teachers called her if she was talking with her friends when she wasn't supposed to, that voice they use when they want to scold or humiliate you. Later, when she married, if she married, it would be Mrs. Something-or-Other. Mrs. Letig. Laura Letig. She had to admit it had a nice ring to it. *Hush now. Stop that.*

Cold again, but not that cold. And Mr. and Mrs. Letig, John and Anne, were ready to go when she got there. He looked at her now, smiled, and was there something else as well? She smiled back, what she hoped was mysteriously.

When they returned around ten o'clock, Mrs. Letig gave her another dollar. It was odd how his wife was the one doling out the money; that had not been the way with her parents. Her father always took care of the money, paid the bills, paid for everything. Even at the Piggly Wiggly or Spenser's General Store, they ran tabs, which her father paid off at the end of each month. Laura wondered vaguely if that was perhaps why John Letig had kissed her, if there was some connection between his wife's control over the money and what happened that night at the Armory.

She got in the car, where he was waiting behind the steering wheel. She smiled, asked easily, "Did you have fun?" She felt mischievous. She wanted to tease him. He nodded. They drove in silence for a few moments, and then he turned on the radio to Bobby Darin crooning about his "Dream Lover." Tapping her foot to the song, she couldn't stop smiling. She felt calm and knowing.

"You surprised me last time," he said.

"Really?"

"Yes, really," he said.

There was a pause, then she said, mock annoyed, "Do you want me to apologize?"

He laughed. "No, no need to do that. I liked it. In fact, I've been thinking about it ever since. Sometimes nothing but. Yesterday I about near cut my hand off at the table saw because of you."

He laid his hand open on the seat and showed her a cut across his palm.

"That's terrible," she said.

"Yep, that's right. It's terrible. But you had me preoccupied."

She felt horrible that she had caused such an accident. She reached down and touched his palm.

"Aaaahhhhh!" he screamed, and his hand flopped on the seat like a fish.

She jumped, her hands flying to her mouth. "Oh, my God! I'm so sorry!"

He started laughing. "I'm just kidding." He put his hand down. "It doesn't hurt."

She reached across the seat and hit his arm. "That wasn't funny," she said, but she laughed hard, then caught herself. "It wasn't."

"Then why are you laughing?"

"Shut up," she said.

"You're very pretty, Laura," he said. "Especially when you scream like that. 'Ohhhhh, my God! I'm so sorry!' " he shrieked.

"Quit it," she said. "You're cruel."

"*Cruel?* I just said you're pretty."

"I don't care what you said. You're still cruel."

But she liked this about him, liked this easy teasing. He wasn't driving her home. He drove past her house and then down a dark, houseless road several blocks away that turned to gravel.

"Where are we going?" she asked, a little nervous.

"Just for a short drive. Is that okay?"

She wasn't sure, but she said, haltingly, "Yeah, I guess."

"I could take you home."

"No, that's okay."

He drove a little farther east of town, out where the houses became farms and ranches and the lights from the town were dim. He turned left, down another potholed road that led to an unlit farmhouse. On the radio, Wilbert Harrison sang brightly about going to Kansas City—Kansas City, here he comes. Letig parked behind the barn. The windows were boarded up, the grass high around the doors. She didn't know if she liked this. He turned off the lights but kept the car running and the radio on, where now the Platters harmoniously complained about the smoke in their eyes.

"I thought you wanted to drive," she said, trying to regain the light-hearted tone from before.

"Not anymore."

"What is this place?"

"This used to be my uncle's farm. I worked here when I was about your age."

He turned the ignition off and cracked his window so that a cool draft blew in. She felt uneasy. He laid his hand across the seat, close to her. "It doesn't hurt. Really."

She reached down and touched his palm nervously, then rested her own hand on the seat next to his. He put a couple of fingers gently on the top of her hand. She wanted to back things up. She preferred the teasing and laughter from before. Everything seemed too quiet now, too charged.

"Why did you kiss me?" he asked.

"I don't know," she said, laughing. "To get you back, I guess."

He nodded. "You're a flirt, aren't you?"

"No." She didn't smile.

"Hold my hand."

"Why?"

"Because I want you to."

She opened her palm to him, and he put his hand in hers. His hand was big, easily twice the size of her own. And there were thin hairs on the back.

He squeezed her palm. She could feel the cut. She remembered when she and Marlene Shopper were much younger, they'd cut their palms with an army knife and rubbed the blood together. Blood sisters.

"That's nice," he said.

He leaned over, and she moved her face away instinctively. He leaned in very slowly and kissed her cheek. She turned away. He reached out with his other hand and gently turned her face back to his. Then he kissed her softly on the lips. He tilted his chin away but kept his forehead next to hers, almost touching.

"What would your wife say about this?" she whispered. She wasn't sure why she'd said it. It sounded like a line from a movie.

"Let's not talk about that."

"But—"

"Shhhhhh." He placed his index finger next to her lips, then dropped his hand and kissed her again. She let herself be kissed, and then she could feel her head moving toward him. It was like easing from the side of a boat into a warm lake. Different from kissing boys, very different. That gravity, a heaviness she remembered from New Year's.

As they kissed, he touched her face again and then slowly moved his fingers down her neck to the top of her chest. She put her hand on his, to hold him, to keep him still. His hands were very different from his lips— big, a roughness to them, despite his long, slender fingers. They made her nervous.

He was gentle, though. He didn't move his hand, just let it rest there.

"Sorry," he whispered. She pressed her lips against his harder. She didn't want him to talk about it. Words only complicated things, made her more nervous. He pulled back. "I don't know what to think about you," he said.

"What do you mean?"

"You *are* a flirt, aren't you?" He kissed her again. "How old are you?"

She hesitated, thought about lying. But didn't. Her birthday was in December. "Sixteen." She almost added "barely," but stopped herself.

He lifted his eyebrows and then leaned his head against the seat. He closed his eyes and made his red mouth into an O and blew out in an exaggerated sigh.

"Ouch!"

He was still holding her hand. She liked the way he looked there, against the seat, relaxed, his eyes closed. He looked vulnerable. She put her other hand up to his face, ran the backs of her fingers across the light stubble of his cheek. He didn't move, didn't open his eyes. She touched his lips, those almost feminine lips, thick with that strange redness to them, his blond mustache above like soft bristle.

Then, abruptly, he pushed her hand away, sat up, and shook his head.

"I better get you home. It's late."

Something had happened. Some line had been crossed. The feeling was not the same.

"Okay," she said quickly, not wanting to agitate him further. "Sure. Fine."

He started the car, turned on the lights. Everything was suddenly about shifting gears, backing up, the logistics of getting her home—like nothing had happened. But something had, and they both knew it. What had felt good just a few minutes ago now felt ugly, unseemly. He wouldn't look at her. He pursed his lips. He was thinking. She could imagine what it might be about but didn't want to say anything. *Don't tamper with it,* she thought, that old phrase of her father's when he was fixing something and the kids were underfoot. She adjusted her dress, pushed back her hair. She felt embarrassed. "Mack the Knife" was playing now, and he turned up the volume, too loud, as he drove, looking straight ahead. He pulled a cigarette from his pocket and lit up. He shook his head now and again. She saw his lips move in the silent gesture of words, but they weren't the words to the song.

"I'm sorry," he said when they reached her house. "I shouldn't have done this. I knew I shouldn't, but I did, and I'm sorry."

She didn't know what to say to that. He was too solemn. Was he implying that it was his fault or hers?

"Okay," she said.

"Would you do me a favor?" he asked.

What, what is it? What did he want from her? "Yeah," she said, "sure."

"Don't say anything about this."

Why was he being so cold about it? It hurt, his voice. "I wouldn't," she said.

"Not to anyone."

"I won't, really. I promise."

She felt insulted. She started to cry. Suddenly the tears were there, and she was angry about it, angry that they were sprouting from her eyes. She turned her head and wiped at her face quickly so he couldn't see. Her throat constricted.

"Hey," he said and turned off the radio. "Hey, there. Calm down."

She laughed, a propulsive sound, too loud for the car. "I'm sorry," she said, laughing again and wiping her eyes with the back of her hand. "It's dumb. It's *so* dumb."

He reached across the seat and touched her arm, a gesture of pity. She resisted, but he pulled her arm toward him and held her hand, squeezing it firmly. She could feel the cut.

"Are you gonna be okay?"

"Yeah," she said. "Yes, sir." A current of bitterness crept in. It was no joke now. She turned to him. He smiled, but in a kind of grimace, his forehead wrinkled, eyes squinting shut.

"Hey," he said. "I'm——"

But she was out the door before he could finish. And then inside. She didn't look back this time.

4

Can't Tell

She didn't want to think about him, but she couldn't help it. He was there on the screen of her imagination. At home, hanging up the laundry on the line, the early-spring wind biting cold, snapping the sheets, she'd see, in the play of shadow and light, an image that looked like him on the deck of the Armory, a beer in his hand, the snow spitting at his receding form. In history class, dozing during Mr. Nelson's lecture on Santa Anna's surrender, she saw his body moving away from her, that athlete's graceful swagger, the muscles of his arms and back and legs and buttocks rippling beneath his clothes. At night, too, she was shaken by dreams, could feel his tongue on her lips, on her neck, that soft mustache over her skin. She soon found herself awaiting these images, disappointed when they weren't there. She went to sleep eagerly now at night in hopes that he would appear, and sometimes she woke before they were over, and she would close her eyes quickly and try to slip into the center of the dream, and occasionally she could do it, and when she woke in the morning, she felt feverish, her body damp and chill-bumped, because sometimes in the dreams he seemed to swallow her whole, envelop her in his big body, like a cat eating a small animal, and at other times, she could hear that exaggerated sigh of his, see his pursed lips shaped in an O, and a cold, metallic film seemed to slip over his face that would exclude or indict her. A dark kernel of shame would grow hard and thorny in her stomach, and sometimes she felt she carried around this shame, visibly, for everyone to see.

She'd look for his pickup on her way to school and walking back home. She waited sometimes by the phone, trying to will it to ring, and one time, as she sat staring at it, concentrating, it did ring; the sharp, shrill staccato alarmed her. She didn't dare touch it for fear the phone might burn her hand.

"Pick it up, goddamn it!" Manny said, but she just sat there, in shock, and he grabbed it, a twist of disgust on his lips. "What's wrong with you?" he asked, covering the phone.

Turned out it was for him, anyway. But it had spooked her.

Finally she wrote him a letter. She started and stopped several times, spending too many hours on it, shredding each draft into tiny pieces before beginning the next. Eventually she wrote one that was as good as it was going to get.

> *Dear Mr. Letig,*
>
> *I'm sorry about the other day. I'm sorry if I embarrassed you. I don't know what I was thinking. I was confused, and it's not like this has happened to me before. I'm not a flirt, and I won't say anything. Let's just forget about it. I suppose I shouldn't give you this letter. I probably won't, except it helps to write it down, and I want you to know.*
>
> *Sincerely,*
>
> *Laura Tate*

When she read it over, though, it seemed wrong still. There was something foolish about it, a sentimental pleading, a defensive undercurrent that seemed to say, *It's not my fault, it's not my fault. I'm really a good girl.* But she didn't know how to get around that, or underneath, or through it. It was just there as a kind of ghost image of the letter. She started to throw it away, but then she quickly put it in an envelope, addressed and stamped it. She didn't put her own address on it. She ran to the post office with it clutched in her hand, and the running seemed to carry a momentum of its own, so that when she got inside, her heart beating rapidly, her legs tingly, the motion of putting it in the slot seemed without consequence, like a wave or a gesture, nothing to it. When it slipped from her fingers, like a quick good-bye, the envelope disappearing into the darkness of the bin, she felt a momentary gasping *oh, no,* but then it was done, and there was no getting it back, and finally it was out of her system, and there was nothing in the damn letter anyway, except an apology. It was over.

As she walked home, a hummingbird hovered in front of her face for several seconds, and it seemed like a sign, a good sign. She felt better, and after that he seemed to disappear from her thoughts, and she slept that night and the following three nights, not dreaming at all, and each morning she woke up, fresh and ready for the day, as if the world were waiting for her to be in it again.

Four days later, however, emerging from the clogged doors of the school with Marlene Shopper and Debbie Carlson, she saw his pickup across the street, sitting there like a huge red exclamation point. He waited until he knew she saw him and then pointed to the street. He drove slowly down the block and turned right. She told her friends she had to go back, that she'd forgotten her history book, that she'd walk on home alone. She went inside the school and then down through the corridor and exited at the south entrance and walked quickly in the direction he'd gone. She got to the end of the block, turned right, and saw him parked in an alley.

"Get in," he said. "Quick."

When she opened the door, he said again, "Quick. And put your head down." She closed the door behind her and did as he instructed. "Down more!"

She crouched on the floorboard with her arms resting on the seat. She felt nervous, sick to her stomach. She thought she might vomit. "What's going on?"

"Ssshhh," he hissed.

He pulled out of the alley, turned, and drove in silence. After a couple of minutes, she couldn't stay quiet anymore. "Is it about—"

"Please, just stay down."

The heater blew on her neck. She could feel the vibration of the truck's wheels in her knees. She was afraid. She should never have written that letter. Never sent it. *Stupid, stupid, stupid.* How could she be so dumb?

"Hey, I'm sorry about the letter," she said. "Just forget it."

"We have to talk about it."

"No, we don't," she blurted out, panicked. "Just let me out now."

"No!"

He drove on without saying anything else. The asphalt gave way to a dirt road and the absence of noise from other cars. He turned left and then left again, then parked. She could see the barn where they had been before. At one time, it had been red. But now boards were out, paint peeling.

"Can I get up?" she asked sarcastically.

"Yes. I'm sorry about that."

She sat back in the seat.

"You can't do that!" he barked, his eyes wide and angry, his finger pointed threateningly at her. "You can't send me letters. You're damn lucky Anne didn't see it!"

She shrank against the door. "I'm sorry. Jeez!"

He sighed heavily and clutched the steering wheel. "No, I'm not saying this right," he muttered to himself and then turned to her more calmly. "Okay, first, I'm flattered, really I am. But we can't do what we're doing."

"We're not doing anything."

"What I mean is that it's dangerous the way I *feel*."

He was agitated, clearly, but it now seemed to be more from his own confusion, his inability to articulate what he wanted to say. She felt less nervous.

"I don't understand."

"I'm almost twice your age."

What did he think she was asking him to do?

"I could go to jail."

"What?"

"It's true."

"I'm sorry about the letter. That was a mistake. I just wanted you to know that I wasn't going to say anything. And that I was sorry—"

"I want to be a good man," he interrupted. It seemed like he hadn't heard what she'd said. "I haven't always been. I want to be now. Can you understand that?"

There was that implication that she didn't want him to be, or that she herself wasn't good. She knew that she wasn't, she knew that, but it hurt more that he thought so.

"I'm not asking you to not be good," she stated, momentarily confused by her own words. And then, more deliberately, "I'm not asking you to do anything."

"Your father is my friend."

"I know."

"And I . . . love my wife."

She didn't want to hear this. "Can I have my letter back?"

"I burned it."

"*Burned* it?"

"Don't write me letters," he pleaded.

She shook her head. She was afraid she might cry again.

"Okay?" he asked. "Do you understand?"

She nodded. He seemed finished. The first wave was over. He had said what he wanted her to hear. And now there was only silence. They sat there, and it seemed strange to her, absurd. She laughed, nervously, and regretted it.

"Why are you laughing? This isn't funny."

"I know, I know. I'm sorry. I sometimes laugh when I'm upset."

"Sorry," he said after a few moments. "I didn't mean to upset you. It's just that your letter scared the shit out of me. Anne almost saw it. I probably overreacted, but it was a very dangerous thing for you to do."

She nodded. He was right. She wouldn't make that mistake again.

"Okay then. I'm sorry I yelled at you."

He reached for her hand. She let him hold it. The clouds had moved across the sun, and now the sky seemed darker, closer to dusk than it really was. She felt suddenly as if the air between them had been cleared. He leaned over and kissed her on the cheek. She put her face to his chest. She could feel him loosening up. And then he put his arms around her tentatively and clasped his hands together.

"What am I going to do with you?" he whispered, almost inaudible.

He sighed again, his chest rising, and then seemed to catch his breath.

But she could feel his heart ticking in his chest. Ticking fast. He was afraid. He was. He kissed her forehead. She watched the clouds through the window, dark now, like torn black blossoms.

"You can't ever say anything," he said.

"I know."

"Not to *anybody*. Ever."

"Okay," she said, though she felt uneasy. The secrecy didn't concern her. That seemed simple enough. But what was she promising? What was she promising herself? She felt like she was crossing over to something she could only dimly envision, some strange place shrouded in fog. *A new world*, her father had said, though it made her stomach turn to think about him at this moment, to think about the way she was using his words. It was her father—as much as, if not more than, John's wife—that she couldn't say anything to.

"Tell me you understand that," he said again, more urgently.

"I understand," she said, though she wasn't quite sure she did.

5

✴

Secret Sharer

*A*nother snowstorm hit Charnelle for four weeks from late January to late February. The town shut down. Pipes burst. No one could even walk to the grocery store. Within a week of the first snows, things reached a desperate point. One widow died when her heat went out. The governor sent the National Guard with huge plows to make the roads passable. Still the snow kept coming. It was like a military zone at first, but then some of the guardsmen became friendly with the people in town. Near the end of February, the worst was over, but the military jeeps were still in Charnelle, and the guardsmen offered free rides.

Laura was happy at first about missing school, but she soon grew weary of the isolation. Although classes resumed once the Guard cleared the streets enough for the kids to walk, bundled, to school, most other social interaction was limited. Her father had lost almost a week of work and had spent most of that time shoveling snow, fixing pipes for their house and Mrs. Ambling's house, uncovering the drifts in front of the storm cellar so they could get to the canned fruits and vegetables, and repairing the heater, which faltered with each new dip below zero. Manny and Gene were often enlisted in these chores, and Laura was put in charge of the house and Rich, cooking meals, trying to do laundry with only cold water. She had to string a makeshift clothesline throughout the house, much more elaborate than what her mother had ever done, in order to dry the clothes, both the ones she'd washed and the ones that everybody wore, which were perpetually drenched from the slush and snow. It was hard, sometimes complicated and tiring work, but she did it without much complaint. She went to bed exhausted, and for a couple of nights she slept as if dead, without dreams, but then once she'd adjusted to the new conditions and grown used to the pace, she found herself bored, ready to return to school, to her friends. It was less work there.

She also longed to see John Letig again. At night, before bed, she found herself thinking of him. She was reading a Joseph Conrad novella, *The Secret Sharer*, for her English class. It was about a young captain on his maiden voyage. He felt alone and estranged from his crew, and on the first night of the voyage he saw a green glow in the water, and out of it emerged a naked man, whom the captain, for reasons he could not understand himself, decided to keep hidden from his crew. He stowed him away in his cabin, fed and clothed him, whispered to him in the darkness. Another ship came by, searching for their first mate, who had killed a crew member, was imprisoned on board, then escaped into the waters. It was the captain's stowaway, but still the captain didn't give up his secret. He wanted to keep the man for himself. Finally, on the verge of going crazy, the captain ran the ship dangerously close to shore to allow his friend to jump into the water and swim safely to a deserted island.

No one else in Laura's class seemed to like the story much, but she found herself mesmerized, as if it were speaking directly, knowingly to her. The mysterious man's name was Leggatt, which startled her to read, as if Conrad were reaching through half a century to grab her by the throat. And, like the young captain, she felt that her Letig had come suddenly into her life not only to complicate it but also to reveal something to her. When she read the passages about the two men together, whispering in the dark, she thought of the last time she and John had been together. After he had sworn her to silence, he held her as it grew dark, and he kissed her and touched her arms and back, and it had been tender and reserved, and as the night fell around them, it had been, above all, secret. As they drove down her street, they saw her father working on his truck in the front gravel driveway, clamp lamps attached to the hood.

"Are you ready for this?" John asked.

She nodded. They pulled to a stop, and she hopped out of John's truck. Her father eyed them suspiciously.

"Where've you been?" he asked.

Before she could answer, John said, "Sorry, Zeeke. I had to get Anne a dress and needed some help picking something out. Saw Laura walking home and grabbed her. Didn't mean to keep her out so late."

Her father looked at Laura for confirmation. "We found a nice dress," she said, smiling. "A blue one with white polka dots."

"Thanks, Laura," John said.

"Yes, sir," she answered casually and then skipped to the door. Inside, she peeked out the window. Her father was at John's truck, his arm draped over the top of the cab. Her stomach tightened. John's face was serious, but her father's head nodded in an easy, familiar way, and she knew it was going to be all right this time. She waved to him. She could tell he saw it, but he didn't gesture back, and she felt suddenly guilty, as if she were betraying her father. But she was also deeply thrilled at that moment.

She turned, and there was Manny, raking a comb through his slicked-back hair, a hand-rolled cigarette dangling from his lips. "What are you up to?" he asked, the cigarette bobbing.

"Nothing."

"Bullshit," he said, smirking.

"Shut up!"

"Are you running around with someone?"

"No."

"Then where were you?"

"With Mr. Letig . . . helping him find an anniversary gift for Mrs. Letig."

"Yeah, I bet," he said and leaned close so that the lit end of his cigarette waggled before her. He puffed a cloud of smoke in her face.

"Get away from me, you idiot." She pushed past him and went into the bathroom. She looked in the mirror. Were her lips swollen? Did it show? She washed her hands and face with cold water, brushed her teeth, then changed into her overalls and went into the kitchen and began making the pork chops she'd put in the icebox that morning to thaw.

Just a week later, the blizzard had hit. She had seen Letig—John—only twice. Once he'd dropped her father off after work. He'd stepped inside, a sash of snow on his shoulders and across his chest, and waited for Laura's father to fetch a tool. Laura came into the living room and saw him standing there, alone, like a declaration. His cheeks and nose were red from the cold, his blond mustache tinged in frost. She had the impulse to go to him, to touch him, to wipe the snow from his coat. He smiled and then his gaze moved upward, over her shoulder, and her father suddenly brushed past her, pipe wrench in hand.

"Hope this helps," he said, holding it out to John. "Remember to turn the water off first before you unscrew it."

"Thanks. I'll get it back to you tomorrow."

He raised the wrench in a good-bye to her father and then nodded in her direction and was gone. There seemed to be a ghost image of him left at the door, and she closed her eyes and could see his silhouette lined in silver against her lids.

The second time he'd come to pick up his boys, after Mrs. Letig had left them with Laura for the afternoon so she could have her hair done. While the boys were playing with Gene and Rich in the backyard, he kissed her on the lips. It was so sudden, it alarmed her. She shook as he held the kiss too long. Only a couple of seconds after he pulled away, his sons bounded into the room, their jackets in hand.

"Ready to go, boys?" he asked cheerfully.

She and John exchanged frightened, exhilarated looks, and then he pulled out his wallet, withdrew a couple of dollars, and handed them to her, his fingers in her palm a few moments too long. "For services rendered," he said, laughing heartily.

She smiled at the double meaning of this. She liked the implication of the phrase, like she was his mistress. And that night in the bathroom after her bath, steam swirling, her hair wet and tangled before her eyes, she wiped the foggy mirror and looked at her flushed body, her breasts and neck and face pink and warm from the heat, water beaded on her skin, and she wondered if indeed mistresses moved in this peculiar space that she seemed to occupy: dark, hazy, warm, a wetly electric charge on the skin.

Now, having not seen him in over two weeks, she found herself thinking of him as the mysterious Leggatt, a green, phosphorescent glow on the water, dangerous. That was his word, too. *Dangerous.* It was dangerous what they were doing. That's what he'd said. And yet worthwhile? Secretly meaningful? She even woke one night and beside her bed was a greenish glow on the floor, and still half dreaming, she swore she saw him rise from this puddle. Then she was awake for sure.

Laura's English teacher asked what the students thought the novella was about.

"It's about an idiot who nearly crashes his ship for a murderer," Gordy Toffler said.

"It's about someone," Marlene offered, "who risks everything for nothing."

"It's about the value of a secret life," Laura said, without really meaning to. It was something she'd written down in her diary about the book and about which she'd been thinking ever since. She hadn't meant to utter the words, but they came out before she could stop them. Everyone turned a head in her direction, eyebrows curiously arched. A blush crept over her face.

"Excellent, Laura," Mrs. McFarland said, raising her own head appreciatively, a knowing smile at the corner of her lips. "Would you care to elaborate?"

6

✴

Arrangements

I have a favor to ask you." It was Mrs. Letig on the phone. "I've got to get away from this town. The snow and cold are depressing the hell out of me. I'm going to take the bus to Dallas to see my sister. I wondered if maybe you could watch the boys during the days while John is at work."

The thought of Mrs. Letig gone for a week flipped a switch in Laura's chest. "Maybe," she said. "I'll see."

"I understand if you don't want to. I realize it's your spring break, too, but I figured you'd have to watch Rich and Gene. Unless Mrs. Ambling's going to do it."

"I don't know," Laura said. "My father hasn't said anything."

She did know, of course. Ever since her mother had left, Laura was responsible for the boys during breaks, though Mrs. Ambling kept Rich during the days when she was at school, and her father was pretty good about letting her hang out with her friends if she wanted to. Mrs. Ambling's husband had died a few years ago of lung cancer, and her children and grandchildren lived in Fort Worth and San Antonio, so she rarely saw them and even more rarely received money from them to help with her bills. Mr. Tate liked Mrs. Ambling—had grown fonder of her since Laura's mother left—and he tried to help her out financially when he could. He paid her a little each month (Laura and Manny debated how much) for watching Rich and sometimes Gene when Laura or Manny couldn't do it, and Mr. Tate and the boys also did the maintenance on her house and mowed her yard. Laura often bought groceries for her when she went to the Piggly Wiggly. But Laura figured she'd be stuck with the boys this spring break because Mrs. Ambling had said just yesterday that she needed to go to Pampa to help her brother, who had broken his ankle.

"I'll tell you what," Mrs. Letig said. "I'll pay you twenty dollars for the week. And an extra ten so you can take everyone out to eat or to something fun, or maybe to the movies if the Somersby brothers open up the drive-in. John'll drop them off in the mornings and pick them up when he gets off, usually around six or six-thirty. What do you think?"

"That's too much, Mrs. Letig. My father would never let me accept that."

"No, I insist. The boys are crazy about you."

Laura liked hearing that. She wanted those boys to like her, though she knew that her reasons for wanting this were complicated and confusing.

"Plus, you're bound to need some spending cash," Mrs. Letig continued, "or maybe you're saving up for something special. And this would be wonderful for me. One of my cousins is getting married soon, and she wants some help with the wedding. And if I don't get out of this dreary town, I think I might go nuts."

Laura was silent and so was Mrs. Letig, as if she realized suddenly that Laura's sister and mother had apparently felt the same way—and had never come back.

"Anyway, you talk to your father about it."

"Okay," Laura said. "Sure thing."

"Oh, thank you so much. You're a lifesaver. You don't know what this trip means to me."

She felt she should say something like "You deserve it" or "Sounds like fun," something encouraging, but the words stuck in her throat. She liked Anne Letig. She did. She remembered a few times, years ago, arriving home from school to find her mother and Mrs. Letig sitting at the kitchen table, drinking coffee, playing gin rummy, Gene and Rich and Jack running around with Fay and the other dogs in the backyard. The two women shared an easy, conspiratorial camaraderie that Laura felt she sometimes intruded upon. This was even before Gloria started dating Jerome, before Gloria eloped, before her mother had grown silent and distant, more mysterious and moody, back when her mother still seemed able to laugh easily.

It also seemed as if what Laura felt for Mrs. Letig's husband was not connected to her feelings for his wife. There was something wrong about this, she thought. But it was not something she wanted to dwell on. The woman needed a break. She wanted Laura to watch her kids. Fine. That could be arranged.

On Monday of spring break, Anne Letig brought the kids over at seven-thirty. Laura's father had already left for work. The bus to Amarillo and then on to Dallas left at nine, but she wanted to get the kids comfortable and give instructions for the week. She wore a stylish blue dress with white polka dots (had John gone over to Thomason's and bought it after all?), cinched at the middle with a white patent leather belt. Her hair was loose, except for a blue hair band. She set down a box of toys and brought in another box of games for all the kids. These were games Laura's family, who was partial to cards, didn't have: Parcheesi, Chutes and Ladders, Yahtzee. She carried in a bag full of extra play clothes for the week so that her husband wouldn't have to worry about bringing stuff over in the mornings. And she'd made three dozen oatmeal and peanut butter cookies and a German chocolate cake, as well as a large tray of lasagna for the icebox. She had a bag of groceries, including sandwich meat, bread, cheese, chips, fruits, and vegetables. Laura helped haul in everything. It was much too much, but Mrs. Letig assured Laura it wasn't.

The boys scampered past Laura into the backyard.

"I feel guilty, I guess," Mrs. Letig said. "I've never been away from the boys for more than a day. This all sounded so great last week. And John encouraged it. But now . . . I don't know. Maybe it's a mistake. I found myself crying over the asparagus in the grocery store."

Mrs. Letig smiled, but the smile seemed bittersweet. Laura felt flattered that she was telling her all this, confiding in her. She wanted to reach out to her but restrained herself.

"Oh," Mrs. Letig said, dipping into her purse, "here's money for the week."

Laura waved her hand. "You bought all these groceries and made all this food. We'll be fine."

"Now, Laura, I already told you that I insist. Besides, I've promised the boys that you will take them to the movies. And you all can have popcorn and cokes."

She handed Laura the ten-dollar bill.

"I'll pay you the twenty-five when I get back. I forgot to go the bank last Friday and won't have time this morning. But that should cover you for the week. If you need more, just ask John."

"It's more than enough."

Mrs. Letig kissed Laura on the cheek. Laura could smell her perfume, sweet, familiar.

"I can't thank you enough for this, Laura. I do think it will be fine. John says stretching the apron strings to Dallas for a week will be good for me, that I might even get to like it." She laughed. "You're a lifesaver. I mean that. Thank you so much."

"You're welcome."

They stood there awkwardly for a second, Mrs. Letig looking at Laura and then staring down at the floor.

"You know," Mrs. Letig said, "I feel bad about . . . something I said on the phone to you—all this talk about leaving. Well, I know we've never discussed your mother or sister. I have felt just awful about it all, and have spent many nights wondering what it must be like for you . . . alone here without them. Anyway, when I said I had to get out of town, I didn't mean any offense by it, you understand."

"It's okay."

"I know you must miss them both. I was the oldest girl in my family. Thank goodness my mother was around, but she was sick much of the time, and I had to . . . well, take over. So I know what you're going through. Maybe not. But I can empathize. . . . Anyway, I'm stumbling with this apology. I just wanted to tell you I was sorry for the insensitivity and to let you know that I'm here, if you need to talk about your mother or about other . . . things. It's not easy for you, I know. All these men and boys around. And to have someone to talk to might help."

"I appreciate that, Mrs. Letig," Laura said, and she smiled but could not look the woman in the eye. Her throat felt tight, and her eyes burned.

"Anne," Mrs. Letig said and put her arms around Laura and pulled her close. "Call me Anne."

Laura could smell the mixture of powder and perfume, a little too fragrant, reminding her of her sister before she eloped. Her mother never wore perfume. But the talcum powder was a constant. She remembered her mother in her bedroom, applying the white cotton puff above her bra, a cloud rising from her chest. Laura felt herself go rigid from the embrace, almost against her will. She wanted to be nice to this woman, she did.

"Okay, enough of this," Mrs. Letig said, and she kissed the top of Laura's forehead and dabbed away the wetness from her cheekbones with her thumbs. "Let me go tell the boys good-bye again." She went through the kitchen to the back porch. "Jack, Willie. Come here, boys," she called. "Come kiss me good-bye."

Laura watched from the window as they rushed to their mother and hugged her. Mrs. Letig grabbed their faces and kissed them each several times.

"You be good for Laura. And for Daddy. You hear? I'll bring you something back from Aunt Anita's." They hugged her one more time. "Oh, I love you soooo much."

Laura felt like there was too much crammed into this moment. Too many layers of emotion and memory. John was there as a ghost, or rather what she felt for him was there, and it complicated and darkened everything because she liked this woman and appreciated her and could see her as someone she might like to talk to in a way she could not talk to her friends or her father or brothers. But she also was glad Mrs. Letig was leaving town. Laura didn't know what would happen between her and John, what this week might bring. They had not spoken a word about it. Maybe nothing would come of it at all. But the possibility of it kept her awake at night. She knew that meant she was a terrible person, sneaky and double-dealing and just the opposite of appreciative. She didn't know what to do with that knowledge, however. Mrs. McFarland had said in class that one of the marks of a mature person was to be able to feel two contradictory emotions and not go crazy. She called it "coming to terms with paradox." Laura wondered if this is what she meant.

At the church here in Charnelle, which they did not attend anymore, not since her mother left, or at Aunt Velma's church in Amarillo, it was simpler. The preachers spoke about dissembling. About coveting. About letting the false face hide what the false heart knows. She understood it all too well, though it was hard to take it *that* seriously.

"Thanks again," Mrs. Letig said. "If it's too much for you, tell John or call this number"—she handed Laura a slip of paper—"and I'll catch the bus back up here, lickety-split."

"Everything will be all right," Laura said. "Don't worry."

7

✳

Anything You're Making

*T*hat night and the following morning and the next evening John picked the boys up and dropped them off, but there was no way to tell what he was thinking. Her father was there all three times. John came in and had a cup of coffee in the morning, a beer in the evening, but he spent most of the time talking to her father about work, how they hated their new supervisor, a young shithead nephew of the vice president of the company who didn't know his ass from a hole in the ground. When John addressed Laura, it was simply about the boys. *Were they good? Did they eat? Were there any problems?* She answered his questions directly, searching for a special inflection in his voice, some coded message that she might discern, but there was nothing she could make out. No "yes, ma'am." No secret smile or brush of his hand against hers. He was efficient and preoccupied, and it seemed that whatever had happened between them before—which, now that she thought about it, wasn't that much—didn't really matter.

On Tuesday night, in bed, she was depressed.

Gene whispered, "What's wrong, Laura?"

"Nothing."

"Why are you crying?"

"I'm not."

"Sounds like it."

She collected herself. "No. I'm fine. Just the sniffles. Go on back to sleep now. You'll wake up Manny and Rich."

"Do you have a cold?"

"I'm fine. Let's sleep."

But she didn't sleep, and the next day, Wednesday, she felt cranky and out of sorts. John was running late and didn't even come in, just dropped them off and let Jack lead Willie inside. She opened the door as he backed out of the driveway. He waved as he left. The truck sped over the gravel, crunching it violently. His arm was back inside, his eyes focused on the road, and then he was gone. Had he done this on purpose? Did he just not *want* to see her?

"Have you eaten breakfast?" she asked the boys.

"No," Jack said.

Willie said, "I want pancakes."

"We've got Rice Krispies," she said.

"I want pancakes."

She stared off down the road. White dust from the gravel still drifted opaquely in the air. The sun was out. It was almost warm. She wished she could go back to bed.

"Rice Krispies will have to do," she said.

That afternoon they all walked the mile downtown for lunch. Gene was off with Manny, shooting cans with friends. She sweatered Rich, Jack, and Willie, and then the four of them sang songs as they walked. It was a pretty day, sunny and cool. Snow from the bad winter still clung to the ground into March but was almost completely melted now, except for a few pockets on the north sides of houses and buildings, and even those were wet-looking, as if they were contemplating evaporation.

There were five restaurants in Charnelle. The Armory, southeast of town, a mile or so from the city limits, served burgers and hot dogs and french fries along with the only liquor you could get between Charnelle and Amarillo; you had to be a member of the club, but the membership cost only a dollar a year. Mr. Thomason's Bar-B-Q, a small, redbrick building on the south side of Main Street, was the last stop before you left town for Amarillo; it was open only Tuesday through Saturday and Sunday for lunch. The Somersby brothers owned Charnelle Burgers, a little joint over on the north end of town, next to the baseball park and the drive-in (which they also owned); however, both Charnelle Burgers and the drive-in were closed several months each year when it was too cold—though it looked like the drive-in might open this week for spring break, if the weather held. Aguilar's, a Mexican restaurant on the west end of town, was really just Mr. and Mrs. Aguilar's kitchen and living room and only opened for lunch on weekdays and all day and evening on Cinco de Mayo; it catered to the four other Mexican families in town and the lunchtime crowd at Charnelle Steel & Construction. The best place to eat in Charnelle, and the only place downtown, was the Ding Dong Daddy Diner—also known as Ding Dong's or 4-D's. Clean and big, it served burgers and fries and shakes, which you could order and eat at the counter for a reasonable price while listening to the jukebox and talking with your pals, but they also had a nice sit-down dining room in back with red leather upholstered booths, where they served high-end meals—brisket, rib eyes, sirloins, chicken, and pork, and sometimes even fish.

Laura had determined at first that she wasn't going to spend Mrs. Letig's money. It had seemed like too much, but now she wanted to spend it all and to even tell her it wasn't enough. Because it wasn't. She was stuck with the boys all day. Marlene had invited her over for a cookout and marathon game of canasta. But nothing doing. She was burdened with these grimy little boys.

Downtown bustled—the lawyers and judges milling in and out of the county courthouse, the kids off for spring break circling the square in their cars. Debbie Carlson and Eddie Stimpson, her new boyfriend, drove by in Eddie's new Chevy, and then circled the square and drove up along the sidewalk where Laura and the boys were walking.

"You coming to Marlene's?" Debbie asked.

"Can't," Laura said, nodding toward the boys.

"Good thing you're getting paid," she said. "I wouldn't be a mother unless they paid me for it."

Eddie laughed, and Laura just smiled, not quite getting the joke. "Don't have too much fun," Laura said, smiling weakly.

"Not without—" Debbie started, but then Eddie pulled away before she could finish her sentence, and she didn't even turn around to wave good-bye, which irritated Laura, made her feel left out.

At 4-D's they had hamburgers and french fries and chocolate and strawberry shakes, so much food that there was no way they could eat it all, especially not Willie and Rich, their shakes turning quickly into glasses of milky mush.

Dean Compson was not working. He was probably off with some other hicks, plotting how to crash Marlene's party. Billy Sidell, the cook, who had once dated Gloria and had been heartbroken when she eloped, shook his head at the waste of food on the table.

"Got your hands full there, Laura." She could tell that he really meant, *Where do you get off throwing away all that food?*

The boys were rowdy on the way home, and Jack ran out in the street once, and a car screeched to a halt within a few feet of him. He looked up, alarmed, and started crying.

She grabbed his arm hard and screamed, "What were you thinking?"

"I'm sorry."

"Are you crazy? You could have been killed."

Then she felt horrible, shouting at this terrified boy. She had to soothe him, and then she had to calm Willie and Rich, too, who had both broken into sympathetic tears. The clouds rolled in and threatened rain during the rest of the walk back to the house. A few drops hit them, but they made it inside, barely, before the downpour.

There was a note on the front door:

LAURA AND BOYS—CAME BY FOR LUNCH, BUT GUESS YOU WERE OUT ON AN EXPEDITION. SEE YOU THIS EVENING.

—*J L*

She didn't expect his handwriting to be as neat as it was, simple but elegant printing, no cursive, except for his initials, which he wrote with a kind of looping flourish. She ran her fingers over her own name and over his extravagant *L*.

———

That evening, when her father and John showed up—late, almost nine o'clock—the two men were laughing in a way that felt contagious.

"Hey, there, pretty thing." John whistled. It was bold but done so deftly, like a magic trick, that he got away with it.

"She damn sure is, isn't she?" her father said and leaned down and kissed her forehead. She could smell the beer on him. "She's growing up too fast. I'm going to have to beat the boys off with a stick soon enough."

"I don't doubt it," John said.

"What are you all so happy about?" she asked.

Her father and John exchanged looks. "I don't know. I suppose if you need a reason," Mr. Tate offered merrily, "we could come up with something."

They both laughed again like this was a real knee-slapper. She figured they'd stopped off at the Armory after work, played some pool, had a few bottles, and shot the shit, as Manny liked to say, with the owner, Luke.

"Your father's having a poker game on Friday. He says you're a shrewd player yourself."

It'd been a long time since he'd hosted a poker game, certainly not since her mother left. He'd taught all of the kids. Manny sometimes got to play with the men.

Her father said, "She's my good-luck charm."

"I can imagine. I'm not that good. I may need some of that luck."

"I won't give her up that easily."

"Hey, Laura," John said. "I have to go over to a buddy's house on Saturday evening to help him overhaul his transmission. Wanted to see if you could come watch the boys that night. Zeeke said it would be okay with him. Unless you have a date."

"She better not!" her father said.

She looked down at her feet. "Yes, I'm free."

"I'll pay extra."

"Mrs. Letig paid too much already."

"No. This wasn't part of the bargain. You'll get more. No arguments."

He winked at her, and to her father it must have seemed natural, but she knew different and was relieved by the wink. She understood what he meant. And she was happy about it.

"I'll stop by tomorrow for lunch to see the boys, if that's okay with you, ma'am?"

"We'll be here."

"Good," he said. "Now, where *are* the boys?"

She gathered them up and walked them to the truck. Jack and Willie clambered in.

"About twelve-thirty," he said.

"What do you like to eat?" she asked.

She meant it as a simple question. She wanted to fix him something he liked. But he smiled at her curiously, his lips slightly parted, his chin dropping, his eyebrows arched.

"Anything you're making," he said.

Lunch. She wore a dress. Just a hand-me-down, one of the dresses Gloria left behind, but nice. A summery, tight-fitting purple one with green diamonds and a V-neck. And she had washed her hair the night before and braided it. She made the boys a picnic and set them up outside at the table, with peanut butter and banana sandwiches, oranges, and some of Mrs. Letig's cookies. He showed up just as she was carrying cups of milk out to them.

"You boys get started," he said. "I'll help Laura make our lunch. Jack, you watch the younger ones."

"Yes, sir."

He shut the door behind him, grabbed her hand, and kissed her.

"The windows are open."

"Where's Gene?"

"With Manny."

"They coming back for lunch?"

"No. They went fishing."

He grabbed her hand and led her back to her bedroom. He shut the door, and she crossed over and drew the blind on the window. He came up behind her, slipped his hands around her hips, and nuzzled his face into the back of her neck. His chin was prickly. The room felt cramped with the three beds—one for Manny, one for her, and the one Gene and Rich now shared—a chest, and a dresser with a mirror. The room embarrassed her. She closed her eyes when he kissed her neck, and then she opened them and could see the two of them in the reflection of the mirror. It startled her.

"I've missed you," he said.

She watched his hands move over her hips. His face was bent at her neck. One hand moved over her ribs. His hands looked huge in the mirror. One nearly covered her rib cage, the other spread across her stomach. She could both see and feel where his pinkie lay. She closed her eyes and listened to her breathing, and his, too, overlapping. She felt, strangely, as if she were acting.

"We better get back to the kitchen," she said.

He moved one hand slowly over her breasts. She did not stop him. He kissed her neck and then reached down for the sides of her dress and slowly inched it up over her knees, then over her thighs. His head was perched on her right shoulder. She thought about stopping him. She put her hand on his but didn't apply any pressure. She watched as her dress rose. There were her panties, white, cotton. She thought for a second about what she'd seen in Mrs. Letig's drawer that time she'd snooped. The frills. This must be boring by comparison. The dress rose higher. Above her belly button. He reached across and held the dress with one hand. The other hand moved across her panties. Gently, down. She sucked in her stomach so that her ribs showed.

"You don't have to do that," he whispered.

She began to shake nervously. His hand moved over her thigh and then between her legs and to her right hip and across her abdomen. She could see the gooseflesh on her stomach and arms. Her arms were now down by her sides. He pressed against her. Her throat was dry and her ears clogged, so that she could hear herself breathing rapidly. She yawned to clear them but couldn't do it. Her body still shook.

"We better get back out there," she said.

He inched her dress down again and then turned her slowly to him and cupped her face with his hands. Those hands. He leaned down and kissed her. She closed her eyes, and his lips touched hers. His tongue was there, over her teeth. She felt awkward, not sure if she was doing this right. She opened her mouth slightly, and his tongue darted softly. He moved her back until she felt Gene and Rich's bed behind her. Her knees bent, and he bent, too, without breaking the kiss and eased her down on the bed and then lay on top of her, continuing to kiss her. She still felt strange, as if she wasn't quite there. His hand was on her breasts, covering them both. He undid the buttons down the front of her dress. And then his lips were on the top of her chest, and then over her bra. She was aware that her breasts were smaller than Mrs. Letig's. Her mother had full breasts, too. Laura's left breast was slightly smaller than the right one, which had always made her self-conscious. He pulled the top of her bra down and ran his lips along the edge of the fabric so that she felt the bristle of his mustache. That was nice. He was heavy, though. She couldn't breathe very well.

"We better go," she whispered.

"What's wrong?"

"It's just that they're out there all alone."

"Okay," he said.

He repositioned her bra with his hand, kissed the outside of the cloth, and then he leaned up and kissed her lightly on the nose and on the lips. She opened her mouth and laughed, not because of nerves but because she felt suddenly light without his weight upon her.

He pulled her to him suddenly, and she kissed him, this time intensely, enough so that the strangeness, the odd displacement she felt before, was gone. She now wished they didn't have to stop. And then she knew, a split second before it happened, that the kitchen door would open.

"Daddy!" It was Jack. "Where are you?"

John opened the door. "In the bathroom," he called. "I'll be right there." He raised his eyebrows in a comic double arch, like Groucho did on TV. He closed the door behind him.

She looked in the mirror, ran her fingers through her hair, repositioned the clips, snapped her dress slowly. She turned to go but then stopped. She reached down to the hem of her dress. She inched it up as he had done, over her thighs, over her stomach, past her ribs. She studied the mirror for a few moments. Her body seemed abstract. Not part of her. Not part of what had happened in this room just moments before. How odd.

She expected to feel a knot in her stomach, electricity skittering over her skin, the nervous shaking from before. But she didn't. She felt calm and easy. She liked this feeling.

"Laura," he called.

"Coming," she answered.

8

Poker Night

*A*lthough she didn't have her license yet, her father let her drive his truck with Gene, Rich, Jack, and Willie to the Charnelle Drive-in. She filled a big paper bag full of popcorn for them all and made a small jug of lemonade.

On weekends the drive-in showed about an hour's worth of shorts and cartoons early, starting at dusk. She parked the truck, but rather than set up shop in the back of the truck, as her family used to do, they laid an old blanket on the grassy area next to the playground. The kids played during the newsreel, then sprawled out on the grass and watched the screen. It was warm enough to wear short sleeves, even in the evening, and everybody had been commenting on the strange hot weather, but what a nice break it was after nearly two months of shut-up-in-your-house wintry blight.

There were several cartoons—Mickey and Goofy and Donald Duck, Yosemite Sam and the Road Runner (her favorite)—and three long trailers for upcoming films followed them. There was an Elvis movie called *G.I.*

Blues, and an Alfred Hitchcock film, *Psycho,* that had the big, double-chinned director giving a slow, droll tour of the hotel and home where evidently the psycho lived with his mother, and a Marilyn Monroe movie, *Let's Make Love.* Laura felt a jolt of excitement from the title of this last movie and wished that John had been sitting here next to her on the blanket when the words flashed on the screen. She didn't like Marilyn Monroe, though, didn't like that fake pout, hated how she always acted dumber than she was, as if that was what made her attractive. And maybe it did make her attractive, at least to some guys. Maybe that was what they wanted—a willing dummy with hips and breasts, sleepy eyes, and thick lips. It made her kind of sick.

They watched the movie, a remake of *Tarzan, the Ape Man.* She liked looking at Denny Miller, so nicely bronzed but not nearly as good or as handsome as Johnny Weismuller. It was clear that this Tarzan was wrestling stuffed animals, and the Pygmies whose village gets demolished by elephants seemed to be American kids. Jane was a pretty but bad actress that Laura had seen once or twice on television. It was really quite awful, this movie, but the boys got a kick out of it, and she did, too, just watching them. Afterward she gathered up everything and everyone, and they headed back home.

Several cars and trucks were in the driveway and on the street outside her house, so she had to park in front of Mrs. Ambling's. She sent the boys to clean up and get into their pajamas. Jack and Willie were sleeping at her house until the poker game was over.

The game had already commenced, all the men crowded around the kitchen table. Jimmy and Bob Cransburgh were there, and her father of course, and Beaver Mitchell, an old silver-haired, deeply wrinkled comic troll of a man who worked at the post office, and Manny and John. It was good to see her father's friends in the house again.

"Hey, there she is. Lucky!" Bob called. "Is she gonna sit on your lap and help you play your hands again, Zeke?"

"Maybe," her father said. "Everybody ante up. Pot's not right. How was the show, honey?"

"Good," she said. "It's really warm tonight."

"Don't we know it."

"What's it gonna be, Zeke?" Bob asked.

"Seven stud, low Chicago."

She got a glass and poured some tea and ate some potato chips from a bowl on the counter. Beers already littered the table, and everybody had a cigarette dangling from his lips, even Manny. There were two packs of Bicycle cards, one red, one blue, and the money. Her father had a rack of chips, which he rarely used. Everybody liked to see the coins and cash, mainly nickels, dimes, and quarters, with scattered dollar bills. Nobody won or lost much at these games. They were an excuse to get together, get a little drunk, and have some laughs.

Before her mother left, the family used to play—even Gene. Her father had taught them all well. And she was sure she could have won in these games, if her father let her play. But maybe not. When her family played, they played for pennies or toothpicks or with the chips. This was too much money for her. She might not be as bold as she normally was if her own money were at stake.

"Jack of diamonds. No help for the Beaver," her father said, part of his usual patter when he dealt, a little song that she hadn't heard him sing in quite a while. "Seven of clubs, possible flush for the boy. Eight—a long stretch on your straight, Letig. Another jack for Jimmy. Jacks are cheap, Jimmy. Uh-oh. Look what we have here: a pair of tens showing for old Bobby. And a dinky little three for the dealer. Bet 'em up, tens."

She watched from the sink, not going too close until asked. John had his shirt undone at the top and his sleeves rolled up. His hair was slicked back except for a messy blond curl that flopped on the top of his forehead. His skin was a little reddish. She flicked her eyes around the table and caught Manny looking at her. He squinched his eyebrows together.

"Bring me a beer, will ya?" he said.

"What's the magic word?" she said.

"Pleeeeeease," he whinnied.

"You keep these boys in line now, Laura," Bob said.

She nodded and got a beer out of the icebox and popped the cap.

"Thanks," Manny said.

John reached out and touched her wrist, and she felt her heart beat fast. He liked to do that sort of thing. Even though he said he worried about the danger, some part of him must have liked the risk. She liked it as well. "Can you get me a beer, too, Laura?" he asked. "Please."

She smiled and stole a glance at her father, who was studying his cards as a thin wisp of smoke snaked between his eyes.

"Appreciate it," he said.

"Okay, pot's right," her father growled. "Beaver's out. Last card up. King, no help for Manny's flush. Don't know why he's still in. Letig's still alive with the straight. Uh-oh: pair of jacks to go with Jimmy's eights. Hard to beat two pair showing. An ace to go with Bobby's tens. And that seven sends me outta here."

"Oh, come on, Zeeke," Jimmy said. "Ain't you gonna wait for the spade in the hole?"

"Not much chance there with all these spades showing. Besides, I think Letig is holding the deuce, the way he keeps betting with that hand. Or Manny's got it."

"Down and dirty, gentlemen."

"Laura!" Rich called.

She leaned into the living room and said, "Be right there."

She watched the final betting. Bob folded, too. There was just Manny, Jimmy, and John left.

"Quarter," Jimmy said, two pair showing.

"Bump a quarter," John said.

"Let me borrow a dollar, Dad?"

Jimmy protested. "Hey, none of that family-bank shit."

"Let me see what you have." Her father looked at Manny's hole cards, then took four quarters from his pile and dropped it on Manny's cards.

"Bump you a quarter," Manny said.

"Fifty cents to you, Jimmy."

"Well, shit," Jimmy said. "Either they got me beat or they're battling for the low spade."

"You can't go out with the high hand," her father said.

"I know, I know." He reluctantly put his money in the pot. "Call."

"Call," John said, and dropped his quarter in the pot.

Her father said, "Show 'em." Manny flipped over his pair of kings and a pair of nines. And a seven of spades in the hole.

"Well, fuck me," Jimmy said.

"Hey!" her father said and motioned to Laura.

"Sorry, Laura," Jimmy said.

"It's okay."

"Did ya get your straight, Letig?" her father asked.

John rolled them over one at a time. Two, three, four, five, six, and a seven to boot. A straight. The four was a spade, and it had been a hole card. He didn't have to split it. It was all his.

"Shit!" Manny said.

"Lucky bastard," Beaver muttered.

John smiled widely. "Sorry, gentlemen." He raked the money toward him. "Hate to take your money like that."

"Yeah, I bet," Jimmy said. "Hustler."

"Are the boys ready to go yet?" John asked her. All the men simultaneously groaned.

"You're not getting out of here after that, you asshole!" Beaver half shouted.

John laughed. He had no intention of going anywhere.

Gene appeared at the doorway and said, "Rich squeezed the toothpaste all over the toilet."

"I'm coming."

"Thanks, honey," her father said.

She read the younger boys a book and put them to bed, and then she and Gene returned to the poker game. Gene stood behind Manny for a few hands, grew bored, and went into the living room and read his comic books. She stood behind her father and watched the game, putting her hand on his shoulder. He leaned his head back, his mouth puckered. She offered him her cheek self-consciously, looking at John, but his head was down, like he didn't want to see that.

Her father won a couple of hands while she was standing behind him.

"Not fair," Bob growled, mock angry, his face flushed from the beers. He'd been guzzling them, she noticed. The trash can was full of bottles. Manny was drinking another one himself; the bottle she'd given him stood empty beside his new one. Bob said, "You gotta share the luck, Zeeke. Pass your daughter around."

The group of men ooooohed, including John, at the insinuation.

Bob smiled lecherously. "Come over here, Lucky," he said. "Come to Poppa."

"Don't go near that old goat," her father said.

"How about me?" John said, a loopy grin on his face. Laura smiled nervously and then looked away. He was flirting too close to the edge, she thought. But she liked it, liked how good he was at it.

"You've been lucky enough," Jimmy said, pointing at John's pile of coins. Several dollar bills were underneath his beer bottle.

"Well, then, that leaves me," Beaver said.

"I'll tell you what," her father said. "I gotta take a leak and say good night to the boys anyway. Laura, why don't you play this hand. Embarrass these jackasses."

"Hey," Beaver said, "she doesn't know what she's doing."

"She'll kick your butt if you don't watch out," her father said. Everybody laughed.

She did kick their butts. They played five-card draw, and she had three nines and drew a pair. She bet conservatively from her father's pile, but Beaver had lucked into three fours, so he kept bumping the pot. When she showed them her hand, they all gasped.

Her father returned. "Well, what happened?"

"No more women at the poker table!" Beaver squalled.

The Cransburgh brothers laughed. Manny just shook his head as he gathered up the cards for his deal. John leaned back in his chair, lit another cigarette, and smiled at her.

"I told you," her father said. "She's something else."

"That's for sure," John said.

Her father let her play a couple more hands, despite Beaver's complaints. Beaver stared suspiciously at her. She didn't win again, but once she had a straight. Manny beat her with a flush. Her father gave her three dollars from his pile, and she watched a few more hands and then excused herself.

Gene had gone to bed, and all the other boys were asleep. She sat in the living room and flipped through the *Hollywood Star Gazette*, skimming over an article about Kirk Douglas's upcoming movie, *Spartacus* (he wore no shirt in the cover photo), and an article on Anthony Perkins, whom she had half a crush on when she first saw him as the Quaker boy in *Friendly Persuasion*, so it was hard to believe that he would now be the psycho in *Psycho*.

Mostly she listened to the game. She loved the sound of it. She tried to imagine John, his movements, his gestures. He didn't speak much. Once she heard him say, "Son of a bitch." Another time he said, "Come here, sweet little momma." He won a couple of pots. She imagined the smoke snaking before his eyes. Drinking his beer, the edge of his mustache a bit frothy above his red lips. It was hot in the kitchen. Half-moons darkened his shirt beneath his arms. His hairline beaded with droplets.

The men made frequent trips to the bathroom. They'd chat with her for a minute, surprised that she was still awake. Everyone seemed to go except John; she knew he'd have to before long. It was almost midnight. She checked in the bedroom. The boys were still asleep, Willie and Jack on the pallet she'd made them between the beds. She pulled the door shut, went back to the couch, and tried to read, but she dozed and then woke with a start. John was leaning over her.

"Hey, Lucky, you still awake?" he whispered, close to her ear. She could smell his beer.

He looked toward the kitchen, where the light splashed. They listened for a second and could hear her father's patter.

"The boys asleep?" he whispered.

She nodded.

"Sure?"

She nodded again. He motioned toward the bathroom. She let him go first, and then she got up and tiptoed to the hallway, looking back to check the kitchen before she turned toward the bathroom instead of her room. He grabbed her hand and pulled her into the bathroom and shut the door, the light still out. He found her lips and kissed her. She put her arms around his neck, and he let his hands slide over her breasts, then down over her hips. They kissed for a silent moment. Then she pushed him away, nervous, thinking she'd heard the sound of a chair moving, someone rising in the kitchen. She'd be trapped in here, caught for sure, if someone waited outside the door for the bathroom. The window was too small for her to slip through, and even if she could, they'd hear her in the kitchen.

They stood still, listened intently. No more sound. She reached up and kissed him again. Their lips smacked together, and she pulled away and almost burst out laughing. He put his hand over her mouth. Then he put a warning finger to his own lips.

"Shhhh," he said as quietly as he could.

He opened the bathroom door, checked the hallway, sent her out, winked at her, and then shut the door again. She moved to the other side of the hallway, right outside her own door. She could see into her father's room. The light was out, but the moon filtered through the blinds. She thought for a moment of her mother, remembered how she used to enjoy the periodic poker games, would joke sometimes with the men for a while and then sit in the big chair in the living room, close her eyes, and listen, smiling, to the poker patter.

Laura bit a hangnail on her index finger. She listened to John urinate. She heard him zip and then run some water. He stepped outside and turned the light off, and for a moment he didn't see her, started out through the hall, expecting her to be back in the living room. She grabbed his arm as he came through the arch. He poked his head back around and then leaned against her, and they kissed, careful not to make the smacking sound. He smiled and then ran his finger over her lips and chin, down her neck, chest, between her ribs, to the middle of her stomach. He kept his finger there a moment and looked up at her. She smiled. A chair moved in the kitchen.

He leaned down to her ear and whispered, "Tomorrow."

She nodded. He stepped into the living room.

"Who won?" he asked in the kitchen.

"Zeeke's runt," Jimmy said and belched.

She quickly opened the door to her room, slipped in, and left the door ajar so she could listen. She felt a surge of pride at her boldness, at what she'd gotten away with, at how she'd surprised him. That was how it was between them, this constant exchange of surprises.

Everyone was still asleep, or so she hoped. Gene was really the only one to worry about. He was old enough to be suspicious, but he was out cold. She lay on her bed in her clothes and listened to the murmur and occasional shouts of the men in the other room as she dozed and woke, dozed and woke.

At about two, the game was over. The men gathered their things, offered their thanks, and drunkenly talked as they made their way to their trucks and cars. Her father and John came into her room, and each quietly picked up one of the Letig boys. She lay still and watched them through half-shut eyes as they tiptoed out of the room. She listened for them outside, heard John thank her father for inviting him, said he'd have to host the next time.

She heard his truck start up, pull out, and drive away, the engine sputtering a little at first. Manny came into the room, noisily removed his boots and clothes, and clambered into bed. He belched a couple of times.

"Did you win?" she asked.

"Nope."

"How much did you lose?"

"What are you doing awake anyway, *Lucky*?"

"Night," she said.

She couldn't have a conversation with Manny anymore without there being some smart-ass accusation, in his voice if not in his words. She didn't want to be accused of anything, especially now that there was actually something to accuse her of. Did he suspect? She couldn't tell. Probably not, but now she worried that she and John had been too careless tonight. The touching over the poker table, the bathroom, the hallway. Crazy. They'd have to be more careful from now on.

She closed her eyes, imagined John's truck pulling into his own driveway, him carrying his boys to bed. Undressing. His jeans unzipped and off. Boxer shorts—maybe those little red diamonds. She could see him adjusting himself like her father and brothers did. Unsnapping his shirt. Running his hand through the hair on his chest. Brushing his teeth with the yellow toothbrush she'd seen in his bathroom. And then in bed, alone, beneath the sheets, the window cracked a couple of notches to let in a cool breeze. Maybe he'd light up a cigarette, smoke it in bed without his wife there, the tip glowing orange as he inhaled, the smoke snaking up in the dark. She imagined him thinking about her, thinking about kissing her, his hands on her body. She felt a nervous thrill slither through her. Did he feel guilty? Second thoughts? She hoped not. She tried not to imagine Mrs. Letig there. *Let him think about me instead.* She closed her eyes and imagined herself with him, which suddenly frightened her. Maybe she needed to set some limits. But if she wanted limits, why not hang out with Dean Compson or Gordy Toffler or some other boy her own age? They were easy enough to keep under control. Could she stop John if she wanted to? Did she want to? It was a kind of sweet torture.

She closed her eyes more tightly and let herself hang suspended between this image of him and sleep, hoping the one would carry over into the other.

PART TWO

Emissaries

✳

Easter Weekend

*L*aura noticed that her mother seemed quieter than usual. Laura believed she was the only one who had noticed. Her father had been very busy, working long hours, taking jobs in nearby towns some weeks, leaving for Amarillo before sunrise and often not returning until after midnight, so he wasn't around as much that spring. When they did see him, he was often too tired for talk, slipping into a doze at the kitchen table or in his chair in the living room. Manny was fifteen and a half, just a year older than Laura, and in high school now. He paid little attention to what was going on with the family. He'd gotten a job at a filling station after school and on Saturdays, and he seemed to spend most of the time he was home primping in the bathroom, greasing his hair and combing it into a meticulously groomed duck's ass—probably to impress some girl at school. Gene, who was eight, and Rich, who was only three, weren't old enough to know when people acted different. They just wanted to have food fixed when they were hungry and be tucked in bed by their mother at night. But Laura did notice what seemed to be happening with her mother. She knew her mother had been hurt when Gloria *eloped, before she even graduated from high school, but that had been a while now, almost a year, long enough to get used to. As Laura watched her mother go about her chores—fixing meals, washing clothes, bathing children—she worried that she didn't smile much, that she didn't say much, that she did everything and did it right, but that something was gone that had been there before.*

Her mother was also more easily angered and strict, quick to punish the younger boys for the least little thing. Laura found herself walking on eggshells when she was home, not starting any arguments, doing her chores before she was asked, even offering to help with the dishes or cooking or laundry when it wasn't her turn. She had been sick throughout the winter and into early spring, feeling feverish, never quite able to shake the sniffles and the itchiness in her nose and throat and eyes. Even school, which she liked—especially geography and English— seemed to limp sluggishly toward the end of the year, like a wounded soldier.

She was relieved that everyone seemed to cheer up when they decided to visit Aunt Velma for Easter. The whole house brightened and straightened into shape, like a clean, snapped-out sheet. Laura's sinuses cleared—ah, how wonderful to breathe normally again. Her father sang bits and pieces of old songs in the shower, and her mother seemed more tender and tolerant with them all, even softly whistling while she hung the wet clothes on the line.

They left for Aunt Velma's shortly after lunch on Good Friday, when Mr. Tate got off work. Mrs. Tate had already packed the suitcases and wrapped the ham she planned to cook for Easter dinner. Fay—who'd been moping about since their other dog, Greta, had run off—jumped around like an excited pup, tongue lolling in a smile as they readied themselves for the trip. She hopped in and out of the truck bed, barking. She was ready to go, right now, let's get on the road and head to the farm—now, now, come on, people, get moving.

Except for Mr. Tate, none of the family had been out of town since last Thanksgiving. Laura didn't realize how good it was to leave until they were on the highway, driving off—Gene, Manny, Fay, and her in the back of the pickup with the luggage and the food, the sky white and breezy and cool, Charnelle dissolving behind them, the bright red brick of Thomason's Bar-B-Q fading, the tall Armory flagpole thinning, thinning until you blinked, and it was suddenly gone.

They arrived just after three in the afternoon. Aunt Velma was waiting in the yard, her strawberry-patterned apron over her dress, her large mop of gray

hair pinned in a loose bun. She hugged and kissed them all. When Laura em-
braced her, she could smell baked cinnamon apples.

Aunt Velma said, "You're just in time to feed the chickens," and she
whacked Gene's and Rich's butts playfully with a broom and sent them off to
the barn, where they scattered the grain and imitated the clucking, head-
bobbing, selfish strutting of the six hens and the rooster.

After a few minutes, Rich ran back up. "I wanna ride Ginger."

"That's fine, honey," Aunt Velma crooned, "but you better ask your par-
ents."

He was off in a waddling run to the house, where he retrieved Manny and
Mr. Tate, who saddled and bridled the older horse, Ginger. Manny rode with
Rich, while Gene and Laura took turns riding the younger mare, Hayworth.

Then, later, Laura and Manny galloped the two horses beyond the pasture,
through the peach and apple orchards, to the open land that bordered the new
highway.

"Hi-yaaa!" Manny yelled, heeling Ginger into a run.

Though nervous—Laura'd almost been thrown from Hayworth the previ-
ous Thanksgiving—she tightened her grip on the reins, clamped her legs
against the mare's sides, clicked her tongue, and pressed her heels into the rear
flanks. The horse galloped faster, and Laura said, "Come on, girl," then
shouted like Manny, and the horse, as if a current of electricity had suddenly
jolted through her, snapped into a run, whiplashing Laura's head.

She nearly fell off but righted herself, leaned forward, and clasped the
reins more securely. The wind whooshed by, and her hair swirled around her
face like a nest of blond spiders. Too scared to let go, she shook her head until
her hair streaked behind her, and she let the horse run for a while before she
started to relax, to ease her body into the rhythm of the horse's gait, to let the
rippling of Hayworth's muscles flow through rather than against her own.

Manny had stopped a couple hundred or so yards ahead, and Ginger was
drinking from a freshwater pond. Laura tugged the reins to the right and circled
in a fat arc toward Manny. She slapped the horse's side with her reins so they
wouldn't slow down. She wanted to prolong this feeling, this wide-open, fast-
galloping looseness. She closed her eyes, took a deep breath, and could feel at
the core of her body a kind of bobbing.

Then, just as she opened her eyes, Hayworth jumped at something, and the
blue sky tilted. Her head bumped the horse's neck. She lost her balance and
could feel herself falling, slowly, like dripping molasses, off the side of the

running horse. She clung to the reins, but they were slipping, slipping, slipping, a hot burn of leather on her palms, and she knew, absolutely knew, in those split seconds when she was perpendicular to the horse, like a spear in its side, that she was going to hit the ground, headfirst and hard. The horse would trample her, and she would be dead, gone for good.

"Are you okay?" Manny kept repeating. "Are you okay?" His hand cradled her head, and around his darkened face was a corona of sunlight that blinded her into a rapid blink.

"What happened?" she asked.

"I was watching you, but then I turned away for a second, and when I looked again, you were on the ground."

"How long have I been here?"

"A few minutes. I thought you were dead at first. You feel okay?"

"I think so."

She sat up and felt a sharp, dizzying spike in her forehead, like when she ate ice cream too fast, but that pain left quickly. Manny lifted her up and helped spank the grass and dirt from her hair and body. Her back and right arm ached, but not enough to gripe about—just stingers that would go away if she didn't dwell on them.

"Don't tell anyone about this," she said.

"Are you sure you're all right?"

"They might not let me ride again."

"Maybe you shouldn't *ride again."*

"I just got her going too fast."

"You shouldn't have chased after me."

"You wanted me to."

"That's not the point."

"It was fun until I lost hold."

The horses were drinking at the pond. She and Manny sat down on the bank, broke off a couple of cattails and absently fingered them. The water was smooth, just a ripple from the horses' mouths, every now and again a light wrinkle across the surface from the breeze. A half mile in the distance, trucks rolled across the highway, and she believed she could smell faintly the diesel in the air, though the horses' sweat was closer, more pungent. The sun had turned from hot white to a liquid red at the horizon, and after it dipped below, she and Manny climbed back up on the horses. She was a little nervous at first, afraid she might fall again. She clasped her thighs tightly against the horse's flanks, and they started back to the barn in a slow canter.

They tethered the horses in the stall, and when they exited the barn, darkness had fallen quickblack over the sky.

Aunt Velma wasn't really anybody's aunt. She was Mrs. Tate's cousin by marriage. Uncle Unser, who was really Mrs. Tate's cousin, died in 1953. During World War II, when he'd served as a captain in the infantry, he lost the vision in his left eye and both his arms up to the elbows when a grenade exploded in his hands as he withdrew the pin. He had metal hands attached at the VA and tried to return to normal life, but he couldn't do the farmwork very efficiently nor of course the fiddle making, which he'd been known for in the Panhandle before he joined the military. He and Aunt Velma had never had children, so they had always treated Laura's family like their own. During the war, he'd sent them odd remnants—pieces of shrapnel constructed into beautiful, strange collages, bullet casings with Italian and Russian lettering on the sides, an Italian military sash for Mr. Tate, a German baby blanket for Laura. And even after he returned from the hospital, he seemed extraordinarily good-natured, letting the kids touch his purple-striated stumps or even play with his metal hands as he sat on a stool or in his big leather chair, smiling serenely.

Mrs. Tate always referred to him as her uncle, as both a term of endearment and because he was almost twenty years older than she was. He'd always been, as she put it, a naturally happy man, quick with a joke or a tease. So they were all shocked when Uncle Unser hanged himself in the barn. No note, no nothing. Aunt Velma found him swinging from the rafters one morning in May. Laura was sure there were explanations, but neither his death nor its possible causes were discussed with the kids. Manny told Laura that he thought Uncle Unser was an alcoholic. Gloria said that was a big fat lie, that he was just depressed, from the war and from his inability to do what he most loved. He just didn't want to live anymore. It was that simple.

But it wasn't so simple to Laura. She could never quite wrap her mind around that notion—not wanting to live—particularly since he seemed so obviously happy. There was some mysterious chasm between the man she had known and the man who had dangled from the rafters, like a secret self had taken over. It had troubled her for nearly a year—she even dreamed of it horribly, this demonic *second self rising out of Uncle Unser's body and knotting the rope, draping it around his neck—but then she had suddenly stopped thinking and dreaming about it altogether. As she grew older, it seemed more and more difficult to remember him very clearly, though every once in a while, especially when they were visiting Aunt Velma's, a charged memory would swim to the surface and overwhelm her for a few seconds—how his suntanned face looked like a sculpture, bronzed and creviced in the sunlight, or the singsong way in which he sometimes spoke, or a snippet of one of his jokes, or his deadpan, teasing manner, his glass eye rolling loosely to one side while his good eye stared straight at you.*

For supper Aunt Velma and Mrs. Tate fixed catfish, okra, black-eyed peas, two pans of cornbread, and an apple cobbler for dessert. The kitchen smelled warm, buttery, sweet, and greasy. After Manny and Laura washed up, they all sat at the table, held hands, and Aunt Velma said an extended grace. The Tates weren't very religious, though they sometimes attended the Charnelle Methodist Church. But Aunt Velma claimed that the church had saved her after Uncle Unser died, literally saved both her physical and spiritual lives, and she had devoted herself to volunteer work and to intensive study sessions with other members of the congregation, particularly those who'd lost spouses, parents, children, brothers, or sisters. Though Manny made fun of Aunt Velma's devotion, and Mr. and Mrs. Tate seemed to tolerate it respectfully, Laura was fascinated and often moved by Aunt Velma's fervor. Regardless of whether or not you believed what she believed, it was clear, to Laura at least, that it had changed Aunt Velma for the better—not like religion did for some people. It made her generous and forgiving, and sustained her as she grew old, lit her from within rather than turning her cynical and ossified, as Laura could easily see happening to someone else in Aunt Velma's shoes. When your husband kills himself . . . well, no telling what could happen to you.

Aunt Velma reminded them that today, of all days, is what they must be grateful for, and she painted a vivid portrait of the frail Messiah, nearly naked, thorns digging into His skull, blood and sweat and dirt streaming into His eyes, which He could barely keep open, the spikes being driven through His hands and tender feet, and how the rabble of the town came to watch Him suffer, to throw stones and rotted vegetables, and as He faded into unconsciousness and then death, the sky blackened. It was a day of torment and abject humiliation, but in this suffering were planted the seeds of the world's salvation.

"Amen," Mr. Tate said, and the rest of them, on cue, chimed in with their amens. Manny looked at Laura and rolled his eyes, smiling, and she smiled, too, but felt bad about it, as if she was conspiring against Aunt Velma.

Then the plates and silverware began to clatter as they all helped themselves. The food was delicious. Laura hadn't realized how hungry she was, or how the events of the day had made her ravenous. She ate two heaping platefuls and had a huge piece of cobbler, and afterward, lying on the floor near the unlit fireplace, a pillow under her head, her eyes closed, she listened to the radio—the Hollywood Star Gazer and then a special Good Friday musical special featuring the New York City Boys' Choir—as her brothers and parents and Aunt Velma sang and chattered and played Chinese checkers around her. She felt sated and pleasantly warm, a tingly buzz on her skin. Truly relaxed and well for the first time in months.

It seemed as if the fall from the horse had shaken whatever was bad or festering out of her, that those few minutes of deadness had made way for this sense of pleasure she now felt. She smiled to think of what Aunt Velma would make of this. In fact, she wondered if she was starting to think like Aunt Velma. She wouldn't say anything to Manny—he'd just make fun of her—or to anyone for that matter. It was just a fleeting thought, anyway, but maybe that's how people like Aunt Velma find themselves, through these odd connected moments, ripened with mystery, like beads on a string—leaving town, falling off a horse, brooding over the dead, eating until you're stuffed—and poof!— through some magical alchemy, you're crazy for Jesus.

"Good night, Laura," her mother said.

She opened her eyes as her mother draped a blanket over her. The windows were dark, and no one else was in the room. Her mother had let her hair down from its bun, and it fell softly around her face, so that she looked beautiful, very much like Gloria, the small network of creases around her eyes and across her forehead smoothed into youth by the dark.

"What time is it?"

"Late," her mother said and leaned over and kissed her. Laura could faintly smell the familiar blossomy scent of the lotion she applied to her neck and hands and face each night.

"I love you," Laura whispered.

"I love you, too." Her mother rose, her long white nightgown billowing like a shroud, and Laura watched her disappear into the darkness of the kitchen and then listened for the pressure of her feet over Aunt Velma's slick but creaky hardwood.

Saturday afternoon Mr. Tate took them all to see The Ten Commandments, a special event since they had never, as a family, been to an indoor movie theater before. Several times each summer, especially before Rich was born, they all went to the Charnelle Drive-in. Mr. Tate would park the truck with the bed facing the screen, and they'd sit on cushions in the back, Manny lying atop the cab, Gloria down front in the grassy area with her girlfriends or later in some beat-up jalopy with another girl and two pimply-faced boys. A sweaty jug of iced lemonade and a huge paper bag full of buttered popcorn (which they'd spent the afternoon popping at home) were wedged beside the wheel hump. Laura's father would clamp the speakers to each side of the truck and turn the volume up high, even though it wasn't necessary, because the sound from the two hundred other speakers in the drive-in could easily be heard. But that was okay with Laura. She loved how strange it seemed, almost dreamlike, hearing the same private conversation being carried on simultaneously all around her while the film flickered on the monstrous, bug-spattered screen. It was both communal and intimate—the smell of hot dogs and popcorn, the collective smacking and munching and swallowing, the stars twinkling overhead like a Hollywood effect. If the movie was boring, she would look around or head off to the bathroom. Sometimes she would spy couples kissing in cars and trucks, ponytails smashed against the windows, and other vehicles parked way in the back, windows fogged over, rocking slightly. It often seemed to her like permissible eavesdropping, a public display of secrets.

The Paladian Theater in Amarillo, however, possessed its own special exoticism. It had just opened its doors, and Mr. Tate wanted to see a movie there because he had supervised a portion of the construction the previous fall. They arrived a good half hour before the film began, bought their tickets, and Mr. Tate spoke to and laughed with the manager like they were old friends and then gave them all a tour of the theater, which seemed as thrillingly majestic as an English palace with its tall, red crushed-velvet curtains, and the gold-and-black rococo curlicues on the facing of the balcony, and the screen towering impressively above them, protected and veiled rather than exposed, like the drive-in screen, to the elements and insects and beer-swigging vandalism of adolescent boys.

Dressed sharply in a white shirt, jeans, and boots, Mr. Tate strode about the empty theater as if he owned it, pointing to the inlaid design of the balcony, explaining the joist work of the three pillars and steel-framed balcony support that he himself had welded, rattling off the cost of the seats and the curtains and the screen, which indicated (Laura couldn't quite tell from her father's tone) either magnanimous wealth or a waste of money. At his insistence, Manny, Gene, and Laura clambered up the carpeted spiral stairs to the balcony and leaned over the ledge, waving down to Rich, who stood smiling like a Munchkin before the massive screen.

They took their seats as other people filed in. Mr. Tate gave Manny and Laura three dollars and told them—in a clownish, mock-hick voice that made everybody laugh—to "oversee the movie vittles." They bought lemonade for their parents, Velma, and Rich and root beer for themselves and Gene, a brick of Hershey's chocolate for everybody to share, as well as two big bags of popcorn, which tasted oilier than their own, scooped from the reservoir of orange-yellow fluff.

The glass-covered lightbulbs dimmed. The red curtain parted as the music from the first short, a Disney cartoon, trumpeted. Unlike at the drive-in, the sound here was not too loud, but it was clear, the picture sharp, brighter, without the crackles and lines and burn holes she had learned to ignore on the outdoor screen.

A trailer for a John Wayne western and then a newsreel, and then the movie itself. It had not come to Charnelle when it was originally released, so Laura was excited to finally see it. She hadn't quite known what to expect—a Technicolor sermon?—but soon she was enthralled by the grand panoramic majesty of it all. It made her want to read the Bible. Who knew it was that romantic, that dramatic?

When they had arrived in early afternoon, it had been hot and cloudless, but when they emerged from the theater over four hours later, the sun had slipped beneath the horizon. The sidewalk and grass glistened with rain, the sky milky purple, as swollen and variegated as a two-day bruise. Laura felt disoriented. It was like falling asleep in the middle of the afternoon and waking in the night, not sure what had happened or even what day it was. Time seemed to evaporate or be kidnapped. She didn't know if she liked this feeling—thick, narcotic, as palpable as an overripe melon.

Aunt Velma loved the movie, though she thought it a little racy for kids. Rich had fallen asleep. Manny loved the fights and the special effects, and Gene's favorite part was when Moses seemed to be walking around in a burning-bush-induced glaze, his face red, his hair suddenly white. Mr. Tate thought it was way too long and had twice stepped outside to smoke a cigarette. Mrs. Tate liked the Exodus—the joy on all those people's faces when they finally left Egypt.

"What did you think, Laura?" Aunt Velma asked.

"I loved it."

"And your favorite part?"

"All of it," she said, but she felt her answer disappointed everyone. They had given specifics, but she still felt too stunned by the experience to talk about it.

Easter Sunday. They rose before dawn and went to the sunrise service at Aunt Velma's church, where the preacher recounted the old familiar story of the Crucifixion, the days of darkness, the stone mysteriously moved from the tomb, Jesus appearing to the women who loved Him and then later to His disciples who needed testing, a hand in the side of His body, and the final glorious ascension—hallelujah, hallelujah, amen.

Laura listened absently. She'd heard this story many times, and while on Friday, during Aunt Velma's dinner blessing, it had seemed vividly alive, it now had lost its power to hold her attention. It seemed, in fact, hackneyed compared to the movie they'd watched yesterday. She bent her head, as if in prayer, closed her eyes, and tried to unfurl the movie in her mind. The most distinct images weren't the ones she would have thought—the Red Sea parting, Pharaoh's army stopped by the pillar of fire. She saw instead the more intimate moments: The princess playing that crazy game, called hounds and jackals, with the pharaoh. (It stunned her to think of biblical figures playing board games like she and Gloria and her brothers did.) The gold dress "spun from the beards of shellfish." Moses in chains in the dungeon, the princess prostrate before him. The dark shine of his sweaty body, half naked and caked in mud, in the immaculate throne room before his father, who turned away from him, who forbade the name of Moses to be mentioned again. Yul Brynner with that black snake of hair coiled exotically out of the side of his bald head.

Everyone suddenly stood and shuffled the hymnals. She opened her eyes and stood up, too, out of habit, and pretended to sing, "He arose, He arose, He arose," while a bright flicker of shame goosed over her because she'd been thinking about the movie, particularly Moses's sweat-glistened chest, instead of being thankful for Jesus dying to take away her sins.

After church they rode Ginger and Hayworth again, played several matches of horseshoes, and then Mr. Tate took them fishing at the pond, but no one caught anything, except Gene, who nabbed a little white perch. Aunt Velma, Mrs. Tate, and Laura made the dinner, and everyone played dominoes and canasta, ate more cobbler, and then listened to a special Easter radio program from the Grand Ole Opry.

After cleaning the kitchen, Laura's mother wiped her hands and said, "I'm taking Fay for a walk."

Gene said, "I want to go." Both Manny and Laura looked on expectantly, like they, too, could use a walk before the trip home.

"No, you stay here," she said, and was out the screen door before anyone could answer.

"Aw, come on," Gene said, moving toward the door.

Aunt Velma caught his arm. "You come sit with me, honey."

"But I want to go."

"Come sit here in this chair with me. Let your mother have a little time to herself."

By eight, Laura's mother still hadn't returned. Mr. Tate, Manny, and Gene were loading the truck for the return trip. Laura helped Aunt Velma dry the last of the dishes and wrap the leftovers they were taking back to Charnelle.

Mr. Tate came in and asked, "Where's your mother?"

"I don't know."

"Well, go find her and tell her it's time to go."

She dried her hands, put on her sweater, and walked across the dark meadow, calling for her mother and Fay. She walked to the orchard where the light from the barn crept to the edge of the trees, but she didn't go into the grove, not at night. She heard rustling off in the branched shadows. She called again. A flurry of indistinct movement, and then some animal—a coyote, maybe—scrambled out of the grove. She sucked in her breath and backpedaled quickly, thinking the animal was charging toward her. But when she glanced again, she saw it lope in the opposite direction, as afraid as she was, moonlight skittering across the edge of its neck and head. It disappeared over a hill.

She felt apprehensive, jumpy, so she walked swiftly, calling again. The evening had cooled; her breath misted in front of her. A twig snapped, and she broke into a run toward the faint light of the barn, where the chickens chastised her as she entered. Ingrid, the Holstein, mooed loudly, and in the midst of this animal chorus, she felt suddenly ridiculous. She laughed nervously and then heard the familiar wheezing of a dog, and said, "Fay? Mom?"

The one-bulb light of the barn was creepy. From the hay-strewn corner,

Fay emerged surprisingly, as if passing through a watery membrane separating darkness from light, and walked up to Laura and licked her hand. She bent down and rubbed the dog's chin, and Fay immediately lay down on her back and exposed her belly for more scratching.

"Where's Momma?" she asked the dog, who closed her eyes and lifted her paws. Laura peered into the darkness and could vaguely make out a still, human shape. A quick, shuddering dread whipped through her.

"Momma, is that you?"

"Yes."

Laura walked toward her and could see her sitting against a bale of hay. Why hadn't she answered her calls or said anything? She wondered how long her mother had been here. Had her mother watched her running into the barn? It frightened Laura, this strange silence. In the shadows, her mother's cheeks shimmered, shiny and wet.

"Are you okay?" Laura asked.

Her mother didn't answer.

"Momma, are you okay?"

"Yes, Laura."

"Why are you crying?"

"I didn't realize it'd gotten so late. Is it time to go?" She wiped her face with her sleeve, then rose and walked into the light.

"You're bleeding!" Laura shouted.

Her mother's yellow blouse was ripped below her left ribs. A blot of darkened blood encircled the ragged hole. Laura reached out and touched the stain.

"Ow!" her mother said, pulling back sharply. "Don't do that."

"What happened?" The blood felt warm and greasy on her fingers.

"I scratched myself on some barbed wire," her mother said. "Dumb. It's nothing. We better get going. Come on, Fay."

The dog stood sleepily, hay clinging to her back, and fell in step at Mrs. Tate's heels.

"You, too, Laura."

"But, Momma—"

Her mother was already through the barn gate, though, striding across the meadow toward the distant light of the house. Laura followed, but her mother moved fast, dissolving into the darkness until both she and the dog seemed merely gold-lined silhouettes.

On the drive home, Manny, Gene, and Laura wore their wool caps and mufflers and huddled together with Fay under the two afghans Aunt Velma had given them. Gene fell asleep, and Manny and Laura watched the shifting stars as the truck hummed north along the highway back to Charnelle. With the wind and the sound of the truck's tires on the asphalt, it was too loud for talk, which suited her just fine, because she liked this time without words. Lying flat in the bed, she could see the headlights from passing cars and trucks shining over them like spotlights. The sky had cleared, and she delighted in identifying the constellations she knew and searching for her own patterns, which she gave foolish names she soon forgot.

She could tell they were close to Charnelle at least ten minutes before they arrived. The traffic going the other way increased, and the sky brightened from the lights. She sat up and peered through the cab window. The tip of her father's cigarette glowed orange and brightened when he inhaled. Rich was asleep in Mrs. Tate's lap, and she had her head turned toward the side window to the low dark hills that rose and toppled as they sped along. Laura rubbed her fingers together. Though she couldn't see them, she knew they were still stained with her mother's blood. In the scramble to get going, she had forgotten to wash it off. She put her fingers to her nose but smelled nothing.

What was her mother thinking about? Laura wondered. She seemed so secretive, ever since Gloria left, almost a year ago now, or perhaps before that— yes, definitely before. Laura wished she could get inside her mother's head for only a few minutes and see what was going on in there, but she knew that was impossible, just as she sensed that others would probably never be able to clearly know what she thought and felt.

Through both the cab window and the front window, she could see the lights of Charnelle spread across the plains like a prairie fire, flickering, blinking, calling them home. Tomorrow she'd be back in school, back to the routines of classes and chores and the chattery, joking banter with her friends. That would be good, but she wasn't there yet, and the weekend itself, the reason they'd gone, the fun they'd had, was over, and there was only this between time of traveling in the dark.

A wave of sadness swept through her. She didn't know if it was the weekend ending, or worries about her mother, or just tiredness. She was prone to these quick spells of sadness or confusion. She often felt a strange, conflicting pull either to give in to the spell—"wallow in it," as her father said—or to resist it, shake it off, get up and do something, anything, which did seem to work. Motion triumphing over mood.

Gene and Manny, asleep on either side of her now, turned at the same moment and tugged the afghans from her, sending a whistling chill through her bones. She pulled the covers back and nestled against Fay. She absently stroked the dog's warm fur as she watched the sky lighten from behind, the town seeming to curl over the cab into the truck bed.

After pulling into the gravel driveway, her father turned off the truck, which rattled and shook Gene and Manny awake. The silence after the drive seemed cottony and thick. Her father said something to her, but she couldn't understand and had to yawn several times to unplug her ears. Without a word, her mother grabbed the box of leftovers Velma had sent home with them and went into the kitchen. Gene wobbled sleepily, and Laura helped him to bed. Her father put Rich in his crib, and after helping unload everything into the living room, Laura slipped into her nightgown.

She expected her mother to say good night, but she didn't utter a sound, just retreated to the bathroom and then her bedroom, the door closing abruptly behind her. Another sign, Laura thought, but of what? In bed, the sadness from before was replaced now by a grateful warmth, the familiar pleasure of the journey finally ended, of returning home, of being home. Still, she felt unsettled, as if this weekend had been trying to warn her of something but she'd not been listening carefully. She tried to recall all that had happened. The fall from the horse, the movie, which seemed, now that she considered it, all about exile and return. Her mother's disappearance into the barn where Uncle Unser's ghost still seemed to reside, her mother crying in the shadows with the dog, the sense of there being invisible barriers between her mother and the rest of the family. Laura felt darkness, glass, and a quietly hostile silence that no one else seemed to register. She believed she was on the verge of understanding something, as if she could almost grasp how a puzzle fit together. But the darkness and the breathing of her brothers in the room enveloped her, pressing down, and the sculpted contours of her mattress held her like a soft hand and urged her to sleep.

9

✳

Inversion

*A*t four o'clock on Saturday afternoon, Laura rode her bicycle over to the Letigs' and parked it in the backyard. Jack and Willie answered the door and lunged against her, almost knocking her over with their hugs. Willie unlocked himself from her legs and ran down the hall, shouting, "She's here, she's here!"

John emerged from the bedroom, wearing his brown work boots, a pair of tight jeans, cuffed at the bottom, and a faded red-and-black-plaid shirt with silver snap buttons, his pack of Lucky Strikes poking out the top of his pocket. He didn't have pomade on, so his blond hair seemed longer, lighter, shaggy.

"Put the boys to bed early. I wore them out this morning. They should sleep hard."

He looked at her knowingly, and at the door he quickly touched her hand so that it seemed an accident. She knew it wasn't.

While he was gone, she and the boys played checkers and Parcheesi, but the boys yawned through supper. Jack complained that his ear hurt, but he seemed fine after she read them two long stories from the Letigs' copy of *Grimm's Fairy Tales*. She put them to bed by seven-thirty, and they were conked out by eight, sleeping hard, as he'd said they would. John returned about nine-thirty.

"Boys asleep?"

"Yeah, they were exhausted."

"I thought they'd be."

He drew the curtains and then kissed her right there in the living room. He'd had a few beers and something stronger. She could smell it on him.

"Be careful," she whispered and stepped back, looking toward the boys' bedroom.

He grabbed her hand, led her to his bedroom, and pulled down the white shades. He didn't speak. He put one arm around her waist, the other around her shoulders, drew her up to him, and kissed her again. She put her head against his chest, and they danced slowly in tight circles. She was excited, but nervous, too, her stomach like taffy, stretched loose, about to break.

"What about the boys?" she whispered. He didn't answer. "What about the boys?" she asked again.

He unwrapped his arm from her waist and leaned over and locked the bedroom door. Then he was kissing her again. He seemed too quiet and intense, and she worried about the liquor on his breath. His face was nestled in her neck, and the heat from his mouth felt good, his tongue fluttering in the hollow of her throat. Then, without warning, he lifted her up, his arms clenched around her legs, his face suddenly buried in her stomach.

"Hey!" She gasped. "Be careful."

He made a low growling sound and laid her on the bed, undid his shirt snaps, which clicked like castanets, and let his shirt fall to the floor. He stretched over her, his mouth moving to hers and then down her throat. He unbuttoned the top button on the front of her dress, kissed below her collarbone, and then unbuttoned the second one. She placed her hand on his to slow him down, but he was insistent as he unbuttoned another and then another until her torso was exposed, and he kissed her ribs and the top of her chest. He reached under her back, deftly unsnapped her bra, and moved his hands over both breasts, placing one of them in his mouth, then the other one, sucking gently at first, but then harder. She tried to guide him back up, slow him down by easing his mouth to her mouth. She was nervous. It felt good, but scary, too. He kissed her stomach, moving his face in slow circles, his mustache tickling. Then he put his hands under the skirt of her dress, moved them over her thighs and across her panties and along the sides of her ribs.

"Hey," she whispered, but he didn't seem to be listening. He lifted her dress up and touched her again, then moved his mouth in circles around the insides of her thighs and her stomach.

"John," she whispered and sat up, reached around his shoulders, but his face was between her legs. He eased her back down with his arms and extended them over her stomach and chest, his hands on her breasts, squeezing. She felt light-headed, dizzy, dizzy. She tugged on his arms, trying to draw him up again. This was happening too fast, though she didn't know what exactly was happening. He suddenly pulled down her panties, breathed heavily. Her head spun, she felt disoriented, confused, and then just as suddenly he was gone. She opened her eyes, and the rest of his clothes were off, which scared her. She pushed him away.

"Hey," she whispered and closed her legs. He pushed her thighs apart. "Hey," she said again and shook her head.

He took her hand and moved it to him, and she knew he expected something, but she didn't know what to do. Then his hand was on hers, moving up and down, and she tried to follow his motion, but he seemed dissatisfied, annoyed, and soon he was on top of her, pressing himself against her stomach, moving back and forth. She could feel him under her ribs, slightly painful, his skin hot against her, and suddenly it was wet hot between them. He continued for a long minute after that, and then lay down upon her with all his weight.

He was heavy, maybe asleep. She couldn't breathe very well. She didn't know whether or not to disturb him. She pressed her arms under his shoulders and lifted a little so she could breathe more easily. Then she heard a knock. He didn't move. She listened. Another knock.

"Daddy."

She nudged John.

"Huh," he said.

"Daddy, are you home?" It was Jack.

"Yes, son." His voice sounded loud in the room, and strange, as if he were drugged. She realized this was the first thing he'd said since they'd entered the bedroom. "Go on back to bed."

"Daddy, I had an accident."

"Go to the bathroom then," he said irritably.

"Is Laura still here?"

She and John looked at each other, alarmed. "No," he said.

"I saw her bicycle outside the window."

He didn't answer. Seemed stumped, in fact. She felt panicky, a wild bird caught in a cage. John was still on top of her. She shivered beneath him.

"She walked home," he said. "Now you go on to the bathroom, son. I'll be there in a minute to help you."

He rose. "Stay here," he whispered. He looked around, then leaned down and whispered, "No. In here."

He opened the closet door. She searched at the end of the bed for her panties and finally found them on the floor. She moved quickly toward the thicker darkness of the closet.

He shut the door, except for a crack, and then she heard the bedroom door open and saw a thin stream of light from the bathroom. She slipped on her panties, redid her bra, and then felt the wetness on her stomach. She crouched down and waited among the dresses and slips and hatboxes of Mrs. Letig. It smelled of perfume in here. Too closed in, too intimate and claustrophobic. He had another private life. She *knew* it, of course, but now she could sense it, smell it. She reached out and clutched one of Mrs. Letig's winter dresses. She ran her hand down the long sleeve, the material silky but thick. She half expected to find Mrs. Letig's hand at the end of the sleeve. The reality of this woman was almost too much to bear. It made her feel suddenly ashamed and lonely. Tears welled hotly in her eyes, and she brushed them away with the back of her hand.

What will happen? Her bottom lip quivered; she bit it. *This is dangerous.*

He'd said that, and he was right. And then, unexpectedly, she thought of that woman her father had brought home a couple of years ago, not long after her mother left. The dark hallway, Laura watching, exchanging looks with the woman. The woman seemed—was she remembering right?—to be a girl. And now Laura *was* that girl in some weird, inverted way.

John came back into the room, shut the door. It was very dark. She couldn't see now. He opened the closet door and whispered for her. She didn't answer at first. He moved into the closet with her, pulled the door shut.

"Where are you?" he whispered.

"Here." She held out her hand in the darkness and felt his face.

"Ouch." He grabbed her hand and pulled her to him, put his lips to her ear. "You have to go home now," he said.

"How?"

"Wait here for a few minutes. Then I'll come get you. You have to walk. I'll bring your bicycle over in the morning."

"Okay." Her throat got tighter; tears streamed down her cheeks.

"Shhhh," he whispered. "It's okay." Her face was against his chest, and she could feel his skin wet from her tears. There was a long pause before he said, "It's okay, honey."

"This is terrible," she whispered.

"No, no, it isn't. Don't think that."

"But—"

"No," he said. "Everything's fine."

"You're just saying that."

"I'm not. Now wait until I come back."

When he returned, he whispered, "Come with me."

They tiptoed through the bedroom and living room to the back porch, where he'd left her shoes. He opened the door and nudged her outside. She felt slighted.

"Go down the alley," he said.

"When will I see you?" she asked, and it seemed to come out as a childish plea. She felt stupid.

"Tomorrow," he said. "Go on. Hurry up."

10

✴

The Trestle

*S*he didn't go straight home. How could she? Her father would be expecting her soon. But she couldn't go back in that house, talk to him, not even the smallest exchange of words. Not yet. He'd know, wouldn't he? She walked north to the railroad tracks. There was a train that ran from Amarillo, up through Dalhart, and on to Denver. Outside, it had cooled, but not too much, and there was plenty of light from the three-quarter moon and the stars. She walked along the tracks and stopped where they crossed a trestle, the Waskalanti Creek running below. Not much water now, even after all the snow had melted, just a thin stream with rocks, sharp and jagged, glinting in the moonlight. She walked out over the bridge, as she and Manny and Gloria used to do before Gloria got married. She sat on the rail and dangled her legs over the side. Then she leaned back between the rails on the wooden ties and looked at the dark sky overhead. She closed her eyes and breathed deeply.

She wished there was someone she could talk to. She thought of Gloria, still in West Germany, her last letter said. She might be coming home this summer for a visit. Their father wanted her to. He had forgiven her now, wanted her to come back. He wanted to see his grandchildren. There was another child now besides Julie—a boy, Carroll. Maybe Gloria would understand. But Laura couldn't tell her. She could tell no one. She'd promised. And she didn't know what Gloria would say. Her husband was older than she was, not that much younger than John, in fact, but it was different, and Laura wondered how much Gloria had changed. Now that she was married and had kids, would she be less understanding, feel she had to protect Laura, as if she'd never been young before? Gloria might even tell their father. Even though Laura wanted to tell someone, in order to make it real, it wasn't worth it, and yes, John was right, it was far too risky. He could go to jail, he said. Though did anyone *really* believe that?

She heard the howl of a coyote. It seemed to be far off, but it startled her. She knew that the coyotes wouldn't bother her, that they weren't really so dangerous, except when they ran in packs. But they made her nervous anyway. There had been an incident once in Charnelle where a coyote grabbed a baby, tried to carry it off but was stopped, the baby unhurt except for a nip mark on its foot, and the rabies shots later. That howl made her think of what happened to their dog Greta.

Lying on the trestle, her eyes still tightly closed, she tried to remember what her mother looked like that day. She wore a pale blue smock that was stained from dirt and blood, and her ash blond hair, laced with silver strands, was pulled back in a scraggly bun that had come loose from all the commotion, long strands falling like scythes down the sides of her face. Her mother sat there on that stump so long, just staring, thinking, waiting, that hard and silent beauty of hers. Then not much later, she left, toting that ragged brown suitcase to the bus station and away from them. No explanation, no letter, no postcard. Nothing. Just gone. Disappeared.

Where was her mother now? Laura hadn't thought seriously about her in so long. Strange, how you get used to it. For the whole first year after she left, Laura could never imagine *not* thinking about her mother. *Where was she now? Did she still think of them? Was she coming back? Was she dead?* All those impossible questions. Her mother maybe in some strange man's room, doing what Laura had done tonight—more, certainly. She could see that now, the possibility of it. She understood that her mother was not just her mother, was not just her father's wife. Did her mother have another child? Enough time had elapsed, and she was still young enough. But wasn't it children, wasn't it them, that she'd run away from?

Laura rolled over on the track and felt the splintery wood against her face. She looked between the ties and could see the thin creek below her, hear it gurgling softly. The white rocks hard, pointy, but shimmering in the moonlight. If she tried, she might be able to fit between these ties. She used to be able to. But she wasn't skinny enough anymore. She'd fleshed out; her breasts and hips would get in the way now. She could toss herself over. It seemed pretty easy, really. You just had to have the nerve to do it, or the stupidity. A boy a year older than Gloria, Danny Lincoln, had done it a few years ago, broken his neck and went into a coma, and he died a week later. Why had he done it? Manny figured he was drunk, but no one else did. His girlfriend had dumped him. It had always puzzled Laura, but right here, right now, in the dark, the water below, she could see how it might happen. She could feel in her own blood the pull, like that one time at Palo Duro Canyon, standing on the edge, that crazy voice inside her head that whispered *jump, jump, jump*.

Headlights shone far away and then suddenly closer and closer. She moved quickly to the end of the bridge. She didn't want to be caught on the tracks over the water; there was an ordinance against it, ever since Danny Lincoln fell—or jumped.

The car stopped, and a man stepped out. She couldn't tell who it was, because the car lights were in her eyes. She looked to her left and right, saw an opening where she might run. He came closer, a flashlight in his hands.

"Laura?" It was Jimmy Cransburgh. "Laura Tate?"

"Yes, sir."

"What are you doing out here?" he asked, approaching slowly, the flashlight on her face.

"Just walking home."

"From where?"

She paused for a moment, unsure how to answer. "Baby-sitting."

"Baby-sitting who?"

"The Letig boys."

"Kind of out of the way, aren't you?"

He was right. Her house was east of the Letigs' house, not north. She had gone a good mile out of the way.

"Just wanted to walk, " she said.

"Were you on the bridge?"

"Yes, sir."

"You know there's a law against that?"

"No, sir," she said. *Plead ignorance rather than guilt,* Manny always advocated.

Mr. Cransburgh didn't answer for the longest time, just shone his flashlight over the bridge and then into the trickle of water below and then back to her face. She couldn't move, felt frozen, her head throbbing with panic.

"Why don't you let me drive you home?"

She put her hand out against the light so she could see. It took her a second to find her voice. "I can walk."

"I think you better let me drive you home," he said and shut off the light. "Come on. Hop in."

In the car, she wondered if he could tell what she'd done. He didn't say anything. But why would he? When they were almost to her house, she asked if he'd let her out at the end of her street.

"I should drop you off at your house."

"No, that's okay."

He glanced at her in his rearview and then nodded. "Listen," he said lightly. "Why don't we just not say anything about this to your father?"

She exhaled, suddenly relieved. "Thank you, Mr. Cransburgh."

He stopped at the corner.

"Stay away from the bridge, you hear?"

"Yes, sir."

She thanked him and closed the door, and he stayed parked there as she walked down the street to her front porch, and then he drove past her house.

Manny was gone. Gene and Rich were asleep. Her father was reading in his chair. He wore his flannel pajama bottoms and a white T-shirt, and his reading glasses were perched on the end of his nose. He was thinking about opening up his own welding shop, and he'd checked out library books, now scattered over the coffee table, on how to run a small business.

"You're back late," he said, looking at her over the black rims of his glasses. "I didn't hear you put your bike away."

"I decided to walk," she said. "It was pretty out. Mr. Letig's going to bring it over tomorrow."

"Everything go okay?" he asked, a worried crinkle in his forehead.

"Yes, sir."

"You're shaking."

He was right. She was shaking. She hadn't realized it. She crossed her arms and rubbed her hands over her shoulders. "It's a little cold."

"Seems warm to me. You feeling okay?"

"I'm just tired."

He pushed his glasses up. "Listen to this," he said and thumbed back through his book.

"I'm really tired, Dad," she said.

He held his hand out. "Come here and let me see if you have a fever."

"I'm fine," she said, stepping around him. "I just want to go to bed."

"Well, okay, then," he said, shrugging. "See you in the morning."

"G'night," she said.

"Love you," he said by rote, his head already back in his book.

11

✴

Easter Again

A month passed without her seeing the Letig family. It was a busy month. Spring break was over, and the rush and daily chores of school and home left the weeks short on leisure. Classes were behind because of the winter snows, the principal said, so the students had to attend school three successive Saturdays so that the summer break would not be compromised. At Easter, Laura's family visited Aunt Velma near Amarillo, as usual, but Velma was not in good health, and Laura felt irritable and distracted while she was on the farm for the long weekend.

Aunt Velma had suffered a small stroke, which had put her in the hospital for a week. She was home now, insistent on doing her work, but there was a slur to her speech, a cobweb of spittle at the corners of her mouth, and she limped slightly. Her arms twitched oddly, and vases and other fragile items were endangered and had to be moved. Aunt Velma had somehow managed to cook a huge meal for them (fried chicken, potato salad, cucumbers in a sour cream sauce), but there were no trips into Amarillo, no movies at the Paladian Theater, no nothing. Everybody just stuck on the farm.

Women from the church had been staying at the house, caring for Velma, but Mr. Tate said they wouldn't be needed while he and the kids were there, and he assumed, as usual, that Laura would just do the work. She was enlisted to help her aunt with her baths, to escort her to the toilet. She resented these tasks. Aunt Velma didn't really want the help, though she needed it. Laura wanted the old Aunt Velma back. This woman seemed like a frail, weathered, half-addled version of herself.

Part of Laura's irritation had to do with the woman's body. Aunt Velma liked to wear long work dresses or long-sleeved shirts, so her skin had never been that exposed. It shocked Laura to see her naked in the bathroom. Her skin was the color of cottage cheese, with a curdled texture and bruises (from falling) of varying shades—purple, blue, yellowish green. Never a skinny woman, she'd always been thick but robust. Now she seemed fat, and in her nakedness the exposed wrinkles and wattled flesh turned Laura's lips down and made her squint. Velma's gray hair floating in the tub of water, the unhealthy folds of flesh . . . Laura tried to look away, but the image stayed as a negative in her mind. She could taste the sneer on her lips, and she did not like this in herself. It felt sad and unseemly and at times sickening in a way that made her lose her appetite.

It wasn't her aunt's fault, she knew. She loved Aunt Velma, she did, but she grew weary, just in their short stay here, of having to remind herself of that fact. The whole farm seemed to be indicative of Velma's age, ill health, and inattention. Gray sheets of paint over the barn were splintering. Everywhere she turned, it smelled like manure—dog crap, cow crap, chicken crap, pig crap. Inside the house, it didn't smell much better. She was used to Aunt Velma's house exuding a freshly baked cobbler or fried okra smell. Now it reeked of Mentholatum. Dust, like a layer of sheep's wool, clung to the furniture, and she kept pulling, in frantic swipes, spiderwebs from her face. Even the beds and couches and chairs seemed to be full of dust. She tossed her copy of *Julius Caesar* onto the living room couch, and a cloud rose above it.

She helped her aunt and kept her mouth shut. But her father told her twice, "Quit that frowning. She can't help it."

At one point, Aunt Velma slipped in the tub and pulled Laura in with her. Both of them screamed, and her father and Manny were suddenly there, opening the door, and helping Laura out of the water. The sight of the naked woman, her breasts sagging and chewed-looking, the folds of fat, the frail ugliness exposed to her father and brother, made Laura turn away in an angry spasm of embarrassment. Once her father saw the situation, he dismissed her brother, but not before Manny's face contorted in disgust, and he looked at Laura as if she were to blame, not just for the fall but for this moment of shameful exposure. She had the fierce, sudden impulse to slap him. As if this was what a woman was. As if this was what it all amounted to.

She can't help it, you idiot, she wanted to spit.

And so, alone, in a room upstairs, or downstairs in the wooden rocker, which didn't seem to be a breeding ground for dust and dirt, she found herself alternately angry, contemplative, ashamed, and sleepy. She tried to do her homework—a geology report and geometry worksheets and reading the interminable *Julius Caesar,* which had a good enough plot, but half the time she didn't know what in the world they were saying. She tried to read it aloud as Mrs. McFarland had instructed them to do—*ta-dum, ta-dum, ta-dum, ta-dum, ta-dum*—but she lost all track of the meaning when she did that. And soon enough she would be staring out the window, wishing she were back in Charnelle, sitting with Marlene and Debbie at their favorite table on the far end of the school cafeteria at lunch, or making fun of Dean Compson with them at 4-D's, or walking with an excited dread down the Letigs' street on her way to school, hoping she might catch a glimpse of him leaving in his pickup.

She had been trying to decide whether she ever wanted to see John Letig again. That Saturday night, several weeks ago, after she got home from his house and the trestle, she started to go to bed, but her two younger brothers were in the room, and all she could smell on herself was him, that pungent, smoky smell. She touched her stomach, and she could still feel him there like a scar. She grabbed fresh underwear and a nightgown, darted to the bathroom, and scrubbed herself in soapy water. Rinsing afterward, she resolved that this was it; it wasn't worth it. She'd had her little thrill, and so had he, but that was it. No real damage had been done, nobody knew, nothing terrible had happened. She'd kissed other boys anyway, and felt them against her at dances, and this wasn't *that* different. If it stopped now, then everything would be all right. Besides, what had happened at his house that night spooked her. She had tried to slow him down, to stop him, but she hadn't, and she wasn't sure she wanted to. She wasn't sure of anything. It all felt too out of control. *Be done with him.* She could almost hear Gloria say those words. And what if her father found out, or Manny, who seemed to suspect her of everything? It could be terrible. She remembered how angry her father was when Gloria eloped with Jerome. It was good they were both out of the country by the time he found out, or he would have gone after Jerome; he was that enraged.

She'd been working over this problem for weeks. The Monday after spring break she was glad to be back at school, where her friends were, and where she could be the unassuming girl she'd been a week and a half before, nonchalant with the boys—ordinary, really. But by midweek she began thinking of him again. In geology, as they were making a topography map out of oatmeal paste, she closed her eyes for just a second and felt again the sensation of being lifted in the dark, his heavy presence on top of her, her anxious excitement. Other times she would close her eyes and would see him with a sash of snow on his shoulder, or licking the droplets of beer off his blond mustache, or the way, when she had asked him what he wanted to eat, he smiled and said—not in a lurid manner, there was something openly lovely about his expression—"Whatever you're making." But then she would forget him again, and the thought of them together seemed foreign, more like an incoherent dream than a memory, and her own yearning felt remote, like it belonged to someone else.

And so the weeks between spring break and Easter had gone like that, back and forth between what she felt she ought to do and what she, well . . . felt.

Here at the farm, in the musty sickness of Aunt Velma's house, she had wanted to drift back to those memories, but suddenly everything associated with the body seemed ugly and bruised, dusty and foul-smelling. And the old woman's body struck Laura as a contorted image of her own, a malignant trick with a fractured mirror.

Best to be done with it. And she finally started to believe it. Under the covers at night, she drifted off to sleep with the self-satisfaction of a sinner determined to sin no more. And the next day it was as if what had happened with John hadn't happened. She didn't even think about it.

On Easter Sunday, Aunt Velma didn't feel well enough to go to church, which was a relief to everyone, though no one said so. Mr. Tate said they needed to be getting back to Charnelle. He arranged for one of Velma's neighbors to check on the farm, and he called the woman from church to tell her they were leaving soon and that Aunt Velma needed someone to look in on her.

That morning, before breakfast, Laura found an old photograph album, the exposed binding lined in dust. She wiped it with a cloth and flipped through it. Her family didn't own a camera. Strangely, they had no family pictures. The only one she remembered was the framed one of her parents' wedding day, and her mother had taken that. Aunt Velma came in, sat down beside her, and began to narrate the story of the pictures. There were Velma and Uncle Unser, not long before he died, with his scissored hands. There were Velma's old mother and father, not long before they died. Uncle Unser's brother and his wife.

In the middle of the book, there was a stunning photograph of a couple standing by a large expanse of water. Laura didn't recognize them. A handsome young man, smiling, wearing one of those full-bodied men's bathing suits, his hair slicked back, a pencil-thin mustache like Clark Gable's. His skin pale but muscled. Beside him was a beautiful, dark-haired woman in a long, body-hugging swim dress, her figure as shapely as old *Life* photos of Lana Turner or Betty Grable. The woman's head was thrown back in high-spirited laughter.

"Who's that?" Laura asked.

Aunt Velma peered at the photograph, rolled her tongue around as if she had something mealy in her mouth that she wasn't sure she liked.

"Hmmm. Who is that?" she echoed and ran her hand shakily over the photograph, rested her crooked index finger on the man's body. She laughed suddenly. "Oh, yes, that's Unser and me. Ha! Right before we got married. In Mobile. No, no, no. Corpus Christi. Imagine that."

"Really," Laura said, surprised, taking the photograph from her. She studied it. Yes, she could see them buried deeply inside the faces, though not the bodies, of those people. It was bewildering.

"You were beautiful," Laura breathed and handed back the photograph. She wondered if that was the right thing to say. It seemed faintly like an accusation. *And now look what you've become!* Wasn't that the implication? But how to correct it? Best to say nothing more.

Aunt Velma just held the photograph close to her eyes again for a long time. She ran her fingers lovingly over the man's body and then the woman's, and shook her head and smiled to herself. Laura felt that Velma was remembering a private moment. It was as if Laura wasn't even there.

12

Lake Meredith

*I*n mid-May, a few weeks before school was out, Anne Letig had to go to Borger for several days because her mother had sprained her ankle. She took the boys with her. Laura heard about this from her father when he got home from work. The phone rang later that evening, and when Manny picked up the receiver, he shook his head and returned it to the cradle.

"Who was it?" Laura asked.

"Hung up."

The next morning she left early for school, walked by the Letig house, saw his truck there, and knocked nervously on the door. The street was busy with activity—people opening their doors, kids in and out of houses. When he answered, wearing his undershirt, his hair floppy and wet-looking, he raised his eyebrows and smiled.

"Come in." She shook her head. An old man across the street was out front with gardening shears. "Okay," he said.

"Did you call last night?" she asked.

"I hoped you'd know it was me. Wait here."

He disappeared into the house. She stood, fidgeting, on the porch. She smiled at the man across the street. He smiled back. After a few minutes, John returned with an old maroon sweater in his hand. Mrs. Letig's.

"Here, take this."

"Why?"

"So Grampa over there thinks you have a reason for being here. There's a note inside. Tell me thank you and that you're sorry for the inconvenience."

She felt confused. "What?"

"Just say loudly, 'Thank you' and 'Sorry.' "

"Thank you," she said.

"Louder," he whispered.

"Thanks. Sorry for the inconvenience."

"Tell your father I said thanks too," he said normally.

"I will."

He winked at her. "Bye, now," he said, and shut the door. She turned and put the sweater in her satchel. A piece of paper fell out, and she reached down, grabbed it, and walked quickly, but not too quickly, along the street. She wanted to run. When she had gone a block, she unfolded the note.

TELL YOUR FATHER YOUR SLEEPING OVER WITH A FRIEND ON FRIDAY AND SATURDAY. SOMEBODY HE WONT WONDER ABOUT. BRING CAMPING CLOTHES. BRING BATHING SUIT. LAKE MEREDITH. COME TO MY HOUSE THROUGH THE ALLEY. TEAR THIS INTO SMALL PIECES AND FLUSH IT DOWN THE TOILET!

He had not signed it, not even his looping initials. She read it again, noting the misspelling of "you're" and the lack of apostrophe in "won't." She clutched the note tightly. She walked to school, went into a stall in the bathroom, and peeled the note from her sweaty palm. She read it again. And again. Two girls came into the bathroom, chattering. She waited until they left. She wanted to save the note, his handwriting. But she slowly tore it into small pieces. The ripping seemed to thunder in the bathroom. She made sure that no sentence could be read, and then the pieces fluttered from her hand into the water and floated there, the blue ink fattening on the pages. She flushed and watched it swirl away. Evidence. Gone.

Once, when she was twelve, she, Manny, and Gloria swam across a huge stretch of Lake Meredith. "Come on!" Gloria had shouted, and Laura and Manny dove in after her.

They just kept going and going. Laura expected they would turn back, but then they were halfway across the lake, and Gloria and Manny were ahead of her. Laura was a good swimmer, but every year the lake had to be dragged for bodies because two or three people would try to swim it and would cramp up or get hit by a boat or caught in the currents. She remembered worrying, as she thrashed after her brother and sister, if something horrible like that might happen to them, but she just kept on swimming, staying as close to them as she possibly could.

They waited for her at one point, treading water near the middle, and when she reached them, Gloria asked, "You okay?"

She nodded, sputtering water from her mouth.

"Too late to turn back now," Gloria said, smiling. "Pace yourself. I'll keep an eye on you."

And then they were off again, this time in a slower rhythm so she wouldn't fall too far behind. Her arms felt heavier and heavier. Twice boats whizzed by, maybe fifty feet from them, not head-clunking distance, but swimming through the wakes was hard, and a coughing fit seized her once when she swallowed water. Every few yards she would stop and see how far she had to go. Her legs felt so weary. She saw Gloria ahead, on her back, facing the sky. She turned over like her sister did, blinked water from her eyes, squinted into the glare of the sun, and floated, scissor-kicking so she'd make some progress. She finally got her wind back and turned over, but the shore still seemed too far away.

Her mother had once told her that drowning was the best way to die. Not nearly as awful as it seemed. Actually quite pleasant. It was a long time ago. They were at Lake Meredith then, too. Rich wasn't born yet, and Gene was only a toddler, playing in the sand under an umbrella. Manny and Gloria were chicken-fighting with two friends in the water, and her father was fishing. Laura and her mother were in the shallows so they could keep an eye on Gene. Her mother lay on her back, her blond hair fanning out in the water like a painting of a dead woman Laura had once seen in an art book—just the pretty, barely wrinkled mask of her face floating above the surface, her eyes closed to the sun, her arms outstretched.

"Your lungs just fill up," her mother said. "You think it's amazing that you're breathing water, and then you're dead."

The thought terrified Laura, both then and now. Her choking earlier had panicked her. She didn't want to breathe water; she didn't want to drown. Each time it sloshed into her mouth, she spit it out immediately, fearing that she might lose the ability to distinguish water from air, and then she'd go under. It wasn't much farther, not much more, and finally she just closed her eyes and mindlessly windmilled until she paddled past the point where she could stand up.

When she opened her eyes again, Gloria and Manny were there beside her, the water just above their kneecaps, each of them with an arm hooked under hers. They heaved her to a standing position. Laura's legs were rubbery, unable to support her body. Gloria and Manny helped her to the bank, where they all collapsed and lay staring into the sky, now overcast. Or was it almost night? Had it taken them all day to swim across the lake? She felt like she might throw up.

"We did it," Gloria said, out of breath, her rib cage heaving. Gloria already had a woman's body, full breasts, beautifully curved hips, which Laura admired and envied. "We damn well did it."

"Fucking-A!" Manny shouted. He was only thirteen then, but in the previous year he'd grown seven inches, his voice had dropped, and hair had begun to sprout above his lips and under his arms. He no longer seemed like her brother, but rather some alien creature that delighted in tormenting her.

Laura felt a sudden sense of alarm at Manny's exclamation, but Gloria only laughed. Laura was too tired to laugh, but she felt proud of herself for having made it. For not having slipped under. After they caught their breath, Gloria stood up, wiped the sand and twigs from her butt, and then held out her hand to Laura.

"Come on," she said. "We have to get back."

Laura looked across the lake despairingly. "I can't," she said.

Gloria laughed. "Walking, not swimming back."

She shook her head.

"Come on. It won't even take us half an hour."

Laura looked at the long, arching ring of shoreline back to where they had left their father's truck. That seemed worse than the swim. But her sister pulled her up. Laura's muscles stiffened and tingled. She felt like a newborn foal, all wobbly spindle legs.

"I don't know," she said, dropping down to the ground.

"Maybe we should walk back and get the truck," Manny said to Gloria. "Let her rest here."

"No, I don't want to leave her here alone," Gloria said. "I'll go. You stay with her."

"I could go," Manny said.

"No. It'll be dark, and you shouldn't drive the truck at night. I'll be back soon. Will you be okay?" Gloria asked.

"Yeah," Laura said.

Gloria set off as Laura sat on the edge of the bank. Manny waded into the water again, floating peacefully on his back for a few minutes, and then he stretched out on the bank a few feet from her and closed his eyes. His body seemed so long.

She watched Gloria walk, barefoot, stopping one time when she stepped on something. It was almost dusk when she reached the truck. Laura could see her barely, a small speck, as she gathered their things, got into the truck, and then disappeared. After what seemed like forever, but must have been only minutes later, she heard the truck on the road behind the bank. Laura was cold by then. Her legs still wobbled when she rose. Gloria helped her put her clothes on and wrapped her in a blanket for the trip home. With her eyes shut, Laura could hear the water in her ears; she felt as if she were tossing again in the wake of the boats. She opened her eyes and watched the horizon so she wouldn't throw up.

"What do we tell Momma and Dad?" Manny asked.

"We don't tell them nothing," Gloria said dramatically. "Nothing. We don't need them worried. You got that, Laura?"

She nodded.

"Tell me."

"Nothing," Laura said weakly.

"Okay, good." Gloria patted her gently on the knee. "You did great today. You know that. Great! You're probably the only twelve-year-old girl who's ever swum that lake."

"You think so?"

"Damn right I think so."

"Yeah," Manny said, putting his arm around Laura's shoulders, surprising her with his gentleness. "You did good."

13

✴

Isabel

By the time she and John arrived at Lake Meredith, it was almost dark. Since school had not let out, there weren't as many campers as there would be in June, July, and August. Still, there were several tents at the first site, fewer the farther they traveled. He drove past any sign of campers and then down a bumpy dirt road that led to a small clearing right by the southern bootheel of the lake. He cut the engine.

"How did you know this was here?" she asked.

"Oh, I've been coming here for years, ever since I was a kid. My grandfather and me and my brothers used to fish here. Hardly anyone knows about it. Too far off the main road. Everybody's too lazy to look for it, which is great. It's like my own private spot. I love it."

She started to ask if he'd brought his family here, but she held her tongue. Surely he had. And besides, she really didn't want to introduce Mrs. Letig and the boys into their conversation. Not again.

She woke that morning feeling nauseous, off kilter. When she arrived at his house with her satchel, sneaking through his backyard, she had asked when Mrs. Letig and the boys would be back. He'd sighed audibly in a way that suggested he would have to settle something and it'd be best if he did it now.

"Let's not talk about them, not for this trip. This is just you and me. We don't have to think about other people. Okay?"

He'd said it gently, without condescension or guilt or any hint of resentment, and she appreciated his directness. It made her feel better. She had nodded, and he pulled her close to him and held her against his chest.

"Let's go, then," he said.

But after that moment there had been the awkwardness of him driving around to the back of his house and her having to skulk to the truck and hunker down in the passenger seat, her head against his thigh, while he drove away from his block and out of town. On the highway, she still felt strange, the same off-kilter sensation from the morning. She figured it was just nerves because they were exposed in the truck, and in a small town like Charnelle, even if you left the town limits, you never knew if someone was going to pass you, waving, curious, but suspicious if you happened to be driving alone with Zeeke Tate's daughter. Gloria's elopement with Jerome and then especially their mother's disappearance had caused quite the scandal, though few people seemed willing to say anything directly to them about it. After Laura's mother left, she grew tired of the hushed whispers in school when she walked by; the covert pointing on the street; the stares; the cars driving by their house, slowing down and then speeding off; the feeling, unsubstantiated but palpable, that her family was the subject of an odd blend of gossip, pity, and scorn; the sense that she—as the only female left in the house—was under particular scrutiny, as if the whole town was waiting for her to follow her sister and mother.

Several miles out of Charnelle, she sat up for a few minutes, but then he thought he saw a truck coming that he recognized, one of the Somersby brothers. It turned out to be a false alarm, but he said, "Why don't you just stay there and sing me a song?"

She was reluctant to sing at first, sullen, feeling as if this trip was a huge mistake, but then he started singing loudly, "I've been working on the railroad," tapping the beat on the steering wheel and on her kneecap, bobbing his head goofily. She loved this boyishness, his obvious delight in his off-key crooning. She looked up at him, the way his teeth slightly overlapped, the mustache that he'd trimmed (for her?), his almost-pretty lips, and that long, beautiful face. She loved him at that moment. She raised up and kissed him quickly on the mouth and then turned on the radio.

For most of the hour it took them to get to the lake, she lay with her head on his thigh, beating a rhythm on his legs and chest, her voice rising above and around his. They sang along to Patsy Cline's "Lovesick Blues" and Elvis's "Hound Dog" and Buddy Holly's "That'll Be the Day," and Bobby Darin's "Mack the Knife," which had been the number one hit last year, and the radio seemed to play it every ten minutes. She propped her foot on the window and watched her toes wiggle in the wind, and it was a good time, loose and easy, as if they'd done this before and were comfortable with each other.

He lit up a cigarette and offered it to her.

"I've never smoked before," she said.

"You want to try?"

"Sure, why not?"

She choked at first, and he told her how to let it just swirl in her mouth and out, and then she did it until her head felt light and tingly, like the way it felt after drinking the champagne on New Year's Eve. She gave him back the cigarette.

"You can keep that one."

"No thanks."

She watched the sky and ran her fingers over the hair on his arm.

"That's nice," he said and smiled. And then, a few minutes later, he told her to sit up; he rearranged his pants.

"Am I hurting you?"

He smiled and said, "No, honey. Not at all."

At the campsite, he turned off the engine and put his arm around her shoulder, and they stared at the whitecapped, reddish lake. The sun had fallen beneath the horizon, but there was still light.

"I'm glad you came," he said.

"Me, too." But she felt dizzy and too hot.

"Let's set up camp before it gets dark," he said, and kissed her softly. He lit the kerosene lamps so they'd have light later, hammered in the tent stakes, and she tightened the lines and helped raise the poles. The tent was small but comfortable, and he'd brought along some old blankets, which he threw down on the tent floor. She was embarrassed when he unzipped two sleeping bags and zipped them back together as one big one. He looked up to gauge her expression.

"Would you rather I keep them separate?" he asked earnestly.

She shook her head.

"I'm hungry," she said. She hadn't eaten lunch, and in the excitement of the trip, she'd not thought about it before, but now hunger seized her stomach.

He scavenged in a duffel bag and brought out some potato chips. "Here," he said. "Do you like hot dogs?"

"Sure."

"Let me start a fire, and we'll roast some."

She poured herself some water from the jug he'd brought and sat on a stump as he gathered the rocks in a ring and then added sticks and leaves. He lit the fire, got it going good, and put a log on top. Out came the franks, and he shaved the ends of two long branches with his knife, put the hot dogs on, and held them out to her. She rotated the sticks while he fixed the buns.

"You like mustard and ketchup?"

"Just mustard."

"They ready?"

She pulled them from the fire, where they had blackened on one side, and she held them out as he grabbed them with the buns. They ate the hot dogs quickly, along with the chips. He pulled out two bananas and a couple of not-quite-ripe peaches, and they ate them as well, and then he opened a tin of homemade oatmeal raisin cookies. She felt guilty eating them, because she knew that Mrs. Letig must have baked them for her husband before she left.

It had been hot during the day, and though it had cooled down with the dusk, it was still summery. John had broken a good sweat. He guzzled water, took off his shirt, and mopped his face. He sat on the ground next to her feet and stretched out with his head against the round boulder she was sitting on. Neither of them spoke for a while, but that was nice. She felt better now that she'd eaten.

"My God, it's beautiful here," he said.

The water was calm and seemed purple and silver in the dusk. Red and orange streaked the sky, still thickly textured with clouds. He jumped up and went to the truck and came back with a small tablet, a little kit, a tin cup.

"What's that?"

"Just some paper and paints," he said.

"You're an artist?"

"I fiddle around sometimes."

He opened the sketch pad and the paints, and he dipped the cup into the lake. She sat beside him. As the light faded, he quickly painted the whole scene. He managed to capture the rich sense of color and the stillness and depth of the lake. In the picture, he'd moved a large willow that was off to the right to the other side so that the leaves created a frame for the water. At the bottom center, barely visible, were a woman's legs—*her legs!*—on the bank, her toes in the water. He'd done all this in less than half an hour.

"You're good!"

"No, not really."

"Yes, really. How long have you been doing this?"

"Since I was a kid."

"Did you ever want to do it for a living?"

"Yeah, for a long time," he said.

"Why didn't you?"

"I guess it seemed frivolous, and when my dad died, my family needed money. I could make decent money as a welder."

"How did your father die?"

"In a railroad accident, when I was about seventeen. He was an engineer for Santa Fe. Cattle on the tracks. The brakeman tried to stop, but it was too late. Engine went right off the rails, flipped on its side."

"I'm sorry," she said and felt a new sense of compassion for him, as if a secret window had been opened to her.

He leaned back against the rock with his hands cupped behind his head and closed his eyes. "Oh, don't be," he said. "It was a long time ago."

"I like this picture," she said, picking it up, studying it though it was hard to see now that night had fallen. "Can I have it?"

"Nah, it's not very good." He propped himself up on his elbow and smiled. "Maybe I'll make something else for you sometime."

A truck rattled in the distance and then it got closer. They turned and saw lights about a hundred yards away. The truck stopped and then the headlights went out. A door slammed, and a flashlight flickered along the path. They both rose and moved toward the truck. John got out his tire iron and gripped it tightly. Frightened, Laura stood a few yards behind him. She wondered if someone had seen them, had followed them here. *Her father? Manny?*

"Who is that?" John shouted, a warning.

The flashlight stopped on the path and pointed up toward the truck. "Park ranger. Okay if I come in?"

"Yeah, I guess," John said, easier, but he still held the tire iron until the ranger came into view. John grabbed his flashlight and shone it on the man, who wore a uniform and a hat.

"Thought I saw your truck drive past. Been looking for you. Not many people know about this spot."

"My grandfather used to bring me here when I was a kid."

"It's a beaut, all right. Solitary. I don't tell anyone. Mostly only rangers know about it. What's your name?"

"Letig." They shook hands. "John Letig."

"Cleavis Peterson." He eyed Laura and tipped his hat. "You the missus?"

She hesitated, didn't know how to answer. John laughed.

"No, this is my niece."

The ranger stepped closer and squinted at them. "Niece?"

"Yep. Whole family was supposed to go camping, but my mother-in-law sprained her ankle, so my wife had to help out. The rest of the family's planning to meet us tomorrow. Isabel and I thought we'd come on ahead and see how the fishing was."

The ranger looked in the back of John's truck. John had brought three poles and a tackle box.

"Anything biting?" John asked.

"The carp, of course." The men laughed.

"Any perch?"

"Not really. The trout on warm days. Some channel cat. Today was pretty warm, so maybe if you set out a trotline, you'll catch something."

"Forgot the trotline—and the boat."

The ranger smiled. "Well, then try about midnight and again around sunrise. Fellow the other day caught himself about a dozen good ones, including an eight-pound cat. All around those times."

"Thanks. Appreciate it."

"You like to fish, Isabel?"

"Yes, sir," she lied.

"Oh, yes. We call her Lucky."

"Is that right?"

Isabel. Lucky. Just who in the hell was she? She was beginning to feel nauseous again.

"She attracts the fish like bait," John said.

The ranger laughed. "Well, good luck to you. I just wanted to make sure you knew where you were and what you were doing. How long you here for?"

"Just a few days."

"Well, okay. I'll get out of here before I scare all your fish away."

"Thanks again," John said.

"You bet. I'm up on the southeast ridge, about four miles from here, the fourth cutoff to the right if you need anything. Bye, miss."

"Bye," she said, too quietly. She could hear the caution in her voice.

"Thanks again," John said. The ranger tipped his hat and then worked his way up the path, got in his truck and drove off.

She was glad when she could no longer hear the engine. She went back to the rock and sat down. The ranger had put her on edge, reminding her of the long series of lies she'd told. She'd never lied so much to her father before. The earlier lies—like back in February, when John had said they were buying a dress for his wife, and then after spring break, when Jimmy Cransburgh drove her home—seemed minor compared to what she'd done today. These had been the most dangerous, because they involved other people. She'd told her father that she was going camping with a new girl from school, Pamela, and her parents. There was no Pamela, but she was afraid to tell him Marlene or Debbie, since he knew their parents and might call them, and then she'd be in for it. She'd given him a made-up telephone number, so that if he called, it would be wrong and she could pass it off as a simple mistake. And when he offered to drive her over or have Manny do it, she said that the girl didn't live far away and she wanted to walk since it was a beautiful day. And her father had raised his eyebrows but agreed, mainly because he'd already sat down to the dinner of baked chicken and potato salad that she'd made him. "Well, okay," he'd said and shaken his head to indicate his resignation to the whims of teenage girls, and she had set out on a circuitous path to the Letig house, practically slinking down the alley and into his backyard so that no one would see her, tapping on his window until he let her in. Driving away, slunk down, wasn't much fun either, a deception through hiding, but then it had been okay, with them singing and her foot catching the breeze from the window, but now again they were almost caught, and if John weren't so quick on his feet, transforming her into Isabel, then they'd be caught for sure. Though what would the ranger have done? It didn't matter. It was all these near misses. They had been sort of thrilling at first, a game, but now this latest close call soured her mood. She felt dizzy again, a little bead of sweat breaking over the top of her lip and around her hairline.

"You okay?" John asked.

"I'm just sick of lying."

"He won't be back, and we have the next couple of days together."

"You don't know that," she said. "He might be back in an hour."

"Nah. They check on you once, and they leave you alone. And we're out on the edges. No one knows this place. Trust me. It's just you and me now. Don't let it bother you."

She didn't say anything.

"Hey, I know what'll cheer you up."

He went to the truck and brought back a large bottle and a couple of mugs.

"What's that?"

"Sangria." He poured some in both mugs and handed her one.

"No," she said.

"It'll loosen you up," he said.

"It'll make me sick."

"No, it won't. It's weak Mexican wine, practically grape juice. You'll like it. It's sweet. Just enough to warm you up. Here, take it." She held the mug but didn't drink. "Come on," he said. "Wonderful on a night like this. Besides, we should be celebrating."

She took a drink, and it did taste sweet, like juice, without any of the bitterness of liquor.

"See," he said. He tapped his mug against hers. "Cheers." They drank.

"Hey, let's go swimming," he said.

"The water will be too cold, won't it?"

"Are you kidding?" He stood up and undid his belt. "Come on," he said.

"Aren't there snakes?" She'd heard a rumor recently about water moccasins, though she'd never seen one in all her previous trips to Lake Meredith.

"Nah. You have to watch out for snapping turtles, though. I heard one bit off a guy's wiener."

"Really?"

He laughed. "I'm joking. Come on."

"Let me go put on my bathing suit."

"You don't need a bathing suit," he said. "It's dark. It's just you and me."

"What if the ranger comes back?"

"He's not coming back. He's up at his station with a flask of bourbon and a big fat cherry pastry in his mouth, listening to a baseball game on the radio."

He dropped his pants and then his boxers, left them crumpled by the fire. The light outlined his body, silhouetted the hairs on his arms and legs. His penis dangled between his thighs. She heard a night bird caw in the trees behind them. It made her jump.

"You go ahead," she said.

"Not unless you come, too."

"Okay. But go on first."

"You don't have to be so shy, honey."

He dove in and resurfaced a few seconds later. "Ahhhh," he called, "Shang-raaa-la! Laura, you have to get in. This is amazing."

The water did look inviting. She was too warm. She slipped out of her jeans and dropped them by the bank. She was hesitant about taking off her panties and bra. But he'd seen her before, and it was dark. He would see her again. Isn't that what they were here for? She both knew and didn't know.

"Come on, Lucky," he sang. "Come on, Isabel."

She moved to the edge of the water. Dipped her toe in. The water was cool but not cold. It felt good. She did love to swim. She stepped back, undid her bra, and placed it neatly on a rock by the water. She bent over and slipped out of her panties. She instinctively covered herself with her arms and hands, aware that the light from the fire must be illuminating her.

He swam up to the bank. "What are you ashamed of?"

"I'm not."

"Don't be." She dropped her arms. "I should paint you," he said.

He held out his hand. She took it as the water edged over her knees. She stepped out so that the lake reached her thighs. He still held her hand, but he kept his distance, as in a dance. She dove past him, swam underwater several yards, and emerged into a banner of moonlight.

"Oh, my Isabel," he said so happily that she had to laugh. Her voice echoed across the lake. She smiled and swam on her back, her body half breaking the surface.

He swam to her, reached under, and pushed up on the small of her back, so that her body broke the plane of the surface. Her skin looked so pale. She put her head back, her hair fanning out. He said something, but her ears were underwater. She just heard the muffled vibration of his voice. And then she heard, from far away, pattering on the water, and then felt a droplet land on her forehead, and then more on her breasts. She opened her eyes. John was still holding her. The water was at his shoulders. The rain landed on her face and body, and with him holding her like this, she felt like part of a ceremony she read in one of Manny's Tarzan novels, a jungle princess sacrificed to rain.

14

✴

In the Tent

They made it to the tent, running through the drizzle, just before it poured. John had to dash to the truck to get towels. He had grabbed the lamp on the first run from the lake. When he went to the truck again, she dimmed the light. He came back with the duffel bag and stopped at the entrance—naked, drenched.

"Towels in there," he said and stood with the water sluicing off his back, so that he resembled one of the pictures she'd seen in her science textbook of a prehistoric man at the mouth of a cave. Then he darted out to the fire, snatched up the sangria and mugs, and brought them inside. "Kick those sleeping bags over so they don't get wet," he said.

She'd already dried off. She threw him a towel. He stepped out of the rain, which increased the volume of the puddle inside the tent. He dried himself and then dropped his towel to the tent floor and let it sop up the puddle before it reached the sleeping bags. Shyly, she held a towel around her and grabbed her bag and pulled out a long shirt. She slipped it over her head before removing the wet towel. He smiled, shook his head. She felt that her modesty was odd even to her. They'd just been outside on the lake, floating on the surface. But she was used to living in a house full of men, sleeping in a room with three brothers. She was used to keeping herself covered.

Through the tent flap, they stared at the rain, watched it douse the persistent embers of the fire so that the only light left was from the lamp.

"How are the sleeping bags?" he said.

"Pretty good." She reached over and pulled them to the middle of the tent again, straightened them out. Only one edge was slightly damp.

"Do we need to get anything else from the truck?" she asked.

"It can wait until tomorrow."

He pulled the canvas flap down. Water dripped from it, making another small puddle. He dried his arm again and cleaned up the mess, clutched the sangria and mugs and crawled over to the sleeping bags and sat cross-legged beside her. He was still naked, and she tried not to look at his lap, but her eyes kept darting there whenever she thought he wasn't looking. She couldn't help thinking it looked like there was simply a small animal hiding in a wet, brown nest.

"I'm cold," she said and climbed into the sleeping bag while he poured the sangria.

She thought at first she wouldn't have any more, but it did taste like grape juice, and it seemed to have no effect on her.

"Thanks," she said as she sipped.

She finished her mug, and he poured her another. He dimmed the light, set the mugs aside, and then he got into the sleeping bag with her.

"Oh, yeah. That's the ticket," he said and scissored his legs a couple of times to heat the flannel even more, his leg brushing against hers. "Come here," he said. "Warm me up."

In the faint glow, under the covers, he pulled off her shirt. She felt exposed, but he held her so close that she could feel the hair from his chest and stomach against her like soft fur. As they kissed, she kept her legs together. He drew her to him, hooking his leg over hers, and thrust against her a few times with a sudden comic force that made her laugh. She had thought about this for the past month and a half, ever since that night at the end of spring break, and she kept reeling back and forth between anticipation and a skittish nausea. On the trip here, she'd been nervous, but it had subsided, come back, and then calmed in the lake so that she no longer felt so anxious. She liked the way he smelled and felt against her, but it seemed like there was this small animal between them, alive, with a will of its own.

He kissed her throat, skimming his hand over her breasts and ribs, and then his head bobbed above her breasts, his mouth on one nipple and then another. His mouth brushed over her ribs to her stomach.

"Ticklish?"

She laughed and rocked back and forth. He grabbed her and blew against her belly, creating a fart noise.

"Don't!" she shouted and then covered her mouth.

"Sshhh," he whispered. "You're going to wake the bears."

"Bears?"

He kissed her ribs, ran his tongue over her hipbones, and circled his mouth around her stomach slowly. The rain was coming down harder now, thumping on the tent and trees, and she shivered. She looked down, saw his head on her stomach, and again felt exposed. She pulled the sleeping bag over his head so that it covered them.

The lower he got, the more intense he became. It made her nervous. The muscles in her legs twitched, pulling together.

"John," she said. She reached for his face, wanting to slow him. "Hey," she whispered. "John."

But he kept moving his face in smaller circles. The stubble from his chin and cheeks prickled. The muscles in her legs felt tight. He looped his arms under her legs, pressing his shoulders against her thighs. She put her arms over his shoulders to draw him back up. She wanted to breathe for a few minutes, settle down. But then he did something with his mouth, something that made her think of the light, rapid flutter of hummingbird wings. She closed her eyes. His head was very still, but his tongue kept fluttering. She felt as if she were levitating. She couldn't quite locate her center of gravity. There was a sound, a low kind of familiar thrumming that didn't seem to be coming from her. She could hear it closer and louder until it was like a vibrating whistle.

He pulled his head away, rose to his knees, and leaned over to kiss her neck. She heard a crinkling sound and felt his hand between them. He kept kissing her neck. She wanted to rest for a few minutes. She felt dizzy again. And then he put his full weight on her.

She said something, "Hey" or "Wait," but maybe he couldn't hear her. She wasn't sure; she could hardly hear herself.

His body pressed tightly against her own, her legs open around his. She needed to catch her breath. And then, in a sudden gasp, he was inside her. She felt a sharp spike of pain shoot through her abdomen and lower back. She could hardly breathe before, and now it felt as if her lungs were about to explode. He groaned, and she thought her breath might return, but it didn't. Her ears plugged, like when she was underwater too long.

She wanted to say something, but there was only this underwater feeling, like she couldn't make it to the surface. She wanted to say his name, but she couldn't form the words. Language seemed on the other side of the surface, beyond the pressure in her chest. She tried to turn to see his face, but even that seemed impossible. She shifted her eyes and could barely make out his jaw. He hooked his arms under hers and moved steadily and then faster, caught in a lurching momentum of his own, beyond her voice.

The rain came down hard now. The drops pelted the top of the tent. She tried to concentrate on the rain, and then, surprisingly, she could breathe again, just short, quick snatches of air. In her head, she counted the drops. One, two, three, four, five . . . twenty . . . fifty. She focused, heard them hit and drip down the side of the tent. She heard him again, his own breathing labored, and then his body tightened into a point of compact stillness.

When he resumed his motion, it was a slow, mechanical rhythm. She no longer felt like she was going to drown.

Finally he pulled away, and she had the sensation that he'd turned her inside out. She felt another spike of pain, worse than before, followed by a throbbing ache that made her whole body stiffen. He rolled beside her, breathing deeply. The rain still came down hard. When she closed her eyes, she felt off balance, spinning. She listened intently to the rain, listened as it subsided. He draped his hand over her ribs, laid his leg over hers. He traced his fingers along her chest and stomach. His touch was gentle again, restrained. But she did not move. She hurt.

"Are you okay?" he whispered, but she didn't think he really wanted her to answer.

The rain settled into a slow drizzle. She lay there, still, and concentrated on the sound of the dripping water from the trees. When she sat up, her stomach cramped. She tightened her muscles until the pain receded and then straightened her back. Had there been a rock underneath her? She breathed to clear the aftereffects of the cramps. She put her hand beneath her, on the sleeping bag. She pressed her fingers between her legs: thick, wet, mucusy. An alarm went off in her head. He'd put something on, hadn't he? She brought her fingers to her face. It smelled like blood. Her first time; there was supposed to be blood, and some pain. That's what she'd heard. So this was normal.

"You okay, Laura?"

He put his hand on her shoulder, moved his fingers over the back of her neck.

"I have to pee," she said.

"Need some light?"

"No."

"Just a little?"

He reached down and turned the lamp up. For a shocking moment, the tent was ablaze, but he quickly adjusted the knob. He reached between his legs and pulled off the condom and tossed it into the corner of the tent. She looked down; the plaid flannel of the sleeping bag was darkly stained. He pushed back the tent flap with a watery thud.

"I think it's over," he said. "It's pretty muddy, though. Be careful. Here, give me your hand." His voice was gentle.

She slipped her nightshirt over her head and bunched the shirt between her legs. She grabbed one of the towels and moved to the opening and looked under his arm to the darkness outside. It sounded like it was still raining, but she realized it was just the trees dripping.

"I can't see."

"I'll take the lamp out and hold it for you."

"No, I can do it myself."

"Sure?"

"Yeah," she said hoarsely.

He stepped over the sleeping bag and grabbed the lamp. He saw the stain on the bag. When he looked back at her, the lamp illuminated his face. Wrinkles lined his forehead.

"Are you sure you're okay?"

"I need to go pee," she said, reaching for the lamp.

"Let me help you."

"Just give me the lamp."

"Here," he said, moving to the entrance. "I'll hold it."

"No!" Her voice was much louder than she intended, with a ferocity that surprised them both. Her voice echoed on the lake. They stood still, facing each other. His face had a stunned, slack expression. He seemed frail and ridiculous, standing there naked in front of her. "Just give me the lamp," she said quietly.

He handed it to her, and she left the tent, stepping onto the cold, wet ground. Blown leaves gathered at her feet. She walked around the tent where he couldn't see her, set the lamp on a flat rock, pulled her shirt up, and crouched. She tried to urinate but felt her stomach cramping again, and then the pain flared hotly in her back. Her hair dangled in her eyes. She lost her balance and pitched forward onto the ground. Mud on her face, a twig lodged in her mouth. She spit weakly and then laughed. What a fool she was. The ground was cool and hard, but strangely comforting. The pain was gone, but she just wanted to lie there for a minute.

Footsteps fast over wet leaves. She thought of a movie she'd once seen, a western, where an Indian scout lay on the ground in the rain and listened for the hooves of the cavalry. She remembered the scout's words, in that truncated movie-Indian language: "They come." She laughed again.

And then he was there beside her, his hands on her face, brushing away the hair from her eyes and mouth. "Laura?"

"Yes," she said. Or thought she said.

"Laura, can you hear me?"

"Yes," she said, louder. She just wanted to rest here for a moment longer.

"Can you get up?"

"Yes." But she didn't move. He placed his hands under her arms and lifted her gently to her knees. "I'm okay."

"Put your arms around my neck. I'm gonna carry you back to the tent."

"I have to pee."

She squatted again and closed her eyes. The night had calmed. The trees continued to drip. The lake sucked against the bank. And then the fluid came from her, hot and burning at first. She felt the wet warmth circle her feet. She opened her eyes and was surprised by the lamplight. He stood by her. He'd not even taken the time to put on a shirt. She was comforted by that thought.

"Done?" he asked.

She nodded.

"Can you stand up?" he asked her inside the tent. "Just for a minute, while I get a towel?"

"Yeah."

She felt wobbly when he let her go, the inside of the tent spinning slowly, but then the dizziness subsided. She watched him set the lamp down and gather more dry towels. He draped one of them over the wet stain where she had been and then brought a couple back and set them on the floor of the tent.

"Let's get you out of that shirt." He gathered it from the bottom with his fingers and began to roll it over her body. It was wet and cool but felt oddly comforting. "Raise your arms."

She lifted her arms, which felt heavy, and he rolled the shirt over her breasts, shoulders, and head and then tossed it into a corner. She teetered.

"Steady, now," he said and clasped her waist with one of his arms and reeled her into his shoulder. "You seem really warm."

"Nope." She laughed. "I'm freezing."

He let go and then was quickly back with a towel. As she tried to dry off, she began to shiver again, so he draped another towel around her shoulders and wiped the twigs and mud from her cheeks, chin, and neck with the corners of it.

"What's the matter?" She laughed again. "Don't you want to kiss me now?"

He ignored her. "You're still bleeding some. Did you bring something for it?"

"No," she said. "It's not supposed to be my time."

He grimaced at that, shaking his head. "Okay." And then again, as if reassuring himself: "Okay."

He got another towel, cut the end with his knife, and ripped three wide strips. He handed the strips to her. "Here," he said. "Use these."

"What?" Then she suddenly realized. "Oh."

She folded one and adjusted it between her legs. She pointed to the end of the sleeping bag. He handed her panties to her, and she slipped them on. He pulled a shirt from his duffel bag, returned, and held it out for her arms. She slowly buttoned it. It was flannel and soft and felt smooth against her skin. He still had not put on any clothes, and again she thought this told her something good about him. He was attentive. The lamplight cast his shadow against the canvas wall as he hunched over her, rendering him, she imagined, a snail with a burden on his back.

"I'm sorry," she said, but didn't really feel sorry. She felt sort of giddy.

"Sshhh," he whispered. "You rest."

"Will you hold me?" she asked.

"You bet." He leaned over, brushed a tangle from her face. He pressed his lips against her cheek, and then her nose, and then lightly to her lips. He wiped his mouth. "Muddy," he said and smiled.

She suddenly wanted to cry. "I'm really sorry," she said again.

"Sleep," he said.

She curled up, her head resting on her hands, and watched him as he stood to dress. He was beautiful. He bent over and slipped on some shorts and an undershirt and then lay down next to her, pulling the sleeping bag over them both.

"Are you still cold?" he asked.

"Not so much anymore."

He propped his head on his hand and stroked her neck and shoulders and face with his other hand. Soon it began to drizzle again, and she watched the drops patter against the tent, and then she closed her eyes and listened to the music of it as he gently kneaded her shoulders. Her abdomen and lower back still felt sore, but not in a bad way, her body weak but no longer shaky. He lit a cigarette and smoked it, using his free hand to stroke her skin. The tent smelled wet and fungal. He was tender with her now, but she wondered if he regretted this whole thing, wished he'd never suggested this trip.

"Maybe we should go home," she said.

"Is something wrong?"

"No."

"Then rest."

"I feel like I'm ruining everything."

"Listen to you," he said, then sighed. "Who should be apologizing?"

She was grateful that he had said that.

15

Bereft

A little before dawn, in the gray light, she woke. He slept beside her but was turned away. She tried to stand but felt dizzy and sick to her stomach, so she crawled across the tent and pushed open the flap. The lake was still and dark blue in this light, and the trees sparkled dimly. A red-and-black bird swooped from a branch by the lake to the top of the tent, turned and seemed to stare at her, cawed, and then flew away. She waited there, hoping it would return. But it didn't, though she heard it caw again farther away.

She walked through the mud to the bushes and threw up. She removed the strip of towel. She was no longer bleeding. She left the rag by the entrance of the tent, wiped her hands on one of the wet towels, and then crept back inside. She swished some water in her mouth, spit it out, and then closed the tent flap. She lay down and felt very awake for a while, listening to the lake come alive. Her back and stomach still ached, and her head felt like a pincushion.

The light intensified, brightening the side of the tent, but she closed her eyes and could see the veins on the insides of her eyelids until they faded into a red afterglow, and before long she slept.

When she woke again, he was gone. The sun made the tent shimmer greenly. It was very warm inside, but she lay under the sleeping bag, shivering, and listened to the lake. She heard footsteps, activity, and assumed it was John. A vehicle approached from the road; then the engine shut off. The click of the door and footsteps on the wet path. She sat up suddenly but felt woozy from the movement and fell back down hard on the sleeping bag. She lay still, trying to clear the fog in her head.

"Hey, there," John said. "Quite a storm last night."

"I'll say." It was the ranger. "Weatherman on the radio said it would be sunny and clear. Tells you what they know."

"Diddly-squat."

"You get rained out last night?" the ranger asked.

"Not too bad. Muddy tent. That's about it."

"Looks like you're packing up."

"My niece isn't feeling too well."

"You want me to take a look? I was a medic in Korea."

"No, it's not that serious," he said. "I'll just get her on home. Thank you, though."

The ranger left. She listened to his boots on the wet path, the truck pulling away. John moved about, gathering things and putting them in the truck. She sat up, still dizzy and sick to her stomach, but no cramping as before. The whole tent, she now realized, smelled foul—like Aunt Velma's that last time she'd been there. Her knees were caked with mud.

He opened the tent, stuck his head in. "Hey," he said. His eyes widened, from the smell, she guessed. He half smiled, half grimaced. "You hungry?"

"No," she said, her voice raspy. "No."

"How you feeling?" he asked without entering.

"Better."

"I've almost got the truck packed. You want to wade in the lake while I fold up the tent." She didn't really want to, but she could tell that it was more of a request than a suggestion. Maybe he didn't want to ride home with her smelling like this, and who could blame him? Or perhaps he didn't want the smell in his truck. It might be hard to get out. He'd have to account for that.

"I guess so," she said. They were silent for a few moments. She faced a dilemma. It was too light out to swim without her clothes on. But she didn't really want to put her bathing suit on now. He guessed at her predicament.

"Here, let me help you out. You can wade in with my shirt on. That'll be easier."

He crouched down and helped her up, and she felt a fresh wave of nausea as she rose.

"Slow down," she said.

He put his arm around her waist as she draped her arm over his neck. "Steady does it," he said.

The camp had been mostly cleared. There was a coffeepot and a skillet with some bacon and scrambled eggs by the fire. The smell of the bacon sickened her. She had to look away from it and tried not to breathe as they passed by. He walked her to the lake, and she sat down on a rock while he removed his boots, socks, pants, and shirt, leaving on only his boxer shorts. She slipped off her panties. He helped her up again and walked her slowly into the water, which was cool and still.

"Oh," she muttered.

"Too cold?"

"No. It's fine."

He held her as she bobbed slowly up and down. The shirt billowed. She stood and wiped her arms and knees with his shirt. She was sore. And dizzy again.

"Do you want to rinse your hair?"

She reached up and touched her head and felt the dried mud and twigs in it. "Yeah," she said, inhaling deeply. She dipped underwater and opened her eyes but could see only a murky green, the sunlight refracting through the water, John's shirt creating an umbrella around her. She closed her eyes and let herself sink for a few seconds. It felt good, the world muffled. The water did not feel so cold anymore. She raked her fingers through her hair a couple of times and then rose to the surface and let the water drip from her face.

"Better?" he asked.

She opened her eyes but didn't answer him. Woozy again. Bile bubbled at the top of her throat. Closer to shore, as the shirt weighed her down, clinging to her, she felt heavy, unsteady. It seemed like a hundred pounds of wet cloth had been plastered to her body. He helped her to a large assembly of rocks that formed a chair, flat stones for the seat and back. The sun beat down, but by the time he returned from the truck with a large white sheet, she was shaking.

"We're out of towels," he said.

She unbuttoned the wet shirt and took it off, and she felt suddenly exposed out here in the light of day, a layer of gooseflesh over her shivering body. He handed her the sheet, and she wrapped it around her and rubbed her hair and legs and arms and then swaddled herself.

"Wait here," he said unnecessarily, then jogged to the tent and came back with her satchel. He unzipped it and asked her what she wanted to wear.

"Give it to me," she said and pulled out a sweater, some panties, shorts, and socks.

She dressed as he slipped on his own pants and boots. She got up to retrieve the panties she had left on a rock but again felt woozy. Although he was shirtless, and it was hot out, she shivered, so he put his jacket over her.

"I made you some breakfast," he said, pointing to the bacon and eggs curdled in the pan. "I can warm it up, if you like."

She shook her head and pulled her knees up to her chest, sitting on the rock in the sun while he packed the rest of the truck and then helped her to it. As she lay down on the seat, he disassembled the tent. When he got in, she propped herself against the window, her head pressed to the glass, as he started up the truck, shifted into reverse, braced his arm across her so she wouldn't fall, and carefully backed out. After a few miles, he stopped the truck and said aloud, "See ya."

The ranger was at the window. "She doesn't look too good."

"Guess she's got what's been going around at school."

"Maybe you should get her to a doctor."

"I'll be okay," she said. "Just the flu."

"Thanks for your concern," John said.

"You bet." The ranger stepped away from the truck. "Get better now, Isabel."

Their original plan had been to stay at the lake all day and return at night when it would be easier for her to move from the truck to the house without being seen, but it was midday by the time they arrived in Charnelle. She slept most of the trip.

"Laura," he said a few miles before they reached town. "We're almost back. Can you lie down on the seat?"

The sun was bright, and she could barely open her eyes. "What?"

"Can you lie down here?" He patted the seat. "You don't want to be seen."

"Yeah," she said, feeling groggy and slightly insulted, though she knew it was for the best. She laid her head down on his leg but felt more jarringly the road beneath them. She stared ahead, watched the motes of light swirl over the console, felt his thigh tighten and relax as he drove, and then nodded off.

He let her out in an alley, shaded by two mature elm trees, a block from her house.

"We have to be quiet about this, Laura," he said. "You understand, don't you?"

"Yeah," she said.

"I'll see you soon," he said vaguely.

She had felt more awake once they hit town, a little better, but now she felt suddenly sleepy again. "Yeah," she said.

She got out, placed the satchel over her shoulder, and watched his truck turn the corner, the familiar sound of the engine humming and then fading until she could no longer hear it anymore. She was suddenly very sad. She had not felt sad before. She'd drifted in and out and had been nauseous and drowsy and dizzy. There had been no time or energy, really, for sadness. But alone in the empty lot next to the alley, the sky still cloudy, she was aware suddenly of being very much by herself. She thought of the word "bereft." She couldn't quite remember what the word meant, though it somehow seemed appropriate at this moment.

She turned the corner and went along the street, walking fast at first, but she was so tired she had to stop before she got to her house, sit down on the curb and put her head on her knees. She needed to compose herself before she went inside. Get her story straight. Her father would surely question her. John had gone over it with her, but if her head clouded up again, she wouldn't be able to straighten it out enough to make things sound plausible.

"Tell him you're tired and want to go on to bed," John had said. "Keep it simple."

Fortunately, no one was home. She was relieved that she didn't have to lie again, not yet. She could take a bath, go on to bed, but it was creepy with no one there. Maybe they'd gone to the movies. Or maybe her father had taken them all fishing. Fay was gone, too, so that was probably it. To Lake Meredith. She smiled grimly at the irony.

There was a knock at the back door. It was John.

"What are you doing here?" she asked.

"Is anybody home?" he whispered.

"No, nobody."

"Are you all right?"

"Yeah. You should go," she said urgently, putting her hand to his chest, pushing. "You can't be here."

"I feel bad." He leaned against the doorjamb. "I should have brought you home. Helped you in."

He still wore the same jeans and shirt he had on at the lake. His nose was slightly sunburned; his eyes were bloodshot. She wondered if he'd been crying.

"No, it's okay," she said. "Really. You should go."

"I'm sorry." His lips were parted like he wanted to say more but couldn't. He swallowed hard, and she reached to his face and stroked it with the back of her hand.

"Don't be," she said.

He grabbed her hand and held it. "I just feel bad about leaving you alone. Are you sure you're okay?"

"Yes."

She suddenly looked toward Mrs. Ambling's house. There was a wooden fence between their houses, but Mrs. Ambling's bathroom window had a straight view to their back door. Chances were she wouldn't look out, but it made Laura nervous.

"Go, please." She released his hand.

"Okay," he said and glanced over where Laura was looking. "You're right," he whispered. "I'll call."

"No, don't."

He leaned over and kissed her quickly on the cheek. "I'm sorry," he whispered again.

"You gotta go," she said. "Please."

He turned and walked quickly to the end of the yard, looking down the alley before opening the gate. He got into his truck, nodded to her, and she waved from inside the house, but she wasn't sure he saw her. And then he rolled away. She turned on the radio to have some noise in the house. Marty Robbins sang sadly about that Mexican girl he fell in love with in El Paso. Her stomach hurt again, maybe because she hadn't eaten. Her legs felt rubbery. She went into the bathroom and took off her clothes, bathed quickly but sensed the dizziness coming again, the heat spreading over her, the clammy return of her fever. She put on pajamas and got into bed. She could hardly even open her eyes when her father and brothers returned home.

16

✦

Emissaries

*T*he next day, Sunday, her fever spiked. She twisted and turned in and out of dreams. Her sheets were soaked. Her father sat beside her with a cool washcloth, saying, "There, there, honey. Everything's going to be okay. Don't you worry now." Then he asked about Pamela. Manny didn't know her. She mumbled something, she couldn't remember what. Her father told her there was no such person as Pamela. He'd checked with the school. "What is this business? What in the hell is going on?" He said Beaver Mitchell thought he saw her in Letig's truck, on the road heading out toward Lake Meredith. "Is that true?" He stood, his long shadow hovering over her bed, removed his belt, snapping it menacingly, as he used to do when they were all little, and then he raised the belt above his head, his face clotted in rage. *What in the hell is going on?*

When she woke, there he was, sitting beside her, asking if she was okay, telling her to calm down. He put a glass of apple juice to her lips.

She closed her eyes, and suddenly it was dark, night, and John crouched beside her bed, and she whispered furiously that he had to go, he couldn't be here, her brothers were in the room, but he said, No, they weren't, they'd been taken care of, and she tried to get him to leave, but he started kissing her ribs and the crook of her arms and down to her wrists, and then he was licking her fingers, and it felt good and warm, but she kept saying, "You can't do this, you can't do this." And when she opened her eyes, it was just old Fay, nuzzling a warm nose in her palm, licking her fingers. She felt disoriented and achy and feared falling asleep because she wasn't sure what might happen there.

She kept expecting her father or Manny to interrogate her again about Pamela, but they didn't, so she wondered if their questions had only been in her dreams. Or perhaps what she had said convinced them, or it no longer seemed relevant. They never pursued it, never called Debbie or Marlene to inquire about Pamela and her family, and then she wondered if perhaps they *had* called around. They knew she was lying, but her father was waiting until she felt better to bring the subject up, so she could be properly punished.

And then she wondered if she was dying. All those pitiful looks on their faces, even Manny's. She couldn't remember the last time she ate. The hot dog, maybe. Her bed felt damp all the time from sweat. That was it. She was dying, and the fact that she'd lied no longer mattered.

Whenever the phone rang, she jumped, alarmed, convinced it would be John or Mrs. Letig. There would be confessions and accusations. *What the hell is going on? Laura and John did what? Where? I'll kill the bastard.*

She knew that her father kept a shotgun in the closet, and she had seen him pull it down from the shelf in one long, sweeping motion.

And then suddenly her mother was there at the edge of the bed. The tattered brown suitcase sat upright by Laura's nightstand. Her mother wore a blue dress with dark red flowers splashed all over it. She had a sheer red scarf tied around her neck. Her hair ringed her face prettily, and her skin seemed softer, the wrinkles etched at the corner of her eyes and around her lips smoother, as if she'd gotten younger. Her mother appeared serene. She stared at Laura without smiling.

"Please don't leave," Laura whispered.

Her mother simply shook her head.

"Please," Laura said and began to weep.

"I'm sorry, honey. It's nature's way."

Her mother reached down and gently brushed away Laura's tears.

"Just nature's way. That's how it has to be, Laura."

And then her mother leaned down and cupped her face and then kissed her on the mouth and held the kiss almost like a lover, her hair falling around both their faces so it seemed like they were in a cave. Then she pulled away and stared at Laura curiously.

"Please don't disappear," Laura pleaded.

Her mother just picked up her suitcase and walked through a series of cobwebs, and then she was gone, the webs tattered and dangling behind her.

Mrs. Ambling watched after her for a couple of days, soaking her in the bathtub with ice in it, changing her sheets. "Maybe she's got pneumonia," Laura heard her tell her father.

There was talk of the hospital.

"No," Laura mumbled, frightened. "I'm fine," she said. "Really, I am."

But Dr. Phelps, who'd delivered all five of the kids, came to the house. He must have been in his sixties by now and had gotten fatter, a bullfrog gullet where his neck should have been. His long gray handlebar mustache hid his lips. He fingered her neck. He thumped her chest and back and felt under her armpits. He pried her eyes open and shone a penlight in them. He shoved a thermometer in her mouth. He asked questions.

"Is she vomiting?"

"Not anymore."

"How long has she been like this?"

"Since Sunday," her father said, his hands crossed tightly against his chest. "What is it? What do you think?"

"Well, it's not pneumonia."

"That's good," her father said, urging him on.

"Probably the flu. It's going around now."

"How long does it usually last?"

"Depends," Dr. Phelps said. "A week, sometimes two."

"What can we do?"

"Keep the boys away. Force liquids. Make her eat, if you can."

He put his stethoscope and penlight back in his bag and then turned to her father and stroked one side of his long mustache and then the other.

"Zeeke, I don't mean to pry, but do you have a sister . . . or aunt or somebody who could come help out around here?"

"Why?"

"It just might be good to have a woman in the house, to help you all out while Laura's sick."

Her father looked as if he'd been punched in the face, then scowled. "Sarah Ambling lives next door. She helps."

"I apologize, Zeeke. I suppose it's not my place. No offense—"

Her father cut him off. "None taken."

"I just thought—"

"How much do I owe you, Doc?"

By Thursday evening, the fever had broken. She ate macaroni and cheese and applesauce and drank some milk, but she was exhausted. Finally she slept soundly, and the dreams didn't wake her in alarm or confusion.

Friday she was better. She got up during the day, while her father and brothers were gone, and walked through the house. It was a wreck: Dirty socks and underwear and various undershirts and pants scattered about, Rich and Gene's toys and her father's newspapers littering the floor. Some greasy engine part propped by the front window. The dishes piled high in the kitchen, a loaf of bread untied, the bag wide open, growing stale. An open jar of plum jelly with a peanut-buttery knife stuck in it. No milk or eggs or butter in the icebox or much of anything in the pantry. She hoped that they would take care of this mess before she fully recovered. She hoped they weren't just waiting for her to get well. Her spirits suddenly flagged. She was reminded of how much she did around here, how much they depended on her to keep things in order. Maybe this is what Dr. Phelps had been referring to. She wondered if this mess was her penance for all her deception. Perhaps it's what she deserved.

She took a bath, changed her sheets, and fell back into bed. She'd missed a week of school, and she'd tried to catch up on the homework that Manny had gathered from her teachers. Exams would begin next week, and she was woefully behind.

When her father and the boys arrived home, around five-thirty, her father came in to check on her. "How ya doing?" he asked, a little edgy. She could tell that he was ready for this ordeal to be over.

"Better," she said. "I think I should get up and do some cleaning."

"Nonsense!" he said, shaking his head. "It ain't your fault you're sick." He kissed her forehead. "Need anything?"

"No, sir."

A few minutes later she heard him call her brothers together in the living room and quietly scold them for the mess, tell them it was inexcusable. He gave orders.

"It ain't my job," Manny said.

"I don't give a damn whose job it is!" her father whispered fiercely. "You're going to do those dishes."

"Ain't it about time she was well?" Manny muttered.

"She'll be well when she's good and ready," her father said definitively.

Then the house vibrated and jangled noisily from their work. She felt guilty, though also relieved, and she returned to her geometry problems, hoping that her brothers would not hold her sickness against her too much.

About seven-thirty, she heard a car pull into the driveway. Then she heard the Letigs in the living room, her father and John exchanging hellos, Mrs. Letig saying they'd heard she was sick, wanted to bring something over for her and the family. Laura felt panicked.

"Anne," Laura's father said, clearly pleased, "you didn't have to do that."

"I don't want you all to go hungry. Laura's the only one who cooks around here, I bet."

"Smells good. What is it?"

"Enchiladas. Half chicken, half beef."

"Oh, my goodness. Mmmm, smells good. Thank you."

"Is it all right to see her?" Mrs. Letig asked.

Why does she want to see me? She'd discovered the truth. Maybe she found some article of clothing that John had failed to put back in her satchel. There would have been an argument, bitter words, tears, accusations, John breaking down, confessing. And the Letigs were here now to tell her father. Her forehead felt suddenly clammy again, her stomach knotted.

No, the woman had brought food. Laura was just delirious—this was foolish panic. She listened as Mrs. Letig gave her father instructions for reheating the enchiladas. She didn't sound anxious or distressed.

No, of course not. She wouldn't know. John would never have confessed, even if Mrs. Letig did find something. They were just here to be nice.

Laura reached down to the end of her bed and grabbed her housecoat, slipped it on. She looked in the mirror. Her hair was a rat's nest. She seemed sallow-faced, with dark circles under her eyes. She ran her fingers through her hair, but they caught the tangles, so she just patted it down. She licked her lips to cover up the cracks. Her mouth felt filmy. The room still smelled sweaty. Her brothers had moved out to her father's room and the living room, so she could have her privacy and so they wouldn't catch whatever she had. She crawled back under the covers.

Her father poked his head in the room. "Laura, you have visitors."

"Who?" What a liar she was.

"The Letigs. They want to see you how you're doing. They brought us some dinner. And they've brought you something."

"I don't know," she whispered, frowning.

"Just wanted to say hello, Laura," Mrs. Letig called from the hallway. "We won't be long."

"I guess," Laura said and tried to smile.

Her father winked and nodded with an expression that said, *Atta girl.*

"You go on, Zeeke. Let me talk to Laura for a minute." He left, and she felt nervous again. "How you feeling, sweetie?" Mrs. Letig said. She handed Laura a copy of the *Hollywood Star Gazette.* "I know you like these," she said.

"Thank you." Laura took the magazine and then began moving some of her books and papers.

"Oh, I can do that," Mrs. Letig said and neatly stacked the books on the end of the bed and sat beside Laura. She wore a sky-blue cotton dress and a matching scarf in her hair. She smiled. "There's a good article about Deborah Kerr in there, and another one about Desi and Lucy."

"I appreciate it."

"How are you feeling?"

"Better."

Mrs. Letig reached over and put her hand on Laura's forehead. It was strange when you were sick, Laura thought. Everybody seemed to think they could put their hands on your body.

"You don't have a fever anymore. That's good. But you still look pale."

Laura nodded.

"Are you going back to school next week?"

"Yes, ma'am. I hope so."

Laura heard her father and John talking in the next room. She tried to make out what they were saying, but their voices seemed muffled, and it was difficult paying attention to both them and Mrs. Letig. At full strength, she would have had less trouble, she believed. She was getting good at doing more than one thing at a time. Lying kept you alert. You could never let your guard down. But the sickness had taken away her powers of concentration.

"That's good," Mrs. Letig said. Laura forgot what she was referring to, so she just smiled. "Your father said the doctor never could quite figure out what was wrong with you."

"Flu, he thinks."

"Well, we won't keep you. Is it okay if John comes in for a minute? He wanted to give you something that he and the boys made. I told him that a young lady doesn't like to have her privacy invaded, especially when she's sick."

She didn't know if she wanted him to see her like this. But he'd seen her worse, hadn't he?

"I guess," she said.

"He won't stay long. Men don't really like sickness, honey," Mrs. Letig said. "They think they can handle it, but they can't. That's why they don't let them in when we have babies. They can't stand to see women in pain. It scares them. They like to think of us in a purer form."

Mrs. Letig turned and smiled sadly and then looked back at Laura.

"I remember your mother used to say that."

"What?"

"Oh, the 'purer form' thing."

They exchanged glances, a question in Mrs. Letig's face, wondering if she should bring up this subject. The woman turned her head toward the door and listened for a second. John and Laura's father were talking about Charnelle Steel.

Mrs. Letig turned back to her and smiled again, wistfully. "I really liked your mother, Laura. Is it okay for me to speak of her?"

"Yes."

"I know it can be a sensitive subject." She glanced again at the door and then said, in a conspiratorial whisper, "And your father never talks about her."

Laura nodded but felt a confused sense of betrayal for doing so.

"Have you ever heard from her?" Mrs. Letig asked.

"No," Laura said nervously.

Mrs. Letig shook her head. "That's too bad. I guess we'll never know why she left. It's a terrible thing. But I want you to know that she was a . . ." She hesitated. "She *is* a good woman. It's important for you to know that, Laura. She loved . . . she *loves* you kids."

Laura didn't know if she really believed that, but she felt there was something mysterious and goodhearted about Mrs. Letig's intentions. She nodded.

"Well, we never got to have that little talk. We'll have to have it when you feel better. I want you to feel free to talk to me about whatever you want." She placed her hands on Laura's and leaned toward her earnestly. "Okay?"

Laura was disoriented for a moment, not sure what Mrs. Letig was talking about, but then remembered that before spring break she'd offered to answer Laura's questions, help her out since Gloria and her mother were no longer around.

"Yes, ma'am," Laura said.

She found it too strange to have her mother returning through the memory of this woman. She tried not to think about her mother much, but in her dreams this week she had come, and even when Laura felt better, when she was more lucid after the fever broke, she had thought of her, remembered when her mother had been there to take care of her when she was sick. And there had been that feeling, during the worst part of the fever, of passing through a membrane to an invisible other world of memory or spirit or something else, a place where her mother seemed to be. Coming out of the fever was sometimes like passing through a dark web to the world of the living. In fact, in her dream, her mother had left those tattered webs behind her. And now there were these . . . these what? These *emissaries* from that other world. That's what Aunt Velma called them. These snatches of memory from the mouths of other people. "God's little signals," Velma had said the Christmas after Uncle Unser killed himself. It made the world seem mysteriously connected, vibrating, and sometimes in weakness, in sickness, was the only time you were vulnerable enough to hear the signals, to dimly recognize the emissaries.

When Mrs. Letig spoke of her, Laura's mother seemed for a second to appear. It was both spooky and reassuring, and Laura found herself wanting to draw close to this woman. She had the crazy urge to tell Mrs. Letig about Lake Meredith, about John. She wanted to be forgiven. She closed her eyes, and the woman reached over and kissed her forehead, and Laura could smell something so familiar that it comforted her until she suddenly realized *why* it was so familiar. It was the smell of the Letigs' bedroom closet, the hatboxes and dresses and powder and perfume.

This was foolish thinking, *absolutely crazy*, to believe that she could confide in this woman. She bit her lip.

"Hey, there," John said.

Laura and Mrs. Letig both turned to him in what seemed like a synchronized motion. He was smiling, but there were anxious wrinkles around his eyes and lips. His hair was slicked back, and he wore a nice western shirt and black slacks, as if they had been out somewhere or were going somewhere after this visit, this courtesy. She suddenly resented them, resented them both for being here, for intruding upon her.

"Hello," Laura said.

"How you feeling?" he asked.

"Okay," she answered.

"Heard you've been out of it for a while."

He stayed on the other side of the doorway. Her father stood behind him. John was nervous. This was hard for him. She could see that. But shouldn't it be hard? Her resentment passed. She felt sorry for him. Squirming there. Poor man, caught between his wife and his lover. In her mind, that word, "lover," seemed foreign and tender and somehow pleasantly deceptive. Did he feel that what happened to her—her sickness—was his fault? That he was being punished? Maybe it *was* his fault. Probably not, but she was no longer sure. She'd not felt good before they went to Lake Meredith, but perhaps he'd brought it on or made it worse. Had he been squirming in his own house, guilty, feeling terrible? But she found herself hoping that he'd still want to see her, that he wouldn't be scared off. She wished she could reach out and touch him, but she knew that was impossible.

"Here," he said and pulled a small box from behind his back and handed it to his wife, who handed it to Laura, and again she had the sensation that Mrs. Letig was an emissary, through whom gifts were being passed. Inside the box was a metal sculpture of flowers with a hummingbird at the center, its bill the only thing connecting the bird to the bouquet. The flowers were blue, red, and yellow. The bird multicolored—green, orange, yellow, purple.

She didn't know what to say.

"John made it," Mrs. Letig said.

"The boys helped me. They said you liked hummingbirds."

Her father looked surprised. "I didn't know you did that sort of thing, Letig."

"Every once in a while," he said.

"Not in a long while," Mrs. Letig said. "Not since I was pregnant with Jack."

"It's good," her father said. "Isn't it, Laura?"

"Thank you," she said. "It's beautiful." He nodded. They stared at each other for a couple of seconds, and then he looked down shyly. "Where are Jack and Willie?" she asked.

"They wanted to come, but we left them with our neighbors," Mrs. Letig said. "We figured there's only so much company you could take. Besides, we're heading over to the Brewers for some pinochle."

"Tell them I said thanks."

Mrs. Letig patted the blanket covering Laura's legs. "You're special to us, honey."

She looked up at John. His face seemed to redden before her eyes. "Get better," he said.

"I will. It's really beautiful."

"Oh, now look what we've done," Mrs. Letig said. "We've gone and made you weepy." She pulled out a tissue from her purse and reached over and wiped the tears from beneath Laura's eyes. "You're just tired. You get some rest."

Laura nodded.

"Good-bye, honey." Mrs. Letig rose and straightened her dress, then reached for her husband's hand. "Come on, John," she said. "We should go."

He quickly glanced at Laura. She couldn't quite interpret his expression. Regret? Embarrassment? Guilt? Love? She didn't know. Just an inexplicable flicker across his face. They said good-bye again, but their voices seemed far away now. Laura could only see the Letigs' hands together, his wife leading him, like a child, away from her room.

PART THREE

Careful

✳

Nature's Way

*T*heir *family had two dogs back then, mongrel collie mixes—Fay Wray, the older female, and Greta, the only pup from Fay's last litter that they hadn't been able to give away. She had some breed mixed in that made her jumpy and snappy around anybody but the family. Laura's father had named her after Greta Garbo, who he thought was the best-looking woman he'd ever seen until he met Laura's mother. He'd always wink and smile when he said that. Mrs. Tate wouldn't look at him. She'd just knead the bread dough or fold the laundry or read Rich and Gene a story, but Laura could see her lips turn upward in the slightest smile and a pink flush spread over her neck.*

In heat, Fay would attract all the neighboring hounds and mutts and alley rovers, who would howl and paw and try to jump the rusting metal fence to get into the backyard, and sometimes they would succeed. Laura and her brothers would watch in fascination as the dogs nipped and bit at each other, the males with their extended pink penises, like flayed lizards, obscene, raw, vulnerable. If a dog got into the pen, Mr. or Mrs. Tate would be out with a broomstick or a rake, beating the dog or shooing it away until it jumped back over the fence, sometimes with its tail between its legs, sometimes snarling at the thwarted opportunity. If Laura's parents were not there, then Manny or, before she eloped, Gloria would fight off the dogs. But on occasion they would all just watch the males tie up with Fay, panting, their tongues lolling wetly from the sides of their mouths, the other males barking and whining and pacing back and forth in the alley next to the fence, Greta either hiding in her shed or barking madly at the coupled animals.

Laura and her brothers and sometimes the gang of freckled fools Manny ran around with would watch the dogs' ritual, laughing at first, the boys wisecracking—Get 'er, stud! Stick it in 'er!—but then they would quiet down and stare with a charged stillness as the dogs labored with a persistence that seemed both grotesque and fascinating. They weren't dumb. They knew that litters resulted from these incidents and that they themselves were the result of their parents' similar activities, but it was not pleasant for them to make the connection in their heads. Laura had never been able to adequately imagine her mother and father tied up, tongues dripping, grunting mindlessly like this. To think too much about it, which she sometimes did seeing the dogs, always made her feel nauseous and sad and strangely frightened.

When Greta first came into heat, two weeks before Easter, rather than wait for the males to jump over the fence, she dug a hole underneath and was gone. The whole family searched down alleys and gravel roads, at the pound, in the fields and parks, on the two highways leading out of Charnelle. They were sure she was lost forever, maybe dead, or had run off with a pack of coyotes. Gene and Rich cried.

"There's nothing we can do," Mrs. Tate said, looking out the window, her arms folded across her chest. It was dark outside, so the light reflected off the window like a mirror. From the big chair, Laura could see her mother's face clearly in the glass.

Mr. Tate knelt down beside the couch, where the boys were sitting. "Maybe she'll come back."

Laura's mother turned toward them. "Maybe she won't," she said flatly.

He gave her a sharp look. "We don't know," he said.

"Exactly. We don't know. She was difficult and a misfit, and she didn't want to be here. It's just as well that she's gone."

"We're responsible for her," he said.

"No, we're not."

"*She ours. She belongs to us.*"

"*She doesn't belong to anyone, Zeeke.*"

There was a pocket of painful silence. He rose from the couch and squared his shoulders. "*She ours,*" he said again.

Laura's mother looked at him for a moment, then turned back to the window and stared into the dark yard. She didn't say anything else.

A few days after Easter, as Laura was going out to feed Fay, she found Greta whimpering by the fence, her fur matted, filthy, cockleburred. Deep, coagulated wounds were gouged in her nose and back right foot. The end of her tail and chunks from her left ear were missing. Laura, her brothers, and her mother fed and bathed the dog, tried to nurse her wounds. She bared her teeth and snapped, put marks in Manny's boots. Mrs. Tate poured some sweet rum inside a butter cake and fed it to Greta to calm her down. Then Manny stroked her coat gently as Mrs. Tate muzzled her with a leather belt so that they could finish tending to her wounds. The dog shook at first, as with a palsy, then relinquished her fear and let herself be cared for.

When Mr. Tate returned home, he removed the muzzle and sat outside with Greta for a full two hours, stroking her, feeling for broken bones, inspecting the wounds and bandages, redoing most of it, soothing the dog with his voice. He palmed her belly, and she snapped again, but he stayed calm, told her that everything was okay, not to worry. He fed her crumbled strips of jerky from his hand, held water up to her mouth, stroked her until she fell asleep. When he came inside, he scrubbed his hands with the gritty rectangle of soap he sandpapered himself with after work. Then he ran his fingers through his pomaded hair and announced, "*I think that dog's pregnant.*"

"*Zeeke, she's too young,*" Mrs. Tate said.

"*I guess not.*"

"*We can't let her. She's not ready.*"

"*We ain't got a choice.*"

"*We do, too.*"

He shook his head.

Mrs. Tate stared down at the knotholes on the floor for the longest time, as if they held secrets that the family was waiting for her to decode. Then she shook her head and stared at her husband. "*This is gonna turn out bad, Zeeke. I'm telling you.*"

"It might calm her down," he said.
She said, "Mark my words."

Weeks passed. Greta's wounds healed until she was well enough to eat by herself and to get on her feet. There was something darkly troubling about the dog, and Laura found herself studying Greta, afraid both of and for her. Her teeth yellowed. She bared them constantly. Her eyes were bloodshot. Fay tried to help Greta, mothering her, licking her wounds, nuzzling her when she was ill, but once Greta grew stronger, she attacked the older dog, biting at her neck, drawing blood, sending Fay whimpering off. Mr. Tate put up a new pen to isolate Greta, who lay in her shed, panting, shifting her head suspiciously from side to side, awaiting intruders. Except for Mr. Tate, she wouldn't let anyone approach her, not even to give her food or water. During the day, she'd gnaw at the hair on her stomach, welting herself. During the warmer afternoons, when she was able, she'd pace frantically in her pen, burning the grass, her belly with its load and the dark, thick, extended teats swaying below her.

At first, Mrs. Tate wouldn't have anything to do with the dog, wouldn't even acknowledge her, was short-tempered with the kids, and silent and sullen when Mr. Tate was home. But as Greta began to heal from her wounds and progressed in her pregnancy, Laura's mother began watching the dog from the kitchen window. When she was outside, while doing the laundry or preparing the garden, she'd eye Greta curiously as the dog lay huddled in her shed, half in light, half in shadow, panting, watching the woman in return.

On a Friday morning in early May, a month before they thought Greta was due, Laura was sick and home from school. She sat at the kitchen table, sipping hot cider, nibbling on buttered toast, watching Rich play as Mrs. Tate did chores in the backyard, hanging up the laundry on the lines, sweeping dried mud from the porch, wiping off the dust from the canned tomatoes and peaches that were in the storm cellar, hoeing the weeds in the garden, which had been recently seeded. It was an exceptionally warm day. The kitchen window was open for the fresh air. Laura heard her mother whistling songs, Bob Wills and Hank Williams tunes that were always playing on the radio. Fay was loose, nosing her way along the edges of the alley fence, sniffing and pissing where the strays had entered her territory. At first Greta stayed in her shed, as usual, though her eyes were open. She seldom slept. After a time, she stood and cautiously inched out of the shed toward her water and food bowls, all the while watching

Mrs. Tate and Fay. Greta drank from her bowl, then looked up and barked.

Mrs. Tate turned to her quickly from the clothesline and arched her eyebrow. "What is it, girl?"

The dog barked again. Fay ambled over to the edge of Greta's pen and cautiously sniffed.

"You don't like my whistling?"

Both dogs looked at her, then cocked their heads quizzically. Greta barked again, followed by Fay. Laura's mother laughed and walked over to the pen with a sheet and some clothespins in her hands. Inside the house, Laura smiled, sipped her cider.

"You out of water?" Mrs. Tate said. She went over to the hose in the garden, which was dripping in the dirt, and pulled it to the bowl and let it fill up. Greta looked at the hose and at the woman and back at the hose in something like a gesture of gratitude. Mrs. Tate tossed the sheet into the laundry basket and sat on the flat stump across from Greta. The clothespins, like two tiny wooden beaks, dangled from her mouth. She watched the dog drink. Greta ignored her, though Fay kept nuzzling under her apron, and Mrs. Tate scratched the older dog's head.

She took some jerky from her apron pocket and let Fay eat it from her palm. Greta looked up, put her face through the chain link of the pen, and sniffed.

"You want some of this, girl?"

Greta stuck her nose farther through the chain link. Mrs. Tate shooed the older dog away, stood up, and slowly approached the pen. Greta withdrew her snout and began retreating, her head low, her ears back.

"It's okay. Calm down now, girl."

Mrs. Tate dangled the jerky and bent toward the bowl. Greta growled low and deep without opening her mouth. Mrs. Tate took one of the clothespins wedged in her mouth, fingered the wood, and opened and closed it methodically. The dog's lips quivered. She growled again, her yellow teeth showing this time.

Fay barked.

"Hush up, you!" Mrs. Tate turned back to the younger dog and spoke to her soothingly, a whispery litany on the theme of "I'm not gonna hurt you." She crouched close to the fence and slowly inched the jerky through the holes, encouraging, "Come on, girl. Come here and get it. It's good."

Suddenly Greta charged the fence and leapt, not at the jerky strip but at Mrs. Tate's face, mouth open, her teeth possessing a malevolent propulsion of their own. Laura's mother sprawled back. The fence rattled. Greta yelped and then, miraculously, stuck there on the fence, her back paws dangling above her water bowl. The wires were stuck between her teeth, and the whole fence bowed with the weight of the wailing dog. Fay commenced a full-scale bark at her daughter. Greta's bloodshot eyes rolled in her head. She seemed to be searching for some way out, expecting something terrible to happen.

Jumping up from the table, Laura knocked off her cider cup. It smashed on the hardwood floor, green ceramic shards splashing. She felt spikes in her feet, but she hopped to the door and out onto the porch, where she saw her mother back-sprawled on the ground, Greta still hanging on the fence.

"Are you okay?" Laura shouted. Fay barked crazily. Greta's wails were high-pitched and hurt Laura's ears.

"Shut up, Fay!" Mrs. Tate shouted. "Shut up!"

"Momma!" Laura called.

"Fay, shut up! Now!"

"Are you okay?"

"Yeah."

"What are you going to do?"

"I don't know. Fay, hush!"

Her mother rose and inspected the caught dog. She grabbed the fence above Greta's face and shook it to free her, but the shaking only served to flop the dog's body in a way that left her shoulder now flush against the fence and her head twisted sideways. Greta whimpered, exhausted.

Laura swiped at her feet. There was blood, nothing serious.

"Laura, go fetch me your father's toolbox. Hurry now."

Rich had followed Laura. She picked him up and put him in his crib. She grabbed the toolbox from the closet and ran out to the backyard. The steel wire had somehow slipped between the dog's back molars and was caught between her teeth and gums. How the wire got there without breaking the teeth was amazing, like the time Laura had seen a magician pull a cloth from a fully set table without displacing the settings.

Her mother took the long flathead screwdriver and wedged it into Greta's mouth, between the tooth and the fence. "Hand me those pliers, Laura. Now hold on to this screwdriver while I work the wire out."

It must have taken only a few minutes to dislodge the dog, but it seemed interminable, with Greta whimpering shrilly, her bloody fangs poking through the fence, Fay jumping around, barking, Rich inside screaming. Mrs. Tate was able to wriggle the wire free from one side. Greta let out a muted wail and hung there by the two molars on the left side of her face. The leverage was against them. Finally Mrs. Tate jerked the wire through the other teeth. They broke, tiny enamel missiles flying past Laura's face. The dog fell to the ground, lay in shock for several minutes, and then passed out. Mrs. Tate sat down on the stump across from the pen and stared at the dog, then sent Laura inside to check on Rich.

She rescued him from his crib, calmed him down, swept up the broken cup, tossed it in the trash, then sat down on the back porch and watched her mother stroke Fay. Greta got up and staggered back to her shed. Blood was matted on her chin. She yelped in pain every few seconds.

"What should we do?" Laura asked.

"You go back in, honey. I'll take care of this."

Mrs. Tate stayed there on the stump for the rest of the afternoon, just staring, not saying a word and not coming in, just opening and closing the wooden pins in her hands. Something's happening, Laura sensed, there's something more to this, but she didn't know how to say it because it was at once impossible to articulate and yet so obvious, hovering in the air like an unacknowledged ghost.

Later, after the excitement had waned, Laura felt weak and feverish again, but she was afraid to disturb her mother. She put Rich down for his nap and then lay down herself. Drifting in and out of a shivering daytime sleep, she replayed in her mind what had happened and tried to figure out what it meant. It had been the same way, she suddenly thought, a year ago when Gloria eloped with Jerome. Gloria didn't say a word about it to Laura, even though they shared a bed. She knew that her sister was in love with the lieutenant. She'd read some of their letters, hidden in a small brown box at the back of Gloria's bottom drawer, beneath her underwear, and Laura figured they might get married soon enough, after Gloria turned eighteen, but the whole family was shocked to find her gone one morning, leaving only a note, saying she and Jerome had eloped to Mexico and that she would write later.

Laura's father was in a furious rant for a couple of months—wanting to hunt them down and throttle them both, grounding all the children as if they'd been party to this conspiracy, even threatening to contact the air force and bring charges against Jerome. But then he seemed to resign himself to the fact of her absence. Their mother stayed silent, as if she knew more about what had *happened with Gloria than she was willing to tell. Not until a week after Gloria's eighteenth birthday did they receive a postcard from Switzerland, saying that she and Jerome would be moving to Greece soon. It wasn't clear to any of them if she was ever coming back.*

"There are no secrets," Laura's mother said mysteriously after the family read the postcard, shaking her head as if indeed there were secrets, and you needed to be clairvoyant to understand them.

It had amazed Laura that her sister could do such a thing. At the time, it had seemed, like what Greta had done, violent and inexplicable. But the more Laura brooded over it, the more she retraced her conversations in bed at night with Gloria, the more she recalled her sister's behavior leading up to the elopement— the secret letters, Gloria working extra jobs and hoarding her money, the way she seemed distracted and worried but also jovial, manic, even—the more it all made sense, as her mother had said, like a clear and obvious path leading backward from this one moment. It made her a believer, though she wouldn't have known how to say it at the time, that there were always seeds of the future in the present, growing, preparing for the blossom.

In mid-May, Mr. Tate went to Amarillo for four days to work on a construction job for the new downtown bank. They didn't expect Greta's puppies for a couple of weeks, but Mr. Tate had already built the whelping pen, an open-topped plywood box, with one side partially cut away and a pull-out chicken-wire gate over the opening. He nailed down old scraps of carpet he'd salvaged. Greta had been relatively docile since falling from the fence. She paced less, didn't growl as much. But she still favored Mr. Tate. He made a small door in the fence so that Manny could feed her without having to go into the pen, and the hose could be draped, as usual, through the chain link into her water bowl. He told the family not to worry about her. She still had plenty of time.

The third day he was gone, however, Greta started her labor. By dusk she'd begun turning in circles, clawing at the old scraps of carpet in her shed. Fay lay in her own shed with her chin on her paws and watched quietly.

"We've got to get her into the whelping pen," Mrs. Tate said. "If she stays in the shed, we won't be able to help her."

When they opened the gate, Greta barked wildly. The hair on the back of her neck bristled. Then she hunkered into her shed and growled, her teeth glowing in the evening light. Mrs. Tate sent Manny to the back of the shed and had him bang on it to get Greta out, but she just barked until he slipped his stick between two boards and prodded her. She snapped at it, then skittered out. Mrs. Tate stood by the door, and after Greta ran through the opening, she guided the dog with the rake into the whelping pen and dropped the gate. Manny then boarded up the opening of her shed with a piece of plywood.

"Should we muzzle her?" Manny asked.

"I don't know if we could if we wanted to. Besides, we got to let her pant. We'll just wait here and see what happens. Gene, go get the newspapers."

Gene brought the stack of old newspapers they'd been saving. Mrs. Tate and Manny dumped the paper in the pen and moved back. Greta clawed at the paper, bunched it together in a pile, sat on it, rose, turned several more circles, and clawed again. She sat back down and began breathing in short, shallow breaths, her belly rising and falling quickly. Mrs. Tate slipped the garden hose through the links and filled the water bowl. Greta lapped at it, but she still eyed them all as if they were to blame for her misery.

"It's okay now, girl," Mrs. Tate said. "Don't you worry."

Laura turned on the porch light, and Manny clamped a floodlight to the pen. It had been very hot, even for this time of year, though when nightfall came, it cooled off, so everyone put on old sweaters. Greta's eyes were bloodshot and runny from labor, with black droplets, like candle wax, in the corners near her nose.

Around eight, after Rich was in bed, the dogs down the alley started barking and howling, aggravating Fay, then Greta, who both barked back. Greta paced the pen rapidly, panting, then turned in tighter and tighter circles. Suddenly she let out a whimpering growl, squatted, and out slithered a watery black sac, the size of Laura's cupped palms. When Fay had litters, she'd always torn the dark-veined sac immediately, bit at the cord, and licked at the puppy's face until the nose and mouth were clear. Greta sniffed at the twisting sac, pushed it over with her paw, sniffed again, but didn't break the thin membrane. Then she walked to the other side of the pen, indifferent.

"Laura, quick, bring me the sewing kit and washcloths!" Mrs. Tate shouted. Laura ran inside and got the kit from the counter and warmed the cloths that her mother had set out.

When she returned, the puppy still lay in the corner in its sac. Manny and Mrs. Tate had entered the whelping pen and were blocking the dog with the stick and rake. Mrs. Tate reached down and grabbed the puppy, backed out of the pen with Manny following. She sat down on the ground and broke the membrane with *her finger. Mucusy fluid dribbled down her arm and onto her sweater. She laid the slick pup on her lap. It didn't seem to be breathing.*

"Manny, get me some thread from the kit. Laura, take one of those cloths and wipe its nose and mouth. Hurry now. But be gentle."

As Laura wiped, her mother knotted the small end of the cord and then took the cloth and finished cleaning the pup's face.

"It's not breathing," Laura said.

Her mother turned it over and patted it firmly on the back, then reached into its mouth with her finger and pulled out a thimbleful of blackish green gum. The pup whimpered. Fay barked, followed by Greta. Mrs. Tate leaned over the fence and set the pup down on the papers in front of Greta. The dog eyed her warily, then sniffed at the wet bundle. Greta reached out and pawed the pup, knocking it on its back. It rolled over and shook its tiny head quickly, rooting. With her hind leg, Greta kicked it across the carpet until it lay against the wall with shreds of newspaper stuck to its wet fur. Fay barked sharply three times. Greta seemed spooked. She turned and growled.

"It's okay, Greta," Mrs. Tate soothed.

But Greta growled again, and then, in a rapid dart, she lunged toward the pup, snapped viciously twice, then raised it over her head and shook it. Blood spewed over Greta's face.

Gene and Laura screamed.

"Oh, my God!" yelled Manny. "She's killing it, she's killing it!"

"Stop her, Momma!" Gene hollered.

Mrs. Tate, who had fallen back stunned, clutched at the rake, knocked it over, then grabbed it again in the shadows and whacked Greta three times on the head until the dog dropped the puppy. Greta bit at the iron brace. They all heard the click of teeth on metal, and then she leapt back in the far corner and crouched into a snarling coil. Mrs. Tate kept her in the corner with the rake's splayed end. Wet, black-red spots darkened the dog's white-and-tan coat.

"Manny, get in there and get the puppy."

"I can't go in there."

"Yes, you can. I'll hold her here. Take your stick."

"But—"

"Do it!" her mother shouted, her voice so deep and ferocious that it stunned them all, even Greta. They turned to her, their eyes wide. They'd never seen her like this before, the lamplight shining electrically over her hair, her face caught in a shadowed scowl.

Manny crawled in. Greta barked savagely, growling, throwing herself against the rake, letting herself be stabbed by the tines, but Mrs. Tate held her in the corner while Manny grabbed the puppy and jumped back out of the pen. Greta snapped at the rake again as Mrs. Tate dropped the gate over the opening.

In the floodlight, they inspected the puppy. The back of its neck had been severed almost clean through. The head was barely connected to the body. Gene staggered backward and vomited on the stump. Laura took one of the warm, wet cloths and wiped her brother's face. Manny went inside and brought back a small paper lunch sack. Mrs. Tate placed the pup in it, twisted the top, and sent Manny to the other end of the yard to bury it. Then she went inside and washed her hands, held Gene until he stopped shaking, and put him to bed. She finally came back outside.

"Why'd she do that?" Laura asked.

"Because I touched it, I think," her mother said quietly. Her anger from before had disappeared. "She smelled me on the pup."

"Is she gonna have more?" Gene asked.

"Yes. I think so."

"What are we gonna do?" Laura asked.

Her mother shook her head and stared at Greta, who lay panting in her whelping pen with her eyes half shut.

"Manny, let's put Fay in the pen with her. Fay will show her what to do."

"She'll attack her," Manny said.

"No, I don't think so. It's me she objects to."

They let Fay into the pen. Greta barked and growled at her at first, but Fay paced the pen away from Greta, then sat and watched the younger dog until Greta calmed down. Then Fay went to Greta and began licking her face and the still-torn ear. Greta snapped at her, but not with the viciousness from before. Finally she let Fay stay beside her.

Within the half hour, Greta began whimpering again. She turned tighter and tighter circles, and then she squatted. Out came another sac. Greta sniffed it, pawed at it, and then, as before, ignored it. Fay nosed her way to the sac, broke it open with her teeth, and began licking the mucus from its face until the pup squealed. Then Fay ate the sac. The pup was lighter-colored than the last one, tan with white-and-black marks, and bigger. Fay nosed the pup toward Greta, who lay in the far corner, recovering. Greta immediately stood up and walked away. Fay lay down next to the pup to keep it warm.

By midnight Greta had delivered five more puppies and lay in the corner of the pen, exhausted and alone. From what the family could tell, at least four of the puppies were alive. One puppy never moved or made a sound. Although Fay kept them warm, they were squealing from hunger, but Greta wouldn't do anything. Manny brought a saucer of warm milk. They let Greta out of the whelping pen, and then Mrs. Tate pulled each pup from the pen and finger-fed it. They waited another hour, but Greta seemed to be through with the births. She licked herself, eyeing Fay every once in a while, growling at Mrs. Tate and the kids whenever they spoke.

By two in the morning, Mrs. Tate told Manny and Laura to go on to bed.

"What's going to happen?" Laura asked.

"It'll be all right. Dogs have been having puppies for years without our help. They don't need us."

"But she's ignoring them," Laura said.

"It just may take her longer to figure out what to do. Besides, whatever happens will happen. I'll stay here awhile. Fay will help her. Laura, check on Rich and Gene, and then you and Manny go on to bed yourselves. You got school tomorrow."

"Let me stay and help, Momma," Manny said.

"There ain't nothing else to do."

"What if she goes crazy again?"

"I said I'd take care of it. Go on to bed."

"But—"

"Don't 'but' me, Manny. I said go on!" That same flash of anger, that same scowl, was on her face again. "I don't want any backtalk now. I want you all in bed!"

"Yes, ma'am," Manny and Laura said in unison.

"And stay there," she said, pursing her lips. They nodded. "If I need you, I'll come and get you."

Manny and Laura went into the house, washed up, then nodded off. About an hour later, Laura heard her mother open the kitchen door and go into her room. Shortly after that, Fay and Greta began barking. Mrs. Tate got up again, then returned to bed, even though the dogs' noise intensified. There were growls, snarling and biting. And then more terrible sounds.

Manny and Laura went to their mother in her bed, pleaded with her to do something, but without opening her eyes, she said flatly, "There ain't nothing we can do. Now go on to sleep."

Her right arm was crooked over her forehead, and she just lay there on top of the covers, wearing the same blood-spattered pants and sweater, her shoes still on. But her eyes remained closed. Laura and Manny watched her for long minute, waiting for some other word or gesture from her, an acknowledgment of their presence. But she didn't move. Laura couldn't even tell if she was breathing.

"Go on now," she finally whispered, her eyes still closed. "Do as I told you."

In bed they listened intently to the squeals and yelps, the snarling, the growling, and that other sound, the sound they couldn't identify but understood the next day. And then, still worse, the black silence afterward. How can she sleep through that? *Laura thought, astonished. That must be what being an adult was about, being able to sleep through suffering, to adjust yourself so it doesn't matter, or matters less, hardening yourself the way roast gets when you cook it too long. From tender to rock.*

The next morning the puppies were gone. Greta had jumped from the whelping pen and lay with her face pointed toward the shed, asleep. They could see her belly, bloated, dried black blood streaked and speckled over her coat. Fay was sprawled in the whelping pen, whimpering, two claw rips across her left shoulder and one above her eye. Her head was on her paws, her eyes closed. The shredded newspaper was dark and wet. Laura was sure she saw small pieces of bloody fur scattered in the pen.

When her father returned home that evening, her mother explained that there was nothing to do but let it happen.

"Nature's way," she said, an edgy irony in her voice.

Mr. Tate shook his head in confusion, then quickly a thin hard shadow congealed over his face, and without a word, just in one long dreamlike sweeping motion, he fetched his gun from the top of his closet, opened the back door, and strode to Greta's pen. From inside the house, they heard the shot, like a thunderclap on a cloudless day, and then a second shot, which seemed even more of a jolt. Mrs. Tate sent Manny out, and he and Mr. Tate put Greta in a potato sack, tossed her in the back of the pickup like a load of grain, and they drove away to bury her.

17

✴

Homecoming

$\mathcal{T}$he letter came in the afternoon mail. It was postmarked from West Germany, and all of them waited anxiously for their father to get home. When he did, they thrust it in his face, but he just studied the envelope for a minute and then set it down on the kitchen table.

"Aren't you going to open it?" Gene asked, incredulous.

"Soon enough," Mr. Tate said. Laura saw the smile at the corner of his lips as he turned away, and she knew he was merely keeping them in suspense.

"Supper ready, Laura?" he asked.

"Almost."

He took a shower! She finished heating the leftover ham, green beans, and applesauce, put a plate of buttered bread on the table, and Manny stuck the letter onto a fork and placed it on their father's plate.

Oh, how he took his time. They heard him shaving, singing to himself in the bathroom. Cruel! Finally he came into the kitchen. Manny, Rich, and

Gene were seated. Laura stood by the icebox. Her father's hair was wet and slicked back. He looked down at the plate, where the letter lay, and smiled. He sat, picked it up, studied it.

"Where are my reading glasses?"

"Here," Gene said.

Gene and Rich leaned in, and Laura stepped closer. Her father put on his glasses and lifted the envelope into the light from the window, then turned it over. He put his knife to the back and slit it halfway, then stopped.

"Let's say the blessing."

"What?" Manny exclaimed.

Mr. Tate folded his hands.

"Open the damn thing," Manny said. They laughed.

"Manny, you can lead us tonight."

"When was the last time we said a blessing?"

Mr. Tate opened his palms on either side of him and smiled serenely. "Laura, Rich, hold my hands. Now, Manny, I know it's been a long time since you've conversed with the Almighty, but it's really very simple. 'Our Father, who art in heaven . . .' "

"You're a ruthless—"

" '. . . *hallowed* be Thy name.' "

"God is good, God is sweet," Manny chanted, "open the letter and then we'll eat."

Gene and Rich fell into a fit of giggles. Laura smiled but looked anxiously at her father. She wanted that letter read as much as anybody.

"Read it," Manny said and tipped his chair back so that he was perched precariously against the wall. "Pretty please."

Her father smiled, picked up the letter, sliced through the rest of the seal, took out two handwritten sheets, and began reading it. Silently.

"What does it say?" Gene asked.

Laura went behind him, wrapped her arms around his neck. "Is she coming?"

He held the letter close to his chest so that Laura couldn't read and then he continued without saying a word, but his expressions changed melodramatically. His eyes grew wide. Then his mouth dropped, and he wrinkled his face up into a comic boo-hoo.

"Well, what's it say?" Manny smirked.

He hesitated a beat before saying, deadpan, "They'll be here for the Fourth of July."

"Next week?" she asked.

"Looks like it."

"Yahoo!" Gene yelled. Manny beat his fists on the table so the silverware rattled.

"Careful," Laura said.

"She's coming home! She's coming home!" Rich screamed, although Laura wondered if he even remembered Gloria. He'd seen the postcards and heard the other letters. But he was a toddler when she left.

"Are they all coming?" Manny asked.

"Yep," Mr. Tate said. "Jerome has a two-week furlough." Laura was surprised to hear him say Jerome's name. It sounded strange coming from his lips, and she figured he was trying to get used to it himself.

"Where will they sleep?" Gene asked, suddenly worried.

"Don't worry, son. We'll figure it out."

Except for occasional pictures, they had not seen Gloria since she eloped. She had tried to come home several times, but Jerome's furloughs kept getting shortened or canceled. Or she was pregnant and couldn't travel overseas.

Laura remembered how furious her father had been with Gloria when she first eloped, even forbade her name to be spoken, threatened to have the pilot arrested or, more outlandishly, court-martialed, but their mother had calmed him down. And after a while his anger subsided, though, before Laura's mother left, he didn't like to talk much about what Gloria had done, and if the subject came up, he'd scowl or leave the room.

He was not a man easily angered, though they all had seen and knew him to be capable of a startling rage. Once, years ago when Mr. Thomason caught Manny shoplifting at the general store, Mr. Tate had whipped him viciously with a belt for almost five minutes, a torturously long time for a whipping, as the rest of them listened in shock in the living room. Manny was quiet at first, but then he cried out and then screamed in pain.

"You ever gonna do that again?"

"No!" Manny whimpered.

"What?"

"No, sir!" and the beating went on until Manny was so tired he could scream no more. Their mother walked into the room. She said nothing, but her silent presence was enough to stop the whipping. And then she came back into the living room where the rest of them sat with their heads down, too afraid and ashamed to look at each other or her. They looked up when their father emerged from the room moments later, the belt in his hand, scowling. They could hear Manny in the bedroom, sobbing.

"What are y'all looking at?" They cast their eyes down again.

That was the worst incident. They never saw him that enraged again, not even much later, right after their mother left, though his whippings were plenty hard, even when doled out judiciously, and you didn't push him.

A few months after their mother left, Mr. Tate finally forgave Gloria. It was difficult to harbor a grudge against her forever. He spoke of her almost as his favorite child, and when others mentioned Jerome's name—which they generally avoided doing in his presence—he no longer frowned, though he still referred to him only as "the pilot."

Gloria had two children now—Julie, who was two, and the baby, Carroll, a boy's name that Mr. Tate thought too girlish. There had been post-cards and letters, which they eagerly awaited. Gloria was a good letter writer. She had a way of depicting herself in a comical light, punctuated by lyrical passages that suggested an intelligent sensitivity, and her letters lived vividly in their imagination, as if she had been designated as the family traveler, the one who sends back news to the home front.

"The life of an air force pilot's wife," Gloria wrote in one of her letters, "is full of glamour and glory." Then she contrasted the wonder of visiting magnificent places—the Mediterranean, Italy, Greece, and Switzerland—with the reality of moving from one base to another, the housing too small ("we've moved into a *lovely* little closet"), the dirt everywhere ("the air force has a policy of shipping all bomb rubble to the junior pilot houses—gives the wives something to do"), the bugs ("flying cockroaches," "horseflies the size of Oklahoma," "mosquitoes who decided to picnic on my legs"), the mediocre base food ("I'd rather kiss Nikita Khrushchev than eat another canned tomato"), the pecking order of not only pilots and officers but also of officers' wives ("who seem to get fat from swallowing pretty little idiots like me").

"Europeans do not believe in ice," she said in another letter and depicted a week-long expedition to get a simple cube for her tea. And then suddenly, in the middle of this riff, she wrote, "Often I find myself imagining Jerome crashing or being shot down. At night when he's gone, I sometimes go outside and study the sky. The shooting stars fill me with dread. I dream of him in flames. I sometimes don't believe it when I hear that he's arrived safely back to base. I hold my breath until I see him upright, smiling. I know we're not at war, but it doesn't feel that way in West Germany."

Gloria wrote letters to each of them at first, but a year and a half ago, she had taken to writing one letter every month, addressed to their father, although the salutation read, "Dear Everybody." Mr. Tate would read the letter slowly or have Manny or Laura read it aloud, as they sat in the living room or at the kitchen table, and then afterward everybody could read the letter again, privately. Gloria would single out each person for a paragraph, asking questions:

"Manny, are you still dating Joannie? Keep that girl. You're lucky she puts up with you."

"Have you lost a tooth, Rich?"

"Gene, are you making Rich give you half the bed?"

"Does Sam Compson's little brother still have a crush on you, Laura?"

When their father finally wrote and told her about the disappearance of their mother, almost a year after it happened and when it seemed clear that she really had left them for good, Gloria didn't write back for several months. When at last they got a letter, it was full of listless details about where they had been restationed, but at the end of the letter, in a postscript, she wrote, "Is she *really gone*???"

After that, Gloria didn't mention it very often, but in the middle of another letter, she wrote, "It doesn't seem real to me that Momma left. You speak of it as a fact that you're used to in your letters, but I can't imagine it, not really." In another she wrote, "Sometimes I look up while I'm out walking, and I will hear an American voice, a woman's voice, and I swear it's Momma's. But it's not. Just some trick. A tourist or another military wife. But it *feels* real. I might cry for the rest of the day then."

She and Jerome had moved three times in as many months. The Tates would get postcards with strange, riddling thoughts on them. "Dresden is a city of ghosts," said one. A letter she wrote when she was pregnant with Carroll ended with this: "Jerome flying over Austria. The days gray and short and always full of drizzle or this strange ashy snow. Julie has mumps and blames me, shoots me looks that say, 'I hate you.' I vomited four times today. I understand now why Momma left."

When she visited Berlin, she had been walking down the street early one morning. There was fog, and she had seen a man climbing the drainpipe on a tenement wall. The man looked at her. "Shots rang out," she wrote, "and I swear the man's eyes went dead before me. I was the last thing on this earth that he saw. Me, a pregnant American woman in the fog. What do I do with that?"

Mr. Tate was strangely quiet after these letters and postcards, never once talking about their mother. Afterward he either left for a while or busied himself in the backyard.

Just after Easter, they got a long, chatty letter that was brimming with details about her pregnancy: "medicine-ball belly," "eating like a horse," "the base doctor has the bedside manner of a drill sergeant." The tone was cheerier. It was spring. She had more energy. They were still stationed in West Germany, where she had more friends in similar circumstances: "The base is full of pregnant women. The joke (not a very funny one) is that they've herded us here like prisoners of war. They pretend to be happy for us, but a couple of the women are spooked about taking a shower! Afraid they'll be gassed. Can you believe it? Me, I prefer a bath anyway. Lets me float the medicine ball. I despise gravity! If Isaac Newton were on this base with all these pregnant women, there'd be a lynching!"

Later in the letter, she wrote, "This election has people buzzing. All the older pilots and officers are pulling for Dick Nixon. They believe the Democrats are soft eggheads like Stevenson. (They use worse language, but I won't repeat it since I'm a *lady*.) They all love Ike and call Nixon 'Baby Ike.' There's a staff sergeant who roots openly for Lyndon Johnson, and he can get away with it because he's from Texas, though we all know that Johnson looks about as soft as a crocodile. I suppose I'd root for him, too, if he ever gets around to getting officially in the race. It *would* be good to have a Texan in the White House. But those ears have *got* to go! (Sorry, Daddy, but they look like cooked cauliflower attached to the sides of his head!) All the wives nod in agreement in front of their husbands, pretend to adore that lovable pooch Checkers, but when they're alone, they all moon over the bootlegger's son from Massachusetts. He *is* awful cute (right, Laura!), even if he served in the navy, goes to Sunday mass, and pronounces his *R*s like a Chinaman."

She mentioned that she and the kids might get to come home this summer. She hoped so. "With the military, though, you don't hold your breath."

But then they received another letter in May. "It looks good for the trip home. Maybe early July. Cross your fingers. Will write when I know."

And now Gloria was coming for the Fourth of July. And all of them, too, even Jerome. One week with his family in Wichita Falls, the other in Charnelle.

Laura shared with John her excitement about Gloria's visit, reading aloud some of her letters, telling him about how her sister had eloped with Jerome and how much she missed her, how glad they all were that she was coming home again.

"You can't tell her," he said. "You know that?"

"Yes, I know that."

Since school let out for summer, John and Laura met twice a week, usually at lunch. He did what he called "fix-it runs" in Charnelle or nearby towns on Mondays and Thursdays and could take lunch on his own. He tried to work fast, and then he'd pick Laura up behind the old abandoned warehouse on Whipple Street, five blocks east of her house, at noon or a little before, and they would drive to his uncle's barn just outside of town until one o'clock, sometimes almost two if they were lucky. In the summer, it was pretty easy for Laura to get away during lunch, easier than in the evening; Mrs. Ambling was happy to let Rich and Gene play in her yard during the day.

He'd fixed up a corner of the barn nicely, with a layer of soft blue carpet, a thin mattress with a gold bedspread that looked like it had been around for a while, and a splintery end table. They'd take turns bringing something for lunch—sandwiches, cheese and crackers, or fruit.

Back in May, about a week after she recovered from the flu, she called to thank him and Mrs. Letig for the food and the sculpture of the hummingbird. He answered the phone, said that he was dying to see her, that he needed to meet her the next day. He took her to the barn, and he gave her a box of chocolates, which they ate together, and he told her how badly he felt about what had happened, that he'd been thinking about her ever since he'd dropped her off that day after Lake Meredith, hoping he'd have a chance to tell her again how sorry he was and that he wanted to keep seeing her. She asked him if they *should* keep seeing each other, if it was worth it.

"Yes," he said urgently, "you're worth it."

It didn't take much to convince her, even though she wondered briefly but uneasily at her inability to say no to him. He kissed her and held her for a while, and then they had to go. He asked if they could meet for lunch in a couple of days, and by then he had cleaned out the barn and fixed it up. There was an ice bucket with some root beer in it and fruit, crackers, and cheese. He'd even set out some flowers in a vase and turned on a transistor radio, so that Patsy Cline crooned softly in the background.

He was very tender with her at first—nervous, almost—slowly touching her, kissing her, his lips softly on her neck and breasts and stomach. And then, when they made love again, it wasn't like before. He was gentle, didn't rush her, slow, controlled.

Her favorite part was afterward when he would sometimes fall asleep. "Just let me rest my eyes for a minute," he'd say, and he'd lie there, heavy and vulnerable. She'd examine his body, his arm crooked over his face. She'd trace her fingers along his jawline, over his mustache and his red, cracked lips, slightly parted, his two middle teeth slightly overlapping, as if hugging. She'd kiss him softly and trace her fingers over the stubble of his neck and into the blond-brown hair of his chest, a light fuzz covering his skin, his nipples small and round and smooth like a child's, and over his rib cage, and down his stomach to the thick brown nest at the crook of his legs, where his penis lay limp and wrinkled, a skein of dried semen over it. She was surprised that her hand could cover it. Sometimes it would grow in her cupped palm, and she'd look up and he'd have that goofy, boyish grin on his face.

"Come here," he'd say, and she would.

And then they would leave, her on the floorboard, talking, telling stupid jokes to make him laugh. He'd drop her off behind the warehouse, bending over to kiss her good-bye, and then he'd be gone, and she'd wait several minutes and then walk home in the bright summer heat, or to the Charnelle pool, where she'd swim and hang out with Debbie and Marlene, playing Ping-Pong or Foosball, yearning sometimes to tell them what she was up to, to see their stunned faces when she made her confession. She felt loyal to them, felt in fact a vague need to repay them for their compassion after her mother disappeared (she had cried one long night at Debbie's house while Marlene rocked her like a child), and to show them as well that she'd gotten over that grief, that she could navigate through an adult world they could only dimly imagine. But she kept her mouth shut about John, as she knew she must, smiling as she swam through the chlorinated water with her friends, laughing confidently as she beat them at Ping-Pong, shouting as she spun the little painted Foosball men, gunning the ball triumphantly in the hole. At the end of those afternoons, she would head home, get the boys from Mrs. Ambling's, make supper and clean up—moving in a light-spirited haze.

"What are you so happy about?" her father asked her one of these evenings, pleased by her good humor.

She simply shrugged her shoulders, smiled innocently.

The family drove to the Greyhound station in Mr. Tate's truck, Manny following in the Ford. Gloria and her family were supposed to arrive on the four-thirty bus from Dallas, but it didn't get in until almost six-thirty. Everyone was hungry, but they didn't eat, because the plan was to take everybody to the Ding Dong Daddy Diner. Finally the bus arrived, and the five of them got up from the outside bench. They could see Gloria in the window. She waved and smiled and turned away for a minute, and then a little blond-haired girl appeared next to her, peering out. Gloria spoke to her, pointed toward the family, and they all jumped up and down and blew kisses.

And then they were off the bus. First Jerome, wearing his air force uniform, carrying the baby in one arm, a suitcase in another. He was tall and thin-faced, with a dark complexion. He set the suitcase down, smiled uncomfortably, and then turned back and held out his hand to the little girl, who wore a yellow dress and tights. Even though Mr. Tate knelt and called to her, she clung to Jerome. Gloria followed them, carrying a bag. Her dress matched her daughter's and was buckled at the waist with a black belt.

Although only twenty, Gloria seemed like she'd aged. The baby fat from her teen years was gone, and her cheeks were hollow, too thin, a little severe. Her hair was done up in a beehive, held together precariously by hair spray and bobby pins. There was a moment of silence, as Gloria and her family stood by the bus and the rest of the Tates stood at the railing. They studied each other as family members who haven't seen each other in a while will do, trying to align the person standing before them with the image in their memories—the little girl, the father, the sister, the brother—and the realignment sometimes takes only a few seconds, sometimes much longer, but that period of adjustment is always there, always a little disturbing, as if time itself were abruptly declaring its passage.

Gloria's family made their way past the railing, where they could be properly greeted, hugged, squeezed, and kissed. There was a moment of polite solemnity as Mr. Tate shook Jerome's hand, held it longer than normal. Mr. Tate nodded and smiled grimly to let the young man know that, though the pilot had stolen his daughter, all was forgiven—though not forgotten—and now that the pilot had provided him grandchildren, he could be counted as a bona fide member of the family. The uniform gave Jerome a regal bearing, and all the kids and even Mr. Tate looked at him with respect. They knew, from Gloria's letters, that though he'd never fought in a war, he'd risked his life many times.

Gloria wrapped her arms around Gene and Rich and Manny and Laura, kissing and hugging them tight.

"Laura? My God," she said, holding her at arm's length and then twirling her. "Look how you've filled out. I keep thinking of you as this skinny little stick. But you're not anymore, are you, Miss Monroe?"

"And Manny. I remember you as this runt I could beat up," she continued. "Good thing I got a soldier to protect me."

"He's just an air force man."

Jerome cocked an eyebrow. "Those are fightin' words, buddy."

"Rich. Can you talk now?"

"Yes," he said shyly.

"I knew that. You come here, you little booger." She knelt down, and he wrapped his arms tightly around her neck, and she kissed both his cheeks, and he hugged her again and wouldn't let go. Gloria lolled her tongue out and crossed her eyes. "He's strangling me, he's strangling me!" she said, and Rich laughed and let go of her.

"And Genie. Oh, Genie. The only sweet one in the bunch."

"You haven't seen the tire tracks in his underwear," Manny said.

"Shut up!" Gene squealed.

"Well, I'll skip that part," she said, mussing his hair. "I have enough diapers to tend to."

Jerome and Manny gathered the suitcases that were in the luggage compartment and returned to the rest of them cooing over the baby, Mr. Tate holding him in his arms and crouching down to his knees, smiling at the girl who now clung to her mother.

Mr. Tate said, "Come here, darling. Give Grampa some sugar."

"Go on, honey," Jerome said.

"It's okay," Gloria urged.

She wouldn't budge. Mr. Tate said, "Come tell me who this little guy is."

"Cawo," she muttered.

"Your big brother?"

"Nooooo!" she protested. "Itto brudder."

"Am I holding him right?"

"No," she said and pointed to her grandfather's other arm.

They all laughed.

"Just like your mother," he said, handing the baby to Laura. "You think you know the right way to do everything." He reached out for her. "Come here and give me some sweet sugar."

Julie finally obliged him.

Then there was the moment that had been delayed, by design perhaps, maybe anxiety, but there it was, the reunion of father and daughter. The prodigal returning to the forgiving parent's arms, the runaway come home. Everyone sensed the decorum appropriate to a ceremony. Gloria's eyes moistened. The rest cleared a path for them, and in the silence that followed, they all could feel the absence of their mother. Laura closed her eyes and could see her clearly, as in that fever dream in May, in her blue-and-red-flowered dress, the sheer red scarf, her mother kissing her and then turning away, disappearing through the tattered cobwebs. At homecomings, Laura thought, the dead or missing always hover like ghosts.

"Welcome home, morning glory," Mr. Tate said. His old name for her.

She walked slowly to her father and put her face against his chest. And they could see her shoulders relax into a sob. He put his arms around her back, and neither of them said a word. Laura's eyes clouded over. She had trouble swallowing. She placed her lips against Carroll's head and smelled baby shampoo.

"Who's hungry?" Mr. Tate said, smiling. Even *his* eyes seemed misty.

Gloria pulled away and laughed as she wiped her cheeks with the back of her hand.

"I'm starving," said Jerome. "Hungry, sweetie?" he asked Julie.

"Uh-huh."

"Hope you haven't been spoiled by all that European cuisine," Mr. Tate said as he leaned over and grabbed one of the suitcases.

"Ha!" Jerome laughed.

"I don't know, Dad," Gloria said. "I may have to ask Ike to ship me a couple of boxes of U.S. Certified Beans and Wienies while I'm here. Can't go a whole week without 'em."

Mr. Tate smiled. "Well, we'll see what we can do, honey. But right now La Palace de la Ding Dong awaits our dinner party."

Laura figured he'd been working on that line all day.

18

✴

Women in the House

*H*er father relinquished his room to Gloria and Jerome. Julie was to sleep on a small portable cot by their bed, unless Gloria and Jerome wanted her to sleep with Laura. A week earlier, her father and Manny pulled Rich's crib out of the cellar. It had been through five children and twenty years of use. They repaired the legs. The mattress was ripped and stained, and when they slapped it, a cloud of dust rose from it and choked them so badly that they had to climb from the storm cellar, gagging, coughing, red-faced. Her father sanded the crib, repainted it bright blue, and bought a brand-new mattress, which stunned all of them. The expense! He never would've done it just for them. Rich, who hadn't been out of his crib for very long, now wanted to return to his refurbished bed.

They had vacuumed, dusted, and aired the house. Old boxes of magazines and newspapers were thrown out. Slipcovers were placed over the cigarette scorches and stains and tattered holes in the couch and the recliner. They cut fresh flowers and placed them in vases. The house had not been this clean in . . . well, not since her mother had lived with them, even though Laura worked hard to keep the house relatively tidy. It was really the first time they'd had visitors come and stay with them in she couldn't remember how long, at least since Aunt Velma stopped coming, and that was several years back. There was her father's poker game last spring, but that didn't really count, because the men didn't give a damn what the house looked like, nor did her father care if they cared.

She liked the new anticipation in their home, the desire to impress, or at least not be embarrassed. It galvanized them all. Dresser drawers and closets were organized to make room. Old clothes and unused toys were placed in boxes and taken to Jensen's Thrift Shop. Manny mowed the yards, and he and her father and Gene repainted the trim on the house, and they all pulled the weeds from the garden and around the foundation. Laura gave old Fay a bath. She hadn't been bathed in—what was it now?—a year; the dog seemed so grateful for the attention that she licked and licked Laura's neck and face, which made Laura decide to brush the dog's teeth with baking soda. The poor thing. She surely didn't have many years left. After the incident with Greta, Laura's father had Fay spayed, though at her age it probably wasn't necessary. She felt sorry for the dog, and perhaps it was pointless to give her a bath anyway. There'd be too many people in the house to bring her inside. But we all need some attention, Laura thought. Even a dirty old dog.

By the time they left for the bus station, the house was as clean as it had ever been, and it was sad, in a way, to leave it. They all just wanted to stand there and admire their hard work. They were more than a little disappointed when they arrived back home, after dinner at 4-D's, and Gloria's first words were "I don't remember the house being so small. How on earth did we all fit in here?" Which seemed ironic to Laura, given what Gloria had said about the cramped base housing.

A nervous, resentful silence thickened the air, and Laura exchanged worried glances with Manny. They both eyed their father—a blush rising from his neck, the corner of his lips twitching. She felt his shame, and her own. She thought of something her father had once said years ago when he'd taken them all to see the new courthouse extension he'd helped build. It seemed like any other structure: ordinary, governmental, nothing that ornate or impressive. "Good work is never recognized and must be immodestly pointed out, or it goes ignored." She came home and wrote it in her diary, impressed by the surprising wisdom of her father.

Laura suddenly saw the house through her sister's eyes, not as their home, the place where they'd all been raised, but as this relic from Gloria's past, a shabby, ramshackle dump in a "dusty, provincial village" (Gloria's phrase) in the Panhandle, something that she, with good reason, could make fun of with the other wives on the bases, in that sharp, clowning way of hers: "You'd never believe the shoe box I grew up in!"

Laura felt suddenly angry, and then depressed and hurt, as if the fault were somehow her own. How could this compare to the places Gloria had been, the exotic countries and famous cities? How backwater they all were. Hicks. She had never really thought about it, didn't really wonder about it, until now, when the slightest expression on her sister's face could confirm their worthlessness.

"We been cleaning it all week!" Rich shouted.

Gloria smiled and said, "Well, I can tell. It looks marvelous! Maybe you should come to my house. It could use a good cleaning."

"You can say that again," Jerome scoffed. Gloria slapped him on the arm, and Gene and Manny chuckled.

"Looks like you repainted," Gloria said.

Mr. Tate said, "Well, yeah, we did some touch-ups." Laura thought, *Dad doesn't get it.*

Laura watched her sister carefully, studied her movements, the way her eyes darted over the rooms. She felt weak, dependent on Gloria's silent judgments and evaluations, her unspoken disappointments and reproaches.

"It's strange coming home again," Gloria said. "It's very strange."

Soon enough, though, the house was just the house, and by that evening, once Gloria and Jerome and the kids spilled into the place with their bags, the polish they'd all given it seemed inconsequential.

But Laura's fascination with her sister did not wear off. She'd almost forgotten what it was like to have another female in the house. Old Mrs. Ambling had been in it, looking after her when she'd been sick, and Mrs. Letig, too, that night near the end of her illness. And that woman her father had secretly brought over after he'd gone dancing, a while after their mother left. But that was so long ago.

Laura had never, that she could remember, had a friend spend the night. (Where would Debbie or Marlene sleep?) It simply hadn't been a possibility, or she had never thought of it as such, though maybe she'd known, on some level, how shameful it would be to have her friends see where she lived, all of them crammed into this house like sardines. It *was* shabby. It *was* embarrassing.

But she had grown proprietary. Now, with her mother and sister gone, this place, in an important way, was *her* house. She cleaned, shopped at the Piggly Wiggly, cooked most of the meals, and did the lion's share of tending to Rich and Gene. While Gloria had once lived here, too, and done what Laura had done, though to a much lesser degree, she no longer had the same rights of ownership that Laura now possessed. And Gloria seemed to acknowledge Laura's status, asking her where things were, asking for permission to make a meal. She didn't have to do that, but Laura liked it that she did.

Laura had spent so much time thinking about her sister that it was weird to have her here in the flesh. In some ways, Gloria was the same as she had always been. There was that high-pitched, cackling laugh of hers when she thought something was really funny. She'd start giggling, and then the sound would trill in her throat, and then there'd be a snort on the end of the laugh, which made you worry slightly for her, but it was also infectious and could make you giggle like a child until tears streamed down your face and your stomach hurt. And she had an animated way about her, acting out an anecdote or story, assuming the attitude and character of whoever was talking. She'd always been good with accents, and she'd acquired some new ones, a thick Viennese one she called Freud, and a ditsy, high-pitched yodel she called the Swiss Miss, and the sultry-eyed, shoulder-wagging arrogant one, with pouty lips and condescending eyes, with a voice like the actresses in *Gigi,* which she called the French Artiste. When she told stories, she was dynamic, her arms and hands graceful, and it seemed so easy and natural for her. Laura both admired and envied her sister, and she knew she'd remember these things and rehearse them herself, as if these ideas and characters were her own, and she'd try them out on Marlene and Debbie, playing Monopoly at their houses, or maybe even with Dean Compson, and most certainly with John, to make him laugh.

When she wasn't the center of attention, telling a joke or a story, Gloria watched them all. Laura caught her observing others—their father, Manny, Gene, Rich, her own children, Jerome, even Laura herself. Gloria carefully scrutinized everything that was happening, and Laura remembered this as well, how it used to unnerve her, as if Gloria was looking for something to mock you with, and Laura had always been careful to stay in Gloria's good graces. She didn't want to be the one teased and tormented. And Laura was aware of this hard, cynical, even selfish part of Gloria, which she both admired and feared. It was what had given Gloria the courage to elope, to defy their parents, to do something so drastic. You needed to be selfish in order to do such things. Gloria was bold, but there was also (wasn't there?), in the boldness, the careless disregard of others and of consequences.

There was a softer side to Gloria as well. She had always been capable of great generosity. She had once bought Laura a brand-new dress at the Amarillo Woolworth's with the last of her money because she felt that her little sister needed some "cheering up." (Laura still had that dress; it didn't fit, but she wasn't about to give it away.) And when she and Gloria and Manny swam across Lake Meredith, Gloria insisted that Laura could make it, even though Laura doubted the outcome. Both during and afterward, Gloria had been tender and encouraging, making her feel triumphant, heroic. Laura could see that her generosity had ripened, with motherhood, perhaps, or being Jerome's wife, into something akin to patience, rough edges smoothed over—the soft nuzzling of the baby, the easy way she tended to Julie, not like when she was younger and had to care for Laura, Manny, and Gene.

There was also, just below the surface, a layer of melancholy. Perhaps it had always been there. Laura could remember her sister crying in bed about this boy or that one (Billy Sidell, in particular), and there had been the anxious quality to her before she eloped, but Laura was looking for the sadness that had come through in the letters—a darker, richer vein of feeling, which made Gloria real in a way that she had never been before. Laura thought she could detect this sadness. She could see it sometimes in a look her sister exchanged with Jerome, the way she deferred to him when he spoke, stayed quiet and a little on edge, which made Laura wonder if Gloria was happy with him or if there were times when she regretted what she had done, felt that this life she'd chosen had now enclosed and trapped her. Laura was looking for the young, pregnant wife walking in the Berlin fog, or the woman who couldn't sleep at night and dreamed of her husband engulfed in flames, or who screamed at her children and wondered if, like their own mother, she would or could abandon them. Those details in the letters had unsettled Laura and stayed with her, like shards of colored glass—dangerous, painful, mesmerizing.

By studying Gloria, she hoped to find answers to her own questions, though what those questions were, Laura wasn't quite sure. She had the feeling that Gloria's being here was somehow meant to teach her something, to show her a direction, a possibility. But it was more complex than that. What people teach is more elusive and indirect and strange, without motive or intention, like the variations and complications of light and shadow during the course of a day. What was there to *learn* in that? You just watch it, absorb it, admire it. *Fall into it.*

In their father's bedroom the next afternoon, Gloria placed the baby, naked after its bath, out on a towel on the bed. Laura lay on the bed and watched her. She wanted Gloria to herself, for a few moments at least, and she was glad that everybody else was outside or in the kitchen, playing cards or listening to a baseball game on the radio.

"Do I seem so different to you?" Gloria suddenly asked.

She'd washed her hair, and the beehive was gone. Her hair now hung around her shoulders, flipped out at the bottom, and she wore an orange-and-white-flowered sleeveless summer blouse and bright orange capri pants that reminded Laura of a picture she'd seen recently in *Life* of Senator Kennedy's wife in a similar outfit—pedal pushers and bright sleeveless blouse and dark sunglasses. Laura wondered if Gloria had seen that picture, or seen Mrs. Kennedy in one of the newsreels, wondered if the similarity was deliberate, if Gloria admired the senator's wife the way Laura and Marlene and Debbie did. Maybe it was just the way women dressed in Europe. Mrs. Kennedy was, she'd heard from Marlene, half French and had lived in Paris. Maybe every European woman wore sleeveless blouses and pedal pushers rather than T-shirts and cuffed-bottom jeans.

"Sort of different," Laura said, but didn't elaborate.

"You keep staring at me. I can feel your eyes all the time. Are you disappointed?"

"No."

"It's odd having me here, isn't it?"

Gloria diapered the baby and asked Laura to hand her a little green jumper from the suitcase.

"No, it's wonderful," Laura answered, handing the outfit to her sister. "Kind of strange. But wonderful. Is it weird being back?"

"A little. With Momma gone."

Gloria glanced quickly at Laura and then down at the baby. This was the first time anybody had mentioned their mother, and they both were embarrassed by it. Gloria busied herself, squirting lotion on her hands, rubbing them together. Then she spread it slowly over Carroll's stomach and arms. Laura felt as if this routine, the deliberateness of each stroke, was somehow connected to the memory of their mother.

"But I'm glad I'm here," Gloria said, raising her head, a melancholy smile on her lips. "Maybe it's just the fact that we're in their room. I don't know."

Carroll squirmed a little on the bed, his mouth puckering. Gloria grabbed the pacifier and eased it between his lips.

"You seem different to me," Gloria said more brightly, as if she was about to compliment Laura, but before she could continue, Jerome came into the bedroom.

He winked at Laura. "How's it going, kid?" he said and then wrapped his arms around Gloria's waist and nuzzled his chin into her neck.

"Stop it. I'm dressing the baby," she said, but her voice didn't say stop it. He started tickling her, his fingers on her hips and waist and then his hand low over her stomach, and Gloria tried to wrestle away, but he held her tight, and then he turned her toward him, pulled her close so that her back arched. Her hair spilled over her shoulders. Gloria put her arms around his neck, and they kissed. It wasn't a chaste kiss either. It was long, and Laura saw her sister's tongue dart over Jerome's teeth. The baby lay on the bed, unfazed, his feet in his hands.

Laura stretched out her leg toward the baby so he wouldn't fall off the bed, and she tried not to look at her sister and brother-in-law. But she couldn't help it. She was disappointed. She felt like he'd intruded. And this seemed inappropriate, in their parents' room, in front of her. Showing off, a lack of courtesy at the very least. Yeah, they were married, but still. She felt her own irritation and distaste.

Why should she feel this way? she wondered. She had no right, but she didn't know Jerome that well (she'd met him only twice before he and Gloria eloped), and though he was nice enough, she thought there was also something insincere about him. She couldn't help but feel that he was on his good behavior, especially in front of her father, saying "Yes, sir" and "No, sir" and laughing a little too much at their jokes, too eager to please, like that Eddie Haskell character on *Leave It to Beaver*. But when her father or Manny wasn't around, when it was just Laura, Rich, and Gene, Jerome seemed different, patronizing and inappropriate. She'd seen him touch Gloria casually on her butt and once, when he thought no one was looking, he squeezed her breasts. Gloria gave him a threatening glance and pushed his hand aside, and when he saw that Laura had seen what he'd done, he just winked at her and smiled in a way that made it seem like he was glad he'd been caught.

"Okay, enough already," Gloria said and pushed Jerome away. "You go in there. You're embarrassing my little sister."

He ignored her, knelt by the end of the bed, and grabbed Carroll's feet and roughly lifted him so that he was upside down. The baby giggled, and Jerome smiled. Men always roughhoused with babies too much, Laura thought. Like they were footballs.

"How old are you again?" he asked, not looking at her. "Seventeen?"

"Sixteen," Gloria said. "I told you that. Don't be so rough with the baby."

Jerome set Carroll down and then rubbed his military brush cut across the baby's stomach, and again the baby squealed with laughter. Jerome leaned over and put both of his hands on the bed, caging Carroll, and then he lifted his head so that his face was suddenly close to Laura's, too close.

"How are things?" he asked.

"What do you mean?" Laura asked.

"You got boyfriends?"

"Don't listen to him, Laura." Gloria slapped his butt. "She's not going to tell you before she tells me."

"God, it's hot in here," he said, pulling away from Laura and standing up. "I forgot how goddamn hot it gets in the Panhandle."

He pulled his T-shirt over his head and mopped his face with it.

"Jerome," Gloria said, frowning.

"What?"

"It's not that hot. Put your shirt back on."

"It's stifling." He turned toward Laura, touched her foot with the end of his shirt. Intentionally, she felt. She pulled her foot back. "Do you mind?" he asked.

She shrugged, tried not to look. His body was muscled and hard and dark, with a dense black triangle of hair in the middle of his chest and bushy outgrowths from his armpits. His waist was narrow, and there was a thick tangle spiraling down from his navel into his pants. There was something hostile about his body. She decided that she didn't like him.

"I better get supper started," Laura said.

"I'll be right there, honey," Gloria said.

Laura pulled the door closed behind her. She didn't really want her father or anyone else to see.

"You know why they get the bedroom, don't you?" Manny said, a conspiratorial hush in his voice. They were in the backyard, Manny sitting in the swing with his head poking over the metal bar of the swing-set frame as Laura took down the clean towels from the clothesline. Fay was digging a bone hole at the far end of the yard. They'd finished dinner, and inside, Gloria bathed her kids while Mr. Tate, Jerome, Gene, and Rich played canasta.

"Privacy," she said.

"So they can fuck," he whispered and then bugged his eyes and obscenely wagged his tongue.

"Shut up!"

"You don't believe me?"

"They have a baby," she protested weakly.

"So what," he said. "Why do you think Julie's cot got moved to our room?"

"You are so crude."

"Maybe, but it's true. It's a biological fact. Travel makes you want to fuck. I think it's rather big of the old man to give up his room like that, letting his daughter be defiled in his own bed."

"SHUT UP!" she shouted and threw a dish towel in his face.

He laughed and then pulled the towel slowly over his face. He arched his eyebrows, and a dark curl flopped over his forehead. He smiled slyly, his imitation of James Dean.

"Don't you think it's *magnanimous*?" He enunciated this word slowly, and she figured he'd just learned it.

"Why are you such a jackass?" she said.

He threw the towel at her. It landed on her shoulder. "You listen to-night," he said, leaning in the swing and then pushing off with his foot so that soon he was moving back and forth, higher and higher. "You'll hear the bedsprings squeaking," he said as he swooped by. "Jerome is going to give it to her good."

"You're an absolute idiot, you know that."

"It's true. I swear to God."

"Shut up. You don't know anything. And besides, I don't care."

"Bullshit if you don't." He laughed and then flew out of the swing and landed about five feet away. He twirled around and then bowed like an actor taking a curtain call.

"I *don't* care!"

" 'I *don't* care!' " he mimicked, then cackled again. He unsnapped his shirt pocket and pulled out his pouch of tobacco and papers, sat on the stump, deftly rolled himself a cigarette, and lit it.

"You want one?" he asked, holding the bag out to her.

"No."

He smirked. "You sure?"

"Yes," she said. She thought about the drags she'd had in the truck with John on the way out to Lake Meredith.

"Suit yourself." He took a long drag, held it, and puffed white rings that jiggled in the air. That, too, seemed obscene to her, an extension of his earlier talk.

"I bet you don't talk to Joannie that way," she said, taunting him.

"She's not my sister."

"You wouldn't say that to Gloria."

"What d'ya mean? *Who* do you think told me all this?"

"Liar!"

He just laughed. Could he be telling the truth? He and Gloria were close. Laura remembered when she was about twelve, Manny thirteen, Gloria almost sixteen, coming into a room to find them laughing, their faces bent close to each other, a joke between them, but when they spotted her, their bodies stiffened, their laughter abruptly stopped. She knew she wasn't wanted, wasn't welcome, wouldn't be privy to their talk. She was young then, and they were probably just protecting her, she realized, but still, they had always been close and even coarse with each other in a way she envied. He knew she would never ask Gloria herself, or if she did, then

Gloria might just cackle, realizing it was one of Manny's jokes. The fool. She hated him sometimes. He thought she was so naïve.

What would he do if he found out about her and John Letig? She had half a mind to tell him, just to show him, just once to see a look on *his* face that would satisfy her the way the looks of shock on *her* face evidently satisfied him. Like zapping him with the end of an electric wire or a cattle prod. *Yes,* she wanted to see him *jump!*

"You're not even glad they're here, are you?" she asked. She knew it wasn't true, but she wanted to accuse him of something.

"Are you kidding?" he said, blowing out another jiggling ring. "Of course I am. I think it's great that somebody's getting laid in this house. It's been too long."

"You're disgusting," she said and started away with the basket of towels, exasperated certainly, but there was also a slight smile at the corner of her lips. She knew he wanted to torment her, but she also wondered if he was as affected by Gloria and Jerome's being here in the house as she was, wondered if his obscenity and cynical attitude, his concerted attempts to rile her, were in his own way an invitation, a yearning to have again a sister with whom he could joke and pose outrageously. She felt a little sorry for him, for what he'd lost, but she also felt older, more mature, beyond his kind of teasing bluster.

"Tonight," he called after her. "You listen, Laura. Squeak, squeak, squeak."

That night she found herself half listening, against her will, for the bedsprings. She didn't want to. But she couldn't help herself. She remembered her father and that woman in his bed, the way the bed seemed like a trough, her father moving over the woman. Laura didn't want to think about Gloria and Jerome together in that way, in the way that John and she had been. It was too strange, seemed a betrayal, but she couldn't help that either. She hated how these thoughts, these images, would be there even though she didn't want them. When she finally did fall asleep, she dreamed of Jerome rocking above Gloria, his face leaning over her, him sucking her breasts, moving into and out of her, their bodies glazed in the thin, white, honey-smelling breast milk. Both of them looked at her and smiled ghoulishly.

When Laura woke, she found herself sweating in the hot night. She felt dispirited. Her head ached, but she didn't want to go back to sleep, not yet. Nor did she want to listen to the sounds in the house. She covered her ears and turned toward the window. The night was still, no wind blowing the willow in Mrs. Ambling's yard, which Laura could see from her bed. The long-leafed branches just hung heavy in the heat like still, slender fingers. She watched the tree, waiting for the leaves to rustle, but they didn't. It was as if the night had been embalmed.

By her bed was the bird sculpture John had made her. In the dark, all the colors disappeared, but if she closed her eyes just so that her eyelashes touched, the sculpture came alive, as if the hummingbird's wings were fluttering. She liked doing this trick, but she could only do it really well at night. The shadows helped create the effect.

She heard her father's door open; someone tiptoed to the bathroom. Manny rolled over and whispered, "What did I tell you?"

The jerk. She didn't respond, just turned back to the window and to the bird and the flowers. She made the wings beat again and closed her eyes, but it was a long time before she slept, and then too soon the early-morning summer sun shone hot on her face.

✳

19

Threats and Intrusions

*A*ll the men and boys went fishing. Gloria, Julie, the baby, and Laura stayed in town. It was nice without the others in the house. Quiet, less chaotic. She was glad they were gone. She felt anxious and excited about having time with her sister, but she discovered there was no need for the anxiety. They lingered in the kitchen after breakfast, Gloria glad to be able to nurse at the table rather than hiding in the bedroom with a cloth diaper draped over the exposed part of her breast. Though Laura remembered the normality of her mother nursing Gene and then Rich, she was embarrassed when Gloria first started to nurse the baby, unhooking her bra, sliding the strap of her sundress over her shoulder, revealing her large breast (twice the size of Laura's), blue-veined, the nipple leaking the watery milk. Laura turned away.

"You can watch," Gloria said. "It's okay."

Her sister pried open the baby's mouth and then forcefully pressed his head against her chest. But something was wrong. Gloria winced, stuck her fingers between the baby's gums and extricated her nipple, turned it up and examined it as if it were a bottle cap or some strange insect.

"Does it hurt?" Laura asked.

"Yeah, sometimes I'm sore for days. Plus, he's cutting a tooth."

Laura winced. "Ouch."

"It's nothing, really. Better than when he doesn't nurse. With Julie, I had a terrible case of mastitis. Like marbles in my boobs. So this is easy."

"Why do you do it?"

"Oh, it's good for the baby. And I like it, most of the time. It's nice."

Laura wanted her to say more about the sensation but wasn't sure how to continue the conversation. "What do you mean, it's nice?" she said after a minute of silence.

"When nothing's hurting, it just feels . . . nice. Also, it's a good form of birth control. My period didn't come back until I stopped nursing Julie, and when it did come back, I got pregnant immediately. I swear it's the best part about being pregnant and having babies. No periods, no cramps. Except for the lack of sleep and sore boobs—oh, and the labor pains—I feel great."

Laura watched her readjust Carroll, and then she watched the baby suck, his eyes open.

"There you go," Gloria cooed and flicked the side of his cheek playfully with her finger. "That's better, isn't it?"

He smiled, and the milk dribbled out of the corners of his mouth.

"Laura, would you do me a favor and cut an apple for Julie? If she doesn't have a snack about this time, she's a bear by lunch."

"Sure." She cut the apple and put in it on a plate, then took it in to Julie, who was coloring in the living room. "Here you go, sweetie."

"What do you say?" Gloria called from the kitchen.

"Tank you."

"You're welcome."

Julie was a sweet girl, docile and able already to entertain herself. Not like the boys when they were young, not even like Jack or Willie Letig. Laura realized, with a dumb shock, that she'd never been around any little girls. Only boys. She liked her younger brothers and the Letig boys, at times seemed to love them all, though she wasn't sure she could trust her feelings about Jack and Willie; they were somehow mixed up with her feelings for John. Having Julie around, though, watching the way she climbed into her grandfather's lap, watching her concentrate so intensely on the pictures she drew, reminded her of herself when she was that age and made her wonder about having her own little girl. Gloria wasn't that much older than Laura when she had Julie, even closer in age when she figured in the pregnancy. *No.* She had to stop that kind of thinking. Having her cute niece and nephew in the house could be dangerous, she realized.

She poured herself and Gloria a cup of coffee, and they both spooned in heaping ovals of sugar.

"It's been so busy around here we've hardly been able to talk," Gloria said. "So how are you?"

"Good."

"Short answers, little darling, are not going to be satisfactory. I'm hungry for some girl talk."

Laura wondered what she could say. She preferred to hear Gloria talk. Carroll had nodded off, his head still cradled against Gloria's breast.

"Daddy said you were really sick a couple of months ago, stayed in bed for over a week."

"Yeah."

"No one knew what was wrong?"

She hesitated, thinking for a moment about all the complications leading up to her sickness, but said, "Just the flu."

"But you're all better now?"

"Oh, yeah," she said, stirring her coffee. "It's hard even to remember what it was like."

Gloria nodded and looked back down at the baby. His eyes were closed, but his mouth worked rhythmically.

"Do you have a boyfriend?"

"Not really."

"I know what 'not really' means. Sam Compson's little brother? What's his name? Come on, give me details."

"Dean? No way! He's got a face full of zits. And he's a bad kisser."

"Aha." Gloria raised an eyebrow and smiled. "How would you know what kind of kisser he is?"

Laura took a big sip of coffee and burned her tongue.

"Doesn't Glenn Thomason have a boy your age? He'd be a good catch. Get 'em rich. Let 'em pamper you."

"Like you did?" Laura said.

"Watch it, smart-ass. I married for *looooove*."

They both laughed. Carroll startled awake, crying. Gloria quickly attached him to her other breast, and he closed his eyes and sucked.

"Nobody," Laura said, shaking her head.

"I don't believe you. You're this gorgeous doll. Boys must be drooling over you."

Her sister raised her eyebrow again and smiled mischievously. Laura liked that Gloria was talking to her as an adult—a friend, another woman. She had the urge to confess. She could feel the impulse, an itch in her mouth. But then she stopped herself, shook her head, laughed like it was a joke.

"I don't believe you," Gloria said again. "Tell me who the boy is."

"No one."

Gloria squinted, cocked her head, and then smiled suspiciously. "Well, I'm sure you're breaking hearts right and left."

Laura turned away. It wasn't true. In school the boys didn't seem to pay much attention to her. Sure, she'd had fun with boys at dances and gone with groups to the drive-in and had even made out with some guys at parties, playing spin the bottle, but no one had asked her out, except for Dean (who didn't count). Marlene and Debbie told her that people knew Manny Tate was her brother and that Zeeke Tate was protective, didn't like his youngest daughter dating. And Laura had intuited the rest of the gossip. Hadn't her older sister eloped with some war hero? And didn't her mother go nuts and disappear? Where'd she run off to? Some other guy, probably. You don't want to mess around with Laura Tate. Her father's still angry. He might take a welding torch to you.

"I can't get over how much you've changed," Gloria said, sipping her coffee. "I guess we all have. But you, you seem like a different person. You were just a skinny little tomboy when I last saw you, and in my mind you remained that tomboy. Now look at you. You've got some curves. It's scary how pretty you are. It makes me wonder if I've changed that much, too."

"Sort of."

"What does 'sort of' mean? Do I look like some old married hag?"

Laura laughed. "No, no. You don't look that different."

"What does that mean?"

"Still beautiful."

"Good answer. Very . . . shrewd! You may proceed."

"It's just strange to see you with kids." She didn't know where she could go with this. She wanted to say something about Jerome, but she was afraid her dislike of him would surface if she talked too much. "You look a little tired."

"Oh, thanks."

"I mean—"

"I know what you mean. I *am* tired. I didn't expect this to be so hard. I'd helped take care of you and Manny and Gene and thought it couldn't be that difficult—not really. But it is! It makes me sleepy. And yet I can't sleep. When Jerome is gone, I swear I'm a nervous wreck. It's awful. Don't marry a pilot if you can't sleep alone."

Gloria gazed out the window, lost for a moment in her own thoughts.

"Do you like it over there?" Laura asked. "Your letters are so funny."

"I like writing the letters. It's not real, I guess, unless I write it down. And then the experience takes on a shape. It's like I get to see my own mind. That's sounds weird, doesn't it?"

"What do you mean?"

"I don't know. On the bases, it's not that different than here. For the most part, it's boring. I like writing the letters. It makes things interesting— and it calms me. I sometimes make copies for myself, like a diary, when I have time, so I can read them again, and then I know what I did or thought. Maybe it's all this lack of sleep. I have trouble remembering things."

Laura leaned across the table, closer to her sister. "They're great letters. We read them over and over and over. Dad was so excited about you coming home. We all were, but he wanted the house looking perfect. It's never been this clean, if you can believe it, at least not since Momma left."

Gloria seemed to flinch at their mother's name. Laura leaned back, suddenly sorry she'd mentioned it. Julie came into the room and said she was sleepy. Laura volunteered to put her down, took her niece's hand and led her to the kids' bedroom, let her lie on her bed. Laura started reading her a story, but by the end of the first page, she was asleep.

"How is he?" Gloria asked when Laura returned to the kitchen. Laura knew that she was talking about their father.

"Good, I guess," Laura said. "He works a lot. And he's thinking of opening his own shop soon."

"I know all that. I mean . . . how . . . *is* he? How did he take it? Does he see other women? Does he talk about Momma? Now that I'm here, I feel her all the time. Like she's around . . . watching us."

"We don't talk about her much."

"Don't you find that *strange?*"

"I don't know. I guess so, now that you say it."

"No one *ever* talks about her?"

"We do and we don't," Laura said, sitting back down at the table. She grabbed an apple and rolled it around nervously in her hands. "Right after it happened . . . I mean, right after Dad came back from looking for her, he seemed paralyzed. We all waited for him to get out of the truck and tell us what happened. But it was like he couldn't answer the most basic question, and Manny finally screamed at him, and Dad hit him, and Manny fell down and just started crying. And then Dad bent down and held him. Pretty soon they were all crying. But after that, I don't know. . . . We got used to it, I guess."

Laura saw a melancholy shadow cross Gloria's face.

"How about Gene and Rich?"

"Gene just reads all the time, comics and tons of books. We have to go to the library two or three times a week. Everywhere he goes, he has a book. You ask him a question and he doesn't answer half the time, he'll be so lost in the book. Dad says, 'Just let him be,' so I figure it's his way of dealing with it. Rich cried a little afterward and slept with me or Dad for a long time, but he doesn't seem to remember much about her."

"And what about Manny?"

"He's meaner than he used to be. He told me a couple of months after she left that he was glad she was gone."

Laura expected Gloria to flinch at that, but she just nodded her head like she understood.

"He said he hated her anyway, which I knew wasn't true. He knew I knew. But there's this hard shell that seems to be around him. He's not the same."

"Huh," Gloria said. "He doesn't seem that different to me. Just bigger and hairier."

She smiled. Laura smiled, too, but she didn't like it that Gloria defended him. What did Gloria know? She hadn't been here.

"We don't get along that well. And I don't see him much. He works at the gas station. He's got his friends. And there's Joannie, too. So he's hardly here."

"Are they serious?"

"Seems so."

"You think they'll get married?"

"I don't know. I feel sorry for her."

"I bet he's nicer to her. Boys are different when they're alone with their girlfriends."

Laura thought for moment about Jerome. And then about John. "Still," Laura said, "he's a jerk sometimes."

Gloria just smiled and shook her head, then eased Carroll from her breast. He was asleep, but his mouth puckered in and out, even after the breast was gone. Gloria put him against her shoulder and patted his back, sniffed his head. Suddenly he belched.

"Does Dad ever go out on dates?"

"No," Laura said, shaking her head. She thought of mentioning the woman he brought home but thought better of it. It was a secret. She didn't want Gloria to think badly of him. Besides, it was so long ago, nearly two years now.

"That relieves me, to tell you the truth. I suppose it would be good for him to see someone, but I'm glad he's not. I couldn't stand the thought of another woman in this house. Some wicked stepmother. It's selfish of me, I know." She paused, patting Carroll's back gently. "He seems so much older, though," she continued, "like he's aged ten years since I left. He's going gray, his wrinkles seem deeper. He looks thin and sad."

"You think so?" Laura thought he seemed younger lately. Happy, even. Gloria hadn't been around a year or two ago, when he really looked ragged and distracted, unshaven and glassy-eyed, as if he'd been drinking secretly or was on the verge of tears that would never fall. He'd snapped out of it, as she supposed they all had. Gloria had missed all that. She didn't know, and there was no way to explain or describe it. You had to be here to understand, to really *know*.

"Maybe it's just me reading too much into it," Gloria said. "Maybe he's over it. But I see him as this sad man whose wife left him."

They both shook their heads and then sipped their coffee, but it had turned cold. Laura retrieved the pot and warmed their cups. Gloria spooned more sugar into her coffee and stirred thoughtfully.

"Where do you suppose she went?" she asked suddenly.

"I don't know," Laura said, not prepared for this question. She felt a catch in her throat. They had been tunneling toward this question, she figured, but still it surprised her. "I don't think about it."

That wasn't true. She thought about it a lot. But now she didn't really want to talk about it. She could feel her own sadness, rising like a water table, and she knew that before long, if they kept talking, it might spill over the edges, and then the tears would come, as they sometimes still did at night, or during the day if she was tired or disappointed or worried about something. She'd learned to watch for the signs now, and there was a line that she didn't like to cross. Gloria was greedy for details—Laura understood why she would be—but Gloria didn't live here every day, in this house. It wasn't a mausoleum. Their mother had left them, and there had been a gaping hole, and that hole had slowly closed. They'd gotten used to the fact that she had disappeared and was probably never coming back. But if her mother reentered, if they *let* her reenter the house, even in their prolonged memories, then the sadness would come again and linger like an untended infection. It was, Laura now understood, the unspoken threat when Gloria returned, the intrusion of these memories from the time before. The threat seemed very real now.

"Are you okay, Laura?" Gloria said, leaning toward her. "I'm sorry. This is hard for you, isn't it?"

"No," she lied.

"You're about to cry."

"I'm okay," Laura said. "Before you went away, did you ever—" She broke off, choking on her words.

"Did I ever what?"

"Did you ever . . . think she would leave? Was there something that made it seem like it might happen?"

"I've thought about that a lot," Gloria said, shifting the baby so that he lay across her knees. She rubbed his back gently and gave Laura's question some thought. "I think I was so focused on what I was going to do, running off with Jerome, that I honestly wasn't paying close attention. You know how she was, so quiet, you could never really read her. She had that perfect poker face. Her eyes would go to stone when she got angry, and she'd go off by herself to do the laundry or walk the dogs. I don't think I ever even imagined that she'd *want* to leave. Who *could* imagine such a thing? It doesn't make sense. Mothers don't do that."

Gloria stared out the window into the backyard. Fay was lying in the shade next to the storm cellar, snoozing away as she usually did most mornings and afternoons. A warm breeze blew in, slightly billowing the curtain.

"I do remember," she said after a couple of minutes, "maybe a week before Jerome and I left for Mexico . . . I was convinced that she knew what I was doing. We were sitting in the backyard one evening. The sun was going down. We were just quiet together for the longest time, but it wasn't awkward. It was beautiful out. The sky was so orange, and the air seemed very warm and still. Suddenly a breeze kicked up out of nowhere. Light at first, but in just a matter of seconds it was blowing hard against our faces. Cold, too . . . very strange.

"I started to get up, but Momma reached over and put her hand across my chest, held me in the chair. 'Don't leave,' she said. My heart was pounding. I thought, *Oh, no, she means don't leave Charnelle.* But then I realized that she was saying not to leave the chair. I didn't say a word . . . just sat there and looked at her. She had her eyes closed, and she put her hand in mine and clasped it hard. 'I want you to remember this,' she said. 'Just close your eyes. This moment's gone, and it's never coming back, Gloria. . . . Now that one. Gone, too. Now that one. . . . And that one. It's all going too fast. And then it's all gone.' She opened her eyes and turned to me. 'Do you know what I'm saying?' she asked, and I said, 'Yes, ma'am,' though I wasn't really sure at all. My heart clanged like a garbage lid, I swear. Then she squeezed my hand even tighter, so hard I could see the ends of her fingers turning white from the pressure. I tried not to wince, but I could feel my eyes tearing up. 'Good, then,' she said. Suddenly she let go of my hand, stood up, and leaned over and kissed me on the forehead. She held that kiss for the longest time, and then she went back in the house without saying another word. I sat there, stunned, shaking. The wind was gone. And the color in the sky had faded, too. Just like that. I sat there until it got pitch-black, worrying about what she knew."

Gloria'd been staring out the window this whole time, but now she turned to Laura.

"A week later I was outta here. But after you all finally told me that she had left, I remembered that moment, and I've been wondering if that was when she first decided that she would go . . . when she would just haul off and abandon—" She broke off suddenly. "Ohhhhh, Laura, I'm so sorry."

Gloria leaned over and touched Laura's face. Tears were streaming down Laura's cheeks.

"Maybe I shouldn't have told you that. I'm sorry. It's not necessarily good to talk about it."

Laura tried to say something, but no words came out. Her eyes burned, and she put her face in the crook of her sister's neck and let the sobs come for a few minutes, until she could stifle them.

The baby fidgeted. Gloria wiped her own nose on the nursing diaper. Then she took the cloth and reached over and wiped Laura's eyes and nose as if she was a baby. Carroll burped again, and they both laughed.

"Enough of this," Gloria said, rising. "Let me go put him down, and then we'll play some gin rummy and maybe go out for lunch. I have some spending cash."

Laura got a dishcloth and finished wiping her cheeks. She remembered when her sister bought her the dress from Woolworth's just to lift her spirits. That Gloria, that sister, seemed back in the house.

That afternoon they strolled Gloria's kids around town, and everywhere they went, people—Sandra Sears, the Garrison sisters, Tim and Ned Stewart, the Cransburgh brothers—were calling out Gloria's name, coming over and talking to her, hugging her, pinching the baby's cheeks, rubbing Julie's head, shrieking idiotically with delight.

"Oh, my God! You look so great! How have you been?"

"My Lord, aren't these the cutest little children. That pilot of yours must be a prince."

"It's impossible to believe that this is Gloria Tate, all grown up. Who'da thought?"

It was like walking downtown with a celebrity. Laura liked it, and she held Carroll as Gloria chatted with her friends, her old teachers, the Cransburgh brothers—Jimmy holding her a fraction of a second too long, so that Laura wondered briefly if there had been something between them. Or was it simply benign lechery? Charnelle was full of secrets. Or maybe she was reading too much into things. Everywhere she looked, there seemed to be clandestine liaisons (she'd read that phrase in a bad romance novel called

Lovely Wednesdays) or secret lives. She knew that her mother's disappearance had been one of the biggest mysteries in Charnelle and that she and Gloria and her father and brothers would always be seen through that prism.

The day was hot and dry, well over ninety degrees, and even in their sundresses they felt the sweat bead over their arms and along their hairlines, between their breasts. Inside 4-D's they gulped down large glasses of lemonade.

"No drink is ever this deliciously cold in Europe," Gloria said, and they ordered a cheeseburger and french fries to split between them, because they were too hot to eat two meals, and then they licked away at some dripping ice cream cones. Once the lunch crowd thinned out, with all those people who kept recognizing her, Gloria nursed the baby again, a cloth diaper draped over her breast and his face, Billy Sidell sneaking some peeks every chance he got.

As they finished, in walked Mrs. Letig with Jack and Willie.

Laura spotted them first. She watched the woman, didn't say a word to Gloria, who was fiddling with the baby's shirt. She hoped Mrs. Letig would not see them. The woman was at the counter, just getting something to go, shooing her boys in behind her. She wore a thin cotton slip of a dress, pale lavender, simple but fashionable as usual. Her arms and the top of her chest were exposed; her skin was smooth and tan, her calves muscled. When she bent over to say something to Jack, there was that thickness in the middle, a couple of loose rolls, unbound by girdle. Mrs. Letig ran her hand over her stomach, pressing out the dress, self-conscious. Her red hair was pulled back wavily from her face and held by two silver fish barrettes (had John given her those?), and Laura thought this looked pretty—beautiful, even—her hair heavy and smooth. Lush. She wished she had not seen her. She wished Mrs. Letig's hair did not look so nice.

Laura said nothing. She hoped Gloria wouldn't notice Mrs. Letig or the boys—she'd baby-sat for them, too, once or twice. Laura slid over a couple of inches in the booth, closer to Julie, so that she was in the shadows, and then turned toward her niece and took a napkin to clean her face, the ice cream stained on her chin and cheeks—hoping not to be detected. *Please, please, please, just go away.*

"Is that Gloria Tate?"

Gloria looked up, but Laura hesitated a fraction of a second and then

turned toward Mrs. Letig, who had her hand over her eyes, peering theatri-
cally from the counter.

"Oh, my God, it is! I knew you were coming in, but I didn't think we'd
see you until the Fourth!"

The Fourth?

"Hello," Gloria said.

"You don't remember me, do you?"

"Mrs.——"

"Anne Letig. You baby-sat this urchin once or twice," she said, patting
Jack's head.

"Yes, of course I remember. Your husband works with my dad, doesn't
he?"

"Yep. Boys, come here. Jack, do you remember Gloria?"

"No," Jack said rudely.

He climbed into the booth next to Laura. She put her arm around him.
"Hello, Jack," she said and pointed to Gloria. "This is my sister."

"You have a sister?" the boy asked.

"I took care of you when you were a little kid," Gloria said.

"And this is my niece, Julie, and my nephew, Carroll."

Willie climbed over Jack, who punched him, and into Laura's lap and
hugged her.

"Willie!" Mrs. Letig said. "Get down."

Laura strained for a laugh. "It's okay," she said, but she wished they
would leave. She felt suddenly nauseous.

"They love Laura," Mrs. Letig said and then asked Gloria how she
was, how married life was treating her, told her that her children were beautiful, asked about the infamous pilot. What was his name? Jerome, that's
right. What is he now, a colonel? Ha, ha. How does the military treat you?
"I always secretly dreamed of marrying an officer, being able to travel all
over the world. I think an exotic life might suit me."

Gloria laughed. "It's not as great as it sounds."

"Well, you know what they say—the grass is always greener."

There was an odd, wistful pause, in which they all felt uncomfortable,
though it seemed to Laura for very different reasons.

"Well, I guess we'll see you on the Fourth," Mrs. Letig said.

"What's happening on the Fourth?" Gloria asked.

"We're all going to Palo Duro Canyon for the holiday. Didn't Zeke tell you?"

"No," Laura said, too sharply.

"Well, you were invited. I assumed you would be coming. We hope so. John's already bought firecrackers and Roman candles and lots of sparklers for the kids. The Cransburgh brothers will be there, too."

"We just saw Jimmy Cransburgh. He didn't say anything."

"Well, maybe he doesn't know you all were invited. I assumed Zeke had said yes. But maybe not. Well, you know what they say about the word 'assume.' Makes"—here she smiled conspiratorially, one eyebrow arched—"an *ass* out of *u* and *me*."

Gloria laughed. Willie was still in Laura's lap, hugging her and touching Julie's hair. Laura pulled his hand away.

"Maybe he forgot to tell us," Gloria said. "They went fishing."

"I know. John met them this morning."

"Really?" Laura asked, though she didn't mean to say it aloud.

"Oh, yes. He's taking them to his secret spot."

Really, Laura thought.

Mrs. Letig noticed Willie pestering Julie. She pulled him out of the booth.

"I better be off. Hope we'll see you tomorrow. You know, you Tate girls are regular knockouts, I swear. Good genes."

Another pocket of silence as the specter of their mother appeared.

"Well, come on, boys. Time to go. Bye now."

After Mrs. Letig left, Gloria said, "I guess we have plans for the holiday. Hey, what's wrong?" she asked, reaching out her hand toward Laura. "Are you okay?"

Laura didn't say a word, just stared down into her plate, the last of her ice cream melting into a chocolate puddle.

20

✳

Fourth of July

They left early the next morning to drive the eighty or so miles to Palo Duro Canyon. They took the truck and the Ford, which Manny was buying from their father, paying him off in monthly installments of ten dollars. They had loaded up the vehicles just after daybreak: Tupperware bowls of coleslaw, baked beans with ham hocks, potato salad, corn on the cob; heaping plates of chicken that Gloria and Laura had fried and cooled in the refrigerator; three full sides of pork ribs to barbecue; jugs of tea and lemonade, a huge block of crushed ice, and a case of Buck's Beer their father would bury, bottle by bottle, in the cool mud of the stream, so that only the brown necks and gold-starred metal caps sprouted above the waterline.

Jerome, Gloria, Julie, and Carroll rode with Manny and Joannie in the Ford. Laura had to ride with her father, Gene, and Rich in the truck, sitting in the bed of the truck with her younger brothers to keep stuff from sloshing out or toppling over.

They met the others at the Armory at seven. The Cransburgh brothers and the Letigs each had a trunkful of fireworks. John's hair was wet, so he must have just gotten out of the shower, and he wore what looked like a brand-new white T-shirt with the sleeves rolled up over his biceps. Mrs. Letig and her boys were in the car, and they waved and smiled at Laura. She tried not to stare at John, but since he was talking to her father, it seemed okay. She kept hoping he'd look her way. Finally he walked over to the truck bed and surveyed the Tupperware bowls and jugs and big metal thermoses.

"You ready for fireworks?" he asked, flashing his toothy grin. She felt irritated. There was a condescending lilt in his voice, the way he had included her in the same sentence with Gene and Rich, as if they mattered equally to him. She knew he had to do that. He was being careful, but still it annoyed her, and when he walked back to his car and got in, she willed herself to look down. This was going to be a long day, she could tell. Her father got into the truck, started the engine, backed out, and Gene and Laura both reached out to steady everything.

"Careful!" she shouted at her father. He put his hand up, nodded his head.

They caravanned down the highway, into Amarillo, where her father stopped to pick up Aunt Velma, but she was not feeling well and decided to stay home. Gloria and her family went in and said hello to her for a few minutes, promised to visit later in the week. And then they drove on to the small town of Canyon, where the teachers college was, the land flat, flat, flat as flat could be, a hot, treeless plain of green-and-tan earth, and above them a blue sky marbled with white streaks—a stark, minimal beauty, the way the horizon stretched endlessly in every direction. And then suddenly (it always shocked her), there was the great hole of Palo Duro Canyon, starting as a small crack, then widening quickly into the gaping crevice. She'd never seen the Grand Canyon, of course, which was the only canyon in the United States bigger than this one. She knew it was much larger and deeper than Palo Duro, but it was difficult for her to imagine anything as spectacular or as large as this hole, or that it had been cut by water and time.

In science last year, she'd learned about the different layers of rock and sediment, had watched as her teacher had pointed out each geologic zone—this-zoic and that-zoic—and for a while the names had stuck with her, but now they had disappeared from her mind, which was a shame. She would have liked to mention them, to show off, to have something to contribute, but then again it didn't matter much, not today. No one really cared about that stuff. They just liked to be down on the floor of the canyon, splashing in the creek, climbing the smaller rock formations, the more ambitious clambering up to the rim. She liked searching out the less well known spots—a curve of beautiful smooth shale that created an overhang above the creek bed, the big cave that you had to crawl around back to get into, and then smaller, secret caves that Manny and Gloria and she knew well and pretended they had discovered.

There would be lots of snacking on chips and cookies and brownies and candy—enough to sicken you if you didn't watch out—and drinking lemonade and tea, while her father, Manny, and the men, and maybe even Mrs. Letig and Gloria and Joannie, drank the beer. Swimming in the cool stream (she wore her bathing suit under her shirt and shorts), naps beneath the trees, imagining what it was like to be here, seventy, eighty, a hundred years ago, the Comanche hiding in the rocks and caves, fighting their bloody battles with the other Plains Indians and then with the Texas Rangers, until one by one the Indians were all moved out or eradicated. That was the word her history teacher, Mr. Nelson, had used. He hated what had been done to the Indians; he had all his classes read Chief Seattle's surrender and showed them photographs of great fields of skinned buffalo, their pelts taken, their bodies left to rot in the sun, though these things weren't on the Texas Board of Education's list of authorized material.

They arrived early enough to stake out the best spot, with lots of picnic tables by the creek bed and near the big cave and Sad Monkey, a large formation that supposedly looked like a chimpanzee, though no matter how many times she stared at it, she could never quite see the resemblance.

"You think Lyndon will catch Kennedy for the nomination, Zeeke?" Jimmy asked as he lathered up a cob of corn with some butter. "Cronkite says he'll formally announce his candidacy tomorrow."

"I hope, but it doesn't look like he can catch him. Seems a shame that he's waited until a week before the convention to officially throw his hat in the ring."

Mr. Tate was standing by the picnic table, drinking a bottle of Buck's Beer that he'd just pulled from the cool mud. John was playing horseshoes within earshot with Gene, Rich, Jack, and Willie. Manny and Joannie took Julie down by the water. Mrs. Letig, the Cransburgh brothers, Gloria,

Laura, and Jerome stood and sat around the picnic table with Mr. Tate. The baby was nearby, asleep on a blanket under the shade of a cottonwood tree.

"It would be quite a ticket if they were both on it," Bob said. He was brushing barbecue sauce on the ribs.

"It would give old Dick Nixon a run for his money," Jimmy said. "That's for sure."

Mrs. Letig leaned over the table and grabbed a leg of chicken. "There's no way Johnson would be on the same ticket with Kennedy," she offered. "At least not as vice president."

"That's what they all say," Mr. Tate scoffed. "Second fiddle ain't all that bad."

Bob said, "But he's got much more clout as Majority Leader."

"Trust me. Vice prez is tempting enough, even if it's a shitty job. But don't listen to me. Ask Gloria. She's the political expert here. How's Kennedy's tan, sweetheart?"

Gloria, wearing jeans and her bathing suit top, which barely seemed to contain her, said, "Better than Lyndon's, that's for damn sure."

"I don't know," he said. "Johnson's got a good tan."

"But it doesn't look as good on a rhino," Gloria said. They all laughed.

"You're talking about our senator, honey."

"I didn't think we were talking politics, Daddy. I thought we were talking about sexual charisma."

Jimmy laughed so hard that he nearly choked on his corncob. He leaned over to Jerome. Slapping him on his back, he said, "You let her get away with that, Jerry?"

"Jerome."

"You let her get away with that?"

"As long as she knows who butters her bread."

"You hear that, Zeeke? Your son-in-law's talking about buttering your daughter's bread."

"She's his wife. He can butter whatever he wants."

"Oh, my Lord!" crooned Mrs. Letig, mocking. "When did you become such a libertine, Zeeke?"

"What the hell is that?"

"It's a liberal that likes his bread buttered," she said.

Jimmy laughed again and began to sputter corn kernels over the table, and Mrs. Letig slapped *his* back a couple of times to unclog him.

"You leave Dad alone," Gloria said. "He'll come around to Kennedy soon enough."

"Sounds like you got a crush on that Massachusetts boy," said Bob.

"Hell, she just says that," Jerome said. "She'll come around to Nixon in the end."

"The *hell* I will!"

Her father turned to Jerome, his face a stone. Everybody was suddenly quiet. "Don't tell me that *you're* voting for Nixon."

Jerome took a swig from his beer and leaned back against the table. "I don't trust Kennedy."

"He served in the military."

"The navy," Jerome said, smiling. "That's not the same thing."

Everybody laughed nervously. Bob said, "Nixon was a navy man, too, you know."

"And Kennedy was a hero," Mr. Tate said, his voice rising. "A hell of a lot more of a hero than Nixon ever was."

"But Nixon knows the world better than Kennedy or Johnson ever will."

"Were you born in Texas, boy?" Bob asked, pointing the long barbecue fork at him.

"Wichita Falls."

Jimmy laughed. "I thought that counted, but maybe not."

"Are you *really* voting for Nixon?" Mr. Tate asked, leaning down.

"I'm voting for Ike's vice president."

"Oh, leave him alone, Dad," Gloria said, putting her arms around Jerome's neck. "They're all voting for Nixon over there. Most of them served under Eisenhower in the war. Or their fathers did."

"We're not talking Ike. Ike just flipped a coin to figure out whether he was going to be a Democrat or Republican. But *Nixon*! Nixon's a mean little bastard. We're talking about the next president of the United States, you know."

"Sorry, Mr. Tate," Jerome said. "She warned me not to talk politics with you. Said you were a dyed-in-the-wool New Dealer."

"Damn straight!"

"It's okay, Daddy," Gloria said, putting her hands over Jerome's ears. "I'm still a true believer."

"Hell, I was pissed off when you eloped. If I'da known he was a Republican, I would've chased you all the way to Europe."

Everybody laughed again.

"Enough politics!" Mrs. Letig said. "Let's go back to talking about Kennedy's tan." She winked at Gloria and Laura. "I'm with you, Zeeke, but no roughing up the father of your grandchildren today."

"Jesus, it's Independence Day. If you can't fight about politics on the Fourth, when can you fight about it?"

"Well, you do whatever you want," Mrs. Letig said. "I'm hot, and I'm going to wade in that water, close my eyes, and think of the Massachusetts senator playing football."

"You hear that, John?" Jimmy shouted.

"She knows who butters her bread," John called, and everybody at the table cackled. Laura put her head down and clenched her teeth. The baby woke, and she used that as an excuse to rise. She picked him up, but he was fussy, so she handed him to Gloria, who quickly calmed him down.

"*Nixon*, for Christ's sake!"

Mr. Tate was hot now. Despite all the joking, Laura could see him starting to seethe. He hated Nixon, would yell at the screen whenever he came on: "You idiot! Idiot!" He was sure that Nixon would get creamed in the election, especially if Lyndon Johnson was running against him. Even Ike had disowned Nixon, barely kept him on the ticket in 1956. When Ike was asked what Nixon had done as vice president, Ike had said, right there on national television, "If you give me a week, maybe I could think of something." Her father had shouted in triumph that day, kept repeating Ike's words to whoever would listen. But now that it looked like "the Catholic rich boy and his debutante wife" (her father's words) would be nominated and alienate the Protestant and the southern votes, her father was edgier, more easily ignited. She felt an undercurrent of fear, watching him and Jerome square off. Hadn't Gloria warned Jerome better? Had she forgotten how riled up their father could get about politics? She was around when Adlai Stevenson had been beaten in '56; surely she remembered how angry and depressed he was then.

"Did you see him the other day?" her father said. "Nixon spent thirty minutes talking about all the places he'd gone and people he'd seen, as if that grocery list was some kind of badge of honor."

"It *does* count for something," Jerome said. "He's been to fifty-six countries, and he did whip Khrushchev in the kitchen debate."

"Okay," Gloria said, "that *is* enough. I'm going swimming. You two can stay here and fight all you want." She reached up and kissed her father on the cheek and handed him Carroll. "While you're sputtering at each other, why don't you smash this banana up and feed him, Grandpa."

And just like that, the tension was defused. Bob pulled a football out from under the table and threw it to Jerome. Laura watched her father sitting there, no one to argue with, his grandson in his arms. Her father frowned at his lost audience. He seemed comical and sad, but then he raised the baby in his arms and Carroll laughed, a string of spittle landing on her father's nose. He shook his head in surprise and then turned to Laura, and she wondered what he would do.

"Look what I get for my troubles!" he cackled loudly, from his belly.

She smiled, too, happy all of a sudden.

The flies swarmed around the picnic tables. Laura swished the air with her hands while she prepared her plate: a chicken leg, a scoop of potato salad, a cob of corn, and some cherry cobbler that Mrs. Letig had made and which Laura, despite herself, had to admit was delicious. She had skipped breakfast, so she was starving, and she ate fast, guzzling down two tall glasses of sweet tea, finishing off another chicken leg and a second helping of potato salad (which she had made herself last night—extra spicy with three dashes of cayenne), before toothpicking the corn kernels from her teeth. Mrs. Letig stood nearby, nibbling at her food—watching her weight, no doubt—and Laura felt secretly pleased that she, by contrast, could eat so much and remain skinny. *Good genes.* After she ate, she stripped off her shirt and shorts in front of Mrs. Letig and waded into the creek with Gene, Rich, and the Letig boys.

It had rained several times over the past two weeks, so the cool water was almost to her waist in some places. They had to keep the younger kids close to the edges, where they made mud pies and waded in only as high as their bellies.

Mrs. Letig followed her to the water, still in her dress, so Laura could see more of her body than she'd ever seen before. Her thighs were pale and varicose-veined above her knees, a little like Aunt Velma's, and Laura felt a secret sense of triumph. She took joy in splashing and parading in the creek in her new blue two-piece, knowing that her legs were thin and hard and tan and that her figure, though not perfect, not as voluptuous as those of the starlets she'd seen in the magazines and on the big screen, was nice-enough-looking, better-looking than Mrs. Letig's. John had told her many times that he thought she was gorgeous, whispered compliments while they made love. She secretly watched to see if John was looking at her and his wife. She hoped he was. She knew she was parading around for his sake. She wanted him to compare. It was not nice, but she nevertheless delighted in her cruelty.

Manny and Joannie joined them in the water. Joannie had not brought her bathing suit, only shorts and a T-shirt, but Manny had stripped off his clothes—he wore his swim trunks underneath—and carried her into the creek, despite her thrashing protests.

Joannie would be a senior, along with Manny, and though the two had been dating since Christmas, she and Laura seldom talked. Laura liked her well enough. They would see each other in the halls every once in a while, nod and smile, and Laura had once hung out at 4-D's with Marlene, Debbie, Joannie, and Marlene's older sister, but Laura didn't talk to her much then either. Joannie's parents lived on the west side of town, and her uncle was Glenn Thomason—the same Glenn Thomason who'd caught Manny shoplifting years ago and who owned the filling station where Manny now worked. The girl was shy and sweet-natured, and she didn't talk to *anyone* very much, and when she did speak, it was in a low, whispery voice, like she was embarrassed to be heard. She was pretty, though Laura thought her tight, dark curls frumpy. Laura had decided that Manny could have done worse for a girlfriend. It somehow redeemed him that he had chosen such a sweet, shy girl—or that *she* had chosen *him*.

"Manny Tate, don't you dare!" It was the loudest sound Laura had ever heard from her.

But once he dropped her in the water, Joannie seemed happy enough, and they splashed each other. Manny was strong, muscular, with some baby fat still and hair scattered in uneven patches over his chest and belly and a wispy black mustache that Laura's father sarcastically called "belligerent." Laura thought of how he always eyed himself when he passed a mirror, spending up to half an hour in the bathroom, combing his duck's ass, rolling up the sleeves of his shirt, sticking out his chest. Yes, Laura was vain about her body, but it was nothing, she thought, compared to her brother's vanity.

Gloria and Jerome waded into the water, too, and then Manny yelled,

"Chicken fight!" and he dove between Joannie's legs and lifted her up on his shoulders. She shrieked in delight. Jerome did the same with Gloria, who was up for any sort of competition. They attacked each other, splashing and wrestling, while everyone looked on, cheering.

Gloria and Jerome had an unfair advantage because Joannie wore a T-shirt and it was easy to grab it and pull her down, which Gloria did, yelling to her husband, "Run, run, run!" as everybody shouted, Joannie toppling backward into the water, taking Manny with her. Spontaneous applause broke out.

"The champions!" Gloria shouted, raising her clenched fists high in the air.

"Yeah, baby!" Jerome slapped her thighs, which were clamped against his cheeks.

"Who's next?" Gloria challenged. "Who dares?"

"How about you, little sister?" Jerome called. "Get yourself a partner."

"No," Laura called, though she loved to chicken-fight.

There was a short pause, and then John stepped to the edge of the water, pulling his shirt over his head.

"We'll take you on," he said.

"All right!" Jerome shouted. He bent down in the water, gulped some creek water, and spewed it as if he were a fountain.

Gloria yodeled: her Swiss Miss.

John still wore his jeans. He took his wallet, keys, comb, and handkerchief out of his pocket and set them on the blanket near Carroll, slipped off his boots and socks, and waded into the water toward Laura. The word "dangerous" popped into her head, but she shook it off.

"You ready?" he said.

"Yeah."

He held his breath, disappeared underwater, slipped his head between her thighs, and lifted her up. She pinned her feet behind his back, and he hooked his bare arms tightly over her thighs, just above her knees. Laura stole a secret glance at Mrs. Letig, who was smiling benignly.

"Ready?" Gloria asked.

"Ready!" John said.

"How about you, Laura?"

"Yeah."

Manny counted quickly: "One, two, three!"

They circled each other in the water. John made a dash, and Laura reached out and grabbed the back of Gloria's bathing suit and pulled as John churned through the water, but just as Gloria was about to fall, Laura lost hold of her, and Gloria righted herself.

"Cheater!" Gloria shouted.

"Get her, Laura!" her father called out. "Make her pay for marrying a Republican!"

They laughed, even Jerome. "So the election is on the line," Jerome called. "What are you, John?"

"My mother once kissed Lyndon Johnson," he said.

"Did you hear that, Dad?" Gloria shouted. "Letig's mother and Lyndon Johnson were lovers."

"Is that true?" her father called.

"Did she say anything about his ears?" Gloria asked.

"You better watch what you say about my momma, girl," John drawled.

Jerome and John circled each other again, Gloria and Laura both crouched low, their arms outstretched, their fingers wiggling, ready to grab. Jerome started one way, and John shifted his weight, but then Jerome turned quickly back the other way and was behind and then suddenly in front of John and Laura. She felt off balance. Gloria grabbed her arm, and Jerome started running. Gloria didn't have that strong a grasp, nothing that should have unseated Laura, but she could feel John relaxing his hold on her legs, and she lost her balance. Then she was sliding, sliding. Gloria pulled on Laura's hand, and she toppled off the side of John's shoulders, face-first into the water, John falling with her.

Before she surfaced, Laura felt his hand slipping between her thighs, his fingers resting for a couple of seconds on her bikini bottom. Panicked, Laura knocked his hand away. As they both rose sputtering from the water, to the shouts of Jerome and Gloria doing a victory lap around them and the smiles of everybody else looking on, including Mrs. Letig, Laura knew that John had done it on purpose, had let her fall so that he could steal this moment under the water. She looked at him in surprise, but he was shaking his head, wiping water from his face, a sly grin beneath his dripping mustache.

"Wanna rematch?" John called.

"You bet!" Gloria said.

Laura was already moving toward dry land, however, against their protests. "I've had enough," she said. She sat on the grass underneath the big oak tree. Mrs. Letig brought her a towel. "Thanks," she said.

"You almost beat them."

John approached, his hair and mustache and jeans still dripping, the water turning the blond hairs on his chest dark brown. His wife threw him a towel.

"She did good," Mrs. Letig said. "You're the one that blew it, buster."

"Just lost hold," he said, his eyebrows arched in a what-can-you-say expression. "We'll get 'em next time."

Laura stared at him for a second and then dropped her head between her knees so that her hair dangled over her eyes. She draped the towel over her head. She didn't think she could bear to look at either of them. The blood pumped thickly through her neck and temples. She could hear her breath as it whistled in and out of her nose.

Her father and Gene, Gloria and Jerome, Manny and Joannie, and John and Mrs. Letig were going for a late-afternoon hike while the Cransburgh brothers prepared the fireworks. Laura was supposed to stay behind, which made her angry, even at Gloria, the way they always assumed she would just watch after the kids, like it was her duty. But Mrs. Letig decided at the last minute that she didn't want to go.

"Come on, Anne," Laura's father said. "It'll be fun."

"I just don't feel like hiking right now."

"Well, then, you just stay here with the kids and Laura can come," John said, annoyed.

"Well, that'll be fine," she said. "I'd rather stay here with the baby anyway. If that's okay with you, Gloria."

"You bet," Gloria said. Mrs. Letig took Carroll, who was napping in Gloria's arms. "The diaper bag's under the table. He probably won't wake for another hour, but just in case, there's a bottle in the bag. Are you sure you don't mind?"

"Are you kidding? It's my pleasure. It's been too long since I've held a baby. You go on. You, too, Laura. I'll keep an eye on the little ones."

By the time Laura turned around, John and her father had already started out, ahead of everyone else. They all walked along the trails, down by the creek and the road. And then, as they turned up the trail toward the big cave, Manny and Joannie slipped off under some trees, and John hung back as the others, chattering, disappeared around a bend. Laura motioned for John to follow her, because she wanted to show him a secret cave. The two of them climbed over the back of the ridge, crouched down for about ten feet, crawled for ten feet more, and then wound up in a large cavern with a small, lighted hole at the other end, where you could see Sad Monkey rock. John crawled in behind her, and then when he caught up to her, he pulled his shirt up so she could see his back—a long red scrape, but no blood. She kissed it. They talked quietly.

"You dropped me on purpose, didn't you?" she asked.

"Nah."

"You did."

"It was exciting, wasn't it?"

"Sort of," she said.

"What do you mean, 'sort of'? It damn sure was. Besides, I was going crazy with you on my shoulders. Did you want me to walk out of the water with my pants bulging?"

"Nope." She giggled.

"Okay, then." He dropped his shirt and winced.

"Does it hurt?"

"I know what will make it feel better."

"Be quiet," she said, slapping him lightly on the arm. "We can't do anything here."

"Sure we can. It's a cave, for Christ's sake. No one can even get in here."

"Manny and Gloria know where this is."

"Just for a minute. It'll be okay."

He leaned against her. His jeans were still wet. They felt cold against her legs. He kissed her, and she let him, and then he tried to slip his tongue into her mouth, but she wouldn't let him, teasing him. He began tickling her.

"Quit it!" she whispered. "We're being too loud."

She wriggled free of him and started crawling back toward the opening where they had come in. He grabbed her foot.

"Let go," she whispered again. She felt his teeth on the back of her ankle. "Stop! I mean it. We gotta go."

"Okay, I'll follow you," he said and reached up and slid his hand inside the bottom of her shorts.

She slapped his hand away. "No, you wait here for a minute. Then you can come."

"I'm about to come already."

"Hush!" she said, laughing.

She crawled through the entry, crouching down lower at one point, aware of the top of the cave that might scratch, and then she got to her feet. Hunched over, she walked out, following the light. She peered back down the mouth of the cave. She heard John, but she couldn't see him yet.

"Are you okay?" she asked.

"Yeah."

"I'm going on," she said.

"Wait for me."

"No," she said. "You wait here for a few minutes."

"You're a tease."

She turned, brushed the dirt off her hands, and then climbed the rock to the top of the ridge, looking only at the handholds in front of her. At the top, right there on the other side, she was shocked to find Gloria.

"Hey!" Laura practically shouted.

"There you are," Gloria said. "I've been looking all over for you. I thought maybe you snuck off to our cave. Is that where you were?"

"Yeah."

"Let's go back."

"It's blocked up," she said. "You can't go all the way in. Let's go to the big one."

Laura hurried past her. She started a miniature rockslide and slid about twenty feet down the hill. She wasn't hurt. She laughed loudly and nervously.

"Are you okay?" Gloria called down to her.

"Yeah, I'm fine," she said and slapped the dirt from her hands. "Come on!"

Gloria climbed more carefully down an alternate path, and when she was almost to the bottom, Laura started off again. She wanted to get her sister away from there as fast as she could. John stood at the top of the ridge. He raised his hand. He obviously didn't see Gloria yet.

"Hey!" he called. "Wait for me."

She didn't answer. She just turned and started down the hill, half running. It was dangerous. If she fell, she might tumble a hundred feet.

"Hey, Laura!" Gloria called. "Be careful. Not so fast. We're down here, John."

"I'm going on," Laura called. She wasn't sure if Gloria could hear her or not. Jumping recklessly down the rock face, she was gone. She didn't look back. At the trailhead, she sprinted the rest of the way, her long hair flying behind her.

"Aren't *you* in a hurry?" Mrs. Letig said when she arrived at the picnic tables, gasping for air, her hands on her knees. She didn't have the breath to answer, which was just as well, because Mrs. Letig was the last person she wanted to talk to. "Here, let me get you some lemonade."

She handed Laura a filled cup. Carroll was still asleep in her arms.

"Thanks," Laura managed, feeling ashamed, not meeting the woman's eyes.

"What's the matter?"

"Nothing," she said. "I just felt like running."

About fifteen minutes later, Gloria and John showed up, with Gene, her father, Jerome, Manny, and Joannie behind them. Laura lay on the ground, underneath the cottonwood, watching them as they approached, trying to guess what Gloria and John were saying. They laughed, Gloria's head thrown back in one of her infectious guffaws. He must have told her a joke. Laura felt relieved. She got up and headed out past the creek, where Rich and the Letig boys and Julie were playing catch with a beach ball next to Jimmy, and then down the trail that led to the big cave.

"Where you going?" Mrs. Letig called.

"I'll be back soon."

Her sister's and John's voices echoed behind her, but she ignored them.

She went down the trail a little ways and sat on a rock, listening to the party. She watched the sun fall beyond the rim of the canyon, and she tried to clear her mind, to not think at all.

Forty-five minutes later, when she returned, it was dark. Everybody was eating big slices of watermelon. The fireworks had already begun. Gloria, of course, said nothing, but Laura could see her looking around at John and Mrs. Letig, and at her father and Manny, too. Gloria was trying to figure out the situation, who knew what and how much, and Laura knew that her sister was a good detective, that she could intuit things about people that others couldn't, and it scared Laura, because no one was supposed to know, and she wasn't sure if Gloria could be trusted anymore—if by virtue of being a parent now, and a wife, a responsible adult in the world, she would forget what it was like to have a secret life, to remember the value of it.

Gloria also had a poker face. She didn't give away what she knew. She laughed and told jokes and did her impressions. The firecrackers popped. The sparklers streaked the night with silver and red striations. The Roman candles burst green and red and blue and gold over their heads, and the air smelled acrid from the smoke. Bob Cransburgh had to stamp out some sparks that flared by the picnic tables.

During the festivities, Laura tried to convince herself that her sister hadn't put two and two together. She laughed and pretended not to be bothered when John wrapped his arms around his wife. Mrs. Letig turned her face to her husband and kissed him for a long time, passionately, and it appeared that John was returning the favor. A firecracker popped loudly. Laura felt like that firecracker.

"Look at the lovebirds." Her father whistled.

Gloria caught her eye, but Laura turned away quickly, smiled like it didn't bother her. Maybe Gloria would see all that and not be sure of what she'd seen earlier. But then, as they were packing the trucks and cars, Gloria caught Laura alone by the picnic tables for a moment, and in the dark, with the creek gurgling beside them, she whispered, "You and me are going to have a long talk tomorrow, girl."

Their father called out from his truck, "Okay, ladies, quit your lolly-gagging. It's time to hit the road."

21

✳

Careful

The next morning, after breakfast, Gloria told everybody that she and Laura were going out. She ordered Jerome to watch the kids, and when he protested, she gave him a look that made everybody tense and silent, and then Manny laughed, offered to help, and then their father laughed and called Gloria "the admiral," and then Jerome smiled, too, but he wasn't happy about it, everybody could tell. Gloria and Laura walked in thoughtful silence to the downtown park, both preparing their arguments.

They sat on the park bench, in the shade of the trees, watching the cars circle the square, kids riding their bikes, playing catch, the county workers returning to the courthouse from their morning breaks.

"He's more than twice your age," Gloria began.

"Jerome's older than you."

"It's not the same. I was older."

"Not much."

"And he wasn't married. With kids. This isn't good, Laura. No matter how you feel about him, it's hard for me to believe that he cares the same about you. Or that he even *can* care the same about you. It doesn't matter how nice and sweet he seems—deep down he's a bastard."

She practically spit the word. Laura was taken aback, not quite prepared for Gloria's hostility. "That's not true!" she protested.

Gloria was quiet for a minute. Then she asked, "How do you do it?"

Laura looked at her strangely. "*Do* it?"

"I mean, how do you meet? Where do you go? Does anyone know? How do you keep it a secret?"

It all spilled out, everything, like she'd just been waiting for someone to ask. Laura told her about their schedule, how she met him before noon behind the abandoned warehouse, and about his uncle's barn, the way he set it up, and how she hid in the truck, scrunched down on the floorboard.

"We're very safe," she said.

And she told about the lies, too, for there had been so many lies, and not to tell her sister seemed wrong. Besides, if anyone knew about lying to her family, it would be Gloria. She'd done plenty of it herself. Her marriage was built on it, Laura thought.

Gloria shook her head. Laura couldn't tell if she was still angry or simply amazed. "I'm sorry," Gloria said. "Go on."

Laura told her about the difficulty of being together, how she sometimes wished they could be out in the open, but of course she knew that could never happen, and she said that was okay with her. And she told her sister about how they met, at the New Year's party, and how it had all started, and about the poker night and spring break and later at Lake Meredith, and in the telling it sounded, even to her, coarse and ugly, slightly sinister. The events themselves couldn't reach what was underneath the events, the other life that lay like bright metal at the bottom of a stream. She could tell, from the look on Gloria's face—her eyes squinted shut, her mouth pursed, a dismissive, judgmental look that reminded Laura of her mother—that she had not told it right, and she wondered if that was the way it always was. When you try to explain yourself and your actions—something that seems inevitable and important and *yours*—then it always comes out a little seedy, as if you were confessing to a crime.

"*Why* do you do it?" Gloria asked.

"I don't understand what you mean."

"Why are you with him? There are plenty of boys your own age. Why would you want to share him with someone else?"

Laura turned toward the street, shaking her head. This was a mistake, trying to make her sister understand.

"You know this can't end well," Gloria continued stridently. "The risks are enormous. Has he made any promises to you?"

"What do you mean?"

"Is he going to leave his wife?"

"I don't know. We don't talk about her much."

"No, I don't imagine you do. Where do you think this is going, then?"

"I don't know."

"How's it going to end?"

"I don't *know!*"

"Oh, Laura," Gloria said, exasperated. "You have to think about these things. I know it seems so exciting now. And you think he loves you, and when you're with him, there's nothing else that matters. But there *are* other people." She looked Laura straight in the eye. "There *are* consequences."

"Don't preach to me."

"This scares me. You scare me."

Laura turned to her sister, angry now. "Are you sorry you ran off with Jerome?"

"Of course not. It's not the same."

"Yes it is, when you think about it! If someone had told you not to do it, would you have listened?"

"No. But it was totally different."

"I just want to enjoy it for what it is. Why does it have to *go* someplace? It's . . . it's—"

"I know."

"No, you don't! It's *different*. I *feel* different. I *am* different. When it's just me and him, it's . . . well, no one will ever know what that's like."

"I hate to break this to you," Gloria said snidely, "but the whole world knows that secret."

"I'm not talking about *that*. You're as bad as Manny!"

She'd had it. She jumped up from the bench and plopped down angrily under a tree, with her legs tucked to her chest, her forehead against her kneecaps.

After a few minutes, Gloria came over, crouched down by her. "I'm sorry," she said quietly.

Laura tried to collect her thoughts. She lifted her head and stared at her sister, whose eyes seemed so much like their mother's. "It's just that . . . just that when we're together, it's not only that no one else is there, but it's that a different— I don't know how to say this."

"Go on."

"It's that a more real me is there. And the rest of what I do doesn't matter. It's not important."

"But it *does* matter," Gloria said, leaning toward her. "Don't you see? It does. There are other people involved."

"That doesn't really matter."

"How can you say that? Of course it matters. Don't you think what you and he are doing has an effect on other people?"

"Not if they don't know."

"But don't they?" Gloria asked.

Laura was puzzled. "What do you mean?"

"Don't you think they know . . . on some level?"

"Not if we don't tell."

"But it breaks everything. If Jerome was having an affair, then it would break things between us, don't you see?"

"What if you didn't know?"

"I would find out sooner or later."

"But if you *didn't,* and he kept on being a good husband to you and loving you? Couldn't he love you and someone else at the same time? Wouldn't that be okay, if you didn't know?"

Gloria shook her head and then sighed as if Laura was a stubborn child unwilling to listen to the obvious. "Our lives would be a huge lie," she said.

"No, that's not true," Laura said more insistently. "I don't believe that. It's the not-knowing. Like when Momma left. We didn't tell you for a long time. And during that time, you were happy. And only when we told you did you become sad."

Gloria stared cautiously at Laura for a minute, mulled over what she would say next. Laura had the feeling that bringing their mother into this conversation was not right, but she didn't care anymore.

"You eventually had to tell me," Gloria said. "I was going to find out at some point."

"What if we had *never* told you? What if you stayed overseas the whole time and never returned and never knew she was gone? Or if we said she just died, a painless death. Then you would have been happier, right?"

Gloria, startled at this line of argument, shook her head vigorously. "No!"

"But you would!" Laura was shouting now. "I *know* you would. I know *I* would."

"Calm down," Gloria said. Two boys playing catch with a baseball had stopped and were staring at them. When they saw Gloria and Laura looking at them, they nodded to each other and, laughing derisively, walked to the other side of the fountain to continue their game.

"The point is," Gloria said, straining for evenness in her voice, "the point is . . . that I would find out, and the later I found out, the more it would seem like . . . like I was being cheated out of something that's mine to know. I had a right to know that. Even if it made me unhappy. It wasn't your right or Dad's right or anybody's right to keep it from me."

"This is different."

"How?"

"I don't know! It just is. I *know* it is!"

"Come here," Gloria said and reached out for her.

Laura pushed her hand away. "You don't see. You think I'm silly or naïve. I can tell by the way you look at me. You see me as this little girl who's getting taken advantage of by this married man. But I'm *not* being taken advantage of. That's just not true. I *want* to be there. I want it as much as he does. I'm not talking about. . . . It's the rest of it. And nobody sees it as real. But it is. It's the best thing. And if his wife and Dad don't know, then it . . . won't affect them. It won't! I know it won't!"

Gloria clasped Laura's hands, pulled them up to her lips, and kissed them. "It will be different later," Gloria said.

Laura still felt that her sister was patronizing her. "Is it different for you?" She could hear the bitterness in her own voice, could hear her desire to hurt her sister. She regretted it.

Gloria looked down at the grass for a minute and then lifted her head and stared directly at Laura. "Yes . . . yes, it is different."

"Does it have to be?"

"I don't know. I guess I've never thought about that. Come here. I want to hold you."

"No," Laura said, still angry.

"Please, come here. Who knows? Maybe you're right about it all. I forget. I still see you as this little girl I need to worry about. But maybe you're right . . . about what's real and what's not. Why don't you tell me what else you want from the world, what else besides—"

"You're just saying that now because I'm upset. Or you think I'm too young to know any better. I'm not. I know more than you think."

"But I still worry about you. Am I allowed to do that? Is that okay with you?"

Laura didn't answer.

"You are my little sister." Gloria suddenly frowned. "Aren't you?"

"It's not funny."

"Yeah, I know. You're right. It's not funny. I'm sorry." Gloria wrapped her arms around Laura, held her for a minute. "Do me one favor, though. Will you?"

"What?"

"Be careful."

"We are careful."

"You understand what I'm talking about, right?"

"Yes. We are."

"That, too. But I mean that you need to watch out for yourself. It may not always feel like this. And when it ends—"

"It's *not* going to end."

"Okay, *if* it ends, it would be better to end it quietly, without anybody getting hurt. So be careful."

"We are."

"And don't tell anyone else," she said. "Don't tell Manny or any of your friends. God knows, don't tell Dad. Who knows what he'd do?"

"I won't."

"If you need to talk to someone, write me. Or if you have to, if there's an emergency, call me. I'll give you a number where you can reach me at the base, and I'll show you how to call and charge it to me."

"You won't tell Jerome, will you?"

"No, I won't."

"Thank you."

Gloria patted Laura's head playfully, trying to lighten the mood. "And I thought you were still a kid. I'm going to have to really start worrying about you now. You know that, don't you?" Gloria put her finger under Laura's chin, lifted her face, and said more seriously, "Please watch out for yourself. Promise me you'll do that."

Laura nodded. She thought she might cry if she tried to speak. When Gloria touched her face, Laura suddenly recognized the gesture as one of their mother's, how she would gently but firmly assure a child's focus. Laura wondered if she would tell her mother if she were here. Would her mother understand what she was going through? Would she listen without judging? Would her reaction be the same as Gloria's? She looked into Gloria's eyes and realized that she could see a glimpse, just a glimpse, of her mother there.

22

✳

Idyll

*I*n mid-August, Mrs. Letig decided to take the boys to visit her sister in Dallas for a week, and John and Laura planned to spend one or two evenings together and, if they were lucky, maybe a whole night. After the Lake Meredith incident, Laura had been nervous about the lies, particularly those involving imaginary others. She had grown weary of sneaking around, and their usual meeting place, the barn, was hot and dusty in the summer. So although she looked forward to the time alone with him, the logistics loomed tiringly before her.

But then her father announced that Gilbert O'Donnell had just caught a twenty-pound bass and a twenty-three-pound catfish on the Canadian River. Her father had been so inspired that he marched into his boss's office and demanded a week off—shocking because he'd not willingly taken any days off since his wife had left. Then he told the family that they needed to get their things together because they were leaving tomorrow.

"I don't want to go!" Laura said, panicked.

"Fine," her father said. "Make other arrangements."

She was shocked by the ease of it. It seemed like a good omen, though she worried that Manny would also choose to stay home, but he was unexpectedly excited about this spontaneous boys' vacation and was able to get off work as well. Later that evening, while her father and brothers were outside, sorting through the fishing gear, she called the Letigs' house. She had a plan for what to say in case Mrs. Letig answered—asking if she could borrow one of their ice chests—but John answered. His wife was out running errands with Jack and Willie in preparation for her trip. Laura told him what was happening.

"Can you believe it?" she whispered, staring out the window at her father and brothers.

"That's great."

"Let's go somewhere," she said.

"I have to work."

"Oh, can't you get off? Just a couple of days before the weekend. Please. I want to be away, far away, where we don't have to slink around. I want to walk outside. I want to go to a movie with you, to a restaurant. Please, John."

"Honey, it's impossible."

And then she hung up because Manny came through the door.

The next day she stood on the porch and waved good-bye to her father and brothers.

"See you soon," her father called from the truck window. "You're fine here?"

"Yes, sir. I'm going over to Nancy's house later this evening."

"Nancy?"

"You know my friend Nancy. I told you."

"Her parents are okay with this?"

"Of course."

"Okay, then," he said, relieved because he was ready to go, and she didn't like to fish, and he knew it, and he even seemed excited about taking little Rich, which surprised her.

She watched the truck roll away, Manny and Gene in back with the gear, and then she sat in the old rickety chair on the porch, not ready to go inside because the house seemed so empty, and she'd never stayed by herself for a whole week, so that seemed frightening. She would have to be careful because of Mrs. Ambling. John couldn't come over here unless he came at night, through the back alley, and snuck in.

All this damn sneaking around. Part of her liked it, but she wished for once that they could be free of it all, free of the constant threat of being caught, but for now that was what they had to do, and it was worth it. It was. There were no longer the clumsy miscues and apprehension of their first encounters. There was an easy, fluid quality to their lovemaking, and throughout the long, hot summer weeks, as she listened to her friends talk about the boys they admired and found handsome, smiling innocently at their excitement and anxieties, she felt secretly superior to them. As she swam in the Charnelle public pool or played Foosball or Ping-Pong in the rec room on the days when she did not see him, she looked forward to the brief times with him and teased herself not only with the thoughts of what they did together now but also of what they *might* do if their life together was no longer a secret.

She tried to convince herself that this made the sneaking around worth it. On weekend nights, though, she would go with her family or friends to the drive-in, and, wandering around, she would see the couples in the cars, their arms draped over each other's shoulders, and it did not matter if they were seen kissing or holding hands. At the pool, she would watch the men and women splashing each other, even the teenagers holding hands, putting homemade suntan lotion—baby oil with a drop of iodine—on each other's back, and too often she felt a twinge of envy. No, it was more than envy; it was a longing for extended time together, for visibility, the openness of affection. She would lie sometimes on the large hill of grass by the pool, with her hat and sunglasses on, and watch in a sun-induced trance, wishing she and John could do as these other couples did. The sun would beat down on her until she felt agitated, and she would jump up, throw her hat and glasses on her towel, dash to the pool, and dive over two or three little kids. The cold water slashed her skin, and she stayed under, her eyes open, the chlorine burning them, and watched the bare legs of all the people moving up and down like slow-motion pistons in the sun-spackled blue of the water, and she would hold her breath until her lungs felt ready to pop, and then she'd kick off the pool bottom and propel herself out of the water like a rocket, the sudden air and sound and water in her face like an explosion. It was that feeling of exposure that she yearned for badly.

She was still sitting on the porch, thirty minutes after her father and brothers drove away, when he called, as if he'd been reading her mind, and asked, "Where do you want to go?"

And she said, as if his question was the natural extension of a long conversation, "Far away, where there's lots of water."

Then amazingly, within a few hours, she was out the door with her bulging bag slung over her shoulder, and down the alley to their spot behind the warehouse where he was waiting in the truck, and they were on their way. And with each mile they put between them and Charnelle, she felt freed of the weight, of the burden of secrecy, and she did not so much rise from his lap as float in the cab. In the dark, with the highway singing under the wheels, Wichita Falls and then Fort Worth behind them, the radio buzzing with Patsy Cline, Elvis, the Big Bopper, the Platters and the Everly Brothers, Bobby Darin and Ray Charles and Marty Robbins, and that silly little song that she couldn't get out of her head, "Itsy Bitsy Teenie Weenie Yellow Polka-Dot Bikini," ice-cold grape and orange Nehis in their hands, she felt like she was levitating, as if the whole truck were levitating. Or as if the truck itself, with them in it, were a song they could sing, a fast-beating melody that they'd been forced to hum quietly for too long, and now they were finally allowed to let 'er rip.

When they arrived in Houston, the barometric pressure seemed to change. The humidity was visible, a gray, misty light over the city, and then, farther south, there was the first smell of sea salt and brine. And through Pasadena and Texas City and across the bridge into Galveston, the air welcomed them like a fat, wet lick of a dog's tongue, and John drove right up to the beach, parked his truck on the sand, ripped off his boots and shirt, and chased her as she ran barefoot, screaming and laughing. He threw her over his shoulder and sprinted, as she kicked and laughed and pounded his back, straight into the morning surf, and on into the surprisingly warm water until a wave knocked them both down and water stung her eyes and tasted like a handful of salt in her mouth.

It was hot and humid, more humid than she would have thought possible, the air thick with moisture, which made her think about her mother at Lake Meredith, her face barely cracking the surface, her hair floating, saying how easy it was to breathe water. The gulf was not lake cold but rather like a lukewarm bath, and the beaches by midday were thronged with swimmers and sunbathers and sandcastle builders and walkers and wet-furred dogs. They put on bathing suits, and John rented an umbrella and spread out their towels, and they slept under the umbrella through the hot afternoon in a pleasant beach sweat, the two of them side by side, her head nuzzled in the crook of his arm so that the smell of his body was part of her. And later in the day, they drank lemonade and waded in the water, the surf curling hypnotically around their ankles. She'd been to many lakes, but she'd never looked out across an endless expanse of water that seemed to drop off the edge of the horizon. It made her understand for the first time what it was like to live before Columbus, what peasants and kings may have believed about the world as they stood on the shore.

They stayed in a small seaside shanty—that was what the place was called, Seaside Shanties—but it was clean enough, with a bathroom and an outdoor spray to rinse off the sand and sea, and best of all, it was thirty or so yards from the next cabin. The sheets on the bed were worn, the towels old but clean, and there was a broom to sweep out the grit—part sand, part salt, always there as a fact of life—which they could not keep off the sheets or the chairs. It was in the food and in their hair and of course on their bodies so that their lovemaking later seemed slightly overspiced.

The humidity was hard to get used to, but John said, " *You* wanted water," and he laughed loudly, such a long, powerful belly laugh that it was infectious. They were both exhausted from the all-night drive and from the boldness of the trip itself, the fact that they'd actually done it, gotten out of Charnelle, and not just a few miles away where they'd still have to worry about being caught, but really *away*, to a new world that was wonderfully and benignly indifferent to them. She'd never heard him laugh like that. It was a laugh that would be impossible in Charnelle. So much of their time together had been swathed, she realized, in silence or whispers. Even their lovemaking at the old deserted barn—at least a mile from any other house—had been muted. This laugh rejoiced with sound, and she, too, began laughing, and before they knew it, the two of them were on the floor, unable to stop. Tears streamed down their reddened faces. Their breaths were jagged rasps between giggles. This laughter was painful and kept on and on until it spluttered out, the giggles coming in smaller, more manageable fits. And when it finally subsided, they lay on the floor, her head on his chest, and they looked out the window, filmy with sea salt, and breathed deeply, as the sun slowly died in the room.

They fell asleep like that, and when they woke, they were starving because they had not eaten anything except corn nuts, Nehi, lemonade, and
some peaches an old, heavily clothed Mexican woman was selling from a
cart on the beach in the afternoon. Their stomachs gnawed and growled so
loudly that the prospect of food took priority over sex.

She did not particularly like fish, but the only place open after nine on a
weekday was Rotten Red's, a barnacle-covered restaurant that jutted out
over the water. The floor was warped from numerous floods and more than
a few hurricanes; the windows were fogged over from seawater, and the
place smelled like it had been steeped in brine. The odor overwhelmed her.
If she hadn't been starving, she wouldn't have eaten anything there, but
John ordered bowls of iced shrimp and lobster tails and crab, none of which
she'd ever tried before, and after she got the hang of removing the shells
from the meat, she devoured the food with the passion of a convert. The
food kept coming, and he ordered margaritas for them, which she loved
also (more salt, more salt), and they finished their meal with slices of ice-
cream-topped cherry pie and sat stuffed in the wicker chairs, shell casings
piled on their table like the remains of a massacre.

They listened to a man with a guitar and harmonica play a strange mixture of Hawaiian music, Woody Guthrie songs, and spirituals. She had
gulped down a second margarita during dinner, and now everything had a
pleasant spinning quality. Her skin was pink and hot from the nap in the
sun. The ocean splashed against the pier beneath them and seemed attuned
to the rhythm inside her body.

In the flicker of the table candles, John leaned back in the chair, glass in
hand, and smiled in a dopey, boyish way. His nose, cheeks, forehead, and the
triangle of skin beneath his collarbone were sunburned pink, and his hair was
puffy from the humidity and gulf water. She felt an outpouring of gratitude
to him for bringing her here. It seemed unreal almost, like one of her dreams,
and some part of her wondered when she would wake up. She knew it was not
a dream, though to call it real, she realized, would not be true either. Of
course, she thought suddenly of the word "idyll," which had been on a vo-
cabulary test last year. She remembered copying it from the dictionary into
her notebook: "a poem treating an epic or romantic theme in idealized terms;
a carefree episode; a romantic interlude." And she remembered the example
that made her think of Gloria: "a summer *idyll* on the coast of France."

"Thank you," she said.

"Thank *you*," he said.

And back at the cabin, with the night and the sound of the ocean surrounding them, their bodies fevered from the day in the sun, they made love with a slow, joint-loosened abandon. Their bodies moved in startling ways. Her skin seemed to expand, strangely malleable, and the smell of salt and the aftertaste of margaritas and seafood and the rhythm of sex were like a hot glaze. She felt like a piece of burning metal—reshaped, transformed by the blue flame.

"I love you," she said, crying. She'd never told him this before and wondered, momentarily, if she was drunk from the margaritas, if she'd made a mistake, not in her feelings for him but in voicing them.

After a pause, he said, "I love you, too," and she clung to him tightly.

Afterward she felt very awake, alert, and the ocean seemed to call to her. "Can we go walking on the beach?" she asked.

Although past midnight, it was still hot and humid. The beach was deserted, the sky clear. If you knew how, you could navigate by the stars. They walked along the shore and then sat on the dune above the tide and studied the waves rolling in, and when the waves broke into white phosphorescence, she began to imagine the Gulf of Mexico as a woman dancing in an elaborate black dress, trimmed in white lace, spinning in the dark to a music that emanated from a churning core beneath the water.

"Yeah, I guess I can see that," said John when she tried to explain it. "That's a nice thought. Let's dance with her."

They dropped their clothes and waded into the surf, out past where she felt comfortable moving in the dark tides. The water here swirled and sucked and pulled you out, away, but John was here with her, and they didn't go too deep, the water never rising, except once, above her neck. They saw the white crests coming in toward them and would hop through the waves. He pulled her to him in the troughs of the waves and kissed her as they bobbed.

Inside, after they toweled off, they didn't make love again but slept naked on top of the sheets. That, too, seemed new and right and welcomed, and they did not wake, despite the light in the windows, until well past dawn, when the sun shone unapologetically on them both.

For the next two days, the mornings and afternoons were lazy and hot and wet. They lay on towels under beach umbrellas or directly under the sun, or waded in the water, or built sand castles, or walked, for miles it seemed, along the crowded beach, and they talked long and easily. She told him more about her friends, described Marlene and Debbie, how tall and gangly Debbie would start wheezing with asthma at the sight of a boy she liked, or how cupid-faced Marlene loved to tell jokes and could do dead-on impressions of their teachers. She told him about Manny and her younger brothers, how hard it sometimes was to take care of them all, how Manny with his preening and obscene taunting and general jack-assedness sometimes irritated the hell out of her, and she told him more about Gloria and her children, and how she didn't much like Jerome. But she didn't tell him that Gloria knew their secret, and disapproved, though Laura felt guilty for keeping this from him.

He talked, too, and it was really the first time, she realized, that she learned much about him. Their time together in Charnelle had been restricted to a hectic hour now and again, and their conversation had been focused more on logistics, which had its own kind of allure—getting from one place to another without being detected, the delight in being with each other again and their plans for their next meeting, the concentrated pleasures of sex. Here, though, with what seemed like an expanse of time yawning before them, they were more relaxed. He told her about growing up in Pampa and Amarillo, about his father, who was always gone on railroad runs, and the effect of his death on their family, especially John's mother, whom he loved but didn't talk to much anymore, and his two older brothers, who had moved to Phoenix to open a steak-and-barbecue restaurant.

He told her that he'd been welding for over a decade, and he believed he should be promoted at Charnelle Steel, that he didn't think they valued his skills as they should, but that was the case with a lot of the workers there, including her father.

"Sometimes in the summer, with the thick suit and helmet, you feel like you're going to suffocate," he said, rubbing more suntan lotion on her back. "I hate that feeling, and I've sworn a thousand times that I was going to quit."

"Why don't you?"

"I don't know," he said. "Maybe I will. But really it's just bitching. I like it when they let me get out for whole days at a time, taking care of the fix-it runs. I'm on my own then, and people are usually grateful. That's good. And I still love the way the torch feels in my hand, the way I can turn metal into this thick liquid and move it around, make it do whatever I want. That still just flat-out amazes me. I love knowing I can do that, that I'm good at it."

"How were you able to get off work?" she asked, her eyes closed, enjoying the heat and sound of the waves, the feel of his hand on her back and legs. She had meant to ask him earlier, during the trip, but in the excitement she'd forgotten.

"I had days coming because of some weekend work I'm doing on the new bank."

"How are you going to explain it to Anne?" she asked, and then wished she could take back her words. Even saying his wife's first name made her feel uneasy.

"I'll tell her I went fishing," he said. "Don't worry about it."

About his wife and the boys, he didn't say much. But Laura had grown more and more curious about their relationship, had wondered about the tension between them at the picnic in July—and about that kiss. And she had been surprised, too, when they visited while she was sick and Mrs. Letig had said that he hadn't done any artwork since before Jack was born. Whenever the topic of his wife came up, there was a whiff of dissatisfaction in his voice, and she had to admit that she clung to that whiff, took a private scornful delight in it, but she was afraid to investigate those feelings too deeply.

She relished the fact that he appeared genuinely interested in and entertained by her stories and urged her to keep talking, and the two days seemed like a long, unbroken river of words from her, punctuated by bodysurfing and naps in the sand, by meals and showers and sex.

The next morning they drove into downtown Galveston. They were looking for a restaurant when Laura spotted an art-supply store.

"Hey," she asked, "did you bring your watercolors?"

"I threw them away. They dried out."

"Let's go in there," she said.

"No."

"Yeah," she said, "come on." She found a medium-size sketch pad, the same brand he'd had at Lake Meredith. "Let me buy this for you."

"No, don't spend your money."

"I want to," she said. She'd brought ten dollars with her—his wife's money!—and this didn't cost much. "Really, let me get you this. You should paint the ocean!"

She convinced him to buy some charcoal pencils and watercolors, and though he was reluctant, she saw a flicker of excitement. Encouraging him to use his talent made her feel closer to him. His wife probably didn't do that, didn't understand that part of him.

He drew pictures of her on the sand, in the water, in bed. At first she was nervous about it, but he didn't make her pose, just kept encouraging her to talk, and then he'd show her a picture—a few strokes, the lines of her face and body, the colors soft and blended, romantic. She felt proud of the pictures, as if she'd inspired him.

"Do you ever think about your mother?" he asked later that day.

It was near dusk, and they were on the beach, he on a towel, she at the shifting boundary where the water lapped against the sand. She was dropping large, liquidy dollops of mud on top of her legs. She didn't answer at first, though she felt that in some way her own words had been moving in this direction, circling around it until she and John had struck through to a different, deeper ring of intimacy. She had rarely mentioned her mother, but the way he asked made her think that he'd given it quite a bit of thought.

"You don't have to talk about her if you don't want to," he said.

But she did want to, and she told him about the day that her mother left, how odd and unsettling it was, and then she started telling him about all the other things, the things she had turned over and over in her mind, that appeared to lead up to that moment. The strange silences, the cryptic conversation about the ease of drowning, Gloria's elopement, and how Laura had found her mother crying by herself in the barn at Aunt Velma's, the same place where Uncle Unser had hanged himself, how she was bleeding, her yellow dress torn. How Greta's craziness upset some delicate balance in the family, set everyone on edge, made her mother more wary and distant, got her talking about "nature's way." And then the lightning struck, and her mother waded through the branches of the fallen tree as if hypnotized, touching the warm, charred bark and repeating, like a chant, the word "hot." Somehow all this led to that next day, when she walked to the bus station with that tattered brown suitcase in her hand. Gone.

Laura had not thought so much or so vividly about these things in a long time, not even when Gloria was back home, nor had she ever put these incidents together for herself in precisely this way, with this string of connections. It was as if this particular context—being away from Charnelle, the openness of the water, the easy rhythm of the beach, the way her passion for John had bloomed inside her—had somehow allowed her to finally say it all out loud, and saying it was a form of remembering but also a way of creating sense. The meanings seemed to appear before her as they never had before. In fact, these words spilling out changed her memories, brought them to the surface, unlike before, when her mother's disappearance had been something inside her that she touched silently and delicately, like a sore tooth, but she couldn't quite reach the actual source of the pain.

Then John asked her if she recalled any good times, last memories of her mother that were pleasant, that she could hold on to. Laura closed her eyes, listening to the comforting sound of the waves, and thought for a minute, and then she pictured their final Easter down at Aunt Velma's. It was the last time she could remember her family happy together, all of them leaning over the balcony at the Paladian Theater, waving and watching little Rich jumping up and down like a Munchkin on the stage. And then she thought of the night before that, when she had fallen asleep on the floor listening to the New York City Boys' Choir, and how it was suddenly dark when she awoke and her mother was there, crouching down by her side, covering her gently with a blanket, leaning over to kiss her, her hair falling around them both. That was the last time her mother told her that she loved her.

"Why do you think she left?" John asked.

For that, though, she had no answer. She merely started to cry, as if even the question were still too much to bear.

"I'm sorry," he said.

"It's okay. Let's get something to eat."

She rose from the beach and dashed into the water to clean the muddy sand from her hands and legs and bathing suit. When she came back, he showed her a quick drawing of her in the water, slapping her butt. It was comical, and she laughed, but then the drawing blew out of his hand and into the water, so that when she retrieved it, her body was smeared into an indecipherable blur.

They ate dinner again at Rotten Red's and sipped margaritas; she liked them better than the champagne from New Year's and much better than the beer she'd tasted. The margaritas made her head spin lightly at first but then warmed her and even made her feel more aware, more intense, and she felt a new empathy for drunkards, could see how you might get hooked on this feeling, like poor Donna Somersby, the woman who reportedly never left her home except to buy bottles of gin from the Armory.

The next morning they woke early and swam, ate a quick breakfast, and then he said, "Let's go to Houston."

She put on a loose-fitting sundress, and he put on his jeans and a short-sleeved shirt, and they headed out past mile after mile of oil refinery that stank of methane and chemicals and hot grease, on into downtown Houston, where they ate lunch at a barbecue joint.

"Know of a company that needs a welder?" John asked the bartender, a short, bald dumpling of a man with buckteeth and wire-rimmed glasses that magnified his eyes.

"Ha. Who doesn't need a welder? If you're any good, you could work all the hours you wanted, buddy."

"Like where?"

"Jason's Steel, for starters. They have the best welders and pay damn good, including overtime. You looking for a job?"

"I don't know. Maybe."

"You from around here?"

"No, the Panhandle."

She sipped her cherry soda and listened carefully. For the first time since they had been on this trip, she felt a wave of fear wash over her. Was this why he'd come down here? Were he and his family going to move? He hadn't said anything to her about this.

"Of course, you could get yourself a job with any oil-rigging crew you wanted. They always need good welders."

"I've done that kind of work. It ain't fun."

"Pays well, though."

"Depends on what you call 'well.' "

"The offshore rigs pay about three times as much as a regular welding job. A man could stash away a little nest egg in a few years if he could put up with it."

"How much?"

"My brother's best friend is a welder. He made a bundle last year with Texaco."

"No shit? As a welder?"

The man looked at the wedding ring on John's hand and then at Laura. She could tell he was guessing her age. "What about your wife there? She looking for work?"

"Nope," John said. "Just me."

In the afternoon they needed to get out of the humid city heat, which was not rescued by ocean breezes. They held hands and walked inside the stores with ceiling fans whirring like helicopter blades. As they crossed the plaza, beneath a grove of tall poplar trees, she asked tentatively, "Are you going to move?"

"What do you mean?"

"You were talking to the man back there like you were looking for a job."

"Just curious." And then he said, pointing to a small boutique sandwiched between larger stores, "Look at that." The sign proclaimed MADELINE'S LINGERIE. In the shop window was a female mannequin dressed in a pink silk nightgown. "Come on," he said.

"No, we can't go in there."

"Why not?"

"We just can't."

"Who's going to care? They don't give a damn who we are. Come on."

Inside, a pretty middle-aged woman wearing an unfortunate amount of mascara and blue eye shadow appeared beside them, asking if she could help.

"Me and my fiancée are looking for some wedding-night goodies, if you know what I mean?"

Laura blushed and slapped him on the chest. "Shut up!"

The woman smiled condescendingly, as if she'd seen these kinds of shenanigans before and they had long since lost their charm. "Just let me know if I can help you."

The shop was full of mannequins dressed so provocatively that Laura was embarrassed to be walking among them, but John kept touching the fabric, talking loud as you please: "I like this, honey," and "What do you think about this, sweetie?" He pulled her close to him behind a rack of colorful lacy brassieres and kissed her.

"John, stop it," she whispered, alarmed.

"It doesn't matter," he said and kissed her again. "We can do anything we want here."

They left the store with a sheer purple nightgown, which she made John pay for while she waited outside the store because she didn't want to exchange looks with the lady. She watched through the window as John laughed, and then the lady laughed as well and seemed to lean in too close to him. A sudden hatred for the woman sparked in Laura's chest. But outside the store he handed her the package, took her in his arms, and whirled her around so that her dress billowed.

"What do you want to do next?" he asked. "The city is yours."

They went to see a movie at a big theater, older but nicer than the Paladian in Amarillo. It was Alfred Hitchcock's *Psycho*. She remembered back in March when she'd seen the trailer for this movie at the drive-in with her brothers and the Letig boys, and how she'd come back to poker night at the house, and she and John had kissed in the bathroom. How foolish they were. How long ago that seemed. Could it have been only a few months? She was just a girl then, she thought. So much had happened since—all of it leading to this moment in Houston.

The movie scared her badly. She curled up in a fetal position, clutching his arm, hiding her face against his shoulder every few minutes. It was excruciating and wonderful, but at the end she felt queasy and ready to be outdoors. She was glad it was light out; the sun still blazed.

They ate dinner at a Mexican place, and then they went to a bar where there was a live four-piece band that played country music. They wouldn't let her in, said she was too young.

"She's my wife," John said. "She's twenty, for Christ's sake."

"She looks about fifteen or sixteen to me."

"Well, she's not."

"Where's her ring if she's your wife?"

"At home."

"You show me the ring, and she gets in."

"Okay, fine. We'll just do that."

So they went to a grocery store and kept buying and opening boxes of Cracker Jacks until they found a ring, and when they returned, the doorman cocked his eyebrow, nodded his head reluctantly, and waved them in. John ordered a couple of beers, but she didn't like the taste of hers, so he got her a margarita. The band—fiddle, guitar, harmonica, and drums—was good, though not as good as the Pick Wickers, and she and John stumbled through a couple of numbers, found their rhythm, and then danced easily over the sawdust-covered floor with under-the-arm twirls and deep-dipping finales.

"Damn, you're good!" he said.

Their faces were beaded in sweat. His shirt was soaked through. They danced for two more hours, jitterbugging, polka-ing, two-stepping, slow-dancing, breaking only to drink and go to the bathroom, but the songs kept getting better, and by the end of the night the crowd began singing along. A drunk woman tore off her shirt and whirled it above her head like a lasso, and everybody clapped while she did it, and then the band finished their last set with a series of slow waltzes, and John and Laura danced close, not talk-ing, their clothing slick and warm from the sweat, steam rising from them both. She could feel him hardening against her, and he moved his hand to the small of her back and then lower. At the end of the song, he picked her up and kissed her.

In the parking lot, inside the truck, with the windows rolled down, they began kissing again, their hands on each other's clothes, the door against her back, mouth and fingers together, and the musky aroma of wet clothing and sweat. Then he was under her dress, his pants down, and soon they were rocking together, and she was almost there, almost, but from far away, and then suddenly very close, she heard a couple shouting, laughing, and then they were standing next to John's truck.

"Where are the goddamn keys?" a woman slurred.

"In your fucking purse," a man said.

"John," she whispered, pushing him away. They slid down in the seat and listened to the couple argue.

"I can do it, goddamn it!" the woman said.

"Well, do it then!"

Finally the doors opened and shut, and the car started and backed out, crunching gravel.

"Let's go," Laura said. John lifted his head, his hair tousled, his face cracked into a drugged smile. The car was gone, but she was ready to go back now to their cabin, to the sound of the ocean, where they could do anything they wanted and no one would disturb them. "I want to swim."

Although they were on the southeast side of Houston, it still took them a while to reach Galveston. With the windows open and the wind blowing in, their clothes dried. She was chilled by the time they drove up to the cabin, and swimming in the ocean no longer seemed such a good idea. Inside, they undressed, and despite the interim, they quickly found their previous rhythm, and the sound of the gulf unleashed something in her, allowed her to give herself to him in a way that was on the verge of frightening. She kept pulling him closer to her. As his mouth and hands and then body moved over her, she felt like she was swimming in air as thick and sweet as molasses.

Afterward they lay exhausted on the bed. Her legs tingled from the dancing, and she listened to the ocean roar hypnotically, the night gulls whimpering. She wiggled her sore toes, rotated her ankles. She looked at John. His eyes were closed. She reached over and ran her fingers slowly over his face and then down his body. She put her leg over his, pressed against him tightly. Without opening his eyes, he moved his arm under her head.

Tomorrow was their last day. She could sense the real world encroaching, the long drive home, her father, her brothers, John's wife and sons. The unanswered questions about his interest in the jobs here, what that might mean. She didn't want those thoughts crowding in on this moment. She counted by Mississippis until she reached thirty and breathed deeply.

"John," she said.

He didn't answer.

"John, are you asleep?"

"Almost," he said.

"I wish it could always be like this," she said.

He nodded but didn't say anything.

"John . . ."

"Yeah, me too," he mumbled.

She listened as he breathed steadily beside her. She wished that she could tell him how she felt, what she hoped was their future, though she was afraid to do that. They'd said more to each other during this time than all their other times combined, but still she feared saying aloud to him that what she really wanted was to never go back to the silence and secrecy of

Charnelle. She wanted to be together like this without the nagging sense of time always running out on them. Perhaps Gloria was right, after all. No matter how much Laura insisted that she wanted to just enjoy this time with John for what it was—wanted simply to let it *be* rather than worry about where it was *going,* what it would *become,* how it would *end*—she could sense a growing attachment to her dreams about their future and a deeper undercurrent of fear that they *were* only dreams.

She closed her eyes and told herself to go to sleep, though part of her wanted to lie awake all night, right here, right now, not allow sleep to rob any more of their time together. But she nestled closer to him, and then soon she was asleep, because, for now, that was okay.

23

✹

Literature of the
American Dream

They had another day together in Charnelle before either Mrs. Letig
or Laura's family returned. They spent that night at the old barn.
It was nice but anticlimactic, which Laura attributed to the arid heat and the
absence of water, the sizzle of cicadas instead of night gulls and insistent
waves. Their backs and shoulders and noses were sunburned, and in the
kerosene lamplight they took turns peeling sheets of skin from each other's
bodies and laying them on the cloth that covered the splintery end table by
the pallet. She had a headache, which the cola and cheese and crackers
didn't drive away, so she slept against him as he read a Jack London book,
The Call of the Wild, that she'd given to him as a gift; she'd bought it at a
dime store in Fort Worth when they stopped for gas and Cokes, and it delighted her to see him enjoying what she'd offered him, caught up in Buck
the dog's journey back to the wild. Though there was a failure of magic on
this final night together, it was comfortable and soft. She had a sense that this
was how it was supposed to be, this slow and easy.

And when her father and brothers returned that Tuesday evening, they were so caught up in telling her their adventures that they never even suspected she'd had adventures of her own. And by the next day, all their routines resumed as if nothing had happened, as if the week had never existed.

Disappeared, she thought. *Disappeared*.

She and John didn't meet that Thursday or the next Monday, and that, too, seemed fine, but by Tuesday depression began to nibble at her.

The days felt prolonged and busy, irritatingly meaningless: watching Rich and Gene, cooking meals for everybody—all that fish to be cleaned and then fried or grilled—and scrubbing the dishes afterward, washing the clothes, clipping them to the lines outside in the heat, badgering Gene and Rich to help, she and Manny snapping at each other again with that unsettling animosity that had grown like scar tissue between them. Her father returned in the evenings from work and would read the paper in his old chair, and they'd maybe listen to the radio—a baseball game or the combination of country and rockabilly on KSNP—or watch television—*Gunsmoke*, *Leave It to Beaver, Rawhide*—all these stupid shows with the sole purpose of helping the evening pass. She reread her magazines. She bought new ones. But they seemed just as stupid, just as frivolous. Who cared about Tony Curtis and Janet Leigh's marriage or about Elvis's time in the army and what lucky girl he fell in love with? The only stories that really grabbed her attention were the ones about Senator Kennedy's wife. She loved one picture she'd seen of Mrs. Kennedy sitting atop a horse, dressed in a riding outfit, long English boots, and a riding cap. It made Laura think of that fall she took that one Easter and how it might not have happened if she'd grown up like Jackie Kennedy, riding Thoroughbreds and wearing sleek boots and fashionable riding caps instead of galloping around (in her tennis shoes) on jumpy, unpredictable mares like Hayworth. She went swimming with Debbie and Marlene, but even that irritated her, trying to pay attention to Marlene's stupid jokes or hearing about Debbie's nails or which boy she now had a crush on.

At the pool, she lay on the grass and listened to the other swimmers splashing, having fun, and she tried to relive her time in Galveston, but it never worked in the way she wanted it to. There were always interruptions, usually Marlene with some idiotic question or comment—"What do you think? Red or pink nail polish?" Or: "Oh, I dread going back to school" (this said for the hundredth time).

Passing the time. That was her mother's old phrase for these kinds of days.

Killing time. That was the other phrase for it. Her father's.

There was no urgency in these phrases, no sense of alarm, unless there was some chore to do. For the most part, these things were said with smiles, at the end of the day, after work and before sleep as they tried to occupy themselves. Time passed away. Or was killed. She began to think of the days and nights as a kind of prolonged death, a murder that everybody seemed strangely happy about.

She fully expected that the trip to Galveston would rejuvenate her, but it had the opposite effect, an unwelcome surprise. She felt like a prisoner granted a week of freedom, and not just grimy, grubby freedom but true, blessed, intoxicating freedom. The prisoner believes that these days will help sustain the rest of the sentence, but instead they make the return all the more miserable. The contrast ruins it. Knowing what is possible but not probable transforms reality into a peculiar misery.

The days plodded along in a weary torpor. But at night she had trouble sleeping. She heard every snore and fart and belch and cough, every twitching in the bed of her brothers. It disgusted her. The cicadas and crickets blared like a fire alarm. When she shut her eyes, trying to transport herself back to her time in Galveston, she would be close to getting the sense of it, the rhythm of it, but she could never penetrate to the heart of that experience, not even in her dreams. Instead she felt on the periphery, as if she were excluded even from her own memories.

Late one night, her thoughts drifted to last year's civics class. Mrs. Conroy had them read Plato's "Allegory of the Cave." The people were all in chains in the cave, facing forward, looking at a wall, upon which shadows from the flames behind them flickered, and the people believed that the shadows were the real thing, and so they were content. But then one person escaped the chains, turned, and saw that the flames made the shadows and that there was an opening to the outside. He went out into the light and was nearly blinded. When he went back into the cave to tell the others what he'd seen, they wouldn't believe him.

In their class discussion, Mrs. Conroy had suggested that Plato's question, the one he never answered completely but posed so forcefully, was whether the people *should* know what the reality was. Or if, because they were content in their ignorance, they should stay where they were. "Was ignorance a kind of bliss?" she asked, dropping her glasses to the end of her nose, staring at them provocatively. Laura understood that the allegory suggested something ambivalent about new knowledge—not just a light but a *blinding* light, made all the more blinding because of so many years spent in the dark.

During that discussion she had thought about Gloria, how they'd kept her in the dark about their mother disappearing, and how happy her letters seemed for a while. Though Gloria had protested this summer that it was her right to know, Laura still believed that Gloria would have been better off if they'd never told her.

But now the allegory took on an even more personal meaning. For hadn't her and John's time in Galveston been a kind of escape into the light? And now this return seemed all the more depressing because there was really no escaping again, at least not in the foreseeable future, and even if it did happen, it wouldn't be the same. Couldn't be the same, in fact, because now she knew that the disappointment of returning to Charnelle, to their normal lives, apart from each other, would be waiting on the other side of any idyll. And wouldn't that knowledge taint the idyll?

Like when you put a drop of black ink in a glass of milk, the whole thing would be darkened.

The fall term began the next Monday, and she was thankful. That first week of school, she didn't get to meet John. They'd spent an extra-long time together the previous Thursday, and then she kept the Letig boys on Saturday, which was the first time she'd watched them since they'd returned from their trip. She felt a new eagerness to be in their company, more appreciative of their desire to hug her and hold her, more tolerant of their fussiness. Tucking them in, she had a quick, dark moment where she imagined Mrs. Letig dying in the hospital or leaving the boys as her own mother had done—Laura moving in, consoling and caring for them and for John. Later, doing the Letig dishes, picking up puzzles and toys, she had to shake her head to clear the scenario from her mind.

He'd driven her home, told his wife he was going to stop by a coworker's house to retrieve some tools he'd loaned him. They had almost an hour then, too, parked in his truck alongside the Waskalanti Creek, the windows rolled down, the sound of the water trickling close by, the dark trees looming above, both of them hurried and fierce so that afterward there were striped lines from the vinyl upholstery on her arms and the backs of her legs. Her lips burned, her thighs chafed.

After he dropped her off, she heard a pleasant buzzing sound in her head. In the bathroom, steam swirled above the tub, rising not so much from the water, she thought, as from herself. Above the buzzing, she kept hearing the lyrics to the Patsy Cline song—"I go walkin', after midnight, searchin' for you"—that had been playing in the truck when they made love, so that the words themselves and the mournful rhythms of the tune transported her back there. She liked this sated feeling, a pampered, exhausted delight, and it seemed to satisfy her for the week so that she didn't long for John or even miss him during those first days of school.

It was actually good to be back, a junior now, with status, not a measly sophomore anymore. There was electricity in the air the first morning, pushing down the crowded hallway, everyone nicely dressed, with summer tans and sun-bleached hair. She had trigonometry, which she slightly dreaded—math had never been her strong suit—though the teacher, Mr. Whitmore, promised to be funny and charming. And English with Mr. Sparling, and home economics, which all the girls were required to take, and chemistry, and American history and civics, and gym, and choir.

She had always liked school and was reminded the first day that she had, unbeknownst to her, missed it over the summer. She liked the discipline, the sense of her mind stretching like a balloon around new knowledge. That stretching had always been easy—a cinch, really. She had seen her classmates, especially some of the boys, struggle, had watched their eyes glaze over, their eyelids drooping with the lectures, and she had never understood their boredom or frustration—or their failure. She never commented on it; she knew she was in the minority. It was not really popular in Charnelle to say you liked school, or to be good at it, so she didn't talk much about it, but people knew she was bright, and she had helped classmates before and felt she had a knack for showing them what the teachers failed to make them understand in class and for helping them see that they weren't dumb. She liked this feeling. She wondered if she'd be a teacher when she got older. She could see herself doing that, though it seemed too early to make any decisions like that about her life.

It was still hot, so after school Marlene and Debbie and Laura went swimming at the pool, which wouldn't close until the following week, after Labor Day. Marlene and Debbie had both been gone the week before school started, traveling with their families, visiting relatives. Though Laura had been so tired of their company during the summer, now she was eager to see them, wanted again the easy banter, the jokes and the teasing and the hushed excitement of gossip.

Marlene confessed that she had fallen in love with her cousin's best friend while in Colorado the past week. He was her age, and they had spent most of the time hiking and climbing the hills and mountains, and she showed them a strip of pictures from one of those photo booths, where the camera takes four for a dime and spits them out immediately. He didn't look all that good to Laura. His skin was pocked, and he seemed cross-eyed and very young. Marlene told the story of their courtship, confessing to hours of kissing, and yes, she had let him go to second base, and Laura and Debbie were the only ones who knew, and they couldn't tell anyone. Marlene felt bad about what she had done, but he was so sweet, and it seemed to make him happy. And yes, she did sort of like it, but only because she loved him.

Laura listened, slightly bored, to the story, looking at Debbie, whose mouth was open. And then Debbie confessed that she, too, had let a boy feel her breasts this summer, that it was no big deal; in fact, he was clumsy and annoying with his rough hands, not knowing how hard or soft to squeeze, yet he believed himself to be some kind of apprentice Casanova. They all laughed about it, and Marlene said it could only happen while they were on vacation, and far away, where no one really knew them. They looked at Laura, wondering if she also had a confession for them, but she just smiled and shook her head like she couldn't believe their boldness. She pretended to be amusingly scandalized, but all the while she thought, *I can never tell them.* They seemed so young to her, but that also reassured her. She would sit quietly, just listen to their stories, as innocent as they were, and let them think that she was awed by what they had done.

Eleventh grade, as mandated by the board of education, required students to immerse themselves in American culture—American government, American history, American literature. Until recently that had been handled separately by the different departments at Charnelle High. But

Dwight Sparling, the juniors' English teacher, had the previous year launched a new, experimental curriculum designed to integrate the three subjects in a more thematically rich way. In assembly, on the third morning of the school year, he provided the overview lecture about this new initiative to the junior class.

Mr. Sparling was a small man with rounded features, a stark white complexion, and a face that didn't seem to go together but was still comically handsome. You could never quite tell if he was serious or not. It was rumored that he had almost completed his doctorate at the University of Texas in Austin but that he had returned to Charnelle because his parents were very ill. Charnelle High had refused at first to hire him because they believed he was overqualified, but he had evidently convinced the principal that there was no such thing as being overqualified in education, so he was given a probationary contract, which quickly turned into a full-status position once they realized what they had. No one really believed that he would be around for very long; it was rumored that once his parents died he would head back to Austin to complete his dissertation and get a college faculty position.

Theirs was the only high school in the county, so all the kids from the smaller towns caught the bus into Charnelle. Assembly, when all seventy of the juniors were present, was held once a week, and it was rowdy because it was the only time the whole class came together. The vice principal, Mr. Burchell, finally quieted the crowd, welcomed them all to the school year, and thanked his staff and made announcements about the new lunch schedule and the redesigned gymnasium, and then he introduced Mr. Sparling. Everybody clapped enthusiastically. They'd all heard, as Laura had, that Dwight Sparling was a good teacher.

He thanked Mr. Burchell and then made a couple of jokes about what an uncivilized crew they appeared to be and how he had his work cut out sophisticating them. He'd heard scandalous stories from their sophomore teachers, and he hoped they could be reformed, but he had his doubts. Everybody laughed, and then he said he wanted to speak more seriously today about what they could expect from the year. He paused, and a boy called out something asinine (Laura couldn't quite hear him), but Mr. Sparling ignored him, and then the crowd hushed, and he looked down at his notes, then up at the students.

Laura leaned forward a little and could see others along the curved row doing the same.

"This is an historic year," he said, "the beginning of a new era in America. A new president will be elected, and though you will not have a formal say in that process, it will affect your lives irrevocably, and you will, I promise you, always remember this particular moment in time. We would like to seize this opportunity not just to meet the board of education requirements but also to engage you in a lifelong inquiry into American life. Not just what it means to be an American citizen but also the economic, political, and cultural process that has shaped who we are—who *you* are—and how that process affects your daily decisions and connects your past to your present and to your future."

He leaned into the microphone, his elbows propped on the lectern, and though he spoke smoothly, even elegantly, with no trace of Texas twang, the rhythm of his voice also had a jittery energy, as if his language and ideas animated him. His eyes moved over the crowd, but Laura felt, even though he was a good distance away from her, that he was speaking directly to her, intimately, as if he were leaning across her kitchen table.

"What links exist between the life you live in Charnelle, the life you lead with your family and friends, and the life of a democracy, of *this* democracy? How do those two worlds impinge on each other? What myths bind us, unite and help either clarify or mystify who we are as a country and as a people? This is what we hope to investigate together.

"Toward that end, we will approach this year, and particularly this fall as the election approaches, as an investigation of the literature of the American dream. I do not mean just literary investigation, though we will do plenty of that as well. There will be opportunities to examine Cotton Mather, Ralph Waldo Emerson, Henry David Thoreau, and Walt Whitman. Nathaniel Hawthorne, Herman Melville, Harriet Beecher Stowe, and Mark Twain. Emily Dickinson and Stephen Crane. And perhaps even more modern texts.

"But we will also examine, with the same kind of precision, other great literary texts of our culture: the Declaration of Independence, the Constitution, the great autobiography by the former slave Frederick Douglass. Lincoln's Emancipation Proclamation and his Gettysburg Address. The Bill of Rights and even Supreme Court decisions like *Brown v. Board of Education*. You will read poetry, political editorials, and comic strips."

This reference brought on a round of laughter, especially from a group of boys—Dean Compson among them—sitting in front of her.

"Oh, yes," Mr. Sparling said, smiling slyly, "the intellectual exploits and philosophical quandaries of Jughead are particularly relevant to this crowd."

This provoked a bigger laugh from the whole auditorium, and Laura grinned at Mr. Sparling's cleverness, his ability to heckle his hecklers. And then, just as the wave of laughter had reached its crescendo, he plunged back into his speech, which induced them all, Laura included, to lean forward more intently.

"You will listen to your mothers and fathers and grandparents as they tell you their stories. You will listen to songs ranging from 'This Land Is Your Land' to 'Oklahoma' to 'Jailhouse Rock.'"

"Go, Elvis!" a boy shouted from the back of the auditorium, and again Mr. Sparling smiled knowingly. After the initial murmur of laughter, the crowd grew intensely quiet, and he used this pause to survey his audience.

"All this, ladies and gentlemen, is part of your literary heritage. These texts are part of you, whether you know that or not. You will begin to see patterns emerging. You will hear the arguments, the texts calling to each other in ways perhaps their authors could not conceive. You will hear the arguments and the calling, and behind that will be a simple contradiction. A capital-letter Yes and a capital-letter No."

He paused to underscore the significance of his statement. Laura let out a little sigh, puzzled but intrigued, and waited for him to continue.

"When you read the first, stirring words of the Declaration of Independence—'When in the course of human events . . .'—you will hear that contradiction. Men saying No to their past, cutting off the ties to a tyrannical monarchy, and you will hear a resounding Yes—humans, for the first time in modern history, not just articulating but insisting on each and every person's fundamental right to pursue happiness. And that simultaneous manifesto of revolt and declaration of freedom, ladies and gentlemen, is at the heart of our collective myth."

Laura felt caught up now, as they all did. She wasn't quite sure what he was saying, what it all meant, but she felt the cadence of his words like a transfixing song.

"You will hear it in the tales of Paul Bunyan and 'The Legend of Sleepy Hollow,' and in Emerson's demand for 'self-reliance' and in Walt Whitman's 'body electric.' You will hear it in Frederick Douglass's eloquent claim that he, too, is a man. You will hear it in F. Scott Fitzgerald's astonishment at the bright green wonder of America and the promise it holds, and in his tragic love story of the corruption of that promise. You will hear it on the radio and on the football field and at the Ding Dong Daddy Diner."

Another cackle of pleasure from the crowd.

"You will hear the world, and even yourself, speaking out of and through this mythology of America, and running, like a murmuring current beneath this talk, will be a simple, triumphant Yes and a simple, antagonistic, often enraged No.

"Yes, this is America, and we can send a rocket into space and maybe a man or woman, and that man or woman could someday be you. You can become a president or a tycoon or Mickey Mantle or Elvis Presley or Eleanor Roosevelt, or you can own Charnelle Steel & Construction or Spenser's General Store. There is no limit. As long as you can imagine it, it is in your power to invent yourself.

"And yet . . ." he said, his voice lower now and more drawn out. He paused and scanned the crowd. His voice had exuberantly rolled through this last litany of Yeses, but now Laura saw that he wanted them all to wonder, as she did, where he was going next. "And yet," he continued, "countering that note of optimism, that great joy, you will hear the No, and that No will emerge from a sense of fundamental injustice. You'll hear it in the songs of Woody Guthrie and the Weavers. You'll hear it in Hawthorne's angry husband, Chillingworth, and in Melville's crazed, peg-legged Ahab and Steinbeck's Joad family. You'll hear it in Biff Loman's anguished cry to his father. You'll hear it in your churches, too, and you'll hear it in your homes as your parents and your parents' friends argue about Vice President Nixon and Senator Kennedy."

"Go, Jackie!" a boy yelled, and Laura grinned and thought, yes, one of the primary reasons for voting for Kennedy was to get Jackie into the White House. Mr. Sparling didn't stop, just rolled right over this outburst, which he clearly didn't deem funny enough to acknowledge, not even with a smile.

"And you'll hear it from the candidates themselves, as they try to articulate for us all who we are at this point in history, where we've been and where we need to go. And I—all of us here—"

He turned and motioned to the row of teachers sitting behind him. Laura could sense he was coming to an end.

"We all want you to listen for those voices in yourself, too. That Yes and that No. Sometimes the Yes and the No will happen simultaneously, and then it's not so simple anymore. And when you hear those voices, they will connect you to that great, complex, historic process of which we are all part, that process that is not dead or abstract or boring but lives and breathes and moves profoundly through whatever you do."

Mr. Sparling took a few final seconds to look over the audience, and then, almost shyly, he said, "Thank you," grabbed his notes, and left the podium.

The spell broke. There was scattered, polite applause, a lot of hushed giggling, and a few cackles. The boys sitting in front of Laura rolled their eyes and elbowed one another. Marlene rummaged through her purse to find her nail file. Laura sat back and watched Mr. Sparling return to his seat on the stage, watched him shuffle his notes and put them in his briefcase, then whisper something to Mrs. McFarland, who was sitting beside him.

Mr. Burchell returned to the podium, told them to quiet down, and then he introduced the football coach, who lumbered to the podium to whistles and loud applause. But Laura just kept staring at Dwight Sparling. She wanted him to go back to the podium. She wanted him to keep talking.

24

✦

Yankee Doodle Gal

*A*fter that day, she went to class and did her homework with a new sense of urgency and focus, searching for the connections, examining her assignments with greater clarity of purpose. Was it true what he had said? She didn't know, but she was smitten with the notion that everything was intimately linked—the books she read, the history she studied, the songs she liked to listen to on the radio, the stupid television shows she watched with her family, the movies she saw at the drive-in, the magazines she pored over, and then ultimately her affair with John, and her relationship with her family, and her memories of her mother—all of it, everything, bound together by this simple tension, this Yes and No that Mr. Sparling had spoken of.

Was it that simple? Maybe so, but it also seemed complex and profound to her, the way she sometimes felt after visiting Aunt Velma, or going to church, that there were these hidden threads binding together the visible and invisible worlds.

She tried to explain this to John one afternoon, a couple of weeks later. They now met only erratically, though usually late in the afternoon on a Monday or Thursday when he returned from a run to Borger. With the out-of-town runs, there was no specific time he was expected back. He'd pick her up after five behind the warehouse and be able to stay with her until almost six-thirty, sometimes seven. She told her father she was studying late, at the library or with friends, and Mrs. Ambling watched Rich and then Gene when he returned from school. On those days, she usually made supper in the morning so her father wouldn't be put out or ask too many questions.

She started telling John about Dwight Sparling's theory as soon as he picked her up. It had entranced her, and she'd been thinking about it constantly, so she rattled on—and then stopped abruptly.

"You don't really care about this, do you?"

"Yes," he said. "And no."

"You're making fun."

"Yes, I am. Go ahead and tell me. I want to hear about it."

So she tried to recall specific parts of Mr. Sparling's speech, and she found that the more she just let herself talk about it, the more she remembered and the more eloquent she became.

"When you read the stirring words of the Declaration of Independence, you will hear that contradiction," she said, her voice low and yet trying to catch that jittery energy of Mr. Sparling's. "Men saying No to their past, cutting off the ties to Mother England, and you will hear a big, huge Yes—people, for the first time in all of recorded history, demanding their right to happiness. And that manifesto of freedom, ladies and gents, boys and girls, is at the very heart and soul of our American myth."

He was lighting the candles and the kerosene lamp, though there was still plenty of light in the room from the window. He closed the curtain over the window, so that it was partly dark in the barn, and he pulled out crackers and cheese from the knapsack he'd brought with him. She followed him around, chattering feverishly, not only about the books they would be reading but also about what they had already read and how she had listened to the radio the night before last and could hear what Mr. Sparling said, about the Yes and the No, in the lyrics of Elvis and Buddy Holly, Dean Martin and Nat King Cole. If you listened, they kept saying, Yes, Yes, Yes. You could hear it in the rhythm and joy of the music. And then she had flipped to the country-and-western station, and the No was in the sweet, sad songs of Patsy Cline, Loretta Lynn, and Conway Twitty, the despair and the righteous sense of injustice and anger, too.

He stood behind her and began kissing her neck. She stopped talking.

"Don't stop," he said, nibbling her ear.

"You're not saying anything. I just sound like a fool, don't I?"

"Not at all. I love hearing your voice."

And so she kept on as he took off her clothes and kissed her neck and back and legs and chest. She talked about *Perry Mason* and *The Rifleman* and even *The Twilight Zone*, and what she heard Kennedy saying the other day about Nixon, joking that the vice president was like an elephant, with a long memory and no vision, following the tail of the lumbering elephants ahead of him. On and on she went, sometimes singing lyrics to songs, and reciting, almost verbatim from memory, a lecture about the Continental Congress.

It was like a gift, everything clearly in her mind and accessible. Soon she didn't even know what she was saying anymore, and it didn't matter. The whole thing was a kind of song that seemed to be pouring out of her mouth as he kissed her body, and it seemed the more she did not concentrate on what he was doing, the more she just let the words flow from her mouth, the more amazing it was what he was doing, as if this physical pleasure were entwined with this other kind of pleasure.

And quietly, behind her, still kissing her neck and holding her close, he moved into her, and only afterward did she stop talking. They lay there on the pillows, and she watched the kerosene lamp burn. It seemed eerily quiet now. Her throat felt scratchy. She reached for the canteen of water on the table, took three long swallows, and then turned toward him and nestled into his body. He put his arm around her. His eyes were closed.

"John," she said.

"Yes, honey."

"Do you want me to read the Declaration of Independence to you?"

He laughed. "I can't think of anything I'd rather you do."

She slipped on her shirt and retrieved the copy from her satchel, and while he smoked a cigarette, blowing jiggling rings in the air above them, she read, as Mr. Sparling had done that very day, the words "When in the course of human events . . ."

When she finished, she looked over and saw that his eyes were closed.

"Are you listening to me?"

"Yes."

"Isn't that marvelous?" she asked.

"I think you're in love with Dwight Sparling," he teased. "I think you have a thing for him."

She hit him with the Declaration, but she was also blushing, because in a way he was right. Mr. Sparling had inflamed her mind, and it *was* similar to the way she felt about John.

"Just for that," she said, "I'm going to read the Constitution."

"Okay, I take it back. I'm sorry."

" 'We the People, in Order to form a more perfect union—' "

"Okay, that's it," he said, rising. "You keep reading. I'm going to draw you."

"No, you can't draw me."

"I am. Keep reading."

With her elbow propped on the pillow, she mimicked Gloria's French Artiste character, which she'd been practicing. " 'Article 1,' " she intoned, lowering her voice, flipping up her shirt to reveal her panties.

"Oh, yeah, baby doll, give me Article 1."

And quickly he sketched. Before she reached Article 10, he laid his pen and pad facedown, leaned across the mattress, and put his lips to her stomach.

"Do you want me to stop?" she asked.

"Whatever you want to do, sweetie."

"The Constitution isn't nearly as interesting, is it?"

"Well, Article 1 was pretty damn interesting. And Article 5 gave me a boner."

"Can I see the picture?"

"Wouldn't you rather see the boner?" he asked, drawing down his boxers.

"Shut up! Let me see the picture."

"Here," he said and handed it to her. He'd not drawn her since Galveston, and he'd made her destroy those paintings and drawings, except for the blurry, indecipherable one that had flown into the water. It was painful to burn images of herself, even though some of them were of her without clothes.

She looked at the picture and laughed. It was a cartoon version of her body reclining on the mattress and shaped like the flag waving in the wind, her shirt covered with stars, her panties with stripes. Her mouth was wide open, square, and nearly as big as the rest of her body. Her teeth were also shaped like the flag. In her hands was a book that said "Declaration of Independence" on it. And above her head, in a curved movie marquee, little lightbulbs all around, were the words, in block letters, all caps: YANKEE DOODLE GAL!

She laughed again. "I have an awfully big mouth," she complained.

"That's almost the best part of you, honey."

"Almost?"

He put his lips to her stomach again and blew loudly, tickling her at the same time.

"Stop it!" she shouted, but he kept on and on, tickling her until she thought she was going to pee. "No, no, no . . . stop it!"

"Yes, yes, yes," he shouted back. She pushed him away. He rolled over on the pallet and threw his arms back against the pillows.

She caught her breath and then picked up the drawing, studied it. It was very clever. "Is this how you see me?"

"Always."

"Let me keep it," she begged.

"No."

"Pleeeeease!"

"What if your father were to find it, or one of those pesky brothers of yours?"

"How would they know it's me?"

"They'd know," he said, reaching for the drawing. She lifted it out of reach. He lay back down and closed his eyes. "It's not safe, honey."

She put the drawing on the table and climbed on top of him, her hips straddling his, her hands pinning his wrists to the pallet. "Please," she said again, letting her hair drape over his face. "Pretty please." She pressed her lips to his, knowing that he wouldn't change his mind, wouldn't let her keep it. She would have to wait until after they made love, when he dozed for a few minutes. She would smuggle it into her bag then. As she kissed him, she could already imagine the picture folded neatly and tucked between the pages of the Declaration of Independence.

25

Options

What is the value of a secret life?

She found this in her English notebook from last year. She read her notes on the Joseph Conrad novella, and they seemed distant, foreign, something about *doppelgänger,* a German word, but she couldn't remember what it meant, and she hadn't written a definition. But she remembered writing that question, remembered that the stowaway's name had been Leggatt and that while reading the book one night, she had dreamed of John rising from the floor of her bedroom, naked and green and glowing phosphorescently, just as Conrad had described it. She stared at the question again, thought about it, closed her notebook, and then, just a few minutes later, Mr. Sparling walked in and wrote on the chalkboard, "What is the value of a dream?"

He underlined the word "value" three times, and she shuddered. It was as if he'd seen what she'd written but had transformed it, turned it into something new and strange. Were *secret life* and *dream* the same? No, they weren't. But maybe there was a connection? How could he have written this, and at this precise moment? So strange how that happened. Aunt Velma's word for this flew into her head. Was Mr. Sparling another emissary?

She paid attention. But he didn't answer the question he'd written on the board, just turned to the class, lowered his head, and peered over his glasses. "What is the *value* of a dream?" he asked them.

No one spoke for a few moments. Jeff Dyer raised his hand.

Mr. Sparling ignored him but repeated the question with a different emphasis: "What is the value of a *dream*?"

Again no immediate answer. Sharon Littlefield raised her hand tentatively. Ignoring her, Mr. Sparling said softly, almost whispering, with an unsettling intensity, "*What* is the value of a dream?"

There were titters. Another one of Dwight Sparling's theatrical stunts. A trick, to provoke them. Was he angry? What was it? No one raised a hand. They waited for him. He examined each of their faces, person by person, maintaining eye contact for an uncomfortable few seconds. And then he nodded and sat down at his desk and began grading papers. He did not look up. There were still thirty minutes of class left. More laughter. He lifted his head sharply. Quiet.

He turned back to the papers on his desk. They looked at one another, uncertain what to do. To indicate Mr. Sparling's insanity, Gordy Toffler twirled his finger near his temple and crossed his eyes. But the other students turned away from him. Soon a contemplative silence filled the room. And then, one by one, they pulled notebooks from their desks or bags and began writing in them.

Laura opened her notebook again. There was her question: "What is the value of a secret life?" She flipped to an empty page in the middle of the notebook and wrote, "What is the value of a dream?"

And beneath that she wrote, in all capitals, OPTIONS.

And below that:

1. Let it die.
2. Don't rock the boat.
3. Wait.
4. Mexico.
5. Disappear.

And then below that she wrote, in big letters, POSSIBLE???

At the bottom of the page, she wrote, YES! And then she wrote it at the top and sides of the page. And around the list. When she was done, there were thirty-seven YESes on the page.

The bell startled her. The other students sat there at their desks, along with her, and didn't move. Mr. Sparling did not look up. Then, one by one, they stood and silently gathered their things and left the room. She waited until everybody else had gone. She studied Mr. Sparling, and then suddenly he looked up and surveyed the classroom, as if he'd been oblivious to his students' departure. He shifted his gaze to her, tilted his head slightly to the right, squinted his eyes, the corners of his mouth lifting quickly. He nodded once, forcefully, and then—was this true? did this really happen?—he winked at her. He dropped his eyes back down to his stack of papers and continued grading.

Had she really seen what she thought she'd seen? She shook her head and watched him, but he did not look up again. Nor did she say a word, but she felt a pocket of energy bubbling inside her chest. She gathered her things and walked slowly out of the classroom, but when she got to the hallway, she moved more swiftly along the tiled floor and down the stairs. The halls were busy with movement and noise, as students rummaged through their lockers at the end of the day. She moved fast, hearing only snatches of conversation that leapt into the air.

"What was *that* all about?"

"I told you he was crazy."

"You had to be there, though. It was amazing."

"Bullshit. He's nuts."

"Did you screw her?"

"Shut up!"

"Let's get out of here."

"Laura, you wanna go—" Dean Compson shouted behind her.

"No!"

"To 4-D's?"

"No!"

"Are you okay?" Marlene called.

"Yes!" she called back.

Outside, she broke into a run, passing Third Street, over to Buchanan, and continued running through the alley to the Charnelle Public Library. Inside, she sped to the bathroom, flung her bag down, turned on the faucet and splashed water over her face. In the mirror, she saw the drops streaming down her flushed cheeks, like rain on a window. The fringes of her hair dripped. She was out of breath, panting. Her temples thundered. Air whistled in and out of her nostrils. She thought of the horse races in New Mexico that her father had once taken them to—a couple of years before her mother left. Her father knew the trainer, and they got to go down to the stalls, see the Thoroughbreds after they raced. The air whistled in and out of their long noses. They seemed different than Hayworth and Ginger, larger, more forbidding. Their eyes were huge and round and black and seemed to stare right through you.

She yanked on the white cloth roll and wiped her hands, yanked again and then buried her face in the cloth, which smelled strongly of bleach. She leaned into the mirror.

"Yes!" she hissed at her reflection.

She gathered her things and found a table in the back of the library, behind the mystery section, dug through her bag, and pulled out the notebook. Turned to the page that read OPTIONS.

1. Let it die.

She had a strong urge to scratch the phrase out. But she decided to leave it on the list because it was an option. A real option, even though she wasn't willing to consider it. And she knew that John wouldn't consider it. She *knew*. It wasn't going to happen. To imagine that it would die might indeed kill it. Like time. You let it pass or you kill it, and then, before you know it, you're resigned, if not content, with the killing. No, they wouldn't let it die.

2. Don't rock the boat.

Was that even acceptable now? Him going home to his wife. The continued secrecy. Forever skulking and slinking and hoping to steal away when his wife and the boys were gone, and her father and brothers, too. That also seemed like a slow death. Yes, some part of her liked all the secrecy, the anticipation of it, the thrill and urgency of what little bits of time they could have together. But how long could that last? Not much longer.

Not now. Not after Galveston. She was forced to admit to herself how much it pained her that he went home to his wife each night. For the last six months, she tried not to think much about his wife and him together, what they did. He spoke so little about their marriage, and she was afraid to ask anything. Or was she afraid? Not really. She just didn't *want* to know. She liked that her life and John's life had these separate containers, and when they came together they were divorced from the rest of the world. But were they? Hadn't she been thinking lately about him with his wife? Did they do the same things that she and John did? How could he go back to her after Galveston? How would she feel if she started dating "some pock-faced boy with a banana in his pants," as Manny put it? Would it drive him crazy? But there was no boy she wanted. She wanted him.

3. Wait.

But it was risky. It was. In the Amarillo paper, she'd read about two cases of statutory rape over the last few months; both had parents bringing charges against twenty-one-year-old men and their teenage girlfriends— no rape at all from what she could tell, just laws for angry fathers. It was real, though. One man went to jail; the other was missing. But she'd also read about sixteen- and seventeen-year-olds getting married—a twelve-year-old girl, even, although that was in Arkansas and she only heard about it because it was so scandalous. She would be seventeen right before Christmas. And if John divorced his wife, then he and Laura could wait until she turned eighteen. Then her father couldn't stop them. That would be about a year and a half. They could keep the secret that long, couldn't they? She knew she could if John would be there waiting. But a year and a half was a long time. Too long.

4. Mexico.

Running off to Mexico, getting a quick divorce. That could be done. Or to Las Vegas first for the divorce and then to Mexico for the marriage. Gloria was only seventeen when she and Jerome ran off. Who said you had to wait? The laws could be bent or broken for love, and in time people forgave you. "Ask for forgiveness rather than permission," Manny liked to say. Gloria proved it. Laura could even write to her and find out the logistics, get some advice. They could settle someplace else, maybe in Europe with Gloria, and then they could return here later, if they wanted, after she

turned eighteen. People got over these things. Look at how her family recovered when Gloria left. When her mother left. It wasn't that hard. It
wasn't. There'd been at least six divorces in Charnelle that she was aware
of. And everybody knew that Dave Somersby, whose wife was an alcoholic, was in love with Tina Fellows. They didn't even try to hide it anymore, would show up at 4-D's together, and people no longer seemed to
care, probably figured he deserved some happiness. Wouldn't everybody
eventually accept what happened between Laura and John? Or would it be
another Tate-family scandal—those crazy women eloping, disappearing,
stealing other women's husbands? Home wreckers.

5. Disappear.

Her heart beat faster just looking at the word. She knew this was it. This
was what she wanted. To just disappear—and never come back. She and
John had done it already. Gone to Galveston, and no one had known, had
even suspected. It was a test run. He could get a job there—a good one, too.
Maybe that was what he was thinking when he asked those questions, said
she was his wife. If not Houston or Galveston, then someplace else. They
could just leave. Just pack up and skip town in the middle of the night, and
they'd have a new life. She and John *could* just disappear. She could get a
fake ID. She'd heard Manny talking about it with his friends, how easy it
was to fake these things. The world *liked* to be fooled. People swallowed
without question what you told them. You could reinvent yourself just by
going to a new place where nobody knew you. This was America. They
didn't even need to get married. And it wasn't like his wife couldn't get
by on her own. She had the money anyway, "the frills." She'd probably
move to Dallas with the kids. The kids—yes, that was the problem. Would
he leave them? *Could* he leave them? Would Laura be some kind of monster
for asking him to abandon them? Would these boys she'd grown to love,
and who obviously loved her, now hate her? And, for that matter, could she
leave her father and brothers, do what not just her sister had done but her
mother, too? She had come to believe that what her mother had done was a
kind of violence, something directed against her father and Manny and
Gloria, Gene and Rich, against herself. Wasn't there some essential mean-
ness or weakness at the core of her action? To wreck the family like that.
That's what Laura believed, if she had to articulate it, which she'd never
had to do. But had she and her father and brothers and Gloria *really* been

wrecked? Was there any lasting damage? People got over these things, didn't they? People were resilient. Her father was over it, wasn't he? Didn't some part of her realize—hadn't she *always* realized—that what her mother did *had* to be done? There was even something courageous, heroic about it, wasn't there? To gather her strength to leave, to head off into a new beginning, a new life, a new world. Cut off from her past—like an animal that chews off its foot to get out of a trap. That's what her mother had done. That was—as Mr. Sparling had said just the other day when they were discussing the ending of *Huckleberry Finn*—the story of America, wasn't it? All these people striking out for a new frontier, a new beginning—thieves, outcasts, runaways, orphans, criminals. All of them risking not just their lives but their *identities,* too. For what? For the pursuit of . . . what?

She stood up, shook her head, went to get a drink of water. The librarian, Mrs. Wickan, who lived down the street from Laura, smiled from the stacks. Yes, she would be leaving Mrs. Wickan, too. All of them. Could she do it?

She felt agitated, clumsy, sitting back down in her chair. She wanted this to be a Yes. In Mr. Sparling's room, she had felt it as a resounding Yes. She was willing to pay whatever it cost to get this dream, pay the value. Weren't *cost* and *value* the same thing? Or were they? She put her head down on the table, covering her notebook. She closed her eyes. She breathed. What is the *value* of a secret life? What is the value of a *secret* life? What is the value of a secret *life?*

She tried to coax back the memory of Galveston, to feel again the rhythm of it, the wet heat. She counted one Mississippi, two Mississippi, three Mississippi. And then held her breath, and it was there, at the edges. She closed her eyes more tightly but tried to remain calm, tried to patiently call it to her. The memory seemed like a skittish animal, hiding in the shadows. *Come out,* she called. *Come out.* She wanted it back. She was confused, and she needed the memory to guide her.

PART FOUR

Traveling in the Dark

August 1958

✳

Thrumming

*I*t was a Saturday night in early August, and Laura baked pork chops and fried potatoes, her father's favorite meal. Manny was camping with his buddies that weekend, so she made less than usual, just enough for her father, Gene, Rich, and herself. As she scooped out the last batch of potatoes, the grease popping and splattering in the pan, her father waltzed into the kitchen, smelling of Old Spice and hair oil, dressed up in his red short-sleeved, snap-button shirt, jeans, and stitched boots.

"Mmmm-mmm," he said and then leaned over and kissed her on the forehead. "I'm starving."

"When will you be back?" she asked.

"I don't know. Late, probably."

"What band is playing?"

"I don't know. The Pick Wickers, maybe."

She nodded.

Gene and Rich chattered through dinner, and her father told them jokes.

They kept laughing and spluttering with their mouths full. She watched silently.

He hadn't been dancing in a long time. She remembered that he used to take her mother dancing years ago. But he'd gone out only a couple of times in the last few weeks—for drinks at the Armory with his welding buddies and fishing once with the Cransburgh brothers. She wanted to believe his going out was a good sign—that he was returning to his old self, back to his normal life, that he could still find ways to enjoy himself even though her mother had disappeared less than three months ago. But she also felt uneasy whenever he left the house. She couldn't shake the unspoken belief that he was somehow responsible for her mother's leaving. He'd done something to drive her away, maybe they all had, but he seemed more responsible than the rest of them because he was her husband and their father, and it was too soon (wasn't it?) to be having a good time.

A shameful heat spread up her neck and over her chin and cheeks. She was as bad as those deacons at the church where they used to attend. It wasn't fair to her father, not at all. He was the one still here, taking care of them. Not her mother. She had disappeared. Not him. Right?

"I don't see why we have to go over to Mrs. Ambling's," she said.

"I told you, I don't know when I'll be back. I may play some cards after."

"I always watch the boys anyway. Why not tonight?"

"I just don't feel right you being here alone at night without me or Manny."

"I'm not a kid," she said. "Manny's just a year older, and you let him do anything he wants."

She didn't like being treated like the younger boys. Yet she also felt somewhat relieved because she hadn't been in the house at night without her father or Manny since her mother had left, and she was a little afraid. She also wondered if he thought she needed watching. Maybe because Gloria had eloped and her mother had left a year later, he wasn't going to take any chances with the last female in the house.

"We already settled this, Laura," he said. "You and the boys clean up, then go on over. I'll get you in the morning."

"Yes, sir," she said obediently.

"You mind your sister now. You hear?"

"Yes, sir," Gene said.

"And be good for Mrs. Ambling."

Rich had potatoes and ketchup in his mouth, but he nodded.

While they finished their meals, she started clearing the table. Her father suddenly stood up and sang "Your Cheatin' Heart," hamming it up until Rich and Gene spluttered again with laughter.

"Hey, good-lookin', whatcha got cookin'?"

He pulled her away from the sink, hugging her close to him, and they twirled quickly on the small kitchen floor.

"Sing for me, boys!"

Gene and Rich sang along and pounded the table. She and her father two-stepped, ended with an extravagant twirl, and then he held her close and dipped her dramatically like Fred Astaire did with Ginger Rogers. Gene and Rich cheered. She laughed and tried to push him away, but he picked her up and twirled her around the kitchen once again, almost knocking over the skillet full of still-warm grease. When he put her down, little sweat beads trickled along both their hairlines. It was hot outside, and despite the windows being open, it seemed even hotter in the kitchen.

He sat down. "Whoa! I need some more tea. Your sister's done wore me out."

He poured himself another tall glass from the pitcher on the table, and they all watched him lift his head and the tea drain down his throat, his big Adam's apple bobbing. When he finished, he shook his head vigorously a couple of times, which made the boys laugh but sent a dark, cold shiver across the back of Laura's neck. The image reminded her, for some reason, of Greta and her puppies.

He reached out his hand to her, and she took it, and he gently pulled her into his lap and said, "Boys, your sister is our little sweetie. Don't you ever forget it."

He nuzzled his clean-shaven chin into her throat and kissed her cheek. It felt rough. Quickly he was up, putting on his watch, patting the boys' heads. Then he was gone.

Watching him rumble down the road in his truck, leaving a gray-white plume of dust behind him, she felt empty. The word forlorn *popped into her head.*

"Gene, why don't you do the dishes."

"It ain't my turn."

"I don't care," she snapped. "Just do it."

On the front porch, she sat in the metal chair her father had welded and listened to the loud buzzing of the cicadas. The evening sun was still hot and bright. She looked at the hole where their old oak tree had been uprooted after it had been struck by lightning the day before her mother disappeared. Her father had not refilled the hole, and it looked like a robbed grave.

She went back inside and helped Gene dry the plates. The three of them went to the backyard, and Rich played in the sandbox and on the swing while she and Gene pulled the laundry off the line.

She checked Fay's food bowl. Still full. The dog hadn't eaten much in the past few months. Although her father said it was because of the heat more than anything else, Laura still believed that it was because of what happened with Greta, followed by the disappearance of their mother. He said that was foolishness. She stroked Fay's side and neck and rubbed her belly. Despite what her father said, she knew why Fay was upset.

She helped bathe Rich, and they all grabbed their pillows and sleeping bags and went next door. Mrs. Ambling answered the door in her nightgown. Her face looked blotchy, her eyes watery, her nose red and runny. She had a tissue in her hand.

"Oh, Lord," she said. "I meant to call. I took some medicine, and it's made me a little dopey."

"What's wrong?" Laura asked.

"I've come down with something. I don't know what. I've got a fever. Has your father already left?"

"Yes, ma'am," she said.

"Well, I suppose you all can just come on in. I hope you don't catch what I've got, though."

"We can stay at our house," Laura said.

"Your father said he'd be out late."

"It's okay. I watch the boys all the time."

"But Daddy said—" Gene began.

"It's okay, really," Laura said. "You don't feel good. We'll be right next door. We can come over if there's a problem."

"Are you sure?"

Mrs. Ambling smiled weakly, clearly relieved, the door already closing on them.

"I'm sure."

She left her father a note on the kitchen table, explaining about Mrs. Ambling, so he wouldn't be angry. The three of them listened to a baseball game on the radio. Later, after Gene and Rich went to bed, she pulled out the letter she'd received from Gloria just this week. In it she'd included a picture of herself, the air force pilot she married, and their baby girl, Julie. In the background was the Mediterranean Sea with craggy cliffs rising dramatically in the distance. Gloria didn't know about their mother yet; they didn't know how to reach Gloria, and even if they could have, their father didn't like to talk about either her mother or Gloria. Her sister looked happy in the picture. Laura wished she could be with her, though she knew that if she was with her, then Gloria would have to know about their mother, and part of what made Gloria seem happy was the fact that she didn't know. Laura missed her sister, but she didn't feel sad anymore that she was gone. Just a kind of sweet longing to be with her again. It was more complicated with her mother.

She picked up the Hollywood Star Gazette, which she'd bought with her baby-sitting money. But the bright, thickly textured pictures of Janet Leigh and Deborah Kerr agitated her. She was only fourteen and felt she was still too boyish-looking, nothing like these glamorous, curvy women. They reminded her, strangely, of her mother, whose body had been made thick in the middle by hard work and children, but she was still womanly enough, and her face had not yet been too hardened by age or the West Texas wind. No movie star, but she was pretty, with large, dark brown eyes and a thin, perfect nose, and sometimes, when she was free from worry and her ash blond hair was loose around her face, she seemed radiant to Laura.

She didn't like to think about her mother too much, especially when she was alone, but sometimes she couldn't help it. The thoughts or images would be there in her mind and wouldn't go away. Her mother was like a ghost who might return at any time, but if she did, what would happen then? Laura tried to imagine where she was now, what she was doing, but without any context it all seemed like that huge hole in the yard. Laura feared she might forget what her mother looked like. She wished she had a photograph. It seemed odd to her that there were no photographs. Her mother had taken the wedding picture with her.

Laura got up, turned the radio to a music station, and sang along quietly to Patsy Cline and a Weavers song and Bob Wills, always Bob Wills and his western swing, and danced around the room. She closed her eyes and imagined herself with Charlton Heston, and then with her father on the sawdust dance floor of the Armory—the smoky, sweaty, sweet-smelling perfume of the couples, the skirts billowing out, the two-stepping, waltzing, fast-twirling, double-dipping couples. She couldn't wait until she was able to go dancing there *herself. In less than a month, she'd be starting high school, and she could go if someone asked her. She'd already picked out the dress she wanted to buy—a green-and-white-striped one with small white satin bows on the sleeves and waist. She was saving her baby-sitting money to get it.*

She spun one last time before plopping down on the couch, sweaty again because it was so hot inside, even with the breeze blowing in. She sat there and listened to the radio until it signed off, and the house seemed eerily quiet, except for the cicadas and the occasional bark or lonely howl of a dog down the alley.

In bed, trying to will herself to sleep, she could hear the late-summer breeze whistling in the branches of the trees. She wondered if her mother had lain awake at night, preparing herself to leave, to not have to think about what would be left behind, toughening her spirit. Had she been planning it for a long time? It seemed so sudden, without warning. Mrs. Ambling said she'd just walked out to the road, carrying that brown suitcase. And she was gone, but of course she wasn't. How could she be completely gone when she was here right now in Laura's mind?

She opened her eyes, tried to keep them open for thirty seconds—one Mississippi, two Mississippi, three Mississippi—which Gloria had told her was the secret to washing away bad thoughts or dreams. Then she closed her eyes again and told herself, Fall asleep, fall asleep, fall asleep, fall asleep, *until the phrase seemed funny. So strange that word "falling," like going over an embankment, standing on the unrailed precipice at Palo Duro Canyon, the vertigo of below, trying to stop the silly crazy foolish impulse to jump, jump, jump. Just an inch—no, not even that much—separating ground from air. And then falling into . . . where? Into air, into nothing. Like being asleep is the fall itself, not the landing. You don't fall* from *or* into *or* onto *sleep. You just fall asleep. Like disappearing. Like her mother. She'd fallen. But fallen where? No. Fallen away—away from* them, *but to what? Into* what? *Or maybe it was like sleep after all, neither away from nor to anything. It was the thing itself.*

And then Laura was asleep, solidly, without thought or dream.

When she woke, it was to the sound of something being knocked over in another room. Gene lay curled on the corner of his and Manny's bed. Rich was stretched out with his feet hanging through the bars because he was too big for the crib.

She heard a laugh, then muffled whispers. She grabbed the pocketknife from her dresser and crept toward the hallway.

The lights were out, but the moon filtered through the sheer curtains. Her father's door was slightly ajar. She heard laughter, more whispering, and she knew then that her father was in the room with a woman. Had her mother come back? *She hesitated in the hallway with the knife in her hand. No, it was not her mother's voice. She felt stupid. She started to return to bed and sleep, but then she heard a little high-pitched yelp, and she stopped and sat down, her back against the wall. The darkness of the house enveloped her. She scooted close to her father's door and sat there on her knees. She closed her eyes. Outside, the cicadas buzzed. The bed squeaked, rocking back and forth. She imagined a small canoe swaying in the troughs of waves. She squeezed her eyes tightly and thought she could hear their lips against each other. Her father's breathing seemed labored and deep and rhythmic, and the woman's voice swelled between his, higher-pitched and sharp, almost whistling.*

She moved her face closer to the door. Her heart thumped in her chest and neck and temples. She felt paralyzed by their laboring. She thought of Fay when she was in heat, the male dogs panting, their tongues dripping. Laura's stomach dropped, but she pressed her face next to the cracked door. She closed one eye and with the other tried to see into the room. It was dark except for a faint light from the open-shuttered window, which cast a slatted splash of yellow over her father's bare, moving back and made a silhouette of the woman. The sheets and covers clung to the edges of the bed.

When her eyes adjusted, she saw the outline of her father's body pressing down onto the woman. The bed did seem to roll, though not with the sea wildness she had imagined. The springs continued to squeak. Their breathing increased in intensity. She could see the woman's white thighs spread wide, like phosphorescent wings perpendicular to his hips, but the rest of her body seemed trapped beneath his, swallowed in the sagging, lumpy mattress and under his long broad body. The woman's arm was slung back against the pillow, crooked over her face, her mouth pinched at the corners in a grimace as his shoulders rubbed against her cheeks. He moved forcefully over her, and his breathing turned to muffled groans. He rocked and pressed so that her body disappeared into the bed.

Is this why my mother disappeared? *The question caught in her mind like a hook.*

The woman shook her head and let out what sounded like a painful moan, and Laura felt sickened by it and unsure if she should open the door and let herself be seen. She wanted to stop this, wanted her father off this woman, wanted him to quit pressing and breathing in this way. But she could not bring herself to do it. She closed her eyes, but the sounds overwhelmed her. She heard the mocking drone of the cicadas outside.

When she opened her eyes again, her heart leapt into her throat because the woman's arm was no longer over her face, and she stared directly at Laura. Could the woman see her there? Surely not. But there the woman was; she just kept staring, her eyes distinct and luminous in the dark. Laura stared back and could see that the face was not womanish but girlish, with chubby white cheeks and a soft, puckerish mouth. She felt a panic billow inside her as her father made more noise, and the bed rocked against the wall, and the woman-girl let out a small groan, muffled by her father's shoulder.

She jerked back. She felt dizzy in the hall and closed her eyes, but all the noise—those crazy cicadas, her father's breathing, the bedsprings—thundered in her head. She felt as if she were being held upside down, and when she opened her eyes, she was surprised to find herself still sitting upright in the hall. She crawled toward her room, shut the door, and slipped into her bed. She put her face into the pillow and covered her ears so she couldn't hear anything except the rush of blood in her temples, which after a few minutes diminished to a steady throb.

She tried to sleep but couldn't. And then she heard a rustling in the hallway. The bathroom door opened and closed. Water ran. The toilet flushed. A minute later, the door opened again, and then there were footsteps outside her own door. It creaked. She kept her eyes closed, fearing what she would see when she opened them. She knew that someone was in the room—her father, certainly, though the presence seemed lighter—and she could also smell something sweet, like warmed buttermilk, so she didn't move. She held her breath and felt a slight pressure by the side of her bed, a rustle, and then the door closed. Feet padded to her father's room, and then his door shut.

She opened her eyes. Beside her on the small bed was the knife. It seemed puny and foolish there. She swallowed hard, her throat scratchy, raw. She reached out and grabbed the knife handle. It was moist. She opened it and pressed her finger against the dull blade. It did not cut her. She closed it again and slipped it between the mattress and box spring, and lay there in the dark listening. After a while, there was rustling in the other room, the click of her father's door, the sound of feet over the hardwood floor, her father whispering. Finally the front door creaked open and shut. Her father's truck rumbled to life.

She tiptoed to the window and watched the truck back out, crunching the gravel of the driveway, the beams from the headlights making small yellow circles in the dark street. She felt the hot summer air through the bug screen, could smell the dust from the road, the ragweed twitching her nostrils, could hear the cicadas still at it.

The night was barely lit now by the clouded moon. She waited until she no longer heard the truck. She didn't return to her own bed but checked on Gene and Rich in the beds beside hers. Even though Manny was gone for the night, Gene was huddled close to his edge, a habit of deferring to his older brother even in his absence. Though only six years older than Gene, she felt sorry for him and angry, too, that already life had taught him to expect so little. She reached out and stroked his head, but he didn't stir. Even his breathing was shallow, as if he were afraid to take too much air from the world. Rich, by contrast, was stretched out in the crib, a space hog, a thrasher, someone who demanded his due without even knowing it. It was just part of his nature.

And what was her nature? What did she look like when she slept? What would she think if she could see herself clearly? The fact that she could not know, that she remained partially blind to herself, bewildered her. Eyes always looking out and then in, but not at. She reached over the crib and straightened Rich, tugged the sheet from beneath him, covered him up. There was no real reason with the heat, but it was a habit of hers, this need to be covered and to cover others at night.

She glided out of the bedroom, into the hallway, and then into her father's room, where the windows were open. She pulled the lamp cord, and a harsh white glow splashed the room, forced her to squint. The covers and sheets lay tangled around the mattress. There was a pocket in the middle of the bed where the woman-girl had been. Laura placed one hand out and down, ran it just a few inches over the top of the sheets, feeling the heat still present from their bodies. She was hesitant at first to touch, to disturb. The heat radiated the entire length of the mattress, from the foot to the pillows, and she floated both hands above the bed and was surprised by the invisible warmth. She reached down to the center, where their hips met, and she touched the sheet. It was hot and slightly damp, but she pressed one palm down flat, her fingers spread, and ran her hand back and forth and then around in a circle. She reached out with her other hand and could imagine the two of them in here, not even a half hour ago, and the quiet stillness of the room was like the buzzing sound you hear in the silence after thunder.

She smelled them here, too, and took a calm pleasure in isolating the *scents. Her father's hair oil and Old Spice, the woman-girl's too-sweet perfume, like that buttermilk smell drifting into her room. There was a faint whiff of the rum her father liked and spearmint gum and something else, something sharp, pungent, the smell of sex, she figured, and lingering above and below and swirling through was the dank, tangy odor of sweat.*

She searched for her mother's own particular smell, the talcum powder like a fine dust on her body, but it wasn't here anymore, not even a trace, and she felt saddened by that loss, a kind of betrayal, but Laura wasn't sure now who was being betrayed.

She opened her eyes, tugged on the lamp cord, and slid her feet purposefully over the hardwood floor so she could hear the callused shwoosh of her feet, out of her father's room, through the narrow hallway that seemed like a tunnel to her—she'd never noticed this before—and then to the living room. It, too, held the smell of her father and the woman-girl in it, and she followed slowly, could trace it to the door, which she opened. She stepped outside to the porch, and even there she could smell them, as if they'd left a vaporous trail. Then the odors dissipated and were gone.

She sat down on the porch, feeling very calm, very awake. She let the breeze brush through her nightgown. It was still hot. She then stood up on her tiptoes, pulled her gown over her head, and, reaching high, stretched out her body, which seemed dangerous, thrilling. She hadn't been outside with so little on since she was a child; she remembered the last time, running around naked in the summery yard, chasing Fay and some of her puppies before they gave them away.

It was dark out, not quite sunrise yet, and no cars, not even the faraway sound of trucks from the highway. She enjoyed this feeling, like a shedding, like an opening up. She thought of the way the rattlers and bull snakes sometimes left long, papery casings in the night for her brothers and her to find the next day. She imagined the snakes slipping away, the new skin wet and vulnerable and free.

She walked over the lawn, skirting the place where the old oak had been, and on out to the middle of the road, where she stood and stared down one end of the street and then the other. Both ends extended farther than she could see at night with only this thin moon and cloud-tangled stars. The ends of the road turned away, bent out of sight, away, away, away into darkness. She stood there and looked at the scattered houses on either side of the street and then at her own small house, where, inside, her brothers and father and she slept, ate, argued, sulked, laughed, dreamed. Where that woman-girl stared at her from her mother's bed. Where her mother was before she disappeared.

No, not disappeared. *Before she* left.

It seemed so small, this place, too small to contain all their lives. She thought about the other houses with their own lives cramped too tightly inside. And the road extended into darkness, the black night high above, the cicadas buzzing.

She felt no fear, not even the cold threat of being caught.

Who cares?

She closed her eyes and, with her arms out, started to spin slowly, then faster and faster until she staggered and fell on the dusty road. It didn't hurt, and she just stayed there for a while, with the acrid taste of dust in her mouth. Then she stretched out on her back and felt the still-warm gravel beneath, sticking like shards into her body, but even that didn't hurt. She stared up at the black sky, traced the constellations with her fingers, and just as the first light of sunrise began its promise, she heard—or rather felt—a sound emanating from her body, a low, vibrating whistle that seemed in tune with the cicadas and the wind and the breathing of the night and the warm road.

She closed her eyes and listened, stayed calmly there as she heard and could almost taste a deep, pressured thrumming inside her head. A tingly heat spread through her neck and chest and stomach and arms and down through her thighs and calves and toes. It seemed as if a shade were slowly being lifted over her closed eyelids.

She opened her eyes and could see headlights, like two pale animals loping around the curve. It was her father's truck, she knew, and she wondered, without worry or fear, what he would do if she stayed right where she was.

Will he see me in time? Will he run over me?

It made her smile to think about it. She imagined that anxious twitch he got around the corners of his mouth when he was confused or worried or sad. She didn't feel afraid, just curious, as the truck zigzagged slowly down the street, still pretty far in the distance. She wished he was gone, would disappear himself for a while, maybe forever, let her stay here like this and let the sun rise fully on her, transforming the world and the house and everything she could smell and hear and see and feel and taste into light and blistering heat. She didn't want to share this feeling. She didn't want to have to explain herself to him or to anyone, just as now she didn't want explanations from him.

As the beams closed in, she rose quickly and felt again that she was gliding as she grabbed her gown. She slipped through the door, into bed, and pulled the sheet up and over her face so that it floated for a couple of seconds before shrouding her. The dust from her body created a layer of fine grit on the bottom sheet.

She closed her eyes and tried to recall the thrumming, coax it back. She breathed slowly, listening to her breath, her heartbeat. She heard her father's truck crunch in the driveway, the rattle of the engine as it died, the front door creak open, then click shut.

Almost there, yes, close, just out of reach.

Her father opened her door. He paused before whispering, "Laura, honey, was that you?"

She didn't answer. She was far away now, far away. She could almost feel it again, the thrum and radiating heat, and she wanted to let it spread through her body. Was this what her mother had felt as she left, this buzz and heat, this pulsing in her own body? Was this what had pulled her, like a compulsion, from the house and to the bus station and away from them forever? Did she find a small, private part of herself where there wasn't room for anyone else? Laura could almost understand that. It seemed sad and mysterious—and even beautiful.

"Are you awake?" her father whispered worriedly, nudging her shoulder. "Why aren't you all at Mrs. Ambling's?"

She could smell the cigarettes and sweet rum on his breath. Her eyes blurred hotly. Still she didn't answer. That feeling, that thrumming, was slipping from her now, drifting too quickly away. She could almost see it, like a brightly colored balloon—rising, rising, and then riding on the wind, growing smaller and smaller until it was barely visible, merely a colored dot in the distance, insignificant.

And then not even there.

26

✦

We'll See

"You've thought it all through, have you?" he asked after she explained her plan.

He'd picked her up behind the warehouse a little before five, minutes before a rainstorm. They drove through the downpour, and once in the barn they made love urgently in a way that reminded her of the loose abandon of Galveston. As they held each other afterward, she realized that the last time they'd made love while it was raining had been in the tent at Lake Meredith. How different this was from that time, how different they both were, how strange to think it was only a few months ago. She remembered her own fear and pain then, how out of control she felt, how odd they seemed to each other. And now it was easy between them, as if it always had been, and she longed not only for the intensity but also for the quietness after they made love, the world slowly coming back into focus, the whistled breathing of John, his face pressed against her shoulder, his arms enclosing her. Listening to the rain pound against the barn, they'd dressed and then lain on the pallet next to each other in the light of the kerosene lamps. Trying to disguise her nervousness, her eagerness, she'd told him about her plan.

"What do you think?" she asked, biting a hangnail.

"Impressive," he said, but he wasn't smiling.

"Do you love me?" she asked and then immediately wished she hadn't. That wasn't the right question. Not at all. Not now. It exposed her neediness.

"You know I do."

It would have been nice to hear the words, but at least he didn't deny it. "We could do it," she said. "We could."

"We'll see," he said.

She couldn't quite read his reaction. The stakes were high, she knew that. Higher for him than for her. She had expected him to argue with her, to play devil's advocate. She had readied herself for a fight; she had prepared herself to persuade him. But he said nothing. He just turned away, walked to the window, and opened the curtain slightly to expose the rain-smeared glass. He reached into his shirt pocket for his cigarettes. He drew one out and put it in his mouth, but he didn't light it. She followed him to the window, wrapped her arms around his chest, pressed her face against his back.

"Are you okay?" she asked.

"Yeah."

She sidled in front of him, pulled the unlit cigarette from his mouth and laid it on the windowsill. Standing on her toes, she kissed his neck and then looked at him. His eyes seemed glassy, his lips not as red as they usually were, too dry and cracked. She felt suddenly sorry for him.

"Come here," she said, taking his hand. "Come with me."

She led him to the mattress and coaxed him to lie down again. He laced his hands behind his head. She stared at him for a long time, until he grew uncomfortable and closed his eyes. She leaned down and gently kissed his lips and then his neck. She ran her fingers along his collarbone and through the tuft of hair rising out of the top of his shirt.

"John."

"We'll see," he said.

He smiled, but it wasn't a genuine smile, just something to appease her. She pressed her body against his, looped her leg over his hips.

"John," she said optimistically, "we can do it."

She lay on top of him, kissed him until he began to respond. She wanted to show him what he could expect. She wanted him to see the possibilities.

27

✳

Go Ahead

he next week John failed once to show up at the arranged time, and
the day when he did pick her up behind the warehouse, he seemed
distracted, hurried, impatient. She tried to get him to tell her what he was
thinking, but he just kept saying, "We'll see," like she was a child who could
be put off indefinitely. She intentionally stood him up the next Monday; she
wanted him to know what it was like to be left there waiting. He had not called
to find out why she wasn't there. She wondered if *he* had even shown up.

By that following Thursday, when he picked her up, she was itching for
a fight. She did not say a word in the truck, felt in fact humiliated, livid
about having to scrunch down on the floorboard yet again. When they arrived at the barn, he lit the lamp, and she stripped quickly and angrily and
then lay on the pallet.

"What's the matter?" John asked.

"Nothing. Go ahead," she said. She opened her legs and stared un-
blinking at him, her lips pursed.

"What the hell does that mean?"

"Go ahead if you want to. I'm not stopping you."

"Are you mad at me, Laura?" he asked, surprised.

She just stared at him. He shook his head slowly and moved toward the pallet, as if he could repair the damage he'd already done.

"Laura, what is the *matter*?"

"You don't want to know," she said, sitting up.

"I do."

"No, you don't."

"Tell me."

"How is this going to end?" she demanded.

"What end? What are you talking about?"

"This. Us."

He sighed as he lifted his eyebrows, pretended he didn't have any idea what she was talking about, that he was not a mind reader. She knew that look. She'd used it herself. She wasn't buying this act. He damn well knew what she was talking about.

"I just want to know," she said flatly. "How is it going to end?"

"It's not ending. Nothing's ending." He pulled a cigarette out of his pocket and started to light it. This irritated her even more.

"Just answer me," she said, more insistently. She stood up but made no attempt to cover herself. She wanted him to look at her. "Answer me!"

"Jesus! We only have an hour."

"And that time can be better spent screwing me!" she shouted.

"*Laura!*" The lit cigarette fell from his mouth, and he had to stamp it out. "Damn it!"

"Well," she barked, "that's all this is, isn't it?"

"No! No, not at all." He put his hand out to her. She crossed her arms. Kept them there, didn't move. "My God," he said, "I've never seen you like this."

"It's been over two weeks since we talked about leaving. You said, 'We'll see.'"

"I did not say that."

"You damn well did too. You said, 'We'll see.' What does that *mean*? 'We'll see.' I want to *know*. I don't *see* anything."

"I'm still thinking about it."

"Bullshit!" she shouted.

"Quit talking like that."

"You're not my father. Don't tell me what to do."

"Please, then," he said, reaching out to her again. She stepped away. He picked up her shirt, handed it to her. "Just calm down. Here, put your clothes on, and we'll talk."

She slapped his hand away. "You don't want to go with me, do you?"

"I didn't say that."

"You don't *have* to say. It's obvious."

"That's not true," he said.

"Then what *is?* What *is* true? You say you want to be with me. But you're never gonna leave here, are you? You're just stringing me along."

"Stop it! That's enough! It's just not possible right now. There are other people to consider here, you know."

"I know it as well as you do." She grabbed her clothes, turned her back to him, and quickly began dressing.

"I don't think you do. It's very complicated. I have a wife. I have kids. I have a job. If I leave, all that's over. Over. I can never come back. Never. You don't understand how much—"

She whirled around, snapping, "Just take me home."

"Laura—"

"Take me home!"

She didn't need his explanations, didn't need him treating her like some selfish, petulant girl. Not now. She grabbed her socks and shoes and headed for the barn door.

"Come back here."

"I want to go home."

"You're the one who said you wanted to talk."

"Not anymore. Just take me home."

"Okay, then!" he shouted. "Fine! If that's what you want, fine!"

He started the truck and backed out, but it made her sick just being on the floorboard again. She'd had enough of that. "I changed my mind. I wanna walk."

"It's three miles to your house."

"I don't care."

"Just let me take you to the warehouse."

"I don't want to go to the warehouse. I'm sick of that damn warehouse."

"It's safer that way."

"Yeah, the secret place where you drop off your little slut."

"Goddamn it, shut up!"

"Let me out."

"No."

She opened the door. The bleached dirt of the road scared her momentarily.

"Laura, what in the hell are you—"

She was stepping out and then rolling, off the dirt road into the grass, but then she landed, surprisingly, on her feet, like a cat. She was grateful for this bit of grace. He stopped the truck, hurtled out, and stood at the tailgate, calling to her, "*Jesus Christ!* Are you okay?"

She just stared at him.

"Get in!"

"Forget it," she said.

"Get *in!*"

She didn't answer him, just walked on ahead of him, past the truck.

He opened his door. She heard it but didn't look back. He eased the truck up beside her. "Please, Laura," he called through the window. "Just get in the truck. Please." She kept on walking. He stopped, and she could hear him getting out again. He stalked behind her. "Laura, goddamn it, get your ass in the truck!"

She said nothing, kept going.

"Is that the way you want it? Is it? Then fine. Walk, then, you little—"

She wheeled around, facing him. He stopped himself. She dared him. She wanted him to say whatever it was he was going to say. When he didn't, she turned around and began walking again. A few seconds later, a rock flew to the side of her, wide, not close, not even really aimed at her, she knew, just meant to provoke her. It hit the road, skipped three times in the dust, as if across a pond. She didn't even flinch. Didn't turn around.

The engine gunned, and then the gravel chomped under the tires. He roared past her, dust billowing in her face.

"Go on!" she yelled. "Just get the hell out of here!"

She squinted against the dust, tried not to inhale the opaque cloud.

✳

28

Lurching

*T*hat night she went to bed thrilled with the excitement of her rage. She did not sleep, nor did she want to sleep. About eleven she got up, changed into her clothes, and slipped out the back door. It was warm still, only a slight breeze blowing, with no clouds. The moon three-quarters full, bright gold, and stars everywhere. Fay woke when Laura opened the door and approached her, growling at first, but when she saw who it was, she put her head against Laura's legs. Laura petted the dog for a long time, reliving what had happened with John, alternately proud and ashamed of her behavior. Fay fell asleep in the dirt by the porch, and Laura wandered around the yard, looked at the foundation her father had been laying for his new workshop. And then she walked down the alley, but the dogs started barking at her, so she went back for her bike.

She pedaled down the alley and then out onto the streets, north to the Waskalanti Creek, racing by the trestle where Danny Lincoln had broken his neck and where she and John had made love at the end of the summer, off the road, under the canopy of trees. She pedaled over to the bus station, which was just off the town square at the intersection of the highways. She circled it three times, stopped and looked off to the highway leading north-west, toward Denver, and then pedaled to the one leading southeast toward Amarillo and stood there trying to imagine the direction her mother had gone, imagining what she must have been looking ahead to.

Staring down the dark highways, she wondered for the first time if her mother's disappearance and her own affair with John were linked, if the one had caused the other. Would she have been at the Armory on New Year's Eve had her mother still been here? Would she have been so able—or willing—to deceive her family had her mother been here? Her mother was always so quiet, so secretive herself, really, but she also seemed to have a direct pipeline to other people's secrets. She even said many times that there were *no* secrets and had seemed to know what would happen with Gloria before everybody else did. Laura's father, on the other hand, was less suspecting, though you'd think he'd be more wary, given what had happened with Gloria and then his wife. Laura was sure she could not have hidden what she was up to had her mother been here. There would have been no Lake Meredith. No idyll in Galveston. And she wondered if John would have been so bold himself. It was one thing to dupe his gullible friend Zeeke, but Laura's mother was, in her hard and silent mystery, more formidable than her father. Her mother's absence had opened up this space for the Letigs to enter her life. And look where that had brought her. To this foolishness! She suddenly felt a hot surge of rage at her mother, something she could never remember feeling before; she couldn't understand the anger her father and Manny felt when her mother left. She could not bring herself to completely blame her mother. She had only felt empty and confused and inarticulately sad, and later, resigned. And then somehow she'd turned it around in her mind so that she was sometimes happy that her mother had left, had transformed her into a hero, courageously doing the unthinkable, reinventing herself, as if her disappearance were something to be honored and admired—like some damn American myth that Mr. Sparling nattered on about in his lectures. *How stupid!* It was all so stupid. The woman had abandoned her family. No explanation, no nothing. What was there to admire in that? *What?* she wondered. Maybe her mother was dead now. Maybe she ran off and killed herself, just like Uncle Unser. Maybe that's what she was plotting in Aunt Velma's barn on Easter. Well, what did it matter now? She was as good as dead to them anyway.

Laura was sick of thinking about it. She was sick of thinking altogether. She got back on her bike and rode hard around the square in the cool evening breeze, until she broke a good sweat, and then practically coasted over to the Letigs' house, where she stood by a tree across the street and stared into their dark windows. It was late, past midnight now. She pedaled to the alley, the dogs barking shrilly at her. But she kept on, making one pass and then another, fast as she could, the rocks on the unpaved alley road crunching under her tires. The Letigs' lights were off in the back windows, too.

She set her bike down in the alley against a trash can. She breathed hard, but from the riding, not from fear. She opened the back gate of their yard. Across the alley, a dog barked once, twice. She turned to it and put her finger up to her mouth, stared at it fiercely.

"Hush," she whispered. The dog shut up.

She walked into the yard, not secretly, but quiet and calm. She didn't fear being caught, and she felt liberated by her lack of fear. She went to the bedroom window and could see those sheer blue curtains she'd admired from inside when she was nosing around in their bedroom. The window was open. The curtains swayed gently in the light breeze. She pressed her face up close, tried to peer in, but she could see nothing at first. She held her breath and listened, could hear the hum of John's breathing as he slept. A light wheezing noise, too—Mrs. Letig. Anne. Anne Letig. Everything else was quiet. She stayed there for several minutes, barely breathing now, just listening to them. They were so still in this house, everybody sleeping and dreaming whatever it was they were dreaming.

She pressed her face against the screen, but all she could see were two lumps in the bed. Not close together. A space between them. Her eyes adjusted, and she could make out Anne Letig, with her thick stomach and her nice fashionable dresses and her cash and her store-bought vegetables and her pinochle games and her hatboxes and perfume and silver fish barrettes and her well-behaved boys and her whining about her apron strings stretching to Dallas and her beef and chicken enchiladas and all those confusing references to her mother, telling Laura that her mother loved . . . no, *loves* you children. What the hell did she know? Who elected her substitute parent? Always sticking her stupid foot in her mouth, acting like she cared, patting poor sick Laura in her bed. *Oh, we love you so much, Laura. You are so special to us!* When what she really cared about was having a dependable baby-sitter so she could drive off to Aspen or Dallas or to the Brewers' for pinochle or wherever else she wanted to go. If she didn't have the money, didn't have the *frills*, would Laura even be in her life? Would John even be in her life? Wasn't that the real thing holding him back now? He couldn't stand to part with the *frills*. What would Mrs. Letig have done back in May had she known that the baby-sitter was so sick because John had taken her out in the woods and screwed her? Would Mrs. Letig have been so sweet and comforting then?

Laura had the impulse to scream at them through their window. Scare the hell out of them both, cackle like a raving maniac. Another crazy Tate woman.

The dog across the alley barked again. *Enough*, she thought. *Enough*. She walked away, out the gate, and to her bike. She started off but circled back down the alley, slowing for one final look. *Enough!* And then off she sped, down the middle of the dark, empty streets, coasting down another alley of barking dogs to her own yard, to Fay, panting by the fence, waiting for her return, glad to see her, licking her hand and then, when Laura bent down, licking her face with that nasty old breath of hers.

The poor dog was starved for love. Laura let her into the house, even though she didn't smell very good, and into her room, where her brothers all slept soundly. It was odd how when you didn't care if you were caught, you wouldn't be, but if you did care, you were always on the verge of detection. Or so you thought. She slipped back into her pajamas and into bed, Fay licking her dangling fingers and then wheezing into sleep. Laura made the hummingbird wings on the sculpture flap one more time but was mad at herself for doing it. It seemed sentimental, stupid even. Then finally she slept.

She didn't go to the warehouse at all that week. But her rage had given way to something more vulnerable and painful. She wanted to see him but felt queasy about it. What would she say? What was there left between them? Throughout the day she would think about John—about his catlike swagger, the way he seemed sometimes to glide when he walked, about his long, angular face and how angry he had been the last time they'd been together, how they'd screamed at each other and he'd thrown that rock toward her and then roared past her, wheeling dust into her face. Everything between them came back to her in vivid detail. The memories that she had struggled to coax to the surface before, when she had wanted them, now came unbidden. She would be working through a complicated trigonometry problem, and she'd inexplicably smell sea salt and was suddenly back at the beach, in the cabin, caught in the crook of his arm, listening to the sound of the waves. Or in English class Mr. Sparling called on her to read aloud from "Young Goodman Brown"—a dumb tale, she thought, about a boy, a girl, and what appeared to be the devil—and in the middle of the paragraph, the words before her were gone. All she could see was a page of dust, John's truck disappearing in the distance.

"Miss Tate," Mr. Sparling had said, "please continue."

"Yes, sir," she said, but she didn't know where she was. Debbie had to reach over and put her finger on the line where she had stopped.

She wanted to talk to him, but it was impossible. She called once. His wife answered the phone, so Laura hung up the receiver. She didn't like this neediness in herself. She had to fight the urge to go to the warehouse in the afternoon to watch from a distance to see if he would show up. She waited in the school library after the last bell rang or walked to the Charnelle Library or downtown to the courthouse lawn and into 4-D's, where she listened to Dean chatter, refilling her cherry soda for free, and she watched the clock until five-fifteen passed. At five-thirty, she would head home, taking back alleys rather than the sidewalks so that he wouldn't drive by and see her, though she also knew that even that was a form of self-flattery. He must be glad to be rid of her, she thought. Glad it was finally over. She had pushed too hard.

But still, she missed him, and at night she would lie awake, unable to sleep, staring at the sculpture, moving her eyelashes so the bird's wings would flap, and in the evenings she would take her diary into the bathroom and read back through the entries, never with his name, never with any details, coded so that only she would know what it meant. One afternoon she found, tucked between the pages, the drawing of Yankee Doodle Gal, and she began to cry. She ran the water in the sink and then the tub to drown out the sound of her sobbing. She took off her clothes. The water was up as hot as she could stand it, and then even hotter, so that the steam choked her, and she stood in front of the foggy mirror and looked at her figure and thought of him, of the ways his hands and body had moved over hers. The sight of her body made her feel even more wretched. She was disgusting. She could never tell anyone about John. She had wanted to believe that it was okay, that there was beauty in what they had done, and that the heat of flesh on flesh was a worthy thing, and sometimes pure, so pure, the closest she had ever come to that invisible life she sensed was on the other side of this life. But now she knew that she had just been deceiving herself.

She let the hot water run. She wanted it to burn. She wanted it to scald her flesh. It took a while before she could even slip into the water, inching her toe, her foot and ankle and calf, the other foot and ankle and calf, and she stood, watching her legs pinkening from the heat, the steam smoking above the water. She bent down and then went deeper, until her knees touched the bottom of the tub, her thighs almost completely submerged. It burned. She covered her mouth, bit her palm. She closed her eyes and readied herself to drop her hips quickly into the painful water. She was afraid she might scream.

But she could not make herself do it. She was a coward. She reached out to the faucet and turned on the cold water, let it run in the tub until the bath was tolerable. She turned it off and sank easily down on her back. She had failed to do what she intended. She closed her eyes, and her thoughts drifted to John and her together. It was vivid and close, and that angered her. She had no control over herself—over her body, over her memory, over anything.

She slipped down in the water to wet her hair, and then down even more until her face was under the surface. She opened her eyes and stared through the refraction at the cracked plaster ceiling, the rusted corners of the pipes. She held her breath for as long as she could, letting the bubbles stream out of her mouth in intervals, and then she held it even longer until her chest started to burn and her eyes bulged. She could see her hair floating like seaweed above and to the sides of her face. Just one swallow. It was easy. The easiest way to go, her mother had said. You wouldn't even know it. One large gulp in the lungs and that's it. She heard her heart thudding loudly in her chest and temples. She held on for another few seconds, and then she exploded through the surface of the water, spitting and coughing.

Someone was beating on the door. "Are you all right in there?" her father barked.

She spit and coughed and couldn't answer.

"Laura, are you all right?"

"Yes," she stammered.

"Your water must be awful hot. The whole house is steamed over." He sounded gruff. "Open the window."

"Yes, sir," she called.

"And get out soon. You need to make supper."

"Yes, sir."

She reached for a towel to cover her mouth. She kept coughing and coughing until tears streaked down her face. Finally she got control. She let the water out and lifted herself, dripping, from the tub and dried off. Her diary pages were bloated. Droplets of water were on the drawing he'd made. The water hadn't ruined the picture, though, hadn't streaked or blotched the image. Her face and body still recognizably there—cartoon-ish, mouth open, a flag—the water just beading on the surface without penetrating.

That night, for the first time since they had argued, she slept well—like the dead, in fact, without dreaming, which is what she wanted. The water had purged the obsession. Temporarily at least.

The next evening, when the phone rang after supper, her father answered. "Hello," he said. "Hello." He hung up and returned to the set of papers he was studying—more loan applications for his welding workshop. He wanted to make some extra money, maybe eventually go out on his own. He was tired of working for Charnelle Steel.

A few minutes later the phone rang again.

"Hello. . . . Hey, Letig." There was a long pause. Her father smiled, and then he laughed hard, as if at a punch line. "That's pretty good." Another long pause, her father listening, and then looking at her. "I don't know what she's got planned. Hold on." He held out the phone. "Laura, it's Letig. He wants to know if you can keep his boys."

"When?" she asked.

"Here, you work it out," he said, handing her the phone.

She put the receiver to her ear but did not say anything.

"Laura, are you there?" he asked quietly.

"Yes."

"I have to see you."

"When?" she said, glancing at her father.

"Tell your dad Saturday for baby-sitting. Can you get out tonight?"

"No," she said.

"I've *got* to see you."

"Dad, can I watch the Letig boys on Saturday?"

"Fine with me."

"Yes, sir," she said in the phone. "Saturday would be fine."

"What about tonight?"

"No, sir."

"Then tomorrow?"

She glanced again at her father. His mind was on his papers. He wasn't really paying any attention to her.

"Please, Laura. I'm going crazy here." They were both silent for almost a minute. "I love you," he said.

"Yes, sir," she said, barely able to control the excitement in her voice. "That would be fine."

"I'll be at the warehouse by four-thirty," he said.

"Yes, sir."

"You don't have to 'yes, sir' me," he said gently, and she smiled. Their old joke.

At the barn the following evening, she was nervous. He looked wild. His shirt unloosened from his pants. His hair seemed greasy, unwashed and uncombed, his eyes bloodshot. His breath smelled of peppermints, and she wondered if he'd been drinking and then chewed candy to cover up the smell.

"I'm sorry," he said.

"I'm sorry, too."

"No," he said, "you don't have to be sorry. You were right. We can't keep on like this. It isn't fair to anybody, not to you, not to me . . . to none of us," he added more vaguely.

"Are you okay?" She was afraid to touch him.

He ignored her question. "You're right," he said. "We can do it. We *have* to do it." He stepped toward her and stumbled. She jumped away. "Oops," he said.

"Are you drunk?" she asked warily.

"No."

"Have you been drinking?"

"No. Did you hear what I said?"

"What?"

"We need to get away from here. This place is *killing* me."

She wanted to remain skeptical, but she felt her own expectations rising, a renewed thrill. "Are you serious?" she asked cautiously.

"I am. I want to go . . . right now." His voice rose strangely, as if he was asking a question rather than stating what he felt.

"You *have* been drinking," she said.

"I want to leave now," he said, moving to her, hugging her. "I mean it. Tonight."

She pulled away. "We can't do that."

"Soon, then," he said and plopped down on the pallet. He took a cigarette from a pack in his pocket and put it in his mouth but didn't light it. "Soon."

"What happened?" she asked, kneeling by the pallet.

"It doesn't *matter* what happened," he said too loudly. He tried to get his lighter to flare, but it wouldn't work. He rapped it angrily against the end table.

"Did you have a fight with Anne?"

"This isn't about her," he said and then shook his head. His eyes were suddenly brimming. She was alarmed. "I'm going crazy," he rasped.

"John, what *happened*?"

"We could go next week."

"Next *week*?"

"That gives us plenty of time."

He dropped the unlit cigarette and the lighter onto the end table and then grabbed her. She could have wriggled away, but she didn't. She felt a little frightened, though. He pulled her close and kissed her sloppily. She had to wipe her face afterward. She smelled the liquor beneath the peppermint. It wasn't just beer.

"A week from Friday," he said, holding her tightly.

"I don't know, John."

"It's what you wanted."

She didn't answer.

He released his hold on her, leaned away so he could see her face. "Are you backing out?"

"No," she said, shaking her head.

"Good, then." He kissed her more tenderly, then said, "A week from Friday."

"Maybe," she whispered.

"Not just maybe. Say yes."

"I don't know."

"Say *yes*."

She wanted to be thoughtful with whatever she said. She felt wary, but underneath she could feel her own joy swelling. "John, I'm not sure anymore."

"Please," he said. "I love you. Come away with me."

Careful now, she thought, *careful.* She reached her hand up to his face, ran her index finger over his cheek and around his eyes and down his thin nose to his lips, those lips. She kissed him softly and then put her head against his chest. He wrapped his arms around her.

"Laura—"

"We'll see," she said.

29

✳

Leaving

Saturday night, after Laura baby-sat the Letig boys, John drove her home, and they worked out the details of their plan. It seemed simple. They would leave Friday morning. His wife was leaving with the boys on that same morning to visit her mother in Borger for the weekend, so Laura and John would have a three-day head start before his wife suspected anything. John would receive his paycheck on Thursday afternoon, so he would deposit it early Friday and withdraw two thousand dollars from his bank account, still leaving plenty for his wife, and she had access to more, he said, from her family. Much more. She would be okay. On Monday and Thursday, when they met, they would bring smaller bags and leave them at the barn, so all of their things would not have to be smuggled out on Friday. She would leave for school on Friday morning, as usual, but instead of going there, she would meet John behind the warehouse, and they would stop by the barn to retrieve the rest of their things and then head out. If they left by ten, they could arrive in Houston maybe by midnight.

Once they got to Houston, John planned to track down the bartender he had spoken to, the bald, bucktoothed one with a brother whose friend worked for Texaco. John would find out if there was a possibility of under-the-table money, work for skilled welders who didn't necessarily want to be on the payroll. John also had contacted an old high school friend of his, who now lived in Louisiana, near Baton Rouge. This friend could create a fake ID for Laura, so there would be no questions until she turned eighteen.

Should they leave notes? She felt that she needed to leave her father something. She didn't want to disappear the way her mother had, her father not knowing what happened to her, worried that she might be dead or kidnapped or something else terrible. It wouldn't be right to leave her father completely in the dark. It would be hard enough as it was, leaving him, leaving Rich and Gene. John, on the other hand, was adamant that no clue should be left behind, not now. They could always send a letter in a week, after they were far away. John had a friend in Kansas City, someone he trusted to keep his mouth shut. They could send the letters first to this friend, and then he could send them to Anne and to Laura's father from there. That way there would be little chance of their being tracked down. John was worried that her father, and perhaps Anne, too, would come after him if they weren't careful.

"This is still dangerous," he reminded her.

Yet she felt uneasy about this part of the plan. She didn't want her father to worry. She remembered when her mother had left, how frantic he was, gone for several days searching for her. She'd never seen him that panicked. She didn't want to put him through it again. At least Gloria had written. And what John and she were doing was more like what Gloria and Jerome had done than what her mother had done.

"Here's what you do," John said. "Tell your father that you are staying the weekend with one of your friends—Debbie or Marlene or whoever. Then you can drop a letter in the mail from Amarillo, and he'll get it on Monday, so he won't have to worry, but it will at least give us a head start. How would that be?"

"Okay," she said, deflated. "I guess."

On Monday she wrote out the letter to her father. She went through several drafts, including a long one in which she tried to explain what she was doing, and that it didn't reflect badly on him at all. He was a good father, and she loved him, and she was sorry about this, but please don't worry. She would be okay. Really she would. But the next day she read it to John, and it seemed too apologetic, too childish, with a whiff, John thought, of weakness that he believed Zeeke might interpret as a signal for him to come find her, to rescue her. She tore up the letter and wrote a shorter one, telling him simply that she had left town with John, that she was fine, he didn't need to come looking for her or to worry, she would contact him later and would see him when the time was right.

She didn't particularly like the letter. It seemed abrupt, cold, with too much left out, but John said it struck the right tone. He also wrote a letter to his wife, which he didn't show Laura. She secretly felt it was unfair that she had shown him the letter she'd written, had even revised it at his request, but that she had no say in his letter to his wife. But after the first wave of resentment, she realized she was simply being selfish. Whatever was between John and his wife was private. It *was* harder for him. And he would have to cope, as her mother probably had, with the knowledge that he had abandoned his family. They would probably never forgive him. So she kept her distance and hoped that while he was writing the letter, John would not change his mind.

And she had her own secret from him. Without consulting John, she wrote a letter to Gloria. John still didn't know that Gloria was aware of their relationship. But she was thankful that her sister knew. Because Gloria had left as well, under similar circumstances, Laura felt that only she could fully understand, even though she might not approve. She wrote a letter to that effect, and she held on to it. It needed special postage. She would try to send it before they left.

On Tuesday, after most of her clothes and things had been packed and smuggled to the barn, she felt suddenly unsure about whether she could go through with this. Had she set in motion something too dark and painful for others?

She could see people now only in terms of the effect her leaving would have on them. Rich, for instance, had a nightmare, woke up yelling, tears streaming down his face, pushed their father away, and wouldn't be consoled until she held him. When she tried to lay him back in his bed, he clung to her and would not let go, as if he sensed that she would be gone for good if he released her. Finally she had to put him in her bed, and he held tightly to her, even after he fell asleep. Each time she tried to move him, he would startle awake and grab her tighter. And so they huddled together, Rich draped over her until morning, and then he followed her around as she made breakfast and dressed, and he looked forlornly out the window of Mrs. Ambling's living room as Laura got on her bike to ride to school.

She went to her classes, knowing that these were her last days. She tried to concentrate, but instead she found herself staring at the other students and her teachers, watching their movements with a nostalgia that made her eyes cloudy all day. Debbie and Marlene told jokes, laughed, gossiped about the Jameson twins, boys they had crushes on. She smiled, tried to join in, but mostly she hung back and observed them, knowing that by Friday she would be gone and that there would be speculation, and then the news would break about what she'd done, and then there would be a flurry of rumors and gossip, and then, a month later, she would be old news. Debbie and Marlene would still talk about her, with a wistfulness she could imagine might last for months, and perhaps a sense of betrayal: *Why didn't she tell us? I thought she was our friend.* But soon enough she would be history.

She felt insignificant. She didn't count, and once she was gone, she would essentially be forgotten. That was how life was. It moved on, relentlessly, back into the ordinary rhythms, and if you fell away, then you . . . well, you didn't really matter much to begin with.

That afternoon she saw Manny and Joannie in the old Ford. They were huddled close, laughing. Joannie pointed to her, and Manny called out, "Hey, Laura, you want to go with us to 4-D's?"

It was the first time he'd asked her if she wanted to go anywhere with him since . . . she didn't know when, and his smile suggested a genuine desire to be in her company, which shocked her.

She hesitated but then said, "Sure."

At 4-D's, he offered to buy her a chocolate shake.

She hesitated.

"Oh, come on. When's the next time I'm gonna buy you a shake?"

He laughed at this, and she wondered for a panicked moment if he knew, if he had gone through her things, had found her letters to her father and to Gloria.

"Two chocolate shakes and one strawberry," he told the waitress.

He smiled again, and it was clearly the smile of the unknowing. It was just a spurt of generosity. *Why now?* she wondered. *He must know something.* But he didn't. As they sipped their shakes in the booth, Manny with his arm around Joannie, him telling a series of jokes, she again felt a sense of betrayal, how *she* would betray *them.* Her eyes glazed over, and she could feel the egg in her throat as she smiled through his jokes, tried to laugh. She would miss even Manny.

The days were getting shorter, and by the time they left 4-D's the sun was almost down, casting the neighborhood in a golden shroud, and even this dusk, she felt, was designed to make her nostalgic. How could she leave this place, these people?

At home, her father reminded them that the first presidential debate was on that night, and so they ate dinner and cleaned up quickly, made popcorn, and sat huddled in front of the television, watching as Kennedy and Nixon squared off. They were civilized and proper, and she had trouble paying very close attention. She watched her father instead, leaning forward in his chair, concentrating hard, his head cocked to one side, his eyebrows knitted.

This was important to him, very important. He had been saddened by Kennedy's win at the convention. He believed that if the ticket was reversed, with Johnson in the top slot, then the Democrats stood a much better chance of winning back the White House. Johnson was the Majority Leader. He was maybe the most effective one ever, especially with a Republican White House, her father argued. He could easily whip Nixon. But Kennedy, with all his good looks and easy manner and Ivy League education, still seemed callow and young, too green, and an easy target for Nixon's barbs about inexperience. And to top it off, the man was an Irish Catholic, which her father didn't personally have any trouble with, except that it promised to alienate a lot of voters. "The senator from Mass" had assumed a new meaning, and Nixon knew how to take the gloves off. Her father recalled with anger the McCarthy hearings and Nixon's nasty role in it all. Nixon was, her father said, a dirty little backstreet brawler when it came right down to it.

So as her father watched intently, she studied him, thinking too about how much she would miss him and how bad it would be when yet another woman from his house, the last one, disappeared. If the Democrats lost as well, there was no telling what might happen to him.

Every time Kennedy spoke, there was a hushed, tense silence in the house, as if they were waiting for him to make a mistake. But he was good, and he looked tan and confident, smiling, relaxed, smart. Nixon sounded good, too, said all the right things, but he looked awful—dark circles under his eyes, a five o'clock shadow, beads of sweat collecting on his upper lip and forehead so that he had to keep wiping his face with a handkerchief, his eyes unsure which camera to look into. He seemed sick. She was amazed that he sounded as calm and assured and intelligent as he did, because it looked like he might throw up at any moment. Manny and her father had made jokes earlier, but then they quieted down and just stared.

She felt sorry for Nixon. She felt more than sorry. She felt like she understood Nixon. The stakes were high for him; this was the most important moment in his life, and he couldn't control his body. She knew that feeling. She had moved through the past few days constantly on the verge of tears, fearful that someone would discover what she was doing, expose her for the fraud that she was. She had thought, more than once, that she was going to throw up.

After the debate, her father seemed happy. He said he was going to the Armory for a beer and asked if Manny wanted to come along. He didn't ask her, which hurt her feelings, especially since she had been the one following the election with him and talking to him about the Declaration of Independence and the Constitution, giving him daily updates on Mr. Sparling's lectures. It was just expected that she would stay home and watch the little boys. They left, and she stood by the window for a few minutes and then turned back to Rich and Gene. She played a game of checkers with Rich and then read him a story, tucked him into bed.

Returning to the living room, she asked, "You want to play some canasta, Gene?"

"Huh?" he said, lifting his head, as if from sleep, from one of his Sherlock Holmes mysteries.

"You want to play some cards?"

"No," he said and dropped his head back into the book.

"Oh, come on, Gene. Please play with me."

"Not tonight," he said.

"Please!" she insisted.

He looked at her, surprised by her intensity and a little skeptical.

"Please play with me."

"Okay, sure."

She almost forgot to meet John on Thursday. She had not slept much the whole week, and she felt weepy and weak from a constant headache. She was at the library when she looked at her watch. It was almost five-thirty. She jumped up, startled, knocking over the textbooks she'd been ignoring. She quickly gathered them into her satchel, ran to her bicycle, and pedaled hard to the warehouse. He was waiting for her. He got out and put her bike in the bed of the truck, and she climbed onto the floorboard, out of breath, panting hard.

"Where were you?" he asked, annoyed.

"I lost track of time. I'm sorry."

"We don't have much time, you know."

"I know."

"Are you ready?"

"Yes," she said.

They drove the rest of the way in silence. At the barn, they gathered their things, and John went over the plan again, and she nodded, tried to focus. She said "yes" and "uh-huh," though sometimes she wasn't sure what exactly he had said. But she knew the plan.

"Are you listening, Laura?" he asked.

"Yes." He looked at her strangely. "I am," she assured him.

"Are you all right?"

She nodded.

"Okay, then."

He kissed her on the forehead and then went over to his bags and opened one of them and sifted through it. He was all business. She lay on the pallet and watched him and then looked out the window, which was growing gray with the fading light. She felt very sad. She turned her head into the pillow and breathed deeply.

After a few minutes, she sat up and said, "John." She wasn't sure what she wanted to say. He was busy buckling something in the corner. They were going to take the pallet and the little table with them. It was their only furniture, and he didn't want to leave it here since he had no idea when or if they were coming back. He'd also purchased a large black trunk that could be locked and would protect most of their things from rain or other bad weather during the drive.

"What is it?" he asked, still busy, his back to her.

She rose and went to him, stood behind him while he finished latching the trunk, and then gestured toward the pallet.

"We can't. We don't have time."

"Please," she implored him.

"Laura—"

"Hold me, then."

"Okay," he said and stood and pulled her into his chest. "Are you okay with this?" he asked. When she didn't answer, he said, "Because we're on that train now. It's pulling out of the station. You better tell me now."

"I know."

They stood there, still, for a few minutes. This is all she wanted, a moment of stillness before the rest happened.

"You with me?" he asked.

"Yeah."

"Good." He kissed the top of her head. "I've got to get home now. Willie's got an earache."

She winced.

"Okay," she said, nodding. "Let's go."

That night she didn't sleep at all. She listened to the house as it creaked and groaned, to her brothers breathing, their light snores, and to the breeze as it moved coolly through the window, billowing the thin curtains. She stared at the statue of the bird.

She thought about her mother, what she must have been thinking the night before she left. Did she have doubts, too? Did she feel this oscillation between a glassy-eyed nostalgia and hardened will? She must have thought for a long time about what she would do. Who knows how long? But maybe not. Maybe the possibility presented itself in a flash of intuition on that particular day. And rather than wait for the inspired moment to pass, she seized it and was gone before she could change her mind, the action carrying its own momentum.

Finally dawn arrived. While Manny and Gene were doing their morning chores, Laura stuffed her bag with a few more clothes, the statue, her diary, and her money, which she had hidden in her bottom drawer.

She scrambled eggs and made bacon and pancakes for them all. Her mother, she suddenly remembered, had made them a big breakfast, too—blueberry waffles and ham and eggs—a final meal. Laura cooked willingly, and they were all surprised to come into the kitchen and see the table set with plates of eggs, bacon, and pancakes as well as cups of orange juice, milk, and coffee.

"My, oh, my!" her father exclaimed, and kissed her on the forehead.

She couldn't eat, but she sat down and watched them, knowing that this would be the last time she saw any of them for a long while—years, maybe, possibly never again. She felt the emotion rise in her. She had to stop these thoughts. She couldn't let herself go to this place. Not today. She washed the dishes, and then she hurried Rich along, took him over to Mrs. Ambling's house and was back in time to see her father and Gene and Manny leave.

Manny asked, "Do you want a ride to school?"

"No," she said. "I'll take my bike."

"Suit yourself."

Then they were off, her father's truck and Manny's car moving down the street and then out of sight. She was left alone in the house. She listened to the radio for half an hour as she walked through each room one last time. And then she went out into the backyard and whistled for Fay. The dog limped over, turned onto her back so she could have her stomach scratched. Laura obliged her. She rose, and Fay rose, too, and licked Laura and nuzzled her legs until Laura told her, "Enough." Then she held the dog's face in her hands.

"Good-bye," she said. Fay was the only one she could actually say it to before she left.

She went inside and washed her hands. She grabbed her bag and school satchel, which had been emptied of books and filled with the last few things she was taking, and then she set off down the alley toward the abandoned warehouse.

She was supposed to meet him there at nine-thirty.

She arrived at nine-fifteen.

By nine forty-five, she began to worry.

And then, by ten-fifteen, she was sure he was not coming at all.

At eleven-thirty, she walked home quickly, the bag and her satchel heavy on her shoulders.

The house felt eerie and silent. She thought she'd never see it again, or at least not for years, so it seemed as if a long time had passed. She waited until noon before she picked up the phone and called the Letig house, but there was no answer. She hung up, dialed again, and let it ring twenty times. No one picked up.

Where is he?

As she put the phone down, she heard Fay barking. She looked out the window. John stood at the back gate. He seemed exhausted, his hair mussed, his long-sleeved plaid shirt untucked on one side from his jeans, his chin and cheeks unshaven.

"Hush up, Fay," she called and then went outside and quieted her.

Laura pointed toward the house, and John quickly crossed the yard and went into the kitchen. She told Fay to hush up again and then followed him in.

"Where were you?" she blurted out. She couldn't keep the bitterness out of her voice. "I waited for more than two hours."

"I'm sorry," he said. "Willie's ear got so bad we had to take him to the hospital. He's been screaming and crying all night long. They had to drain it. He's still there. I just got away for a few minutes."

"What are we going to do?"

He was clearly irritated by her question. "I don't know. We can't do anything right now. He's in the *hospital!*"

She didn't say anything, just turned away from him to the sink.

"What do you want me to do? I can't leave like this. I feel like enough of a shitheel without doing that to them. For Christ's sake, no one abandons his kid when he's in the hospital."

"No," she whispered. "I understand."

"Do you?"

"Yes," she said, nodding. She turned to him. "You should go back."

He sighed heavily and pursed his lips. "I'll call you tomorrow," he said.

"Okay."

"We'll work it out."

"Yeah."

"I gotta go."

She nodded. "I know."

There was a short pause, and she wondered if he would at least hug her or perhaps reach out and touch her, but he just opened the door, and Fay began barking crazily. He stuck his head back in.

"Can you keep the dog quiet?"

She called Fay to the house. The dog came slowly and hobbled up the steps and into the kitchen. "Go on," she said to him.

"I'll call you tomorrow."

She nodded, and they stared at each other for a moment, and she felt as if more should be said, as if something would die between them if more was not said.

Then he left, walking with his head down, and when he was out of sight, and she heard his truck come to life and roll away, she let out a long sigh. Something that had been wound tight in her body suddenly released. It had been crazy to believe that he could ever do it, that he would ever be *able* to do it. She had sensed that something might happen to prevent it. She had even half hoped that something would stop them. And now that it had, she felt strangely relieved.

30

*

Election

Yes, it had been foolish, their plan. Over the next five weeks, they agreed that there was no way it could have worked. Willie's sickness had been a sign. It would all be easier in a year or two, much easier, John told her. Laura knew, however, that it would never happen. It would never be like Galveston. She still fantasized about it sometimes, but she realized it could never be the way she had imagined. There would be too much hostility, too much opposition and upheaval. His boys would hate him, hate her. His wife—who knew what she would do? And her father? She couldn't even think about his reaction. It wouldn't work, and she resigned herself to that.

She also tried to savor what they still had together, because she knew it had to change into something else, and she was afraid, too, of the way it would change.

Things were already different. When John picked her up on election night, she tried to make small talk as they drove to the barn. She told him what she was studying—a novella by Herman Melville called *Bartleby the Scrivener* (all that preferring not to—a definite No), sines and cosines, the Lincoln-Douglas debates—but he just nodded his head absently, feigned interest. She knew he was bored. At the barn, they drank some Nehis, listened to the radio. He smoked a few cigarettes, and then they took off their clothes. She felt strangely sad, though, and maybe he did, too, because he could not keep an erection long enough to put on the condom, and he finally just rolled over and put his arm over his eyes. She lay against him, but he nudged her away.

"Let me sleep a little," he said.

She put on her shirt and stared out the window as the light faded to different hues of black. Even with the kerosene lamp, the inside of the barn seemed very dark when she turned around.

"John," she whispered. "John, wake up."

"Just let me rest a few minutes more."

She finished dressing and waited silently by the window for a while, and then she knelt by the pallet, noticed the dark circles under his eyes, the deepening worry lines at the corners of his mouth.

At eight-thirty, she woke him so they could drive to the Armory, where people from Charnelle Steel and the town were meeting to watch the election results. She had told her father that she was going to a football scrimmage and then the library and would catch a ride to the Armory to watch the results with him, as part of her homework for history class. Her father seemed delighted.

John dropped her off about a block from the Armory. He drove on, parked, and went in. By the time she got there, he was eating a sandwich, drinking a beer, and talking to some men who were shooting pool.

Her father was perched at the bar in front of the television, drinking a beer himself. Walter Cronkite was shuffling papers.

"Who's winning?" she asked.

"Too close to call yet," her father said. "A nail-biter."

There was half a cheeseburger and some french fries left on his plate.

"Can I have that?" she asked. "I'm starving."

"Sure, go ahead. Hey, Luke, can you heat this up for my daughter?"

"That's okay, Dad. This is fine."

"Nonsense. It's cold. Hey, Luke."

"Yeah."

"Will you put this back on the grill for a minute? My girl is hungry. And give her a root beer, would ya?"

"Sure thing," Luke said.

"Thanks," she said.

As she ate and sipped her root beer, she watched John in the mirror over the bar. He shot pool with Beaver Mitchell and the Cransburgh brothers, concentrating on his shots but then laughing and cracking jokes, attempting impossible behind-the-back shots to the oohs and aahs of the men. Showing off, it seemed. For her? Maybe. Though perhaps this is how he was at work, with the men he knew. Every once in a while he would glance over to see if she was looking at him, but there was no special sense of urgency. There'd be no secret kissing behind the Armory. Neither of them was up for it. Tonight she was simply Zeeke Tate's teenage daughter, the baby-sitter.

She wanted to go home, but her father was determined to stay until the end, even though it was a weeknight. The election was too close to call. The popular vote seemed neck and neck, though Kennedy had a slight lead in the electoral college. Her father stayed glued to the television, even though the reporters said the election might not be settled until the morning. He called Mrs. Ambling, arranged for the boys to spend the night at her house.

At a quarter to ten, John grabbed his coat and announced, "I gotta get home."

Beaver Mitchell bellowed, "The old ball and chain calling, Letig?" The few men and women still at the bar laughed, including her father.

"You got it," he said, smiling. Laura grimaced at his response.

"Can you give me a ride home?" she blurted out suddenly, hopping off the stool, grabbing her coat.

"I don't know." John shot her a look that said, *What are you doing?* "I suppose so," he said calmly.

"Now, wait a minute," her father said, his hands up, his voice suddenly gruff. "You're not going anywhere, little lady."

John's eyes darted nervously back and forth between her and her father. She felt panicky for a moment, wondering why her father would protest. She'd pushed their luck. How ironic would that be—after all that they'd gotten away with, to be caught like this?

"Who's been lecturing me for two months now about the American dream?" he said loudly, wrapping his arm tightly around her shoulders. She looked at John to gauge his reaction. He just grinned at her father, put on his coat and his hat. "Well, here's the American dream in action, honey," her father continued, pointing to the television set propped on the end of the bar. "And we're gonna see it through to the bitter end."

John shook her father's hand, tipped his hat to her, and then lifted up his collar and started for the door. She wanted him to turn back around, but he didn't. She could see his silhouette on the porch, where he hesitated before heading down the steps, maybe a little drunk. Who could blame him for hesitating? she thought. Going home to his wife. The ball and chain.

A little after eleven—after almost everyone in the Armory had left except for Laura and her father, the Cransburgh brothers, and Luke—the vice president and Mrs. Nixon finally appeared at campaign headquarters.

Nixon said that "if the present trend continues, Senator Kennedy will be the next president of the United States."

The crowd at his headquarters started chanting, "We want Nixon! We want Nixon!"

But Nixon just smiled and held up his hand. He thanked them for their support and was gracious, more gracious than he had seemed throughout the campaign, her father said.

"Look at that old phony, plastic smile," Luke said. "You know he's torn up inside."

Wiping the froth of beer from his upper lip, Jimmy Cransburgh said, "Serves the bastard right."

Even though, like her family, she had been rooting for Kennedy and Johnson, and she thought maybe her father was correct about Nixon, that he was a dirty fighter, she couldn't help but feel sorry for him again. She kept watching Mrs. Nixon standing by his side—stoic, grim, trying to smile, the cords in her neck tight. Mrs. Nixon's face seemed like it was about to crack open.

Up on the screen, the election results were posted. Still very close, and she wondered if Nixon felt he'd made a mistake, conceded too early. On the television screen was a photograph of Kennedy and Johnson holding their hands up high in victory. The screen switched to Nixon's headquarters. No one there. Balloons littered the empty floor.

Her father laughed. "The aftermath," he said. "You lose and the party's over quickly."

"Yep, everyone disappears fast," Luke said.

She was depressed, just wanted to be in her bed, asleep. She said, "Can we go now?"

"We gotta hear Kennedy's victory speech," her father said happily and ordered another beer from Luke. "Why do you look so glum, sweetheart? We won!" He propped his elbow on the counter and leaned toward her, touching his forehead to hers. "Aren't you happy?"

"I guess so," she said.

"What do you mean, 'I guess so'?"

"I feel sorry for Nixon."

"Ha!" Her father laughed and then called down to the end of the bar, "Jimmy, Luke, Bob, did you hear that? She feels sorry for Dick Nixon."

"You're a softy, sweetheart," Luke said.

"Yep," her father said and grabbed her hand. "Just an old softy." He kissed her hand. "Somebody's gotta lose, honey. Politics isn't about who's nice or whose feelings get hurt."

"I know," she said. "But that doesn't mean I have to like it."

Her father woke her right before two o'clock. She had gone to lie down on the old couch behind the Armory bar just after midnight. This was the second time he'd woken her with an update. The first was about some controversy with the Illinois primary. She had nodded her head and fallen back to sleep.

"It's gotten closer," her father said now, animated, sitting by her.

His eyes were glassy, and she didn't know if it was because of lack of sleep or because of the beers he'd been swigging.

"Kennedy won't give his speech until he hears personally from Nixon. They say it may be morning now before we know for sure."

"Okay," she answered, and then he was back at the bar with Luke and Jimmy. She kept dozing in and out of weird, groggy dreams. She and Senator Kennedy were at the barn, lying on the pallet together, she with her arm over her face. She couldn't stop sweating. She asked Kennedy, who wore a green cardigan sweater, if she could rest a few more minutes, just a few more minutes. Standing at the window, staring at them, Mrs. Kennedy wore bright orange pedal pushers and her riding boots and an orange cap, her hands resting on her pregnant stomach.

Her father woke her again and said that Kennedy was about to speak. Her back felt sore, her head ached, and her clothes reeked of cigar and cigarette smoke. She staggered to the bar and climbed up on a bar stool. Luke pushed a stack of warm pancakes and syrup and a glass of tomato juice her way.

A tired but grinning Senator Kennedy appeared and praised Nixon for being a good citizen. He assured the nation that the vice president would continue to serve the country in an important capacity but declared that this victory symbolized a new generation of leadership and a new hope. He then put his arm around his young, pregnant wife, who looked tired but smiled benignly, and said he needed to go now, "to prepare for a new administration and a new baby." The reporters chuckled.

Kennedy's simple speech momentarily lifted Laura's spirits. She watched the Kennedys leave the podium, his hand touching his wife's back. The way things should be, she thought. She poured the syrup over her pancakes and took a bite and thought again of the Nixons. She still couldn't shake the image of Mrs. Nixon from her mind, standing by her husband's side. *Bereft.* It must have been a bitter night for her, Laura thought, for them both. More bitter days to come.

31

✳

Accident

*L*aura knew that she would have to be the one to end it. He wouldn't do it. Knowing that the end was near made her want to hold on to and protect this time even more, but another part of her just wanted to get it over with. They had not met much in the two weeks following the election, and the sense of failure from that evening still clung to her. She did not want to see him, did not want to have the conversation that she knew they needed to have. So she made excuses. She would show up late at the warehouse on their scheduled days, pretending to be tired, and would hurriedly tell him she had to go, she couldn't get away this night or the next night, and no, she couldn't keep the boys on Friday. She had a cold, she'd say, wiping her nose, pretending to sound sniffly and congested. She had to cook supper. It was Marlene's birthday, and she was having a party. Even with the legitimate excuses, she felt like a phony, and though he accepted her excuses without question and kissed her quickly on the lips, she could tell, by the way he shifted his eyes, that he didn't believe her. She realized that it was easy for her to lie now, even to him, and it began to make her sick. She knew that she was avoiding the inevitable, and finally, after two weeks, she resolved that it had to be over. Why continue with it if it seemed like a senseless duty?

But the end did not happen as she imagined or planned.

Her period was late. Two days. Three days. She was pretty regular, unlike Gloria, who always said she never knew when it was going to hit. So she began to panic, even though she knew they had been careful. She didn't know what to do. Should she say something to him?

And then it was four days, and then five.

Mrs. Letig called, asked if Laura would watch Jack for her the next afternoon. She had to take Willie to the doctor; she would drop Jack off after Laura got home from school. John would pick him up when he got off work.

"Of course," Laura said.

She worried all day about whether or not she should tell him. She felt on the verge of tears, her eyes brimming every few minutes, and she was sick to her stomach but didn't know if it was an indicator of pregnancy or just nervousness. She stared out the windows at school, ignoring her teachers. She skipped her choir class, spent the first few minutes in the bathroom vomiting, and then walked outside and sat in the stands at the south end of the football field. It was cold, the temperature dropping rapidly, the sky dark and turbulent. The wind kicked up and blew off her wool cap so that she had to chase it down the bleachers and felt sick again. It began to snow, and she sat there shivering, with her hat pulled low over her forehead, her hands thrust into her pockets. The snow just lightly spit at first, but the wind blew harder and the snow grew heavier, coming down at an angle. It had been warm just yesterday, a sunny autumn day in the mid-forties, but that was the way the weather was here, turning suddenly and violently. She thought she should go back inside, on to Mr. Sparling's class. They were discussing *The Scarlet Letter* now, but she'd struggled with this story about a woman branded with shame, raising her daughter on the outskirts of town while the woman's lover continued to deceive everyone. She had started it several times and had only just last night been able to get through it all, though it pained her to do so. She believed it was, on some level, an evil book. She didn't want to discuss Mr. Sparling's theories about Hester the martyr, stoically keeping her secret, proudly wearing her shameful brand, a heroine for the simple fact that she got pregnant and kept her mouth shut about the father.

The snow fell harder now, and it was sticking, starting to collect on the bleachers. She fled from the field and grabbed her bicycle from the racks, wiped off the seat, and then headed for home, moving as carefully as she could over the back streets, slick with falling snow, hard to navigate. By the time she arrived home, she was soaked, chilled to the bone. She took a hot bath, staring down at her stomach, which didn't seem any different. She ran her fingers over her taut abdomen, wondered if there was life there, wondered what she could do.

She had heard a rumor that Mrs. Aguilar, who operated the Mexican restaurant on the west end of town with her husband, helped girls in trouble. What exactly she did, Laura didn't quite know, the rumors never specific, and she had no idea how you solved this kind of problem. She had heard, too, about a home in Amarillo and another one in Dalhart, where girls were sometimes sent. Debbie Carlson's cousin, who lived in Borger, had been sent away to the home in Amarillo for several months, and then she'd returned to school like nothing happened. And one of Gloria's friends, Janet Cornwall, had disappeared for months as well—supposedly to visit her sick aunt in Brownsville, but Gloria had hinted that she was really in Dalhart. She missed half her senior year, returned skinnier, and then never graduated, apparently too ashamed to go back to school.

And plenty of girls from Charnelle got married right after graduation, and sometimes, she knew, their wedding dresses couldn't hide their growing stomachs. Gloria herself was one of those girls. Julie had come into the world only seven months after her parents eloped.

Gloria had cautioned Laura to be careful. And they had been, hadn't they? Evidently not careful enough.

At three-thirty, Laura retrieved Rich from Mrs. Ambling. The snow had turned to sleet for a while, and the path between their houses was slick and treacherous. Mrs. Letig showed up a few minutes later and brought Jack inside.

"Man, oh, man, is it getting bad out there," she said, stamping on the welcome mat, taking off Jack's coat. "John's going to try to get off work a little early. He should be here about five."

"How's Willie?" Laura asked. He was sitting in the Letigs' snow-covered car, which was still running.

"Oh, he'll be fine. Another earache, but he seems better today. This is more a checkup than anything."

Mrs. Letig wore a thick black overcoat and a red wool scarf over her head. Laura felt suddenly angry at her, felt that somehow this whole mess was Mrs. Letig's fault—everything, all of it. If she'd been a better wife, maybe her husband would not have seduced the sixteen-year-old daughter of his friend. Would have knocked up his wife again instead. Laura looked at the woman's face, her eyes lined darkly with mascara, her lips glossed with lipstick the color of her scarf, her dark red hair pinned neatly under the scarf to protect it from the elements. Made up, painted, a phony. Underneath her coat, she was no doubt wearing one of her expensive dresses. Laura felt the urge to slap her.

"I better get going. We're late," Mrs. Letig said, backing out the door, waving. "You be good, Jack." And then to Laura, "Thanks, honey."

So this was how it would end, she thought. *Messy.*

When John showed up that afternoon, a little after five, before her father got home, she couldn't contain herself. Manny and Gene were gone. Rich and Jack were in the kitchen playing checkers.

"Hello," John said, knocking on the door, his collar up, a wool cap pulled over his head.

She burst into tears.

"Hey," he said, grabbing her by the arms, bending down to see her face. "What's the matter?"

"I'm late," she whispered.

"What?"

"My period hasn't come."

Jack and Rich appeared at the kitchen door. "Go get in the truck, son," John said.

"What's the matter?" Jack asked.

Rich frowned at her. "Why are you crying?"

"It's nothing," she said, but then she ran to the bathroom, put her face into a towel to muffle the sound.

"What's the matter?" she heard Rich ask John.

"I don't know," John said. "Rich, why don't you walk out to the truck with Jack?"

"Laura wouldn't let us go out because it was snowing."

"You can get in the truck with him for a few minutes. Are your brothers home?"

"No, sir," Rich said.

"Get your boots," John said. "Bundle up, boys." And a few minutes later she heard the front door open.

He rapped the bathroom door lightly. "Laura," he said.

She didn't answer. She ran cold water and splashed it on her face.

He knocked again. "Laura, where are Manny and Gene?"

"Manny's at work. Gene's at the library. My father's picking him up on his way home."

"Come on out. Your dad will be here soon, then."

She opened the door and stepped into the hallway. He leaned against the wall with his arms crossed. There was a layer of snow on the side of his wool cap. His jacket was wet, his face flushed red. She didn't know whether to reach out to him or to stay where she was. She crossed her arms as well, stared at him.

"How late are you?"

"Five days."

"Shit," he said, shaking his head. "Did you count right? Maybe you messed up the math. Anne did that a few months back."

The mention of Mrs. Letig made her stomach flip, and the "few months back" reference made her feel even sicker. "Yeah, I counted right. I counted a hundred times. That's all I've been doing."

"We've been careful, though," he said.

"I know."

There was a long pause, and then he grimaced. "Is there somebody else?"

"What?" she shouted and then shoved him. "No!"

"I just meant—"

She punched him on the chest with her fist, hard. "Why would you say that?"

"I'm sorry. I didn't mean it that way."

He reached out for her, but she backed into the bathroom. "*Why* would you *say* that?"

"I'm sorry."

Then they heard the front door open. Her father. She slammed the bathroom door shut. She leaned against the wall and slid down, her head in her hands.

"Where's Laura?" her father asked.

"In the bathroom."

"The boys said she was crying."

"Yeah."

"Why?"

"I don't know. When I came in to get Jack, she was crying and then ran to the bathroom. I sent the boys on to the truck so I could try to find out what was wrong."

He sounded bad, she thought, nervous.

"She won't talk to me, though," he said. "Maybe something happened at school today." His voice seemed more in control now, more convincing.

"I thought I heard a door slam," her father said.

"Yeah, she opened the bathroom door and then slammed it shut again. I don't know, Zeke. I'm no expert with teenage girls. Thank God I have boys. . . ."

She hated that he said "teenage."

John continued, "I'm glad you're here. I'm sure she'd rather talk to her dad. Besides, I gotta get home and check on Willie. Anne took him to the doctor today. Can't seem to get rid of that earache."

Silence. She could imagine the look on her father's face, the corners of his mouth twitching of their own accord. He never knew what to do when she was upset. Laura wondered if that's when he most wished his wife were still here, to deal with situations like this. Though *this* was too complicated for any of them, and she wasn't sure she would have wanted her mother here anyway. The blood pounded in her temples. She breathed deeply, and then she unwound some toilet paper from the roll, wiped her nose, and listened.

A knock. She didn't say anything. What could she say? She wanted them both to go away now.

"Laura?"

"I gotta go, Zeke," John said, trying to make his getaway.

Good. Get out of here.

"Bye, Laura."

She started to answer. What could she say, though?

"Good-bye, Zeke," he called.

"See ya, Letig. Careful out there. It's coming down hard now."

"Hope everything's okay," John said.

And then he was gone. She turned on the water to let her father know she was fine. She heard his footsteps as he walked into the living room, where he told Rich, "Take your boots off and go wash up in the kitchen."

"I gotta go to the bathroom."

"You'll have to wait."

"Why?" he whined.

"You want a spanking, son? Just do what I said." Footsteps again. Her father rapped on the door. "Laura," he said, irritation in his voice.

"Yes, sir."

"Laura, what's the matter?" he asked.

She kept the water running. "Nothing."

"Doesn't sound like nothing."

"I didn't do very well on my history test," she said. "But it doesn't really matter, Dad. I just don't feel good. . . . I'm sorry, I just . . . don't want to talk right now."

"Well, okay, honey," he said, more gently. "You can tell me about it later if you want, though. You know that, right?"

"I'm fine, Dad. Please. It's okay. Really. It's nothing."

"I'm just saying that——"

"I don't want to talk!" Her voice sounded too sharp. It echoed in the bathroom. "Please," she added softly.

"Okay, okay. Later, then. You let me know."

"Yes, sir."

After a few minutes, when she heard him in the kitchen, she went to her bedroom, shut the door, and locked it. She could hear her father telling Manny and Gene, in whispered tones, about her behavior.

"Give her some room," he said.

"Is she on the rag?" Manny asked.

"Keep your voice down. I don't know."

She got out her calendar and counted the days again. And then again. Yes, five. And then she curled up on the bed and tried to calm down. She closed her eyes and breathed deeply. It would be okay, she told herself. She shouldn't worry yet. Not yet. And she definitely should not have told John.

Stupid, stupid thing to do. She looked out the window at the snow, mixed with sleet and ice, the sky metallic and gloomy. It was ten till six. She closed her eyes. She heard the clattering of pans as her father prepared supper.

The phone rang. She rolled over so she could hear who it was. Would he call her? To find out if she was okay?

Her father answered. "No, Anne. He left here forty-five minutes, maybe an hour ago."

She looked at the clock. It was nearly six-thirty. She must have dozed off.

"No, he said he had to get home. If I hear from him, I'll give you a ring. . . . I don't think it's anything to worry about, Anne. . . . Have you tried the Armory? . . . What about 4-D's?"

There was a long pause. It should have taken John only five minutes to get home, maybe a little longer in this weather. She could get there by bike in ten minutes, twenty minutes at most, when she walked. She got up and stood by the door so that she could hear better.

"Yes, Anne. Yeah, I know the roads are bad, but he's a good driver. . . . Well, maybe he dropped by the grocery store. . . . Anne, it's okay. . . . You want me to go out and find him? . . . Okay. . . . Yeah. Don't worry. . . . You're welcome."

He put the phone down.

"Where are you going?" Gene asked.

"Manny, you finish supper."

"What happened?"

"I'm going out to see if Letig's stuck in the snow somewhere."

"You want me to come with you?" Manny asked.

"No. You boys stay here. Gene, check on Laura."

"You might need some help, though, if he's stuck," Manny said.

"Stay here. Finish supper. I'll be back soon."

From her door, where she had listened to all this, she moved to the window and watched her father trot to his truck, his head bent, his hood covering his face. He opened the door, turned on the lights, slashed the blades across the icy windshield. In his headlights, the sleet shot past like burnt film on the drive-in screen, silver and white spikes exploding on the ground. The street was dark but glistened from the ice, a thick white membrane collecting along the sides of the street and the lawns. She watched him back out of the driveway. On the street, the end of his truck fishtailed when he accelerated. He slowed down and drove cautiously away, the exhaust pipe spewing a milky cloud behind him.

✴

32

Momentary Silence

*S*he was not pregnant. Her period started before her father even arrived back home, and that seemed a terrible irony. She was in the bathroom when Gene called out, "He's back. I see him."

It was nearly eleven, and she was at the window in time to see his truck rumbling slowly into the snow-packed driveway, the beams from his headlights catching the hard lines of sleet and snow still falling from the sky. He didn't immediately turn off the lights and the engine. Rich was asleep, but she, Manny, and Gene all stood by the window, waiting for him to come in. He finally cut the engine, the lights flicked off, a dim yellow afterglow still visible in the globes. He opened the truck door and walked too slowly through the snow and sleet to the porch, with his head down, his hood draped darkly over his face.

All of them stood silently, peering through the window to the porch, as he pulled back his hood, scraped his boots on the step, and stamped a couple of times on the mat outside the door. Then he stepped in and was surprised to see them there, as if he'd forgotten them or figured they would not have waited up.

"What happened?" she asked. Her voice sounded like a lamb's bleat, but no one laughed. It was not funny.

He just shook his head and inhaled deeply. They did not rush him. He took off his coat, shook it out on the porch, and then hung it on the peg by the door. His jeans were wet and darkened up to his coat line. His boots, too, were soaked, as were his gloves, and his hair was wet as well. They watched him patiently as he dripped, a puddle encircling him on the Home Sweet Home mat inside the door, the snow and water spreading out to the hard-wood floor, so that it darkened, too.

He would tell them soon enough. She thought she knew what he would say, and she knew that once he said it, it would be truth, and that until he spoke, they all still existed in this world of suspenseful ignorance. Part of her wanted to stay there, didn't want to hear her father's voice, and was thankful for his momentary silence. She swallowed, and it hurt.

Finally he turned to them, sighed heavily, began to speak, and everything changed.

33

✳

Charnelle in Grief

*T*he snow and sleet that began falling on Thursday had come down heavily throughout the afternoon and night. The temperature rose, and the sleet turned to rain, and then the temperature dropped, making the roads slick with black ice. Seven accidents occurred that night in Charnelle alone, and cars and trucks were stranded along the highway leading into Amarillo, where the snow and ice had shut down the city. Two rigs jackknifed and spilled crates of California citrus across the frozen highway.

Only one person, however, had died in the Texas Panhandle because of the weather. On Monday, the Tate family attended his funeral.

Friday, schools had closed, the town of Charnelle shut down, except for the plows, which Laura heard grinding and scraping, metal against asphalt, the sound of an accusation. The snow and sleet continued through Friday morning and afternoon but stopped Friday evening. Saturday and Sunday, the sun was out, the temperature kept rising, reaching close to sixty degrees. The snow and ice melted quickly, and by the day of the funeral there was little evidence of the damage, just patches of snow on the shady north sides of buildings and ditches.

Laura and her brothers didn't go to school. By two o'clock, when they had to leave for the church, the day was bright and warm. They didn't need sweaters or jackets. And this, too, this sunshine, this heat, seemed like cruel irony.

They sat in the middle section of the Charnelle First Methodist Church. Gene sat next to their father. Manny and Joannie sat next to Gene. Laura sat on the other side of her father, with Rich between them. She wore a black-and-white dress that was a little too big for her—really more of a summer dress, one that her mother had left. She put a dark burgundy shawl that had been Gloria's over her shoulders. Her father and Manny and Gene owned only navy blue suits, so they wore them, though that morning their father bought them all black ties at Thomason's. Rich wore a dark green sweater and green corduroy pants, hand-me-downs from Gene.

She had been to only one funeral in her life, Uncle Unser's. And that was many years ago. She remembered very little. It was a graveside service. Just fifteen or twenty people there. Uncle Unser's coffin was closed. Everybody seemed embarrassed. Their heads were down all the time. Maybe because he'd killed himself. Afterward her brothers, Gloria, and she went home with her father while her mother stayed with Aunt Velma for a week.

The church was now nearly two-thirds full. Mrs. Ambling was there, in the pew behind Laura and her family. Jimmy and Bob Cransburgh were there. Beaver Mitchell was there. Most of the men who worked at Charnelle Steel & Construction seemed to be there. The Somersby brothers and even, more surprisingly, Donna Somersby (who seldom left her house) were there, sitting three pews away from Tina Fellows, Dave Somersby's girlfriend. Billy Sidell and Dean Compson were there, and Debbie and Marlene and their families were there. Several of the teachers were there as well, including Mr. Sparling and Mrs. McFarland, and the librarian, Mrs. Wickan. Laura didn't understand why they had come, how they knew the Letigs. Luke from the Armory bar and Mr. Thomason were there, as were Mr. and Mrs. Aguilar, Mrs. Aguilar wearing an elaborate black silk dress, gloves, and a veil that covered her entire body. There were other families from town, who had lived here as long as Laura could remember.

John's mother and his aunt and uncle had driven over from Pampa, and his two older brothers from Phoenix. John's mother was thin and seemed frail, walking with a cane. His brothers looked like John: the same athletic bodies, long faces and red lips, blond hair. They both wore thick beards that made them seem foreign. They sat solemnly in the first row, which was reserved for the family.

Mrs. Letig's mother was there from Borger, and her sister and her husband had come up with their kids from Dallas. Laura knew all these people because she'd seen pictures in the Letig home, framed on the walls and in meticulously organized photo albums.

The coffin was made of black walnut, and it glistened beneath the lights in the church. It was three-quarters the size of a regular coffin, but it still seemed too big. It sat atop a long communion table draped with a red velvet blanket. The lid of the coffin was half open, from the head to the waist, and the inside lining was made of ruffled off-white silk, but from where Laura sat, she could not see the boy's face.

The funeral was supposed to begin at two-thirty, but it was nearly three before the door by the baptismal opened, and out stepped the preacher, a tall, dignified man in his mid-fifties. Laura had often seen him around town, but she didn't know until now that he was a preacher. He held the door open, and behind him came John, Anne, and Willie Letig.

Mrs. Letig wore a black dress and hat, her face partially hidden behind a sheer black veil. John carried Willie, who was crying. Both the man and the boy wore matching black suits, and Laura wondered for a brief moment if they had bought them today. John's hair was slicked back, dramatically revealing the results of the accident. Three jagged gashes, scabbed over now, lined his right cheek. Abrasions waffled his chin and forehead. Both eyes were black and puffy.

The preacher nodded toward one of the ushers, who stood by the door, and he helped the Letigs to the first pew. The preacher approached the pulpit and waited until the family was seated. He paused solemnly for another moment in the silent church for them all to register why they were here.

" 'Suffer the little children to come unto Me,' " he began.

His voice was even and smooth, though ordinary; he didn't have the usual singsong bombast of other preachers. He could have been a banker or an accountant.

"What exactly does Jesus mean when He says that? It is a translation that has always, quite frankly, troubled me. When He spoke those lines, He meant them literally, as His disciples were sending mothers and their children away because they didn't want them to bother Jesus. For the translators in King James's time, it meant simply, '*Allow* or *permit* or *do not forbid* the children to come to Me.' And yet '*Suffer* the children' is one of the phrases we most remember from the New Testament. We still cling to the archaic usage of that word, partly for the poetry but partly because the word still speaks to us in a profound way, especially at a time like this.

"I remember, before my own study of the Bible began, I thought that Jesus was saying that the children must suffer. My youngest sister died when I was fifteen, and I saw what happened to my parents after her death. Even now, to me, as a parent and as a minister who has had to comfort those who have lost their children, I can't help but believe that those lines are also Jesus's solace to parents, His promise that the suffering will pass, the redemptive consolation that the children are moving from our hands to His, our world to His.

"But still, despite that solace, it seems a terrible injustice to lose a child. It is so difficult because we believe that our children are meant to outlive us. Our parents may die, our grandparents and uncles and aunts, sometimes even our friends, but those losses do not carry the same jarring, unnatural blow that the death of a child brings to a parent. We cannot quite fathom it, no matter how many times we hear reports about children dying, or read about it in the papers, or even worry about it, as parents always do. It is still an awful and not-quite-believable tragedy when it happens in our community."

He paused for a moment, looked down at his notes, and seemed to collect his thoughts. Laura stole glances at the people in the pews, some with their heads bowed, some with handkerchiefs pressed to their faces. Manny, Gene, and her own father wiped their eyes. She breathed deeply and listened.

"John Raymond Letig Jr.—Jack, as he was called—was only five. Five and a half, as he would have said. He would have been six on March twenty-first. I am sure that those of you here—family, friends, loved ones, members of the community who have come to pay your respects—join with me now to extend our prayers for John and Anne Letig, and to little William, too, as they try to bear this burden and prepare for the even harder days, weeks, and months that surely wait ahead for them.

"I have spent the past two days with this family, precious few hours, and I know they love each other. I want to urge them to persevere in their love. In the end, it must sustain them. But it is also in times such as these, when we are united in suffering so elemental, so primitive, that it seems beyond articulation . . . it is during these times that we can either renew our faith or discover our spiritual selves, that secret chamber of our hearts that may remain dormant until a tragedy such as this pries it open and reveals the hidden depths within.

"Without that renewal, without that discovery, we will most certainly flounder. We will lose our way. I know this for a fact. I have seen it happen again and again. We can easily give in to this despair. And while I offer this warning in hopes that it will not happen, I know all too well, both firsthand and in my work as a minister, how difficult it is to learn that lesson, and even to relearn it. Suffering renders us dumb and blind. We must remember this.

"Ultimately, however, our grief can purify us, as Jesus Himself promised and by His example revealed. But first there is a kind of death through which we must pass, and it is not an easy or safe passage. The journey is fraught with more hardships and with a dangerous pull, like an undertow, toward self-destruction and heartache."

He paused again and looked down at the front row, where the Letigs sat huddled together with their heads bowed. Laura tried to see past the men in the pew in front of her, but she could only see the backs of the Letigs' heads. She wanted to see their faces yet dreaded it as well.

"So John and Anne and Willie, we join now, in this assembly, to be with you in your tragedy, to let you know that you reside within a circle of prayer. And I ask that we all now bow our heads and pray together for this family."

Laura bowed her head and could feel, as a kind of collective heaviness, the heads of others dropping, too. She closed her eyes.

"We need not pray for Jack. He has already come unto You, Lord. We pray for this family, who suffers his loss, and who may find in their grief the threat of despair, and the temptation to find fault with one another, and to search in their hearts for blame and their own guilt. We ask You to help them in their suffering and guide them to You, and to one another, and to those they love. And that You help them navigate the treacherous waters through which they inevitably must pass. Help them remember that they, too, are Your children, and that their sufferings can be, must be, rendered unto You, and they will find the peace that eventually awaits us all. While there can be no easy remedy for their sorrow at Jack's passing, we ask that You please help that sorrow, in time, turn into strength, into compassion for one another and for others who also suffer. In Your name we pray. Amen."

The gathered murmured solemnly, "Amen."

The preacher looked down again from the pulpit at the Letigs and then motioned for the usher who had helped them to their pew to escort them to the coffin for the final viewing of their son. John and Anne Letig, with Willie between them, walked slowly to the coffin. John was first. He placed his hand over the face of his son, and then his back and arm seemed to shake visibly. The crowd sat, hushed, afraid of what could happen in this moment.

He then withdrew his hand and picked up Willie, but the boy did not want to look at his brother. He buried his face in his father's shoulder and began sobbing.

Mrs. Letig lifted her veil and turned back for a brief moment to the audience. Laura could see her face for the first time. It was a face Laura realized she would never forget: a spiderweb of grief, not just wrinkled but shattered. The preacher went to her, held out a steadying hand, but she pushed him away, gently, and then placed one hand down on her son's chest. She bent over and kissed his face.

John put his other arm across her shoulders. She hovered over her child in the coffin, and Laura wondered how long Mrs. Letig would stay there, if she would not allow him to be buried. But then she rose and placed her face in her husband's shoulder, wrapped her arm around Willie, and the three of them stood there, in front of the coffin, as if they were on display. But it also seemed appropriate that they stand there before their son, with everyone in the church as witnesses, many crying audibly now into handkerchiefs.

Then the preacher tapped gently on John's elbow, to let them know it was time to go. They stood there, still, for a few more seconds, and then the three moved awkwardly, as if attached, for a few steps, before Mrs. Letig broke free, dabbed her eyes and nose with her black handkerchief, and then dropped her veil down again. Neither John nor his wife turned around, but Willie, from his father's shoulder, lifted his head and looked back at the coffin, and his face seemed strangely shocked, the same expression Laura remembered from months ago, last spring, when she had walked all the boys to town, and Jack had stepped off the curb and into the road and was nearly hit by the screeching car, and she had grabbed him, pulled him back, and scolded him sharply, making him burst into tears. That was the face. The exact expression. As if that moment had been superimposed onto this one.

Throughout the funeral, Laura had not cried at all, but this moment triggered her own grief. She felt it swell in her face as she watched the Letigs leave the church with the preacher.

The rest of them were then led in a procession, row by row, toward the casket. She didn't want to go, but she was in line, and she didn't know how she could just walk away without embarrassment. None of the others had excused themselves. The procession moved by the casket, most paying their respects with simply a nod, others moving quickly on, not looking at all.

When his face came into view, she thought she might throw up. His eyes were closed, as if he were asleep, but she had seen him asleep many times, and the combed hair, the pale pink lipstick, the peach-colored blush on his cheeks made him seem like a cartoon version of a child, not the boy she had known, with his cowlick and his splotched skin and his father's angular nose. He had a scarf around his neck to cover the jagged gash. That was the only wound, though it had been enough. She couldn't look again. She turned away and then followed the man in front of her, out into the vivid, painful sunlight.

She saw the car where John and Willie and Mrs. Letig were. The windows were tinted lightly, but she could see them huddled in the backseat, heads down. She watched unabashedly. And then John turned to her, as if he knew she was looking, or as if her stare had compelled him. His face didn't change, though. It seemed frozen. Finally he blinked twice. Then he turned, expressionless, back to his wife and child.

Laura's father and Manny were pallbearers, and she watched them, along with the other men—John's brothers, Mrs. Letig's brother-in-law, three other men she didn't know—as they carried the closed casket slowly to the hearse. They stepped aside while the driver shut the door. The engine of the hearse started, and then her father motioned for her and Gene and Rich, who held her hands, to follow him. They walked quickly to the truck.

Along the way, the automobile engines, in a fitful commotion, started, the bodies of the cars and trucks shaking slightly. The beams of light came on, one by one, but you could barely tell in the harsh sunlight, only a dull silver sheen over the globes and the bumpers in front. And then finally, slowly, the phalanx of humming vehicles followed the dead boy to his grave.

34

✳

Letig in Grief

*E*very day since the funeral, she walked to the abandoned warehouse and waited. He didn't show up. She really didn't think he would. But each day she went with an electric sense of hope and dread, and she waited, telling herself, *No, he won't come.* Her breath quickened when each new car or truck turned the corner, and she could feel the pressure in her chest, thinking, *Yes, this will be him,* and when it wasn't, she thought, *Of course it's not him,* and she chastised herself for going back and forth, like a yo-yo. Her need to see him was, in part, practical. She still hadn't been able to tell him that it was a false alarm. She figured he'd want to know, would need to know, and so she kept coming day after day, as a kind of formless obligation. She'd rehearsed how she would tell him and had tried to predict what his reaction would be. She could even imagine him striking her, and at first she tried to dispel these thoughts, but soon she willed herself to think about that possibility because maybe she deserved it and so should prepare herself for its inevitability.

She was afraid to call again. She had worked out what she would say if Mrs. Letig answered the phone, and she had dialed the number and let it ring. Mrs. Letig answered, her voice dark and dull, as if drugged, and Laura knew that the lies from before would not be so easy now. She hung up.

She thought of sending him a note. Just something unsigned in code: "False alarm" or "Everything's okay." But then she remembered his reaction to that first letter she'd sent. She'd wait it out. She'd just keep coming to this spot, or she would one day go with her father to their house, to take a meal, and she would tell him then. Slip a note to him, or whisper something in the hallway or kitchen when no one else was around. And then it would be done. Everything would be over. She longed for it all to be over. Some part of her never wanted to see the Letigs again. They would always remind her of this year, this accident, and her part in it. But she also felt bound to them in a way, and drawn to them as well, as if they were a powerful planet and she simply a moon orbiting them.

Her father had gone over twice to visit the Letigs, but he'd not asked her to go with him, and when he returned he seemed stunned and vague. She wanted details, specifics: *How did they look? What did they do? What did they say?* But she didn't feel it was appropriate to ask.

He just said, "It isn't good," and shook his head. "It's sad," he said. "They're having a rough go of it." And he went to wash up for supper.

How? What do you mean? Tell me!

So she kept coming here to this place, hoping he would show up, telling herself that he wouldn't, but secretly believing that one day he would.

Waiting for him, in the increasing cold as the sun dropped lower in the horizon each afternoon, she relentlessly brooded over the events leading up to the accident, as if this time of waiting should be her penance. She had begun to wonder if Jack would still be alive if she and John had left. It seemed to her as if their staying had set in motion a chain reaction that had resulted in his death, and if they had gone, as they originally planned, if they had headed out of Charnelle, if they had started their lives over anonymously, even if their guilt over abandoning their families had torn them apart, creating only divisive shame and isolating regret, even if they had been permanently exiled from Charnelle, even if all of this had occurred, it would have saved Jack because he would not have been in that truck with John that terrible night. He would have grown into a man, perhaps a man who hated his father, who hated Laura, who hated what they had done to his mother and his brother and himself, but all that bitterness, all that anger and pain that each and every one of them would have felt, would have been worth it because he would be alive right here, right now, and on into the future.

And why, she wondered, did Willie have to get sick, his ear so bad that he had to go to the hospital on that particular day and stop them and make them think it was a sign, a sign that had saved them from their own foolishness? Why had her period not come for so many days, alarming her and causing her to alarm John so that he could not concentrate on the icy road, and then why had it started just hours later? Why had Mrs. Letig asked her to watch Jack on the day that an ice storm descended so suddenly and unexpectedly on the Texas Panhandle? And why, out of all the accidents that occurred that day—the rigs turned on their sides, the spilled oranges across the white highway, the truckers stalled in the black ice and snow outside of Amarillo, the seven accidents that happened in Charnelle alone and the ninety-eight that happened that night in the Panhandle—why out of all of these accidents had the only fatality been this guiltless little boy, who did not deserve to die, and whose only wound, whose only scratch, had been a thin, jagged gash across his neck from the broken windshield?

And going back further, why had she and John met on that snowy New Year's Eve, and why had it been snowing then, almost as white and cold as the night of the accident, a warning, it seemed to her now, and why had she let him kiss her, and why had she kissed him the next time she saw him, urging him on, and why had they kept meeting when it was so clear that this was no good for either of them or their families? And why had she continued to see him after everything that happened at Lake Meredith, and why had she not heeded Gloria's warning to end it, to end it then and there, because, if prolonged, it could only result in disappointment and heartache? And why had he not heeded his own warnings of danger, danger to himself, to her, to their families? And why, for that matter, had they not been caught before this, when there were so many opportunities to be caught? There had been close calls, and it was miraculous, really, that they had not been caught, by Bob Cransburgh at the Armory that very first night, by her father during his poker game, or by Manny, who suspected something, she

knew, or by Rich or Gene, or Willie, or Jack, who came the closest that
night while she hid in the Letigs' bedroom closet. Why didn't she heed the
signs then? Why hadn't she just jumped off the trestle over the Waskalanti
Creek, just jumped like Danny Lincoln when she felt the impulse to do so?

They had been lucky, she thought, so lucky, and yet what kind of luck
is it that leads to this? She could imagine her father's rage, Mrs. Letig's an-
guish, John going to jail because of what they had done, could even imagine getting pregnant and desperately searching out Mrs. Aguilar or going
shamefully to Dalhart or Amarillo and living with other teenage girls who
didn't want, or wouldn't be allowed, to keep their babies, and it all would
have been better than this.

And why, she finally wondered, had circumstances allowed them to go
to Galveston together, giving her a maddening glimpse of what it would be
like to have him to herself, making realistic a fantasy that propelled them
into their crazy plan to escape Charnelle? And why did they continue to see
each other after the huge failure of that fantasy, even though they both
knew it was over? And why did they just keep passing the time, killing the
time, refusing to end it cleanly, until all of these significant and insignificant
events conspired to murder this little boy?

Two weeks after Thanksgiving, on a clear, chilly afternoon, she heard a car
turning the corner, but she didn't look up at first. She had trained herself to
wait before she looked, as if the waiting would lessen the disappointment,
and when she did look, she saw the dark green Chevy, Mrs. Letig's car,
rounding the corner. She darted behind the warehouse where she couldn't
be seen, but when the car got closer, she could see it was John. Of course it
was John, of course it would be the Chevy. The truck had flipped three
times, the windshield shattered, the front end squashed like an accordion.
She had driven with Manny and Joannie to see it at the junkyard, where it
sat propped on blocks, like a county-fair spectacle. Bloodstains were still on
the seats. It had been hosed down, but the stains had not come out. She expected Manny to make some bad joke, but he seemed as shaken by the sight
as she was.

When John pulled up, she opened the door and got in, hunching down
onto the floorboard.

"Are you pregnant?" he asked immediately.

"No," she said.

He put his forehead on the steering wheel. He stayed that way for a long time, with the car engine idling. She didn't know what she should do. Get out? Stay there?

"John, I'm sorry—"

"No," he said sharply, lifting his head. "Don't talk."

"But—"

"I mean it. Don't say anything."

Okay, she thought, *okay. So this is how it will be.*

Without looking at her, he shifted into drive, pressed the accelerator. She studied him. His hair was oily, and it shot out in different directions. He must not have washed or even combed it for days. His face had a small layer of bristles that covered the three raised scars on his cheeks. The scars were purplish red now but no longer scabbed over. Only a few dimpled dots of abrasions were left on his forehead and chin. Under his eyes were faint, green-yellow shadows. He didn't smile. He squinted ahead. New wrinkles seemed to have sprouted around his eyes and the corners of his lips—a network of faint, crosshatched lines. *Grief lines,* she thought.

He wore his brown leather jacket, a flannel shirt, and a T-shirt under it. His knuckles seemed unusually white on the steering wheel, and the sight of them made her feel suddenly afraid. He was not going fast, and she could see the familiar landscape of trees and houses and buildings and poles that she was accustomed to seeing from the floorboard of his truck, though because the car sat lower to the ground, she saw more roof lines than usual. She felt the shift from asphalt to gravel, and then, a couple of miles later, he turned and parked behind the abandoned barn.

He did not say a word to her, did not even look at her, just shifted into park, turned off the car, and got out. She rose from the floorboard and watched him walk to the barn and go in, the door left open behind him. She cautiously followed him inside. He had turned on the kerosene lamp. Now he stood by the window, smoking a cigarette.

"John," she said, like a question, but he ignored her.

No words.

She approached him slowly and touched his arm. He turned around, didn't say anything. He didn't seem angry, but there was a coiled look about him and that inscrutable blank stare. His face was swollen, his eyes dead in the lamplight, as if he had been punched several times and resigned himself without complaint to the beating. It was chilly in the barn, not cold, but when she removed her jacket, goose bumps rose on her arms. He stubbed out his cigarette on the windowsill and then reached over and pulled off her skirt and her panties.

He pressed her down on the pallet and then took off his own pants and underwear. He took a condom from his shirt pocket. He began to slip it on, but then it got tangled or torn or something, and he flung it into the corner. He lay down over her and held her arms against the pallet with his hands and opened her legs with his knees. He pressed against her, breathed heavily. And then, in a sudden painful thrust, he was inside her.

"John," she whimpered, "please."

No response. He kept thrusting. Tears creased her eyelashes, but she made no sound. He let go of her arms and pressed his body tightly against her. He was heavy, and she could hardly breathe. He began to shake as he kept moving his hips roughly, pushing more deeply and then drawing almost all the way out, and then plunging fully into her. He pressed his cheek hard against her face. She could feel the bristles where he had not shaved and the raised texture of the scars. Then she felt his tears, hot on her cheeks.

"John," she whispered again.

The motion of his body continued. And then a choked, guttural cry issued from his throat, a painful, ugly sound, one she had never heard from him before. Abruptly, he pulled out of her, lifted above her on all fours, and she felt the wet heat on her stomach. He leaned back on his knees, covered his face with his hands so she couldn't see his expression. And then he rose without looking at her. He dressed quickly, pulled a cigarette from his pocket, flicked the lighter, and the flame leapt before his face. He inhaled, the orange tip brightening. And then he grabbed his coat and walked to the car.

She strained to hold back her tears. She breathed deeply, but even the sound of her breath seemed offensive to her now. She closed her eyes and tried to remember other times they had been here, a time, not long ago, when she had believed that they loved each other. She realized how terrible she had been to think that they could run away together, how awful and deceitful she was, even to herself, how she had deliberately plotted to bring grief to so many people.

Now she could feel tears spilling down the sides of her face, and she felt even angrier with herself. *What in the hell are you crying for?* she thought. *You don't deserve these tears.*

She heard the engine start. She was afraid for a minute that he was going to leave her there. It was dark and cold now, and she didn't want to walk all the way home. Not just because of the dark. She didn't want to have to explain a further delay. It was already past the time she was expected home. She quickly slipped on the rest of her clothes, grabbed her socks and shoes, and ran to the door of the barn. The car lights were off. He sat behind the steering wheel, staring blankly ahead. He did not even seem to see her. She turned off the lamp, grabbed her coat, and shut the barn door behind her. She ran to the passenger side, opened the door, and slid quietly inside the car.

They sat in silence for a long minute. Finally she said, "John."

He didn't look at her, didn't even seem to register her presence.

"John," she said quietly, "are you ready to go?"

He put the car in reverse, and without looking at her or even looking behind him, he backed the car out so fast that the ground moved violently beneath them.

"Lights," she said softly. He pulled the knob, and two thin beams shone ahead. His shoulders were slumped, his eyes seemed to be on the road, but she wasn't sure he saw it.

When they hit the main street, she crouched down on the floorboard as she had grown accustomed to doing in the truck, and she watched him. He still had that same expressionless stare she had seen first at the funeral and ever since he'd picked her up, a blankness that seemed to her dangerous because she didn't know how to read it. He sped up, and she wondered if he would deliberately wreck the car, if he was determined to kill them both. *It would be what we deserve,* she thought.

She watched the trees and buildings and houses and telephone poles and streetlamps blur. Despite the speed and his apparent recklessness, the drive seemed to take forever, and when she looked above her, the trees and sky also seemed strange, foreign. He'd gone too far. Where was he going? He turned twice but barely braked, the tires squealed; and she found herself holding on tightly to the door handle, bracing herself hard against the dash.

When he finally stopped, the car jerked forward and then back. She lost her balance and slid, her head tapping the glove box. It hurt, but she was relieved that at least he'd stopped. He did not turn off the engine, did not say a word. She rose from the floorboard and discovered that they were in front of her house. She scrunched back down onto the floorboard, alarmed.

"What are you doing?" she whispered.

He didn't answer.

"What do I say?" she asked.

He didn't respond, just stared ahead. She sat up, opened the door.

"John," she said, thinking at that moment that she would, most likely, never see him again.

Before she could say anything else, he pulled away. The door shut by itself, nearly knocking her over. The back wheels spewed pellets of cold gravel onto her jeans and over her shoes. She watched the red taillights receding. Her stomach knotted. She turned, reluctantly, toward her house. An amber glow blossomed in the living room. Her father's truck was not in the driveway, but the old Ford, the one Manny now drove, was, and she could see her brother in the window, staring out at her.

35

✴

Telling

She walked toward the porch, her face congested with dread. He stood at the window, fingering his small mustache. She knew he'd start in on her with the doggedness of an interrogator: *Where have you been? Why did Letig drive off so fast? What's going on?* She was in trouble. She was in a lot of trouble. It was her fault. She was to blame. Even if her father wasn't there, it would only be a matter of time before Manny would tell him, just to see his rage, just to increase her grief, everybody's grief.

But before she reached the porch, he opened the door. His face was not twisted into the taunting mask she had imagined. His forehead instead was furrowed with worry; his mouth twitched anxiously, like her father's.

"Laura," he said gently, "are you okay?"

She was so surprised that she tripped on the steps. He caught her, then helped her into the house, took her coat, and sat her on the couch.

"Where is everybody?" she asked.

"They went to get the Christmas tree. What's wrong? What happened?"

There was no accusation in his voice, only urgent concern. He was worried. She almost wished he would accuse her. His tenderness made her feel vulnerable. And when she tried to speak, her voice cracked, and then the flood of tears came. She covered her face with her hands. He sat beside her and put his arm around her.

"Hey," he said softly and then again, "Hey." After a moment, he asked, "Were you baby-sitting for the Letigs today? Dad didn't say anything about that. What's wrong, Laura?"

"I can't tell you."

"You have to."

"I can't tell anyone. It's terrible. It's a terrible thing." She put her face back in her hands. She wanted to hide.

"It's okay," he said. "You can tell me."

"You'll tell Dad."

"No, I won't."

"I can't," she sobbed.

He drew her hands away from her face, wiped her eyes with the sleeve of his shirt. "Tell me," he said. "Maybe I can help."

"No one can help. It's all my fault."

He stood up. "You weren't baby-sitting today, were you?"

She shook her head and watched the truth dawn on him.

"Whoa!"

He handed her a handkerchief and then brought her a glass of water. He started to say something, hesitated, then asked quietly, "Did he hurt you?"

"Yes," she said, and then, "No." And then, "I deserved it."

She didn't know how to explain this night, only that it was complicated and painful and must have been somehow necessary. There was no way she could ever describe it.

"I'm terrible," she said. "I'm a horrible person."

"No, you're not."

"I am," she said and then lowered her head back into her hands, ashamed to look at him.

She felt Manny's hand on her shoulder. "It's over, isn't it?" he asked.

Then they heard the front door open. They hadn't even heard her father's truck in the driveway. The sound was so sudden that they both jumped up. She dropped the glass, but miraculously it didn't break.

"Manny, give me a hand with the tree," her father called.

"I'll be right there," he said.

Her father went back outside, leaving the door open behind him. A cold draft swept through the house.

"You can't tell," she whispered.

"I won't."

"How do I know you won't?"

"Joannie and I are getting married."

"What?"

"She's pregnant. About two months now. After New Year's, we're going to tell Dad and her parents. You're the only one who knows. Joannie would kill me if she knew I had told anyone. That's your collateral."

"What?"

"That's how you know I won't tell." He squeezed her hand, assuring her.

And then her father and Rich and Gene were on the porch. The tree filled the doorway, so huge and thick and tall that it seemed, despite their tugging and prodding and complicated maneuvering, fallen needles spraying the floor, that there was no way, even with the whole family helping, that they could pull it through.

36

✳

Mrs. Letig in Grief

*M*rs. Letig answered the door in a dark green floor-length robe, her hair wrapped in a blue towel. She wore no makeup. Her eyes were puffy and bloodshot, her nose red, her cheeks blotchy. Laura had not seen Mrs. Letig since the funeral, and she had not seen her face that day except for that one terrible moment when she had lifted her veil. Mrs. Letig had called this afternoon to ask if Laura could watch Willie. Laura didn't want to, had told her father, who gave her the message, that she couldn't, that she was going to the library with Marlene to prepare for a debate in her history class, but he was angry with her, said that she could cancel whatever she was doing with Marlene, that the Letigs needed their help and, by God, they would do what they could. She was surprised by his anger. He even called Mrs. Letig back himself and said Laura would be there, that he'd bring her over. Reluctantly, Laura agreed. She rode over on her bike, worried. She felt relieved that the Letigs' car was not in the driveway. She wouldn't have to see John.

"Am I too early?" Laura asked nervously.

"No," Mrs. Letig said, staring blankly at her. "Come in."

Laura stepped across the threshold. Mrs. Letig shut the door behind her. The house was a mess, unfolded clothes piled on the furniture and Willie's toys scattered all over. Two plates of partially eaten lasagna sat on the coffee table, the fork tines buried in the congealed cheese, beside several glasses with syrupy residue in the bottom, water stains underneath. Laura had never seen their house this way.

"Where's Willie?" she asked.

"With Mrs. Langston across the street. I'll go over and get him soon," she said. She stared at Laura for an interminable minute and then sighed heavily.

"I could go over and get him for you now," Laura said, eager to leave.

"No, no, no," she said. "I want you to stay here with me. Besides, we never had that talk. I want to talk with you." She patted Laura's shoulder, then hooked her arm inside Laura's. "Don't you want to talk with me?"

"Yes, ma'am."

"Oh, listen to you. You are so polite," she said, releasing Laura and then stepping past her. "You don't have to call me 'ma'am.'"

"Mrs. Letig—"

"Anne," she corrected. She turned back to Laura and adjusted the towel on her head. "Call me Anne, please."

"We don't have to talk right now," Laura said. "I know you're upset."

"You do, do you?"

"Well . . . I mean," Laura stuttered. "I mean—"

"No!" She spoke sharply, pointing her finger at Laura. "Let's not talk about *that*. Please."

"I'm sorry."

Mrs. Letig grabbed Laura's hand, squeezed it, and then leaned in close to her and smiled again. "I want to talk about *you*. We never had the opportunity, and I promised you."

Laura didn't know what to say. She felt uneasy. She was supposed to be here to baby-sit, but Mrs. Letig seemed in no hurry to get Willie.

"Just for a little bit," Mrs. Letig said, releasing Laura's hand. "Why don't you come on into the bedroom. We can talk while I dress."

"I can just wait out here for you," she said, not moving.

"Oh, don't be ridiculous." She pulled a handkerchief out of the pocket of her robe, wiped her eyes and nose. "I don't have time to dress and then talk with you later."

"Where's Mr. Letig?" she asked.

She did not want to see him, not in this house, not with his wife there, not after what happened. But she felt she needed to know if he might be coming back. She needed to prepare for it.

"John's out. You don't have to worry about him, honey. He won't be coming back anytime soon. It's just us girls," Mrs. Letig said, grabbing Laura's hand again. "Come on, dear. Come in here with me."

Mrs. Letig led Laura into the bedroom. Her dresses, slips, bras, and stockings lay scattered on the bed and floor. The top of John's dresser was completely empty. Something had happened.

"You sit on the bed there. I'm going to have a glass of wine. Would you like one, Laura?" Mrs. Letig smiled with her mouth but not her eyes, and there was a rise in the pitch of her voice.

"No, ma'am."

"You are *too* polite. Now, come on. How old are you? Seventeen?"

"Almost. My birthday's in a couple of weeks."

"So only sixteen. That's right. I know Zeeke, though. He wouldn't mind if you have a little glass of wine. Or maybe a beer."

"No thanks."

"I insist," she said, leaning forward, too close.

"A glass of water, I guess. I could get it, Mrs. Letig."

"*Anne,*" she said.

"I know you're in a hurry."

"I'm not in a hurry, Laura." She cocked her head. "Are you wondering if you're getting paid for this time?"

Laura shook her head, worried she had offended her. "No, ma'am."

"Well, you are. Getting paid, that is. Consider yourself on the clock."

"No, I didn't mean that."

"I know you didn't, dear."

She patted Laura's hands again and stared at her for an uncomfortably long time, her bloodshot eyes beginning to brim. Laura looked away, embarrassed. Mrs. Letig sniffed and then breathed deeply.

"I'll be right back," Mrs. Letig said. "Don't you go anywhere now."

Laura sat on the edge of the unmade bed, the wrinkled sheets and spread hanging off the ends as if they had been kicked off. She searched the room for more clues. Mrs. Letig's vanity table was not in its usual order, lipsticks and nail polish bottles tipped on their sides, a wad of her red hair ratted in a wire brush. Two empty wineglasses with dried purple residue in the bottom stood amid the strewn makeup. Laura had never seen their room like this. Was this grief or something else? She had to find a way to excuse herself, to get out of this house. She could not be here. It was a mistake her coming, letting her father bully her into coming. She wanted nothing more to do with the Letigs. She'd done enough, hadn't she?

Mrs. Letig returned, the hem of her green robe dragging the floor. She carried two glasses of wine, both of them full. She handed one to Laura. "Here."

"Mrs. Letig—"

"Anne, please."

"I can't."

"Yes, you can. Drink it." This seemed like an order, and so Laura took the glass, but she just held it. She did not dare drink.

Mrs. Letig sipped hers twice and then set the glass down on the vanity table, next to the empty ones. "Drink, please. This is good wine. None of that cheap Armory stuff. I got this in Dallas last spring when I visited my sister."

Laura hesitated. Last spring, when she had watched Jack and Willie while Mrs. Letig took a vacation. She took a sip of the wine. It tasted bitter.

"See, isn't that better? Isn't this cozy?"

Mrs. Letig sat at the vanity table and removed the blue towel and threw it on the bed. Wet and hanging down in tangled ringlets, her red hair seemed almost black. She took the wire brush from the table, removed the wad of hair in it and threw it on the floor, then ran the brush roughly through her hair.

"So . . . your mother," she began.

"We really don't—"

"No, no, no," Mrs. Letig said. "I *want* to talk to you about your mother. That's a good theme, don't you think? Motherhood."

"Pardon?"

"You know, I have given your mother quite a bit of thought, Laura. What makes a woman walk off and abandon her family like that? I have thought about it more than I care to admit. I have come up with several theories. Would you like to hear them?"

She said this lightly, and again Laura felt a strong sense of incongruity, as if her actions and her words didn't go together. Laura didn't want to hear Mrs. Letig's theories about her mother.

"I don't know," she muttered, staring down at the floor where a black slip lay rumpled by the legs of the vanity table.

"You don't know? Hmmm. I'll take that for a yes. Okay, first theory, pretty obvious: She was crazy. Of course, I never remember thinking that about her. She seemed such a practical woman. Quiet, yes. Hard to read her. No one could, I guess. A lot of people thought she was strange, arrogant. I know she had a crazy uncle. And perhaps she fell into some kind of spell, walked off, and that was that. Maybe she's in some nuthouse, even as we speak. What do you think? Does that hold water?"

Laura continued to stare down at the floor. This was not good. Where was she going with this?

"Second theory—and this was certainly a rumor—is that she was murdered, though I guess we have the bus depot man's testimony and the bus driver's as well. And your neighbor saw her leave with a suitcase in hand. So that pretty much rules out that theory."

Mrs. Letig looked into the mirror and continued brushing.

"Three is hard. Theory number three is this: She'd had enough. With Zeeke, or with you all. That was difficult for me to comprehend at first. A woman. No money. All five of you kids, or four kids, I guess, since Gloria had flown the coop already. Four beautiful children. Well behaved. They say, 'yes, ma'am' and 'yes, sir.' They help with the chores. Good kids. But maybe that's just how they *seem*."

She paused and turned toward Laura, raised an eyebrow. The brush was still in her hand, and she held it like a weapon.

"Maybe they're actually terrible," she said. "Or she believes them to be terrible, or maybe she believes herself to be a terrible mother. And she has to leave before she does something awful. Something she won't be able to forgive herself for. Perhaps it's an act of charity, her disappearance."

"Mrs. Letig—"

She clicked her tongue and wagged a finger in front of Laura's face. "Anne," she said.

"Anne, I don't want to—"

"Please," she said, smiling. "Indulge me for a while longer."

Laura didn't know how to stop this. Mrs. Letig took another drink of her wine and straightened the folds of her robe. Laura set her still-full glass on the bedside table and then crossed her hands in her lap and felt strangely like a little girl, waiting to be punished.

"Now, where were we?" Mrs. Letig continued, too brightly. "Theories. Theories about your mother. Theory four is that she killed herself. I was sure of this for a long time," she said, nodding her head. "That mysterious uncle. She just made it seem like she abandoned you all, but then she just didn't want to saddle you with the burden of her death. But what is *worse?* I've often wondered. To kill yourself and have your family live with that shame, that burden? Or to have them think you hated them so much that you just up and left—started over but didn't kill yourself? It's a toss-up. Very difficult choice. But what mother hasn't felt the desire to just walk away sometimes? Men do it all the time. It's more difficult for women, though. Your children are part of you, you see." She suddenly stood. "You still have the scars. Your body is one big scar. Look at this, Laura."

She opened her robe. Beneath, she was naked. Laura, shocked, put her hands in front of her face and closed her eyes. "Mrs. Letig!"

"No!" the woman said sharply and then reached over and grabbed Laura's chin between her fingers, turned it toward her body. "You look at this," she demanded. "I want to *show* you, so you know what motherhood does to your body. Girls should be shown this so they know. Look, look here at these marks! You see them. Those are scars. When John and I first married, I was as thin as you. But this is what they did to me. See—"

"Mrs. Letig, please don't—"

She ignored Laura's pleas. "Look, damn it! Look at these hips. Look at this belly. Not pretty, is it? Not very sexy. And this is just two children. I can't imagine five. And look here, look at these breasts. They used to rise of their own accord, just like those movie stars you daydream about. I used to be a looker. I was. But see them now? Look at them, Laura!"

She sat back down on her vanity stool but did not close her robe. She took another long, deliberate drink of her wine.

"It's not pretty, is it?" she said calmly. "Your mother was still pretty, honey, but her body had lost the war. And Zeeke, well . . . your father, he was no saint. I bet you didn't know that, huh? Or maybe you do. Here, you want to touch?"

"No!" Laura rose quickly and darted for the door.

"Wait!" Mrs. Letig shouted, grabbing Laura's wrist and jerking her back into the room. "Here," she said. "I want you to feel the scars."

"No—"

"Touch them. I want you to touch them!"

She was strong and quick, and she forced Laura's hand onto her stomach, ran it over her skin. Laura fell to her knees, but Mrs. Letig held tightly to Laura's hand and pressed it against her body.

"Do you feel that?"

"Stop it! Please, stop it! Why are you doing this?"

She let go of Laura's hand, closed her robe, shut the bedroom door, and sat back down on her vanity stool. Laura lay on the floor, crying.

"I'm sorry, Laura. I don't know what got into me."

Laura started to get up from the floor. "I'm going."

"You're not going anywhere."

"I know you're upset," Laura sobbed.

"*Upset?*" Mrs. Letig seemed puzzled by the word.

"In grief," Laura amended.

"What do you know about grief?" Mrs. Letig asked. No anger, no bitterness. A legitimate question. She leaned over to Laura, still on the floor, and touched her arm. "Here, come sit down. And please tell me what you know about grief. Tell me what you know about mourning."

Rising, Mrs. Letig's hand supporting her elbow, Laura brushed the tears from her face, tried to collect herself. "I need to go."

"No, you don't. You don't need to go anywhere. You need to be here with me."

The door was right there, but Laura could not move. She stood, frozen, near the bed, staring at the woman. "I think you've had too much to drink," she said.

Mrs. Letig released her arm and then pointed toward the bed. "I'm paying you to be here. Now sit down."

"I can't," Laura said, still standing. "I have to go, Mrs. Letig."

"I told you to call me Anne. Please."

"Anne . . . I really think I should leave now."

Mrs. Letig nodded and then reached out for Laura's hand again, squeezing it more gently than before. "Maybe I have had a little too much to drink. I used to never drink. But I've recently developed a taste for it. I'm not drunk, though. It's important that you know that. I'm not. I'm sorry about what happened before. I really am," she said. "Just sit back down. Let's finish our conversation."

Laura didn't know what to do. How did she let herself get inside this room?

"Sit down. I didn't mean to scare you. Now sit down, please."

Reluctantly, Laura sat again on the edge of the bed. Mrs. Letig picked up her wineglass, saw that it was empty, so reached over to get Laura's glass from the bedside table. She poured half the wine into her own glass, spilling some on the floor. She didn't seem to care.

"Now where were we?"

"Mrs. Letig—"

"Anne."

"Anne, I'm so sorry about Jack."

"This isn't about Jack. This has nothing to do with Jack," she said, taking another drink. She closed her eyes, as if to relish the taste, and said, smiling, "You know what this is about, sweetie."

She had been a fool to think that this was all about grief. "I'm sorry," Laura whispered. "I really am."

"No, you're not the least bit *sorry*," she said, shaking her head, talking quietly but very deliberately. "You're only saying that because I've got you here, and you can't really bear that I know the truth."

"I am sorry—"

"I think, honey, it would be better if you didn't talk. He told me everything. Well, maybe not *everything*. I don't think I could have handled everything. But enough for me to get the picture. It was a very tearful confession."

"I am so sorry."

"No!" she said, rising again, grabbing Laura's face with both her hands. "Stop right there. Listen carefully to me. I want you to stop saying that. You are not *allowed* to say that. Do you understand? Say 'I hate you, Anne Letig.' Say 'I'm young and stupid and selfish.' But don't tell me that you're sorry. We are not lying right now, you and me. My son is in the grave. And I'm staring at the girl, the girl I entrusted with my children, with my dead boy . . . and I learn that this same girl has been screwing my husband for the past year, that in fact he ran off the road because you told him you were pregnant. Why you told him that, when it was not true, I do not know. But my son is dead. That's what I do know. We are past the point of lying. You got that? We are only telling the truth now. Do you understand me?" She shook Laura's face. "Answer me."

"Yes," Laura said.

Mrs. Letig let go of her and sat back down. Laura felt a sickening dread. She realized she had expected this moment, had been waiting to finally be accused directly. Mrs. Letig was right. She was responsible.

"Good." Mrs. Letig drank the rest of her wine and then took Laura's glass. "Good."

"What are you going to do?" Laura asked.

"You don't really have the right to ask that question, now, do you?"

Laura shook her head. She no longer felt concern for her own safety. She was instead suddenly worried for Mrs. Letig. "Are you going to hurt yourself?"

"You flatter yourself, girl," she said, laughing. "That would be convenient, wouldn't it?"

"Anne—"

"Mrs. Letig!"

"What?" Laura asked, confused.

"Mrs. Letig. You call me Mrs. Letig."

Laura stared at her for second, then said, "Yes, ma'am."

"If I were to kill myself, then what? You marry John? You raise my son?"

Laura shook her head. "No, I didn't mean—"

"Well, what *did* you mean?"

"I just don't . . . want you to . . . hurt yourself," she stammered.

"Well, what you *want* doesn't really count for a whole hell of a lot anymore. Does it? If things were different, then maybe. Maybe I would kill *you.* Or kill John. If there wasn't Willie. Well, then, it might be a possibility. Maybe a probability. But . . . Willie's too important. And I am not going to mess up his life because of another trampy little slut of John's. Oh, I'm sorry. You probably think you're the only one."

She threw her head back and laughed sharply.

"You're not the first one, honey. Did he tell you that? Did he tell you about the other little peccadillo? After Jack was born? She was a little older than you, and he, of course, was younger, and so it was more serious. He actually did leave me and Jack. For two weeks. Ran off to Kansas City. But I wouldn't give him a divorce, and he didn't really want one. Mr. Letig decided he loved Mrs. Letig after all, and he was ready to settle down and be a good boy. But I guess he wasn't such a good boy after all, now, was he?"

Laura didn't move.

Mrs. Letig leaned forward, waiting for an answer. "Was he?"

"No."

"No, he wasn't. And I suppose I should have known, should have suspected. The way he sometimes looked at you. All those shenanigans out at Palo Duro Canyon on the Fourth. I should have known. Fool me once, shame on you. Fool me twice, shame on me."

She pulled her robe more tightly together, closed her eyes, and ran her fingers through her hair.

"And he's still not a good boy, but he came to me. He's a sweet boy, a *charming* boy. But not *good*. I'll give him this, though. In the end, he's an *honest* boy. He told me. And now what am I supposed to do with that information? My son is dead. My husband has been . . . with a girl half his age. *Jesus!*"

She shook her head and laughed again. Then she stared at Laura, squinted her eyes. "What would *you* do if you were me?" Laura didn't know if the woman really wanted her to say anything. "Well?"

She hesitated and then muttered, "I . . . I . . . don't know."

"No, you don't. Of course you don't. You have no idea. I thought, absurdly, before you came over, that I might just shoot you. Why not? But I couldn't do that. I don't have that in me. I have to do *something*, though, don't I? That's why John told me. So I would *do* something. He wants to be punished. He wants *me* to punish him. But the irony is that he doesn't want to be punished for what he's done with you. He wants to be punished for killing his son."

Laura began crying again. "That's not true," she whispered, though she realized as she said it that Mrs. Letig was right.

"Oh, yes, it is. He knows I would never accuse him of that. It *was* an accident. So he tells me this other thing, this thing about you, because he knows I *will* punish him for that. He knows he *can* be punished for that." Mrs. Letig took the last drink of her wine. "So how?" she continued. "How do I punish him? What would you do?"

Laura looked at the floor, shook her head.

"Well, of course you must know what some of my options are. You must have considered them. You've kept your pretty little mouth shut for the past year. John must have warned you. Maybe he threatened you. This was dangerous business, you understand."

She nodded.

"He can go to jail if I want him to. You know that?"

"Yes, ma'am," she whispered.

"Don't *yes, ma'am*' me! That's a term of respect. You say that to someone you respect. You got that?"

Laura flinched, afraid Mrs. Letig might strike her. She didn't answer. Language was not her ally.

"So you know that I could pick up the telephone and call the authorities," she said, her voice quietly threatening. "I could explain, very calmly, what happened. And John would go to jail, maybe not for long, but perhaps long enough. It would happen. He wouldn't even contest it."

Laura nodded again.

"And you, you would be humiliated. We *all* would be humiliated. But you *are* just a girl, aren't you? And perhaps you are a victim in this."

Mrs. Letig stood up and began pacing the room but never got far from the door. "Jesus, I can't even remember what sixteen was like." She waited for Laura to respond, but when she didn't, Mrs. Letig eyed her carefully before she spoke again, standing now beside John's chest of drawers.

"Or we have option number two: If I don't want to publicly humiliate myself, if I don't want more pity than I already get as the mother of the boy who died in the accident, then I could just tell your father. What do you suppose he would do? Huh? Tell me, Laura. What would he do?"

"I don't know."

"I'll tell you what *I* think he would do. He would, at the very least, beat the shit out of my husband. John is bigger than Zeeke—stronger, younger. But John would let himself be beaten. And beaten badly. A married friend seduces a man's sixteen-year-old daughter. That sort of thing might drive a man crazy. And then what would your father do to *you?* Have you thought of that?"

Laura nodded.

"I guess you have." She paused and ran her fingers through her hair again. "Then there's option number three: I could leave him. I could take Willie and just go. I have money. You know that. And besides, even though he did not kill our son, he is *responsible* for his death. It's hard for a marriage to survive that sort of burden, you know? People would shake their heads, but they would understand, wouldn't they? None of us would have to endure the scandal. Not me, not you, not even John. Although he would lose me—and Willie. Just a clean break. And then he could do whatever he wants. He might even decide to kill himself, if our leaving is not punishment enough."

She crossed to Laura at the bed and knelt before her. Laura leaned back again, afraid. She could smell the wine on Mrs. Letig's breath.

"Or he might run off with you to Mexico, or Galveston, or wherever the hell you want, like your sister did, and *maybe* marry you. But what do I win? I raise Willie on my own. He grows up without a father." She stood up. "And who will he blame for that? It won't be John. Will it?"

"I don't know," Laura said, crying again.

"Oh, I think you do," she said and slapped Laura on the cheek.

She finished Laura's glass of wine and sat back down at her vanity table.

"You're smart. And yes, you've had your own grief, your own little sadness. I know that."

Laura didn't nod or shake her head, didn't even touch her cheek where Mrs. Letig had slapped her.

"Option number four," she said. "Do nothing. Perhaps that sounds too weak. But I'm not so sure. We stay together. But we live in a cold house. I could make it *really* cold. Don't let him come to my bed. Force him to punish himself. But what do *I* gain by doing that? Perhaps watching him slowly suffer would be enough?" She looked in the mirror. "Now, is that it? Do you think those are all my options?"

Laura looked down. She did not want to hear any more.

"Answer me."

"I don't know," Laura said.

"Look at me." Laura raised her head, looked squarely at her. Mrs. Letig said, "Well? What do you *think*?"

"I don't know."

"No, I suppose you don't. Because there *is* another possibility. Something you're much too young to even imagine." She leaned in toward the mirror and spoke to herself. "I forgive him. John wants to be *punished*. He doesn't want forgiveness. But what if I *do* forgive him? That's a choice, you see. A strategic choice. The Christian thing to do. If I forgive him, if I keep silent, if I say nothing to your father or the authorities, or to my family or his, or to Willie when he gets old enough to understand . . . if I tell him it's okay and take him back into my bed even though I know where he has been . . . if I do all that, then what? Do you think that makes me weak?"

She paused, and Laura watched as Mrs. Letig studied herself in the mirror and contemplated her own question.

"No. If I forgive him, then he is in my debt. And it would ensure that Willie has a father and that the three of us are not humiliated any more than we have already been humiliated. It's what women have been doing for years." She turned to Laura. "Your mother even did it. For a while, at least. And then maybe she couldn't stand it anymore. Left him with the kids, with his own guilt. That took true courage, I believe. Or desperation. Or both. One seldom occurs without the other."

She leaned toward Laura, took Laura's hands in her own and said sympathetically, "You *are* just a girl. I know that. I even feel sorry for you, and I don't know if that makes me a good woman—or a pathetic one. These are difficult choices, Laura. Aren't they?"

Laura remained motionless. She was reminded of the evening back in May when she lay sick in bed, and Mrs. Letig had sat on the edge next to her and spoken softly about her mother, and Laura had felt—what?—as if Mrs. Letig was an emissary, a woman through whom gifts were being passed.

"But do you want to know the one thing that is clear, Laura? The one thing I know for certain? Go on, nod your head. Because you *do* want to know. What I know for sure is that *I* get to make the choice. I didn't *want* to make the choice. I didn't *have* to know, and I think I might have been happier if I'd *never* known. But now I do know. The secret is out. And it's my choice. Not John's. Not yours. *My* choice. And mine alone."

Still holding Laura's hands, the woman stared at her until Laura did not think she could stand it anymore.

"You can go now," Mrs. Letig finally said, releasing her and turning away. Laura sat there for a few seconds longer, not sure if she should move too fast. "Go. Go on," she said. "Get out of here."

Laura moved slowly to the door, opened it, and then turned back. She caught Mrs. Letig's eyes in the mirror for a moment, and she ran out the door and then out of the house. She got on her bike and waited for some sound, some indication of what was going on in that room. But there was no sound. It was foolish to think there would be. She hadn't really understood what Mrs. Letig was saying if her first instinct was to listen for some sound of tragedy.

It was dark but deceptively warm for December. She pushed down on the pedals. She pedaled hard four or five rotations, her head down, focused on the road beneath her tires. The air whisked over her face. She wanted to look back, but she thought, *No*. She thought of Lot's wife, unable to keep herself from turning around, her body suddenly a pillar of salt—as if she had disappeared and something completely different, some nonhuman element, had taken her place. She thought of her mother, walking down their street with that tattered brown suitcase in her hand, not looking back. What if her mother had turned around? Would she still have been in Charnelle, but changed, a pillar of something that wasn't really her at all?

Laura kept her head forward and down. She watched the road glide by beneath her. She pedaled hard and navigated through the dark streets. She was relieved that it was so dark. She didn't want to be seen by anybody. She just wanted to keep going and going and going and never look back.

✳

37

Traveling in the Dark

*C*harnelle was the first stop on a wide arc around the smaller Panhandle towns in Moore, Hutchinson, Roberts, and Carson counties before the bus wheeled into Amarillo, where you could catch other buses to more distant places. The afternoon bus out of Charnelle left at two-thirty. A ticket to Amarillo cost only four dollars. Laura had forty-two. She would go there first and then decide. She carried her bag and satchel to the bus station, bought her ticket, and then boarded the bus and sat by a window in the back, one of only four passengers, none of whom she knew.

She fell asleep right after they left Stinnett, and when they stopped again, it was dark, so it seemed as if a long time had passed. She wasn't sure what day it was or where exactly she was. She thought at first that she must have stayed on the bus too long, wound up in God-knows-where. She asked an old woman sitting across the aisle where they were.

"Amarillo, honey."

Relieved, she gathered her things. The bus station felt grimy and warm as she studied the departure times for Dallas, Houston, San Antonio, Austin, Oklahoma City, Tulsa, Little Rock, and Albuquerque. She didn't know where she wanted to go, and the least expensive choice would cost her another seven dollars.

"Is there a place I can sleep?" she asked the attendant, a stiff-backed man with glasses and graying hair at his temples.

"There's some motels down the road." He looked her over. "But they ain't too nice."

She motioned to the row of benches. "Can I sleep here?"

He cocked an eyebrow, examined her more carefully. "I wouldn't advise sleeping here. It's not all that safe, not for someone like you."

"How about those motels then? Do you know how much they cost?"

"They're not too expensive. Maybe two or three dollars, but like I said, they ain't all that nice. Don't you got someone you can stay with?"

"No," she said.

"Let me get you a taxi to take you to a better part of town."

"No, I'll be fine. Which way to those motels?"

Outside, it started raining—the streets black and shiny, the buildings slick, grainy, fluorescent. He pointed out two motels, the American Inn and the Red Motor Lodge. Both were run-down, seedy: shingles missing from the roofs, beat-up cars and trucks in the parking lots. The American Inn was either missing a final *n* or was misspelled, so that it read the "American In." She walked across the street to the lodge. The desk clerk, a tall, rangy man with a purple scar on his forehead, wore a dirty straw cowboy hat tipped back on his head. When she asked how much rooms were, he didn't immediately answer. Instead he leaned over the counter and looked at her bags and then at her.

"You're awful young, ain't you?"

"How much is a room?" she asked again.

"Two bucks. Three if you're staying the whole night."

She thought this was odd. "I'm staying the whole night."

"You have to pay in advance."

"That's fine," she said and took out her coin purse. The desk clerk tried to see into it. She lowered it below the counter and quickly withdrew three dollars.

He rang up the amount on the cash register, took her money, and then gave her a large key with a green 29 on it. "Upstairs to your right," he said.

"Thank you." She pulled her bag and satchel over her shoulders and traipsed up the red-carpeted stairs, which were stained with spills and cigarette burns.

The room immediately depressed her. It stank of smoke. She had to open the window to get some fresh air. The chair was bloodred, the arms and cushion both tattered, the white stuffing oozing out like intestines; the bedspread was yellow-green, discolored over time and also worn and damaged with burn holes and loose threads. She pulled back the covers. The sheets looked old. They smelled clean, though. The bathroom wasn't filthy, as she expected, but there were rust stains around the faucet and the drains of both the bathtub and the sink. A black-and-white television set, with long rabbit ears, sat precariously on the end of the dresser. She turned it on and was surprised to get a clear picture. On one of the stations, a variety show she'd never seen featured perky country music, and she left it on, just to have some company in the room as she washed her face and brushed her teeth.

She got into bed before she realized she hadn't eaten since breakfast. She didn't want to go out or spend any more money, but she felt she had no choice. She was starving. She couldn't believe that she hadn't thought to bring food with her. It had been the last thing on her mind. It would have been so easy to make a couple of sandwiches and pack some fruit. It would have saved her some money.

She changed into blue jeans and put on a sweater. She hadn't thought to bring an umbrella. She asked the clerk if there was some place she could get a hamburger, and he pointed across the street to a joint he said had decent food for pretty cheap. He seemed friendlier than before.

"I could make you a sandwich," he said.

"I appreciate it. But I want a hamburger."

"Suit yourself," he said. "Feel free to drop in when you get back. We could have a couple of beers."

She nodded. He offered her an old newspaper to put over her head. She thanked him, and he touched the brim of his hat and smiled, his two front teeth rimmed in gold.

The café was cloudy with cigarette smoke, the customers mostly men. The few women wore too much makeup. She asked for a burger and fries to go and waited on the bar stool with her head down as the cook fixed and sacked it for her. The woman who took her order was old, large, her face ravaged by wrinkles and liver spots.

"You from around here?" she asked Laura.

"No, ma'am."

"Where you from?"

"Charnelle."

"Where you staying?"

Laura pointed across the street.

"How long?"

"Just for the night."

The woman leaned back and cackled loudly, as if this was a joke. "So you're the girl from Charnelle."

Laura felt confused, as if the woman had mistaken her for someone else. "Beg your pardon?"

"You be careful, you hear."

Laura, still confused, paid the woman. When she turned around, several of the men stared at her. Hungrily, she thought. The rain had subsided into a drizzle, so she abandoned the paper and ran with her bag and drink, darting inside the motel lobby. The clerk had left his desk, a relief. The stairs creaked loudly, even though she walked on her tiptoes. She locked the door, and then she positioned the red chair under the doorknob, as she'd seen it done in a movie. The room didn't smell as bad as before, so she shut and locked the window and then turned on the television and watched *Rawhide* while she ate and then turned down the volume but kept the television on so the room wouldn't feel so lonely.

She read from the book of American short stories that she had brought home from school. She should have left it at her house, but at the last second she decided to take it. She'd already done enough—what did it matter now if she stole a schoolbook? Besides, she wanted something more to remind her of Charnelle. She'd brought clothes and her diary and this book. She would miss school, would miss Marlene and Debbie, and would also miss Mr. Sparling, the way he kept them focused on their reading, made them think hard and clearly about the meaning of the stories, not just their plots but the stories underneath the stories, the Yes and the No of the American dream, which her classmates had grown tired of hearing, and she had, too, for a while, but not now. He had said that when the Yes and No were together, when you experienced them simultaneously, then it was no longer so simple, and she felt he was right, felt that she knew this firsthand now.

She opened the book and started rereading a story she liked by Nathaniel Hawthorne, whose writing she generally did not like. But she was fascinated by "Wakefield," about a man who leaves his family, just disappears, but in reality moves only a couple of blocks away and spies on them for years, watches them as they recover from their grief, as their lives fold over the scar of his absence. The story reminded her of "Rip Van Winkle," but it also, more importantly, reminded her of her mother, made her wonder if perhaps her mother had been lurking around Charnelle, watching them, spying on them. She wished on some level that it was true, though she knew that it wasn't, that her mother had left for good, and they would never—no matter how many theories they devised—know what became of her.

Mr. Sparling had asked them to write an essay detailing the various reasons that not just Wakefield but that other characters left their communities. When he said this, she could feel her classmates stealing covert glances at her, but she ignored them, no longer cared what they thought. She put her head down and wrote about Wakefield and then about Huck Finn, striking out for the new frontier, fleeing civilization. She wrote about Bartleby, so politely preferring not to, removing himself more and more from the world, until he at last died. She wrote a paragraph about Hester living on the outskirts of town, shunned and humiliated. But what she was really thinking about as she wrote was how Gloria had escaped Charnelle to be with Jerome, to start a new life in a different place, far from home. And how perhaps that's what her mother had done as well. When she wrote the essay, she and John were about to strike out themselves, and she had imagined, though of course not written about, that journey for herself and John.

Rereading the story now, she thought about how she had finally left Charnelle after all, and not because she could no longer imagine living there but because she felt that she no longer belonged there, that she had lost her privilege. She remembered reading *Oedipus Rex* last year, how he had gouged out his eyes for what he'd unknowingly done and had asked for death, but his brother-in-law had given him a punishment worse than death—a wandering exile. When she read it, she thought about her mother, wandering in exile, which sounded exotic, but now, the day after leaving the Letigs' home, she realized that exile was a form of shame, and shame was what had made her ride so fast through the dark Charnelle streets, hoping she wouldn't be seen. She was determined to disappear, just run away from them all, like her mother had done, convinced that it was better to remain a mystery, to say No and, if you could, begin your life over rather than remain in the place where you had caused so much grief.

Traveling on the bus, dozing, unsure which town she was in, she also felt as if leaving was a way of discovering her mother, felt in some ways that she was traveling down a path her mother had already laid for her, as if the very act of leaving might lead her to her mother's doorstep in a strange city, in another world. *A new world.*

But now, not even seventy miles from home, lying in this dingy bed, she felt more confused than ever about her own motives, what a stranger she was even to herself. And she was afraid as well, and wondered what kind of timid traveler she would be—no longer welcome in Charnelle but not welcome anyplace else. Perhaps that was what exile was and what she deserved. Had she been a coward for leaving, abandoning her family, abandoning her responsibility in the Letigs' tragedy? Wasn't that the coward's way out? Wasn't running away the easy thing to do? Wasn't it much harder to stay? She wasn't sure anymore.

She drifted off fitfully but woke again to the sound of drunken stumbling in the hallway. Then she heard a key in her own door. She jumped up and saw the doorknob jiggling but not opening. She ran to her bag, reached in, and searched for her pocketknife. She pulled it out and then scurried over to the far wall and watched the knob rattling.

"Damn door!" a woman's voice called.

"Let me try," a man said. He turned the knob, but it didn't open. "Shit," he said. Then he kicked the door several times.

"Cut it out," the desk clerk shouted from downstairs.

"The damn key doesn't work, Tim!" the woman shouted back.

"What number is it?"

"Twenty-seven."

"What door you at?"

"Oh, shit. Sorry."

"Keep it quiet," the clerk called. "I got real customers tonight."

"Come on, sugar," the woman cooed.

The next door down opened, and she could hear them mumbling and then laughing through the walls. Then she heard what sounded like a struggle, and then, a few minutes later, the wall next to her bed began shaking, as if someone were hammering on it. She moved away, watched the wall vibrate, the cheap, framed paintings above the lamps threatening to fall. It was all over in a couple of minutes.

There was silence, and then more laughter, and then the pipes from the bathroom next door whined. The door opened, and the man said, "Thanks, Jenny," and stomped noisily down the hallway and the stairs.

"That was fast," she heard the clerk say.

"If you can't be good, be quick," the man said.

Laura wished she had a radio. The pipes whined again, and then, moments later, the door opened and closed. Laura moved the chair and looked through the keyhole but saw only the gold-dressed torso of the woman as she walked by. She heard her half stumble down the stairs.

"You want a beer, Jenny?"

"You're a sweetheart, Tim. I can't, though."

"Come on. You got time. That brute was fast. Come on. Just one. It's cold. I got my icebox fixed."

"I guess just one wouldn't hurt."

Laura packed her things and waited for daybreak.

Although it was still early in the morning, Velma was already awake, dressed, and outside feeding the chickens when Laura arrived in the taxi. She had not called beforehand. She wasn't even sure what condition Velma would be in; she hadn't seen her since July, and then only briefly. Velma put her hand over her eyes to block the morning sun and watched as the taxi pulled up in front of the house.

When Laura stepped out, Aunt Velma called, "My Lord, girl, what are you doing here?"

Laura paid the driver and gave him an extra quarter, which seemed extravagant, but he frowned and didn't even thank her.

"What are you doing here?" Velma asked again, hugging Laura.

"I just wanted to see you."

"Where're your father and brothers?"

"Charnelle."

"How did you get down here?"

"The bus."

"Just to see me?"

"I missed you."

"Well, come on in. Let me fix you some breakfast."

Aunt Velma seemed almost back to normal. The left side of her face was still partially paralyzed, which made it difficult for her to articulate carefully, but she talked plainly enough, and she didn't seem confused by language, as she had before. She walked with a slight limp, but you might not notice it if you didn't know she'd had a stroke.

Laura's father had believed the doctors when they said that she would have to be put in a nursing home, but Aunt Velma had been adamantly against the idea, convinced that she would recover in no time, with willpower and prayer. She was right. The women from the church who took care of her after the stroke now came by only once a week to check on her, and Velma did most of her own chores around the house and the farm. There was a man from down the road who came every day and milked the two cows, taking half the milk for his labor, and he mended fences and helped feed the other animals in exchange for the use of Velma's pastures for his cattle.

The house was clean again, not the wreck it had been last Easter. Laura remembered her disgust from that time, the smell of animal crap and medicine, but none of those smells permeated the house, and even if they had, they would have seemed benign now after the motel Laura had been in, which had looked even more decrepit in daylight, though not as sinister. Velma even had her Christmas tree up and decorated, with a few gifts underneath for Laura and her brothers and father.

Laura had almost called the taxi in the middle of the night but had promised herself that she would stick it out, and she couldn't think what to tell Aunt Velma if she showed up at midnight, scared to death. With the daylight, she felt better. She had even gone back to the bus station and written down times of departure and prices, but for now she wanted to see a familiar face, someone she loved, someone to whom she would not have to explain herself.

Driving down the road to Aunt Velma's farm, however, it seemed inevitable that she would return to Charnelle. Who was she fooling? She had little money and no plan. It had been ridiculous to leave as she did, and she was still confused about exactly why she'd done it, except that she felt she had to be gone from there, that in some crucial way she had given up her right to be in Charnelle.

Aunt Velma scrambled some eggs with cheese and Tabasco, fried some bacon, and toasted two pieces of bread. The milk was fresh from the morning milking, and though it had been put in the icebox, it was still warm. Laura ate heartily, still starving from eating so little the day before.

"Does your father know you're here?" Velma asked.

"No," she said.

Velma smiled. "I'm glad you came to see me, sweetheart."

"Can I take a nap?" Laura asked.

"You betcha. I'll take one with you."

She slept through the morning and startled awake, disoriented at first and then relieved to find herself on the bed in Aunt Velma's spare room, where Laura's father (and when she was with them, her mother) usually stayed. She had never been to Velma's without the rest of her family. She was glad to be here now.

Velma was still sleeping, so Laura left her a note, telling her she had gone for a walk. She went to the barn, which smelled of hay and the stink of the animals. Only Ginger was in the stall. She wondered where Hayworth was. She stroked Ginger's nose and then grabbed some carrots from the box and fed them to her until she whinnied and snorted.

Laura opened the stall and put the bridle, a blanket, and the light saddle on her, cinched it, and then led the horse out of the barn. She climbed atop and then walked her past the orchards and across the pasture, which was still wet from the previous day's rain. Laura breathed deeply. She loved the smell of wet grass. She prodded the horse into a trot, and when she saw the pond a few hundred yards in the distance, she squeezed her legs against the horse's flanks, leaned forward, and heeled Ginger into a gallop. She loosened the reins and let the horse find her stride. The band on her hair fell off, her hair streaked loose behind her, and her shirt pressed tightly against her chest. It was still warm out, but a breeze had picked up and brushed against her cheeks and eyes.

She rode past the pond, over the wet grass, to the far north fence line, and, seeing the barbed wire ahead, she tugged the reins so that the horse angled toward the highway. As they approached it, they ran beside the fence, racing one and then two and then three cars and trucks before she pulled on the reins and slowed Ginger to a canter and then a walk. The horse's red neck and mane were sweaty. Laura, too, was hot, but the sweat felt good in the breeze. She stopped the horse and watched the cars pass by. Ginger snorted, so Laura took her to the pond and let her drink.

Laura remembered that Easter, before her mother had left, and she closed her eyes and could still feel and hear and see that vivid moment when she was falling, falling, right before she hit the ground and was knocked unconscious. That was the last time she had ridden a horse. It was Hayworth then. Where was Hayworth?

She was proud of herself for not falling this time, and not being scared either. She had lost so many of her fears, or maybe they had been replaced with others. Maybe she needed another fall in order to knock what had happened in Charnelle, with the Letigs, out of her, to drive away the bad luck. Regardless, she was glad to be right here, right now, at this moment. It seemed almost as if everything that happened had led to this small happiness.

Ginger finished drinking, and Laura walked her back to the barn. She took her to the stall, unsaddled and unbridled her, and then brushed her.

"Thanks," she said to her. Ginger stared down her long nose, those big, black marble eyes reflecting Laura back to herself.

Aunt Velma was out on the porch. "Did you have a good ride?"

"Yes," she said. "Where's Hayworth?"

"She broke her leg. Had to put her down. What do you want to do now?"

Laura thought for a second and then said, "Can we go to a movie?"

G.I. Blues was playing at the Paladian, and she remembered seeing the trailer at the drive-in many months ago, during spring break. It was odd seeing Elvis on that screen. There seemed something faintly sacrilegious about watching him on the same screen where she had seen *The Ten Commandments*. And she didn't like him as much in his uniform and short haircut. She preferred the younger, wilder Elvis of *Jailhouse Rock* and the sweet, light-haired Elvis from *Love Me Tender*. Here he was, brawling and flirting his way through Europe, and every once in a while he'd break into song. It was silly, but she enjoyed it nonetheless and liked seeing places where she thought Gloria might have been.

Afterward Aunt Velma drove them home. Her driving was precarious, and Laura found herself holding her breath during both the trips to and from the movie theater. Velma refused to signal when she was turning and seemed slow to react, so her old Studebaker jerked along. Twice other drivers honked at them.

It was time for supper when they got home, and Laura helped Velma make a chicken and noodle casserole and a pecan pie. They ate in silence, which was fine and comfortable. Laura didn't want to talk, and Aunt Velma seemed to understand that something had happened to her that necessitated silence. Laura had always admired this sweet patience about Aunt Velma, this intuitive awareness of when people needed comfort and when they needed to be left alone, and she felt bad when she remembered her own impatience with Aunt Velma last Easter, how she had been confused by her and John's relationship, and how Aunt Velma's incapacity disgusted her, made her feel ashamed and nervous and angry. Now Laura felt only gratitude toward this woman—for offering her a home, for asking no questions.

That night they looked through the old photo albums, and she found the picture of Aunt Velma and Uncle Unser when they were younger, at the beach in their bathing suits. She remembered how Velma had traced her finger over the photo. There were pictures of Laura's mother when she was a child, and Laura studied those, too. She didn't have any pictures of her mother at home, and except for her dreams she could not keep the image of her mother in her head. These pictures of her mother as a child were similar to the woman Laura remembered, but not the same. As she studied them, she tried to discover the seeds of the future in her face, some faint trace of loneliness or courage or anger or despair or shame or simple cowardice that had prompted her mother to leave. She thought for a moment that she could see the clues, but then she lost them, and it amazed her that the girl in the picture could be her mother at all, that like some molting insect her mother had transformed into something so different.

"Your mother was a beautiful girl," Aunt Velma said.

"Yes."

"You know, she came to see me after she left Charnelle."

"What?" Laura said. This news stunned her.

"She came and stayed here for a night. I thought she had just come to Amarillo for a visit. She had breakfast with me before she left the next morning. I didn't know she hadn't gone back to Charnelle until your father showed up."

"I never knew that. How did she seem?"

"No different."

"*Really?* No different at *all?*"

"Oh, I knew she was upset about something, but we ate supper and talked like we usually would. I think it was just a farewell for her."

Why, Laura wondered, had her father not told them? He never said a word about it, made it seem as if there were no clues whatsoever. Perhaps he thought it would make them feel worse, knowing that she had not said anything to them but had said good-bye to Aunt Velma. It made Laura believe that her mother was alive somewhere, and it also made her strangely happy that her mother had not left without saying some final word to a member of the family. It was not a complete escape. Laura now regretted that she had not left a note for her father or brothers, had left just as her mother had done, without a clue.

"Laura, can I ask you a question?"

"Yes, ma'am."

"What are you running away from?"

She looked at Aunt Velma but did not answer.

"You don't have to say."

Velma circled the back of Laura's chair and kissed her on top of her head. "I'm going on to bed, sweetheart. We'll go to church in the morning. That'll make you feel better."

"Yes, ma'am."

"You look at those pictures. They are full of people who love you. Turn off the light when you're done."

Laura flipped through the photos of her family but then stopped and stared at one of herself as a tiny girl, standing on Aunt Velma's porch. She studied the face, the eyes, but, as with the picture of her mother, she could hardly recognize this girl in the person she was now.

When she and Aunt Velma arrived back at the farm from church the next morning, Laura's father was waiting for them in the driveway.

He was not angry, nor did he ask her any questions while they were at Aunt Velma's, and for that she was thankful. He was gentle and patient, as if her trip to Amarillo was something they had agreed upon, nothing out of the ordinary. She wondered if Manny had told him what he knew. Or maybe her father had called the Letigs and asked if they'd seen her, and Anne Letig had told him what had happened, though it was difficult to imagine that conversation. She figured that Aunt Velma had called him not long after she showed up at the farm and assured him that everything was all right, perhaps even encouraged him to wait a day before coming down, and to go easy on her, not push.

That afternoon her father helped with chores around the farm— mended a fence, caulked the bathtub, cleaned out the drain, checked the septic tank. Laura helped Aunt Velma make supper—fried chicken, mashed potatoes and gravy, coleslaw, biscuits, and apples baked in cinnamon—and then they sat down to eat, Aunt Velma holding her and her father's hands and leading them in a simple blessing that made Laura's eyes blur with tears. Afterward they wrapped the leftovers in tinfoil and Tupperware, and at dusk they said their good-byes. Velma told them to hold on a minute, and she retrieved the photos Laura had been looking at the night before, the ones of her mother and herself as children, and one more of her family, all together, when Rich was just a baby, all of them lined up by the old Ford in Aunt Velma's front yard, squinting against the sun, smiling as best they could.

"I figure you need these," Aunt Velma said, putting them in Laura's hands and pulling Laura tightly to her. "An early birthday present."

"Thank you," Laura whispered, and then she put the pictures between the covers of her diary and closed it up in her bag.

"See you at Christmas," her father called as he backed out, and by the time they hit the main highway leaving Amarillo, the sun had fallen below the horizon, and the sky was soon pitch-black. They drove in silence for a while, her father smoking a cigarette, Laura staring out the window to the dark horizon ahead of her.

She remembered that trip home from Aunt Velma's more than two and a half years ago, shivering in the back of the truck with Manny and Gene and Fay, staring up into the night sky and naming stars, then sitting up and looking into the cab of the truck at her mother, who held Rich and stared out the side window, thinking her own dark thoughts. Laura remembered the

feeling of isolation that overwhelmed her then, her own yearning to eaves-
drop on her mother's thoughts, to understand the unsettling silence that
had descended on her and seemed to preface, now that Laura thought about
it, the silence to come.

"What are you thinking?" her father asked, his voice surprising her.

She turned to him. "Do you ever think about her?"

"Who?"

"Momma?"

He took a deep drag from his cigarette, seemed to hold it for a long
time, and then exhaled it out the window. "Yeah," he said quietly. "Of
course I do."

"What do you think when you think about her?" she asked.

She wanted him to talk about it, but this was new territory for them
both. She tried to read his expression, but it was so dark that she could see
only the shadow and silhouette of his face.

"Mainly stuff when you kids were younger," he said slowly. He did not
seem upset by her question. "And before any of you were born, when we
were courting. She was such a beautiful woman—with her long blond hair
and those thrown-back shoulders and that lovely face that seemed as mysterious as a sphinx. I remember long ago better than more recently. I'm not
sure why."

"Do you miss her?"

"Hmmm. I don't quite know how to answer that." He took another
drag and then stared ahead at the road. "I don't really *want* to miss her,
Laura. I try not to think about her. But I do, of course, especially sometimes early in the morning, before any of you get up. Or when I look at
you, or when we saw Gloria last summer. You both seem so much like her
when she was a young woman. So pretty. Or the way Gene hiccups and the
way he looks when he's reading. His concentration, his quietness . . . it re-
minds me of her. Lots of things, I guess."

She smiled, but then they fell silent again, and she found her thoughts
slipping darkly toward her mother's disappearance, the nagging whys that
she had not wanted to think about but kept thinking about and that Anne
Letig had forced her to pick at like a scab that can't be left alone.

"Why did she leave?" she asked.

Again he was slow to answer, glancing over at Laura in the dark. He
sucked on his cigarette and then said quietly, "I don't know. None of us

could have predicted that she would just vanish like she did. No one *does* that. But I guess on some level I wasn't totally surprised. I wasn't the greatest husband, Laura."

She nodded, not to agree with him but to encourage him to continue.

"I guess you're old enough to know that. I didn't always treat your mother right, and so some part of me felt I had it coming. That she did it to spite me, and I deserved it. I believed it was my fault."

Laura didn't remember her parents arguing too much when they were married, but she did remember the woman he'd brought home a few months after her mother left. And Mrs. Letig had insinuated that there had been other women, that her parents were not happily married. Laura knew there was a longer story here, but she didn't really think it was her business to know it. Parents and children did not need to know everything about each other, she thought. Some things were better left unsaid.

"Do you still think it was your fault?" she asked tentatively.

"No," he said. "But I did for a long time. And my guilt got all mixed up with my anger. Eventually I felt that *she* was to blame. It wasn't right what she did, to abandon us all. But it especially wasn't right what she did to you kids."

He paused here and seemed to be remembering something.

"But now . . . I guess now I don't blame anybody. I don't see the advantage in it. Or the truth of it. We sometimes do things in our lives that seem like deliberate choices at the time, but really, when we look back on them, they weren't choices at all. People do things because they have to do them. It's *in* them already."

"What do you mean?" Laura asked.

"I think your mother *had* to leave, that some part of her always wanted to leave, to be alone and maybe even to be somebody different. She'd always been mysterious. Always something of a loner. That was why I fell in love with her in the first place."

Laura closed her eyes and tried to imagine the young woman he'd married, the girl she'd seen in those pictures that Aunt Velma had given her. Was her father right about this? Are our actions always in us? She remembered thinking something similar way back when they were having all those problems with Greta. She remembered watching her mother sitting on the stump staring at the dog pen, and she wondered later if the seeds of the future are always there, in the present, just waiting to bloom. Maybe

that's what her mother had meant when she told her father that it was nature's way. Laura didn't know if she believed this, that our natures were always waiting to have their way. It seemed such a sad philosophy.

"Do you think she'll ever come back?" she asked.

"No, I doubt it."

"If she did, would you take her back?"

He kept his eyes on the road. She held her breath, and her throat felt
tight. She wanted him to say yes.

He shook his head. "This is starting to sound like an interrogation."

"Would you?"

"That's a big *if*, Laura. But if she came back . . . well . . . I'd have to
say no. No, I wouldn't."

"Why not?"

"It couldn't be the same. We could never go back to how it was
before."

"But I thought you said you didn't blame her anymore."

"That doesn't mean I could forget what she did. And I guess I'd always
be wondering when she would leave again. I couldn't take that. Once was
bad enough. And I don't think it would be, in the end, very fair to all you
kids."

"Do you still love her?"

He paused again, took a deep, contemplative drag off his cigarette,
held it in, and let it curl out of his mouth in a long, white stream that filled
the cab.

"No," he said. And then, "That's not true. And it's not fair, really. I
suppose I will always love your mother. Or maybe it's just the memory of
her when we both were younger that I love. I'm not quite sure. . . . That's a
hard one, honey."

They were both quiet then. The wheels of the truck whistled underneath them. What had she expected him to say? Something clear and defin-
itive? But that wasn't the way things really were. She felt a sudden sense of
failure sweep through her. She thought about how strange it was to be coming back, in the dark, to Charnelle. Doing what her mother wouldn't or
couldn't do. In some way, she believed she was coming full circle, but the
idea depressed her. She began to cry, softly at first, just tears welling in her
eyes, but then soon she was sobbing.

"Hey, now," her father said. "I'm sorry. I didn't mean to upset you."

"I miss her," she said, staring out the window at the dark, flat nothingness of the Panhandle.

"Is that why you ran away?" he asked.

This was such a complicated question, made more complicated by her tears. She had left because she felt that Mrs. Letig was right, that she had helped to bring about their tragedy. Though when she boarded the bus, it was not that clear—just a need to be gone, out of her house, out of Charnelle, to be away from them all, far away, where she couldn't be seen by people who knew her. These thoughts had coiled in front of her, as alarming as a rattlesnake.

"I don't know. Partly, I guess."

He passed her his handkerchief, then put his hand on her shoulder. She looked out the front window. She could not see Charnelle yet. The gray highway lay ahead of them like a river, leading them back to the town where she had spent her life, where so much had already happened, and where the Letigs, as well as her own family, lived with their grief and their shame. Where Anne Letig hovered before her mirror, pouring more wine and sorting through her options. Where Jack lay in his grave. She was grateful now, despite all that had happened, that she and John had not run away, that her life was still her own. Yet she knew she would always carry some burden of guilt, the knowledge that she had been, for a period of time, at the secret center of the Letigs' grief. For them she would always be the girl from Charnelle, the one they wouldn't mention again but could never forget.

And they, too, had penetrated the secret center of her life. She imagined that she would always think and even dream about little Jack, his eyes closed in the coffin, and then the coffin itself closed and placed in the ground, the hole covered with dirt. Some part of her had disappeared with him, would always be gone, buried deep inside the Letigs' marriage.

"Do you think we're punished for the things we do?" she asked.

He took a last drag of his cigarette and then tossed the butt out the window. He seemed to think about her question for a long time. She turned to him, watched the silhouette of his face in the dark as he stared ahead at the highway, his arm perched over the steering wheel.

"I think," he finally said, "that we usually punish ourselves."

Her throat felt thick and tight. She remembered again watching her mother through the cab of this same truck, wondering if she would ever really know her. It had dawned on her back then that such a connection was almost impossible. Was it only in our cruelty, intentional or not, in our shared pain, that we ever penetrate other lives? Was it only in grief that we ever really touch someone else? She hoped not. She hoped that time would bring, for all of them, less pain, less memory of pain.

"Slide over here," her father said. She buried her face in his shoulder. His flannel jacket smelled of smoke and something else, a good smell she couldn't quite describe but knew immediately as her father's.

"I love you," he said. "You know that, don't you? I'll always love you."

He held her tightly for a few seconds until she calmed herself, and then he let his arm drape loosely over her shoulder. He rolled the window all the way down, so that a steady stream of crisp, chilly air filled the cab.

After a while, he began humming. The melody sounded comforting and familiar, although she couldn't remember the name of it. The rhythm of the tires rolling over the newly patched highway provided accompaniment, as did the steady beat she could hear in his chest. She felt enormously thankful for this small pleasure, and soon she was able to swallow and then breathe again.

"I love you, too," she whispered, brushing away her tears.

When she looked up again, she could see in the distance the faint glow of Charnelle, little dots of jittering yellow and white lights. She wanted to prolong this part of the journey home, this short time of traveling in the dark with her father. She closed her eyes for a while, listening to him, listening to the wheels beneath them, knowing and yet not knowing this melody he was humming, and hoping, despite the fact that she knew the lights up ahead were growing brighter and more distinct with each mile, that they weren't too close to Charnelle, hoping, even though they were on their way home, that they wouldn't arrive just yet.

ACKNOWLEDGMENTS

I first want to thank the two Jennifers in my life: my agent, Jennifer Cayea, whose faith, good cheer, honesty, intelligence, and stubbornness made all the difference; and Jennifer Pooley, who is everything a writer could want in an editor—critic, advocate, and cheerleader.

Thanks to the MacDowell Colony, Vermont Studio Center, and especially Blue Mountain Center and the Corporation of Yaddo for residency fellowships that allowed me valuable time and solitude to write and revise most of this novel. I also appreciate Dave Hanna and Lisa Floyd-Hanna for the use of their Durango home and Ronald Regina for his Palm Springs home, and my annual writing-retreat pals, Tim Crews and Wayne Regina, for their inspiration and abiding friendship and all the fertile discussions about nitrogen fixation, legumes, differentiation, multigenerational emotional processes, postmodernism, entity extractions, narrative strategy, and *lucerne* coincidences.

I am deeply grateful to Prescott College for their support, especially in the form of sabbaticals, and my many Prescott College and, more recently, Spalding University friends, colleagues, and students, who nurtured me in ways they probably don't realize. I particularly want to thank the Arts & Letters Program, Deb Ford, Roseanne Cartledge, Gret Antilla, Jamie Mehalic, Tricia Goffena, Sena Jeter Naslund, Jesse Schwartz, James Daley, David Siegel, and Aram Yardumian. Special thanks to Rick Russo, Bret Lott, Hannah Tinti, Silas House, Joan Silber, Harriet Barlow, Juliann

France, Ben Strader, Hilda Raz, Kelly Grey-Carlisle, Jennifer Klein, and Ladette Randolph. Abby Koons, Paula McLain, and my great friend Joe Schuster read all or portions of this book and offered invaluable feedback and/or encouragement.

Many thanks, too, for their love and friendship to the Thomason, Cook, Menefee, and Speegle clans, and particularly to Lena Cook-Kellison, Gail and Larry Menefee, Melanie Carter, Amanda Menefee, Janet Bicknese, Sarah Crews, Don and Judy Sulltrop, Raymon and Linda Thomason, Anna Burchell, Red Thomason, and Mike and Marianne Thomason. (As I promised, Mike, this is *all* about you.) My deepest gratitude and love are reserved for Anita, Brandy, Carson, Tristan, Vivian, and little Lena, and of course Charissa Menefee, the grace in my life, who read this novel more times and more closely and in more incarnations than any person should have to do, and who played many roles in its evolution: muse, midwife, nursemaid, coach, critic, collaborator, dramaturg, and editor.